TRANSCENDENT

Book 2 of Ascendant

By
Craig Alanson

TABLE OF CONTENTS

CHAPTER ONE

The evening breeze blew a stray lock of hair into Nurelka's eyes, and she brushed it away in irritation. The light, swirling breeze danced the lock of hair straight up, then back into her eyes. Huffing in frustration, she took firm hold of it and tucked the end up under her scarf, tugging the scarf down to secure the hair in place.

The guard next to her leaned over in his saddle to whisper "You missed a-"

"I know," she whispered back, more loudly than she intended, and ignored the stray hairs as best she could.

The man looked stung, and turned away.

"Sorry, Duston," she said to the man, "I didn't mean to snap at you. I am only, oh, how many nights are we going to do this?" She nodded toward the setting sun, toward the silhouette of the young crown princess, sitting still and silent on her horse, with another riderless horse beside her. The crown princess of Tarador was gazing sadly into yet another sunset.

"Until it's enough," Duston announced with the wisdom of his years. "Until she decides it is enough."

"It will never be enough," Nurelka declared, "not until that boy returns."

"He's no boy," Duston replied, twisting in the saddle to ease his stiff back. "Not anymore. Not after all that has happened to him. Not if he is out there, on his own."

"He is out there?" Nurelka asked, not expecting an answer.

"Most likely. The wizard says he would know if Koren were dead. I don't know how he would know, he seemed pretty sure of it, I tell you. Best to stay out of the affairs of wizards."

"It's best," she agreed. "Still, I don't know as to why Lord Salva is so concerned about one servant running away. He's had many, over the years."

"Any of them ever been accused of injuring the princess?" Duston asked. "Or being a jinx?"

"No, but-"

"That's why the wizard cares. Something's going on with that Koren. I don't know whether the wizard feels guilty that he is somehow at fault for Koren leaving," Duston frowned. Someone in the castle knew the full story, and whoever they were, they weren't talking. "Or that he didn't stop the Lady," he meant the Regent Carlana Trehayme, "from accusing Koren of being a dangerous jinx."

"Is he?" Nurelka asked.

"A jinx?" Duston rubbed his beard. "Talking to the soldiers who were with him and the wizard, when they were attacked, most of them think Koren's quick action saved them. He certainly saved the wizard, all by himself. Others, ah, they're not sure. It was certainly very odd bad luck to be attacked, deep inside Tarador, on a fine, clear spring morning. That was bad luck, you could say they were jinxed. So, I don't know. The wizard says there is no such thing as a jinx-"

"You'd expect a wizard to say something like that, wouldn't you?"

"I suppose. Yes, they would have to say something like that."

The two, the former royal guard who now watched over the young crown princess, and the woman who had been Ariana's maid since the girl was little, sat silently on their horses a moment, looking into the setting sun. Looking at the princess, who was alone. Alone, except for two trusted personal servants just out of earshot. And a hundred members of the royal guard, mostly staying out of sight but forming a secure perimeter around their precious charge, the future leader of Tarador.

"She never smiles anymore," Nurelka sighed. "She used to smile all the time. It was such a joy to see her happy."

"She didn't smile for a long time after her father died," Duston observed. Her father. The man Duston knew as the king of Tarador, back then. Duston reached over to the maid and gave her shoulder a reassuring squeeze. "She will smile again, someday. Someday, you'll see, Nurelka," he added with a smile that he didn't feel.

"It had best be soon, Duston, before the enemy falls upon us. None of us will be smiling then."

Duston nodded grimly. After the enemy attack on the court wizard, the whole nation seemed to be holding their breath, waiting for the enemy to strike again. "Soon," he said, "it will be soon."

As the sun touched the horizon, Ariana almost held her breath. She had done that, holding her breath, the first time she watched a sun set after Koren had fled. At the time, she had told herself that Koren would return, if only she could hold her breath from the moment the bottom of the sun kissed the horizon until it disappeared entirely. That first time, she had gasped for breath in panic before the orb had sunk halfway, alarmed at how long it took for the sun to set. Usually, it happened within seconds, it seemed! Perhaps time slowed when you held your breath. Knowing she was likely being silly but desperate to do *something*, the next time she was able to view a sunset, she had timed it with a glass. Over three minutes! Could she hold her breath that long? No matter, it was silly anyway, something she did for herself and not to help Koren in any real way. The time for her to indulge in silly things was long past. She needed to put little girl things aside and lead her nation to victory. Or, survival. Survival first, then perhaps they could begin thinking of eventual victory. Survival, in her lifetime, might be the best she could hope for.

Not taking her eyes off the setting sun, she reached out with her left hand, and Thunderbolt stepped close enough for her to pet the horse's head. After Koren left, the horse had been frantic, nearly breaking out of his stall. The stable master had not known what to do, he had been almost in tears the day Ariana visited the stables. Ariana had ordered that the great horse be released from the stables into the high-walled paddock, and allowed to wander in and out as he pleased. No one, Ariana decreed, would ever put a saddle or bridle on Thunderbolt, until Koren returned to do that by himself. Ariana leaned over to scratch the horse's mane, which was tangled and needed brushing. Thunderbolt only allowed two people to groom him; Ariana and Lord Salva, both of whom were extremely busy, and both of whom came to the stables several times each week anyway. Ariana enjoyed spending time with Thunderbolt, she felt close to Koren while she was grooming the great horse. As she tussled the horse's mane, and he leaned in close to her, the last rays of the sun fell behind the western hills; the sun had set on another day. Another day when Koren Bladewell had not returned. "What do you think he's doing right now?" She asked the horse. "Is he watching the sun set?"

Thunderbolt tossed his head, looked at her with one eye, and snorted sadly.

Lord Paedris Don Salva came back to awareness with a gasp, pulling himself from deeply within the spirit world. His eyes not focusing properly, he blinked and looked around, wondering where he was. Then realized with a shock, and looked to the west. He was at the platform on top of his tower, and the sun was almost touching the horizon. "Cecil!" He tried to shout, all that came out was a thin croak. How long had they been there? They had begun the spell after mid-day. Hours? They must have been there, unaware, for hours.

"Cecil!" He swallowed to soothe his raw throat. "Mwazo! Lord Mwazo!" He shook the other wizard, who lay slumped on the platform, having fallen off the bench they had been on. The man did not respond, even when Paedris shook him. Glancing at the sun, which had now slid down so that its bottom edge was below the horizon, Paedris felt fear. The darkness of night was the province of the enemy; Paedris knew that Mwazo was in grave danger. He gathered his strength, thinly stretched as it was, touched a palm to the man's forehead, and delivered a shock. Strong enough that Paedris felt the shock up his own arm to his shoulder and neck.

It worked. Mwazo gasped, his eyes fluttering, as he was rudely pulled from the spirit world. "Wha-" he choked, rose onto one elbow, and collapsed.

"Rest, my friend," Paedris managed to say, and pulled Mwazo's head into his lap. "Drink," he said, as he pulled the cork from a flask of water and held it to Mwazo's lips. The other man drank sloppily, most of the water pouring down into the platform. No matter, Paedris had plenty of water. "We were gone for far too long. That was foolish of me."

"S-sorry," Mwazo stammered, his mouth still parched.

"Sorry? For what?" Paedris asked, as he opened another flask of water and drained the whole flask. His hands shook so much that half the water spilled out onto his clothes. He was weary, weary deeply into his bones; he knew that he and Mwazo would be weak and exhausted for many days.

"I failed," Mwazo explained. "Even with you lending your power, I could not discern the enemy's mind." The wizard had traveled the spirit world, seeking to penetrate the enemy's mind, to learn the thoughts and plans of their ancient enemy. "All I can tell you is that I received an impression of great eagerness, a terrible impatience, a longing. The enemy will strike soon. Beyond that, I cannot tell you anything. I'm sorry."

"Cecil, you tried to enter the mind of a demon from the underworld. You could have been lost to us, forever. You did not fail, my friend," Paedris assured the other wizard, and he watched the last rays of the setting sun. "I lack the ability to see into the enemy's mind, only you can do that. It is perhaps past the point where even my power can make any difference."

"Perhaps," Mwazo agreed. Lord Salva's power was truly impressive, beyond anything Mwazo could imagine. But the enemy's power was greater still, great enough to evade even Mwazo's skill. To penetrate the shield the enemy had around its mind would take the power of a wizard more powerful, far more powerful than Paedris Don Salva. There was only one such wizard Mwazo knew of who had that much power, and that young wizard had fled Tarador. "I am certain of one very important thing, Paedris," Mwazo said quietly.

"What is that?"

"The enemy has not captured Koren Bladewell."

"No," Carlana Trehayme, Regent of Tarador, said. Then she sighed. "Must we have this argument every time we talk, General?"

Grand General Magrane was as weary of the argument as Carlana was. "Every time you seek my advice in military matters, yes. The enemy is poised for attack along our border. Our scouts, and wizards," he glanced out the window to Lord Salva's tower, "report that the enemy is massing forces in three areas, and that wagon trains of supplies extend back at least thirty miles. They will attack this summer; such a large force cannot be sustained in the field indefinitely. So, again, Your Highness, when you seek my advice I will tell you that we must attack. We must strike before the enemy is ready, if only to conduct a raid for the purpose of throwing off the enemy's timing. To remain on the defensive, especially pulling back our main force to defend the capital, is certain to fail. We must go on the offensive, we must seize the initiative, take the fight to the enemy. Then we can dictate the terms of the fighting. All my years of military experience tell me this; yet when you seek my advice, you ignore my council."

"Seeking advice does not mean always agreeing. I have many advisors, General," Carlana looked out the window to where the sun was approaching the horizon. "The decision ultimately rests with me."

"Then, again, I offer my resignation."

"And again," Carlana managed a hint of smile at their little dance, "I refuse. Your nation needs you, General. An old soldier like you would not shirk your duty in time of war."

Magrane nodded curtly. As long as there was a chance, any chance, that he could prevail in his ongoing argument, he would remain in command of Tarador's army. "If we are done, Your Highness, I will take my leave of you?"

Carlana nodded, and turned her attention to a pile of scrolls on her desk. Magrane bowed slightly, strode purposefully out of the room, walked down a long hallway, and stepped through a door onto a battlement. The guards there saluted stiffly, and backed away, to give the general privacy. With hands scarred from many battles, and calloused from years of hard toil, he gripped the edge of the stone that was also worn smooth from years of use. Looking into the setting sun, he knew that same sun would soon be setting on the enemy's forces to the west, just across the border.

The enemy would be coming, soon. And Tarador was not ready.

Kyre Falco was also standing on a battlement watching the sun setting on a bitter day, only Kyre was atop the outer wall of his family's keep, not the royal castle in Linden. After the attack on Lord Salva, Ducal families had been allowed to bring their eldest children home from Linden, to make preparations for war. Kyre's younger brother Talen remained in Linden, as hostage against his father attempting to use the Falco's ducal army to overthrow the Trehaymes, it had always been that way. The fact that the royal family needed hostages to avoid a civil war, Kyre thought sourly, was a sign of the divisions within Tarador that made the realm weaker in the face of the enemy. In the case of his father, he had to admit, the Trehaymes were wise to require a hostage; his father burned inside to take back the throne that he thought rightfully belonged to the Falcos.

"Don't you worry about it, young sire," The soldier said quietly enough so that only Kyre Falco could hear him. "Your father will see your qualities soon."

Kyre turned away from gazing at the sun, which had just touched the hills to the west. "Jonas," he addressed the man by name, something that his father would never have done. Regin Falco would consider knowing the names of the common soldiers in his army to be beneath him. "Thank you. How is your son doing?"

Jonas brightened. "Much better, thank you, Your Grace." His son had been injured when a farm cart fell against his leg; Kyre had sent the Falco's personal surgeon to look after the young boy. That was another reason Regin Falco was not happy with his son, and had spent much of the afternoon railing against Kyre's weakness and lack of focus. "He was walking this morning, he will be healing right soon, thanks to you."

"Thank our surgeon, Jonas not me. I am only sorry that he was called away on an urgent matter." There had been no urgent matter, and Kyre and Jonas both knew that. When Regin Falco learned that the family's personal surgeon had been sent to care for the son of a lowly foot soldier, the Duke had called the man back to the keep, and angrily instructed both Kyre and the surgeon never to do such a thing again.

Jonas coughed. "Yes, Your Grace. No matter, my boy will be fine, up and around in a week, the surgeon told us." The man glanced quickly left and right, assuring they were still safely out of earshot. "There are others who," he hesitated, seeking to choose his words carefully, "appreciate when a leader sees that loyalty runs two ways, not one."

Kyre looked at the man sharply, thinking he was being baited. Seeing the almost pleading look on the man's face, Kyre relaxed slightly, and nodded. Jonas had been with Kyre on the night that Kyre had given up his tent, to let a sick soldier get a comfortable night's rest. Regin had not been happy about that either, but the majority of his soldiers had heartily approved, and word had spread quickly within the ducal army. "With war coming," Kyre responded, choosing his own words carefully, "we will need to rely on loyalty more than ever."

Jonas nodded silently, and stepped back to give the ducal heir privacy, as they watched the last rays of the sun disappear behind the hills.

Inside the secure walls of his keep, Regin Falco stepped back from a balcony, and closed the door behind him. He stood facing the window, watching the sun set over hills that defined the border of his ancestral lands.

Once, all of Tarador belonged to the Falcos, before the upstart Trehaymes used a crisis to greedily seize power, and they had held the throne ever since. Seeing the shrunken border of his land only made Regin angry, he sought to use that anger as energy to feed his resolve. Regin was in a foul mood, having once again been compelled to correct his eldest son and heir. Kyre, who had as a young boy been so promising, had grown soft during his years in Linden. The boy had fallen under the influence of those people in the capital who sought to curry favor from the Trehaymes; weak people who had no minds of their own. Regin himself had experienced such influence when he was a boy in Linden; he had resisted the usurper Trehayme family's attempts to make him betray his legacy. Regin had stood fast and remained true to the Falcos, never wavering from the family's cause that had consumed every duke and duchess for hundreds of years; recapturing the throne. Now, Regin feared that Kyre, because of weakness and self-doubt, preferred the false comfort of popularity to the hard path of power. Regin knew his son was popular with some soldiers in the ducal army, popular for the wrong reasons. Popular because Kyre was soft on the men, because he took the easy path of popularity, rather than maintaining the distance a commander needed. What did Kyre think would happen, Regin asked himself bitterly, the first time the boy led men into battle, the first time he had to order men forward to their deaths? How popular would he be then, when the soldiers saw their fellows lying dead on a battlefield, knowing Kyre's actions led to their deaths?

Not so long ago, Regin had high hopes for Kyre, that the boy could gain the favor of princess Ariana, and the Falcos could regain the throne through marriage. Now, Regin concluded bitterly, his heir might someday catch the eye of the princess, but it would be due to Kyre's softness and weakness, and he would no longer truly be a Falco. Any alliance between Kyre and Ariana, Regin saw, would be the Trehaymes seeing a way to absorb and corrupt the Falcos. The opposite of what the Falcos had sought for centuries.

As the blazing sun touched the horizon, Regin spoke. "Forne. Tarador will not survive this coming war, with Carlana as Regent."

Niles Forne could not argue with his duke. He could not argue, both because he agreed with Regin on the issue, and because he knew Regin blamed Niles Forne for the growing softness of Kyre. "Yes, Your Grace."

"We must act." Regin's hands clasped tightly behind his back. "For the good of the nation, it is our patriotic duty. We cannot stand by while Carlana does nothing."

Forne cleared his throat quietly. "The Regency Council may be in the mood to replace the current Regent, but not, I judge, to accept you as her replacement. The political stars are not aligned for you to become Regent, Your Grace."

"Forne," Regin smiled for the first time that day. Occasionally, he was able to surprise his own adept political advisor. "You must think more subtly. The time is not right for me to assume the Regency," and effectively the throne, "but there is another candidate we can put forward."

"Who, Sire?" Forne asked, with curiosity and dread. Whatever plan Regin intended, the Duke would expect Niles Forne to make it happen.

"Ariana's uncle."

"Her uncle?" Forne almost laughed in surprise and horror. Leese Trehayme was a drunkard, a man who had never taken responsibility for anything in his life. Given a monthly stipend by the royal family, the man had left Linden to live a life of leisure and debauchery, surrounded by people who plied him with drink and, it was rumored, stronger substances. "That would be," Forne considered what to say to avoid insulting his Duke, "rather surprising, Your Grace."

"The man can be controlled, Forne. All we need is a figurehead, a symbol for the nation to rally around. He would not be expected to bear the burden of making the hard decisions, for that, we would provide guidance."

"It might be difficult to persuade him to return to Linden, Sire. He left because he could not stand the thought of his young niece being ahead of him, in line for the throne."

"Inducements can be provided, Forne. Flattery. If there is a strong call for Leese to return, to lead us in such dire times, how could any man not respond to such a summons?" Regin smiled wryly. "He should be reminded, also," the Falco Duke added darkly, "that these are dangerous times. How many attempts have there been on the life of our crown princess already?"

Forne sucked in a breath. The doors and windows were closed, no one was listening to them. Still, he was surprised to hear his Duke even broadly hint at such treason. "Many, Sire. Our crown princess is in great danger at all times."

"And in greater danger, as long as her mother holds the Regency. To protect our crown princess," Regin could not prevent his lip from curling, "we must act. Although," he shook his head sadly, "there is only so much we can do. If Ariana were to suffer a terrible fate," he looked into the fading sun, "someone must be ready to lead this nation."

Chu Wing stood in the stirrups to stretch her legs, and to relieve the pain in her aching backside. After living in a comfortable cabin on a sailing ship, during the journey from Tarador to Ching-Do, with a stop at Indus, she was unused to riding a horse. When the message from Lord Salva reached her, she had concluded her official visit to Indus, and had been about to board a ship for the final leg of her journey home. Immediately, her hosts had turned the coach around, and she had raced, day after day, through the landscape of Indus. That time of year, the winds blew strongly in the wrong direction for a sea voyage from Indus to Tarador. A ship would have to slowly beat back and forth all day to progress a few miles, and on some days, all the skill of captain and crew could only hold the ship in place. It was faster to make the long, arduous journey overland. When hills turned into mountains, and roads narrowed then disappeared, she had left the bouncing, coach behind to ride a series of horses. The Indus Empire had a string of stations across the remote mountainous area, where imperial couriers could change horses, in their swift race across the sparsely populated wilderness.

"Halt!" The captain of her escort shouted in warning, holding up a fist. Wing pulled her horse to a stop, and stood again to peer into the setting sun. They were in a broad mountain valley between two towering mountain ranges, peaks thickly covered in snow and ice even this far into the springtime. The mountains here were referred to by the Indus as the Roof of the World, and Wing could understand why. Even where they were, in a valley, the air was thin and cold; the horses huffed loudly to fill their lungs even when merely walking.

Banners flew atop staffs to the west, almost within the disk of the lowering sun, and Wing squinted to see what lay ahead of them. Even with her wizard-enhanced senses, she could only discern it was a party of people on horses, perhaps a dozen. Banners were carried by two of the horsemen, the cloth flailing in the brisk wind making it impossible to tell what the banners signified.

The captain of her Indus escort drew his sword, and shouted commands to his men. The captain's orders, written directly by the Raj himself, were to deliver Madame Chu to Tarador safely, even at the cost of the men's lives. This remote part of the Empire, lands only loosely controlled by the Raj, held vicious bandits who preyed upon travelers and merchant caravans.

Wing closed her eyes, and let her senses fly on before her. Concentrating, she swayed a bit in the saddle, the balance of her body wavered as her consciousness was briefly projected elsewhere. Smiling, she opened her eye and spoke. "Captain, you may rest easy. Ahead of us are Rangers of Tarador. They have come a great distance to meet us."

Her escort remained on alert, though swords were sheathed. The sun had slid halfway down behind the horizon by the time the Rangers arrived; their leader came on ahead, hands up in peaceful greeting. Seeing the wizard, he dismounted from his horse and got down on one knee, bowing to the powerful wizard from Ching-Do. "Chu Wing? Madame Chu, Her Highness the Regent of Tarador, and the wizard Lord Salva, thank you for answering their call in our time of great need."

"You are?" Wing asked.

"Lieutenant Tems of the Ranger Corps, ma'am. We are here to escort you to Linden. There is a full complement of Rangers several leagues back, we could not bring our full strength, due to lack of fodder for our horses in these parts," he nodded back to his men. Behind the saddle of every horse were bags of grain to feed the horse; the sparse springtime grasses in the high mountain meadows meant the horses would otherwise have to spend most of each day eating, rather than traveling.

"Thank you, Lieutenant Tems. Captain Rashesh of Indus will accompany us to Linden," she announced. Seeing the look of surprise and not a little wariness on Tems' face, she hastened to add "the Raj has ordered them to see to my safety. His Imperial Majesty the Raj will be sending an army of five thousand soldiers to defend Tarador, but they will be arriving by sea, and the winds this time of year are not favorable."

Five thousand skilled imperial soldiers could make a great difference on behalf of Tarador. If they arrived in time. "The winds?" He was familiar with the seasonal winds and ocean currents between Tarador and Indus, having served on a Taradoran naval ship early in his career. "When does the Raj expect his troops to arrive in Tarador?"

"Likely not until the leaves are falling," Wing said sadly.

Tems looked grim. "I fear to say, that might be too late, ma'am. With your strength and skill, and that of Lord Salva, we may yet prevail."

"We may," Wing looked at the last flash of the day's sunlight. "It is two miles, I believe, to the way station, and it grows dark. Lead on, Mr. Tems. We have a long way to go, and no time to tarry."

Captain Raddick winced as thorns scraped his face and snagged in his hair. He pushed the rose canes aside slowly, carefully, lest the movement catch the eye of the enemy below. They were in a bad position, for the setting sun to the west illuminated the slope they were on, while looking into the glare made it difficult for Raddick to see his quarry. Against the orders of the Regent, and following the hinted desires of Grand General Magrane, Raddick had crossed the border into Acedor with only four men. Traveling light and swiftly, they were now on a rock-strewn slope, wrestling with thorn bushes that provided their only concealment. To get into position had taken all day, stealthily crawling up the hill, avoiding poisonous serpents that were sunning themselves on the warm rocks. Only now were they in position to view the enemy, and what Raddick saw dismayed him.

Campfires. Many campfires, filling the valley below him. Campfires stretching along both sides of the river; orcs on one side, foul men on the other. Two armies, building up strength to invade

Tarador. The last light of day fell on a train of wagons coming from the east, bringing more supplies for the enemy's forces.

Raddick turned his head and looked at his lieutenant, catching sunlight barely glinting off the man's eyes.

Soon. The enemy would attack soon. The coming summer could be the last for Tarador.

And for the world.

Shomas Feany was on his own long voyage, although he was able to travel in relative comfort aboard a ship, instead of a bone-jolting ride on horseback. Relative comfort was a relative term; sleeping in a swaying hammock, trying to walk on a heaving deck, and eating what sailors considered good food had made Shomas yearn for the ship to get into port as quickly as possible. Yet, there he was, back aboard the ship, with sailors climbing the masts to unfurl more sails. Beginning a voyage as the sun was setting did not seem wise to Shomas, but the sailors explained they must take advantage of the tides, and sailing at night was nothing unusual. The ship was barely making way at the moment, under half sail and still within the main harbor of LeMonde. The main harbor was a fine anchorage; wide, deep enough that heavily laden ships need not fear running aground, shallow enough to securely anchor. Hills ringing the harbor and a reef offshore, protected it from summer storms that sometimes raged with little warning. It was the safe anchorage of the harbor, and its location in the main shipping lanes off the coast of Tarador, that had made the little Duchy of LeMonde a wealthy and prosperous nation. Despite her title of ancient origin, the Duchess of LeMonde was a queen in all but name; she answered to no one but her subjects.

Although that was not quite true, and that was the reason Lord Feany had made the uncomfortable sea voyage. The Duchess of LeMonde allowed two small offshore islands to be used as bases for pirate ships, pirates supported by Acedor. Not allowed, exactly; the Duchess did not encourage Acedor to use two of her islands, and she did not allow ships flying the flag of Acedor to enter the main harbor. She had also done nothing to remove the pirates from the islands. Tarador, in years past, had for centuries maintained a strong naval presence in LeMonde, at the invitation of that Duchy's rulers. No more did Tarador protect its smaller neighbor; ships and troops had been pulled back to the mainland, leaving the Duchy to defend itself. And so, the current Duchess turned a blind eye to piracy, even to Acedoran ships flying false flags using her fine harbor. Those ships paid an anchorage fee, and their crews knew to keep their visits ashore brief and quiet.

The purpose of Shomas paying a visit to the Duchess was to discretely inquire what support from Tarador she would need, in order to act against the pirates. The answer he received, from a chilly and skeptical Duchess, was not encouraging. Unless Tarador could station a substantial force in LeMonde; a half dozen ships, perhaps five hundred soldiers, the Duchess would not do anything to risk an open invasion of her little country by Acedor. As Tarador appeared to be unable, or unwilling, to protect even itself, the Duchess was not optimistic of a renewed alliance between her Duchy and her once-powerful neighbor across the sea to the north.

The problem, thought Shomas as he watched the sun settle into the sea to the west, was Tarador's current Regent. As long as Carlana Trehayme refused to risk her armed forces in battle, the outcome was inevitable. When he returned to Linden, he needed to discuss a taboo subject with Paedris; the Wizard Council may need to take action, lest Tarador be defeated before the battle had begun.

Koren or, as he now called himself, Kedrun, was also on a ship, though his ship was gliding slowly into a harbor far to the south of LeMonde. That same island had been Koren's first landfall after departing from Tarador. It was the northernmost of the South Islands, and a popular trading port. The harbor held a half dozen ships at that moment; two weeks ago, Koren had counted fourteen ships anchored in the warm, clear water.

He stood at the rail and looked down; even in the golden light of sunset, he could see the white sandy bottom of the harbor. As he watched, a school of multi-colored fish flashed by and under the ship. He inhaled deeply, breathing in the scent of something that was still new to him. New, and wonderful and delightful, and so invigorating that every time the scent wafted past his nose, he smiled. It was the scent of what sailors called the tropics, and so indescribably wonderful that Koren could never have imagined it. The scent was a combination of things called pineapples, and coconuts, and papayas, and guava fruits, and sand baked by the midday sun, and of sunlight glinting off crystal clear waters. The balmy evening breeze caressed his bare arms; he had followed the advice of fellow sailors, and cut sleeves off one of his shirts as the air grew warmer on their sea voyage south. The tropical breeze also carried from land the dry rustling of palm fronds, so unlike the sound of wind whispering through the pine trees that Koren remembered from his childhood.

"Beautiful, isn't it?" Alfonze asked as he came to stand by the rail next to the young man he knew as Kedrun. With the ship gliding into the harbor on almost bare poles, with all sails furled but one, there was not much for the sailors to do right then. The ship's momentum was carrying it slowly to its selected anchorage. In a few minutes, the captain would call for the sailors to back the single sail, then furl it, and the ship would come to a stop for the night.

"It is," Koren admitted enthusiastically. "Alfonze, when you told me about the South Islands, I didn't believe you, not all of it. I could never have imagined this."

Alfonze breathed in deeply, filling his lungs with the enticing scent of land, welcome after many days at sea. "A man could be happy here, Kedrun."

Koren nodded silently in agreement. He could be happy here. He *was* happy here. Aboard the ship, he had found a home; his fellow sailors were a band of men who knew nothing of his past, knew not that he was a jinx, did not think him a coward and a deserter. Indeed, his jinx had not arisen since he had been aboard the ship; nothing bad or even odd had happened. As each day passed without incident, Koren was beginning to dare hope that he had left his curse behind in Tarador. This, maybe, was where he belonged; far from those he had injured, far from his curse, far from his home. This place, this tropical paradise, could become his new home, if he embraced it.

Then he frowned, a shadow passing across his face. There was a ship, between his ship and the land, the shifting breeze had just lofted that ship's flag. Koren could now see it was the flag of Tarador. The last time Koren had been in this port, rumors had flown that many sailors from his homeland were answering the call to come home. The taverns had been filled with men from Tarador, some of who had not seen home shores for many years, they were now leaving to take passage north. To serve in their homeland's navy, in their nation's time of dire need.

Alfonze saw the look on Koren's face, saw the young man was looking at the flag which fluttered lazily from the stern of the other ship, glowing in the golden light of the setting sun. Alfonze knew what the young man was thinking, and the sailor clasped a calloused hand on Koren's shoulder reassuringly. "Don't you worry about them, Kedrun. The war between Tarador and Acedor has been raging for a thousand years, if tales be true. Oh, they will tell you about duty, and honor, and noble causes, and none of it puts food in your belly, or coin in your pocket. I've seen war, Kedrun. I've seen war, and it's all only spoiled kings and queens who have too much, and lust for more. They live in their castles, surrounded by every luxury, and all the land they can see belongs to them. And they are not happy, because lands they cannot see do not belong to them. So, they send men like you and me to fight and die." He spat in the sea. "What do royalty think of their duty to us? Nothing, that's what. I tell you, the troubles up north amount to nothing down here. Tarador has been fighting for a thousand years, this dust-up is nothing new, mark my words. Whatever happened up there, whatever you did, whatever happened to you, put it behind you."

The young man did not appear convinced, so Alfonze continued, looking at the sky where stars had begun to shine. "Tell me this, Kedrun, what do they owe you?"

"Nothing," Koren said quietly.

"That's right. And that's what you owe them. You're a young man, you need to make your way in the world. Leave strife and glorious quests to others, eh? The South Islands are peaceful. Tell you what, we won't be paid until the day after tomorrow, but I have coins in my pocket. When we get to shore, I'll buy you one of those drinks you like, served in a coconut and all."

"No rum in it, please," Koren grinned at the thought. Alfonze was right. He had left his homeland to protect the people he cared about from his jinx; he owed nothing more to Tarador. He could be happy here.

And he would.

CHAPTER TWO

Cully Runnet was walking across the courtyard of the royal castle, with a basket of freshly cleaned and folded laundry for the court wizard, when he saw a girl standing in front of the wizard's tower, staring up at it. Cully guessed that she was about his age, 14 or so, and she had the lightest blonde hair that he had ever seen. Although her clothes were fine, with a nice cloak tied around her shoulders, her shoes and the bottom of her dress were dusty and dotted with mud. She must have traveled from afar and just arrived at the castle, Cully supposed. Why, he decided, it was certainly his duty to offer help to a weary traveler. The fact that she was a pretty girl, well, that never crossed Cully's mind. Or maybe it did, a little.

"Hey there!" He shouted, waving at the girl. She had a heavy satchel with her, and she had bent down to pick it up and walk closer to the wizard's tower. Newcomers are so stupid, Cully thought to himself, shaking his head. "Hey there! Don't you go in there," he warned. "Don't you know, that's the wizard's tower!"

The girl dropped the satchel on the ground and smiled at him. Cully was instantly in love; her smile outshone the morning sun. "Yes, I do know," she said. She reached inside her cloak and pulled out a card made of a heavy paper. Handing it to Cully, she introduced herself. "I'm Olivia."

Cully studied the card, it was like the 'calling cards' that rich people used when visiting each other's houses. He thought that a silly custom; if people weren't home when you were there, why bother leaving a card? Sometimes it seemed like the Quality sort of people made a contest of how many cards they could leave at other people's houses, without actually ever having to speak to anyone. Still dazzled by the girl, Cully read the card carefully. "Olivia Dupres?" He said, pronouncing her last name as 'Doopers'.

"Doo-PRAY", she laughed. "It's Dupres. Everyone seems to calls me Doopers."

"Oh," Cully was so embarrassed he would have sunk straight into the ground and disappeared if he had been able to. "Sorry about that, Miss Du-pray."

"And you are?" She asked with an amused tilt of her head.

"Cully," he snatched off his cap and ran a hand through his tangled hair, now wishing he had taken care of it that morning. With him scheduled to haul firewood and work in the Royal Army stables that afternoon, he had not seen any point to bathing before such hard work. "Cully Runnet. I take care of his lordship the wizard," he added with pride, puffing out his chest and standing tall.

"Oh, I," she was at a loss for words. "I am sorry. I was told Lord Salva did not have a servant."

"He doesn't," Cully was quick to explain. "Not a proper one. Not since Koren ran off, and, well, I guess that's a long story, if'n you haven't already heard it." Cully was still upset that Koren Bladewell had not said anything to Cully before leaving the castle. "Seeing as his lordship doesn't have a servant, I've been filling in." As Cully spoke, a lock of Olivia's hair was caught by the breeze swirling around the base of the tall, narrow tower. The strand of hair, like finely-spun gold, danced around her face, utterly mesmerizing Cully. He shook his head, realizing that Olivia had said something to him. "I'm sorry, Miss, what did you say?"

Olivia suppressed a laugh. "I asked if Lord Salva was at home this morning."

"Yes, he," Cully panicked. The wizard had been there that morning, when Cully brought in breakfast and heated water for the wizard's bath. Seeing as Paedris was a wizard, who knew where he could have gotten to while Cully had been tending to laundry duties? He desperately wished to impress Olivia; telling her the wizard was in his tower when he might be elsewhere would be embarrassing. "He was, this morning. I have his laundry, you see," Cully lifted the basket he was carrying. "Lord Salva did say he might go out for a ride. I can see if he is receiving visitors? You have business with his lordship?"

"Yes," Olivia answered with a smile, "I am to be his new servant."

"His new-" Cully was stunned. The thought of a lovely girl like Olivia placing herself in danger while working for the sometimes-cantankerous wizard horrified him. "Miss, are you sure you want to do that? Wizards are different from you and me. There are dangerous things in there. Have you ever been around a wizard?"

"I have," Olivia opened her right palm, and a tiny, flickering flame suddenly danced there. "I am familiar with wizards, you see."

"Oh!" Cully was stricken with fear. He went down on one knee and stared at the cobblestones of the courtyard. "I meant no offense, Your Ladyship."

Olivia laughed, it was a happy sound. "Cully, please, stand up," she touched his shoulder. "I am only training to be a wizard. They sent me here to be Lord Salva's servant, nothing more." Although she had supposed all along that the Wizard's Council wanted Paedris to have a young wizard as a servant this time, figuring that a wizard would be less likely to get into unintended trouble. Or to run away, as Lord Salva's servants had a tendency to do. "Please, stand up. And you don't have to call me 'ladyship', you're making me feel old. Can you take me to the wizard?"

"Oh, yes," Cully stuttered. Then he brightened. "I can carry your satchel for you."

The satchel was heavy, and Cully already carried a basket of laundry, but Olivia knew not to refuse the offer. Cully needed to feel useful; she should let him carry the satchel. "Thank you. My shoulders are already sore from carrying it."

Cully grabbed the handle of the satchel, then hesitated. "There's not any, wizard, dangerous secret things in here, is there?"

"No. I told you, I'm not a wizard yet." Now she regretted showing off by having created a tiny fireball in her hand. A real wizard would not have done that; real wizards were not supposed to use their power to impress other people. Magical power is a gift that should never be abused, she had been taught over and over.

"Um, sure," Cully still avoided her eyes. He picked up the heavy satchel and grunted, leaning to one side. "Right this way, Your Ladyship," he said in a strained voice. They weren't even going up the stairs yet.

"Cully," she caught his arm as she opened the door at the bottom of the tower. "Please don't call me 'Ladyship'. People are going to do that when I'm a wizard, *if* I become a wizard. I would like to be a normal person as long as I can."

"You're not a normal person," Cully protested. While many of the 'Quality' people he served did not deserve his respect, wizards did. They had special powers, and they helped people. They protected Tarador from the enemy.

"Cully, starting today, I will be picking up dirty dishes and laundry. And carrying firewood, and scrubbing floors. A real wizard," she winked, "doesn't do that."

"I suppose," Cully grunted. "This," he heaved the heavy satchel up the last stair to the landing, "will be your room." With his arm shaking, he carried the satchel along, barely off the floor, and set it down next to the bed.

"This is where Lord Salva's servants stay?" She asked, looking around the cramped room. If she ever needed a reminder that she was not yet a wizard, seeing this room every morning and evening would do that for her. "Is this where Koren stayed?"

"Yes," Cully said simply, massaging his sore arm. "I cleared out his stuff, there wasn't much of it. Lord Salva has what is left. I'll show you where to put this laundry later, let's go meet the wizard."

"You are sure Lord Salva is here?"

"I'm sure," Cully managed a smile. "You'll see." When they were in the courtyard, he had seen a flash of orange light from the window of the wizard's workshop. Paedris was blowing something up again.

When they reached the level of the workshop, Cully paused to straighten his jacket and smooth his unruly hair. Then he stood up straight and knocked firmly on the doorframe. "Her Ladyship Olivia Doopers," Cully announced proudly, before cringing at mangling her surname.

"Eh?" Paedris asked, noticing them for the first time. The air in the workshop was a thin cloud of curling orange smoke, and smelled of burnt fruit. The wizard's face was streaked with dark soot. He turned from his workbench and saw Olivia. "Oh, you must be, what did you say your last name is?"

"Dupres," Olivia pronounced it correctly.

"Ah, my new protégé." Paedris replied, waving smoke away from his face. "Good, good, come in, then." He coughed. "You are to be my new servant, for now?"

"Yes, Lord Salva," Olivia looked from one end of the room to another. It was a mess, a cluttered mess. If she were asked to straighten it up, she would not know where to start.

"Excellent, then. Oh," he pointed at the clutter on the floor. "You can start here."

Bjorn Jihnsson paused at the top of a hill, breathing heavily, his legs shaking from the strain, his shoulders burning from holding the heavy log he had carried up the hill. And back down, and up, and down again, and then up. How many times he had hoisted the log across his shoulders and climbed the hill, he couldn't remember. It didn't matter. What mattered was the effort. What mattered was the pain. The pain that was his revenge against his own weakness, the pain of weakness being forced from his body and mind, with every step, and every breath, and every drop of sweat that fell onto the ground. With every bead of sweat that soaked his clothing, or ran down his face and off his chin to splatter on the ground, he sweated out not only the weakness of a body too long inactive. He sweated out self-pity, he sweated out fear. Fear that he would, as he had once before, failed in his duty. Fear, worse, that when the people who loved him most tried to comfort him, tried to explain that he had not failed in his duty, that no one could have won against such terrible odds, he had been more afraid of accepting the truth, than of death.

Bjorn had been one of the best, one of the elite, chosen personally to guard the King of Tarador, and the king had died in battle. What had frightened Bjorn the most that terrible day was not the prospect of death, nor even the fact that he and his fellow guards has failed in their duty to king and country. What frightened him the most was the uncertainty. If all of his dedication, training and bravery had not been enough to save the king, what else that Bjorn believed would be revealed to have no more substance than wisps of fog?

Right then, he needed some certainty in his life. He needed to know there would be food on the table the next day, he needed money, and he needed work. Perhaps more than the money work would provide, he needed the labor and the enforced discipline, to drive the remaining weakness from his mind and his body.

Having made the decision, Bjorn tossed the heavy log aside. He no longer needed it. There was a stream with a deep pool at the bottom of the hill, he could wash there. And down the road was a village where he could seek work. But before that, something to eat. He was hungry.

"I need work." Bjorn announced simply, looking around the cluttered blacksmith shop, which was in desperate need of cleaning and organization. Half-finished pieces were scattered around randomly, none of the raw materials were arranged for quick or easy access. Tools that should have been well-oiled were rusty, handle grips that should have been smooth leather were tattered or missing entirely, exposing the bare wood or metal. None of the tools were hanging where they were supposed to be, according to the barely-visible outlines drawn on the walls. He surveyed the mess with a critical eye, keeping the disgust off his face. "It looks like you need work done around here."

"Work?" The blacksmith scanned the stranger top to bottom, peering at the sun-reddened skin that still had the sallow tone of a person who was ill until recently. The man had the look of one who had been in great physical shape, formidable even, in the past, until some misfortune had claimed him. Although, with a second look, the man's bare arms had toned muscles. "You have experience? What kind of work are you looking for?"

"I've done some simple field smithing in my time," Bjorn said. "I can certainly organize this mess." He knew exactly where he was going to start. The shop must have produced good work at some point, or the owner would not have been able to afford so many tools. Some misfortune had befallen the shop, perhaps the man had lost a critical assistant. Or the man here was himself that assistant, who had taken over the shop and so far failed to run it successfully by himself. That seemed more likely, seeing that the shop had a volume of work waiting, which indicated customers were used to good work in the past. There was a table in the corner, with finished pieces that were tagged and ready for customers to pick up, Bjorn could see that the work was top quality, meticulous. There was potential here. He walked over to the table and picked up a part for a wagon axle. It was well made, the metal lighter than he would have expected for a piece so strong. "You do good work, what you've been able to complete," he said as he set the piece back on the table. "All I ask for is a roof over my head, and three meals a day. Let me work here for a fortnight, and if you're not pleased, I'll be on my way."

The blacksmith scratched his belly as he considered. Clearly, the newcomer had seen better times. Though Bjorn clasped his hands before him, the little finger on his left hand trembled slightly. The blacksmith scowled. "I'll not have a drunkard working around my forge."

"I don't drink." Bjorn fairly snarled in anger. "I don't touch it. If you see me drinking, you throw me right out into the street, and I'll thank you for it."

The blacksmith was taken aback by Bjorn's vehemence, his apparent hatred of alcohol. "You're old for an apprentice." He protested, not yet convinced.

"And not as stupid, or as clumsy around a forge as an apprentice. Nor as given to daydreaming when I should be working, nor chasing after every girl who walks by your shop. I'm not an apprentice. I told you, I've done some simple smithing in my time; field repairs when needed. I have enough experience at it to know I'll never have the patience or the skill to make a living as a blacksmith." He pointed to the finished pieces on the table. "You do have the skill. I want to work, I want a roof over my head and food in my belly, I don't want to take up your time teaching me to work metal. I have coins, but my funds are running low, and as you've guessed, I've been ill." That was true enough. "I need a place to live while I recover, and I need hard work to build my strength. If you want a steady, reliable man who is strong enough to be useful, and smart enough to stay out of your way, I'm your man."

Ariana arrived at the wizard's tower for their weekly meeting, an event that had become a well-practiced ritual. She walked across the courtyard with her personal guard Duston, two younger guards, and two maids. The maids carried a tea set with them; when they reached the door of the tower, Ariana and Duston took the tea set between them and slowly climbed the winding, circular steps of the tall, narrow tower up to the room that was the royal court wizard's study. Ariana walked slowly for the sake of Duston; the man's aged knees could not climb stairs as well as they used to. That was also part of the ritual; Ariana paused at each landing of the stairs, pretending that she needed to catch her breath, so that Duston could rest. She also told the man that he should not be carrying the heavy tea set, even though it was the princess who had the burden of the teapot and plates; all Duston carried was a tray with two cups and a small bowl of sweets.

When they reached the wizard's study, Paedris rose from his chair by the fireplace, or stepped away from the table by the window. Even though the crown princess and wizard had been meeting for months at the same time every Thursday morning, half of the time the wizard acted surprised to see them. The wizard always took the tray from Duston first. Then the old guard bowed, asked if the princess needed anything, and assured her that he would be right outside the door. Ariana and Paedris knew that Duston would go one floor below, to nap on the large couch in the wizard's library.

The next part of their ritual was the pouring of tea, and Ariana inquiring how the wizard would like it, with the princess knowing full well that the wizard liked a spoonful of honey. The only variation was that Paedris sometimes liked a slice of lemon in his tea, if that fruit was available. Sometimes, Ariana thought that what Paedris truly enjoyed was simply seeing a juicy yellow lemon with the tea set. Since the long-simmering war had grown hot, exotic fruits from lands to the south had become rare. There had been weeks recently when Ariana's maids had reported that there was not a lemon, nor an orange for sale in the markets of Linden, not for any price. Renewed attacks on merchant ships by pirates, pirates either sponsored or emboldened by Acedor, had cut commerce across the southern sea by half.

After tea was properly served, and they each nibbled at a small sweetcake, it was time for the next part of the ritual. The part Ariana liked least, although she had started it. "Lord Salva," she said quietly, staring at the fire, "has there been any news of Koren?"

The question was not necessary and they both knew it. If Paedris had any important information about his former servant, he would have told the princess immediately. The wizard's answer was always the same. No, no news. He and his fellow wizards continued to search for the young man. As did the Royal Army. And none of them had any idea where Koren had gone, nor word of his fate.

This time, however, Paedris took a sip of tea; tea without lemon because there were no lemons on the tray, or anywhere in Linden. He cleared his throat, and surprised the young woman who would inherit the throne of Tarador. "News? If you are asking whether Koren has been found, then, no. Nor do I know where he has gone. I do, however," he said with a raised eyebrow, "know where he is *not*."

Ariana froze, afraid of spilling tea in her lap. She set the cup down carefully and folded her hands in her lap. "Where, where he is not?"

"Yes. I am fairly certain, now, that he is not in Tarador. Fairly certain. As certain as I am that it snows in Linden each winter," he said with a wink intended to amuse the princess. Her anxious expression did not change, and Paedris regretted the attempt at humor. "Yes, well, you see, we, that is, wizards, you understand, have just this past week completed a survey of Tarador. It has been a slow and painstaking process, and it has yielded a result I both expected and feared. Koren is not within our borders. He has fled." Seeing her eyes begin to well with tears, Paedris hastened to offer her a handkerchief and continued. "He is not in Acedor, of that we are also certain. We are most certain of that. The enemy does *not* have him."

"Where could he be?" She asked softly, dabbing at her eyes.

"Inquiries I have made to the dwarves, leave me confident that he has not gone north into their lands. And he certainly would not have ventured into lands controlled by foul orcs, either. There are caravans travelling to the east, even all the way to Indus. Inquiries have been made there also, but as you are aware, there are too many merchants from too many lands to keep track of them all. And not all caravans seek to be noticed," he added with a quick glance at his future queen. Paedris thought that if Koren had sought to travel with a caravan, he would most likely seek to join smugglers. A young man who wished not to be seen would join a group accustomed to moving around unseen. Although local sheriffs might know hidden paths in the wilderness used by smugglers, no sheriff had the resources to track them all. With the war driving up prices of everything, merchants traveling overland had increased in numbers, and smugglers abounded. "In my opinion, I do not believe he traveled to the east. I do not think he went by land at all."

"How do you know?" Ariana asked hopefully, expecting that a powerful wizard had ways of knowing things.

"Highness, it is merely a feeling I have, nothing more," he shook his head sorrowfully. "I tried to think what I would have done, at Koren's age. If he sought passage on a ship, that would carry him away most swiftly; and a ship could carry him very far away. Also, although he does not know this, the water of the sea has an effect of dampening somewhat the senses of a wizard. Highness, when I became aware that Koren had," he had been about to say 'fled for his life', "left us, I searched for him. As you know, I was still weak then," from his battle with enemy wizards and then chasing an assassin across the palace rooftops. "So, my ability to project my senses were not at their greatest. Still, if he had been anywhere within my reach, I should have been able to sense *something*. Even aided by my fellows," Paedris meant the wizards who had answered his call and gathered in Linden, "I could not detect any trace of Koren. Traveling by land, he should have still been within my reach. Traveling by sea, where my senses are not so keen, he could have gone far beyond my reach. Also," the court wizard added with a wry smile, "a young man leaving home, who is seeking a fresh start and perhaps a bit of adventure, might very likely choose the sea. Young men," he said with another wink, "are drawn to adventure, whether they understand it or not."

That remark drew a smile from the princess. "Young women may seek adventure also, Lord Salva."

"Yes," Paedris said quickly. "Our society is, perhaps, not as welcoming for young ladies traveling on their own. Highness-"

"Please, call me Ariana. I am not yet anyone's queen."

"Er, yes, Ariana," Paedris responded uncomfortably. He had known the girl since she was an infant, but she had not been merely 'Ariana' to him since the day her father died. The day she became Tarador's ruler-in-waiting.

Ariana looked back at the fire. "If he went by ship, then he could be-"

"Anywhere." Paedris finished her thought. "Yes. The South Sea is vast." It had been vast when he crossed the sea, many years ago, on his voyage from his homeland of Estada to Tarador. "Highness," he wished to change the subject. "You mentioned that you are not yet queen. I regret to report that I have completed my search of the royal archives, and I do not see any legal means of you becoming queen before your sixteenth birthday."

"I must. I *must*," the crown princess insisted. "The enemy is at our gates, and my mother does nothing."

Paedris winced, torn between what he knew as the court wizard, and not wanting to encourage strife between mother and daughter. Ariana and Carlana, daughter and mother, crown princess and Regent, were not speaking to each other. The relationship between the two had become strained to the breaking point when Ariana had learned the truth about Koren; learned that her mother had known the truth all along. Her mother had known Koren was a wizard, a vulnerable young wizard, and as Regent she had done little to protect the young man. Worse, it had been Carlana's falsely and very publically accusing Koren of being a jinx, that caused him to flee the castle. To flee the place that he had come to think of as his home. Paedris had explained to Ariana that the deception surrounding Koren was the fault of Paedris, and Paedris alone, but the princess had been beyond listening at that point. When the enemy attacked across the border, and the only response of the Regent had been to pull the Royal Army back, Ariana had entirely stopped speaking with her mother. Now, the two communicated only through servants and written notes. Paedris took a sip of tea before answering. "You *must* become queen soon? There is a difference between *should* and *could*, Your Highness. You know that I fully support you taking the throne sooner than your sixteenth birthday. Soon. *Now*, if possible. I do not see that it is possible."

"No law is perfect," Ariana spoke from experience. "There must be a way."

"It pains me to say, but at this point, I believe you need to consult an expert on the law. An attorney. I can make inquiries to find someone discreet," Paedris frowned. An attorney who was discrete, and also reckless. An attorney willing to take the crown princess as a client, and risk incurring the wrath of Tarador's current ruler. If the attorney failed to find a way around the law, he or she could be charged with treason by the Regent. "Someone-"

"No." Ariana shook her head. Then, to the surprise of Paedris, she smiled. "I know a legal expert."

"Cap'n wants everyone on deck," Alfonze announced while rapping his knuckles on the timbers overhead.

Koren blinked sleep out of his eyes; he had been taking a rather pleasant nap in his gently swaying hammock, as the *Lady Hildegard* rested at anchor. All the ports were open, and a tropical breeze wafted through the lower deck, which was nicely shaded from the hot afternoon sun of the South Isles.

"Did he say why?" Renten asked with a yawn from his own hammock. Many of the crew had been sleeping during the hottest part of the day, a practice that their Estadan crewmate Diergo called a 'siesta'. Renten didn't care what it was called, he enjoyed a break after lunch. Besides, there wasn't much to do aboard the ship, nor had there been for the past eight days. When they reached Antigura, where the ship was now moored in that island's harbor, they had endured several days of hard labor to unload their cargo. Sometimes the back-breaking work of unloading was immediately followed by loading new cargo in the ship's holds. Sometimes there were a few days of leisure ashore, when the crew could relax and spend their money in taverns, or other places of amusement that were only too happy to take a foolish sailor's hard-earned coins. But this time, it had been eight days since the ship's holds had been emptied from their previous trip, and no cargo was waiting to be loaded. In the excellent harbor of Antigura, many ships swung idly at anchor, waiting for contracts to carry goods, and it was getting to the point where many of the crews had begun to grumble. Merchant sailors were not paid if there was no cargo to carry.

"No, he didn't say why," Alfonze scoffed. "Captain Reed doesn't confide in me, nor you, you lazy lout. Now get on deck, and make it quick."

Koren joined the somewhat bleary-eyed group of sailors who made their way through the lower deck to the hatchway, and up to the ship's main deck to stand blinking and shading their eyes in the bright tropical sunshine. Usually, the *Lady Hildegard* had some cargo lashed to the deck; crates or barrels that could stand being exposed to the weather, and would not fit in the cargo holds. Now, the deck was empty of anything that was not necessary to make the ship move. While they were idle, Koren had been practicing tying knots, and learning how to maneuver the ship. How to set what sails in a particular wind, how to adjust sails when the ship was going with, crosswise to or against the wind. Koren's head was spinning with terms like reach and run and tacking and beating and wearing, and he was certain that he would never understand all of it, or even enough of it. How expert ship handlers like Captain Reed remembered all the myriad things they needed to know, Koren could not imagine, but the captain and first mate and others made it look easy. To them, it was second nature to come up on deck, feel the breeze on their faces and simply know exactly how to get the best speed out of their somewhat awkward and slow merchant ship. Alfonze told Koren that, after he learned the basics of seamanship, he could attempt to learn navigation. Navigation, that apparently magical art of knowing where the ship was, on the open sea with no land in sight. Privately, Koren told himself that his poor brain could never hope to learn navigation; his greatest ambition at the moment was to be an instinctive sailor like Alfonze, who scrambled up and down the rigging like a monkey. Alfonze thought nothing of walking out along one of the upper spars during a storm to reef sails; with the ship bobbing up and down and side to side, and every motion exaggerated the higher a sailor climbed from the deck. Koren was as yet trusted only to work the lower set of sails; to climb to the first set of spars. Someday, soon, he hoped to join the rank of sailors like Alfonze who worked the topsails.

"Gather here," the first mate's voice boomed out, louder than necessary as the ship was gently floating at anchor with only a light breeze wafting over the deck. The first mate had developed his speaking voice to be heard all the way at the top of the mast during a raging storm, and the man did not seem to know any lower volume.

Koren and the others shuffled their feet, to crowd in front of the quarterdeck where the captain stood in front of the wheel which steered the ship. A wheel that had been lashed stationary for the past fortnight. At first, the wheel had been immobilized so work could be performed on the ship's rudder, but that had taken only two days. Now, it remained lashed because the ship was not going anywhere.

Captain Reed stepped forward and took off the broad-brimmed hat he usually wore when the sun was overhead. With the ship resting at anchor, the crew had rigged an awning that covered most of the deck, shielding them from the sun's burning rays. Even so, Koren's neck itched where the collar of his shirt touched his reddened skin. He needed to listen to the sailors who had spent many years in the tropics, and cover himself better when the sun was scorching down on him. "We have a cargo," Reed announced simply, and the crew cheered. The captain held up a hand for quiet. "The cargo is for Istandol."

The crew around Koren murmured and grumbled, shifting their feet and looking at each other. Before Koren could ask Alfonze about Istandol, Captain Reed continued. "You know what that means; a high potential for profit, because we'll be taking high risk."

"Pirates, he means," Alfonze said quietly.

"With the war up north," Reed gestured in that direction, "business here is bad. There's less demand for cargo, and more piracy than I've seen in all my years at sea. We could stay here, where the pirates haven't ventured yet, but there's no money here to pay our costs. Too many ships," he pointed to the harbor where more than a dozen ships were idle, "chasing not enough profit. So, we're going north, to Istandol. We won't load cargo for another week yet, I want to careen the ship, scrape the weed off her bottom."

That prompted some appreciative nodding of heads among the crew. A slow merchant ship like the *Lady Hildegard* had a difficult enough time trying to outrun light, fast pirate ships. If the ship's hull below the waterline was cluttered with barnacles, mussels, seaweed and any other form of sea life that clung to wood or rock, her speed would be cut further. What the captain was proposing was to take the ship into shallow water, where a low tide would cause the hull to lay aground and exposed. Until the tide began to rise again, the crew would scrape away any unwanted growth, and take the opportunity to inspect and repair the timbers. It would be hot, dirty work, but it would give the ship a better chance to evade pirates. "Anyone," Reed said while looking in the eyes of his crew, "who wishes to leave the ship, can do so with no hard feelings."

"I have a family," Renten said just loudly enough for the men around him to hear. "I didn't sign up to fight pirates," he stared at the deck.

"Aye," Alfonze clapped a hand on Renten's shoulder. "You need to think of your family first. No hard feelings, as the captain said."

Captain Reed spoke for a few more minutes, detailing the bonuses that would be paid upon delivery in Istandol, and they were substantial. Perhaps enough to change some minds among the crew; Koren could see some men counting on their fingers, imagining the coins they would receive at Istandol. Then the first mate dismissed them, with a warning that the ship would begin moving toward the careenage spot just after noontime the next day.

"What do you think, Alfonze?" Koren asked. He had seen battle, and he did not seek to experience it again. At least on land, soldiers were able to retreat if faced with superior force. On the sea, if the *Lady Hildegard* were chased by faster pirate ships, Koren's fate would be in the hands of the captain's skill, and luck. He would have no place to go other than his assigned station in the rigging. And he would be virtually powerless to control what happened to him.

Alfonze scratched his head and thought for a moment. "I think the captain is doing the best he can. All these other ships are sitting idle, with weed growing on their bottom, and pay for the crew running out. If we swing here at anchor too long, we may as well let her sink and be done with it."

"Are you going?" Koren asked anxiously.

"I don't know as I'm sure yet," the big man mused, looking longingly at the shore. "I'm going into town, talk to other crews. See if any other ships have a berth for an experienced sailor, and a less risky cargo. But I doubt it. Will you join me?"

Koren smiled wryly. "You want me to come with you, so I can lend you coins for rum."

"Rum? Me, drinking rum?" Alfonze grinned and cuffed Koren lightly on the head. "Ah, you're young. What else are you going to do with the coins that are burning a hole in your pocket, eh?"

CHAPTER THREE

Royal Chancellor Gustov Kallron strode purposefully down the broad hallway of the royal palace, the robes of his office flowing around him. Guards stiffened to attention as he approached, and held their posture until the royal chancellor had gone around a corner. With the throne vacant and a Regent ruling Tarador, Chancellor Kallron was the second most powerful person in the kingdom. Some said, as the Regent was weak and indecisive, that Kallron was *the* most powerful. Although, he could not get the Regent to take action against the enemy, so what good did his power do for him? Or for Tarador?

Kallron paused outside the door to the private chambers of the crown princess, catching his breath and straightening his robes. A meaningful glance by one of the guards flanking the door drew the Chancellor's attention to a tiny piece of lint caught in a fold of his robe, he clumped it and tucked it into a pocket. With a curt nod, he signaled that he was ready; the guards thumped their staffs on the floor, opened the large double doors and announced him. "Chancellor Kallron to see Her Royal Highness Ariana, as requested."

Kallron stifled a smile of amusement. Ariana. A girl he had held on his knee when she was a baby. A girl who had spit up on his expensive robes, many times. And now she was a young woman, learning how to rule her nation.

"Chancellor Kallron," Ariana said in a cool and unfriendly tone, and Kallron stiffened. Sometimes when the crown princess called for him, it was because she wanted him to do something behind her mother's back, and Kallron had to prepare himself for a struggle between his competing responsibilities. But even when Ariana was making trouble for him, she always had a friendly smile. Not this day. Kallron's mind raced through the past several days, since his last meeting with Ariana. That meeting had been a quick lunch, an opportunity for Ariana to complain about her mother, and to ask Kallron's opinion of issues her military tutor had raised. What could have happened in the past few days to sour Ariana's mood? She had met with the court wizard the previous day, but Ariana met often with Lord Salva, and Paedris had not said anything about it to Kallron. The Chancellor considered Paedris to be a friend and ally; if something was amiss, he would have expected the wizard to tell him. Unless the wizard himself did not know what was troubling the crown princess? Ariana's mood had been volatile since the wizard's servant had fled from Linden and, apparently, from all of Tarador.

There was something more to that story, much more than Kallron knew. And that drove the Chancellor to many sleepless nights. The court wizard, the Regent, and Ariana knew something about why Koren Bladewell had fled from the castle; something very important. And none of them would tell Gustov Kallron, although he had hinted that the Chancellor of the Realm certainly needed to know anything important.

Kallron had many guesses about why the Royal Army had been sent out to bring Koren back, or kill him if he had been captured by the enemy. Had Koren stolen something from the wizard, something dangerous? Did Koren know a dangerous secret? Kallron could only guess, and his guesses failed to satisfy him. He had interviewed soldiers who had served with Koren on their ill-fated expedition, when Lord Salva had been attacked by enemy wizards. Other than the fact that Koren had been falsely accused of desertion and cowardice, Kallron had learned little to explain why the three most powerful people in the realm seemed almost desperate for Koren's safe return. Captain Raddick also knew something about Koren, Kallron suspected, although Raddick was not talking, and had requested duty in the field where he was far from intrigues around the royal palace.

Kallron bowed from the waist; the correct amount of bending owed by a senior royal official to the future queen. "Your Highness."

"Kallron, you serve the crown," Ariana said in an unfriendly tone.

No, she was not unfriendly, Kallron told himself. She was nervous. Whatever it was, it made her uncomfortable. "I serve your mother. Or, officially, I serve the Regent," he corrected himself.

"Chancellor Kallron, you disappoint me," Ariana said with an exaggerated pout. "You serve the Regent, but your service is at the pleasure of the crown. I *am* the crown."

It was not often that Kallron found himself surprised. He truly did not know where the conversation was going. "That is true, Your Highness," he said in a neutral tone. "It is, the best term perhaps is a 'legal fiction' that my office serves at the pleasure of-"

"No." Ariana declared flatly. "It is legal. It is the law. It is not a 'legal fiction'. You serve Tarador. I am the head of state, whether my mother holds the Regency or not. You serve at my pleasure, Mister Kallron."

It was even less often that Gustov Kallron found himself at a loss for words. He could not recall when last it had happened. Ever? Had it ever happened? When he finally found his voice, he managed to say "Have I displeased Your Highness?"

"You have displeased us," Ariana replied; using the royal 'we' that reminded the listener that in this case, she *was* Tarador.

"I, I am sorry, Your Highness," Kallron stammered. "What have I-"

"It displeases us that, while you serve my mother, you cannot truly serve me. And, Uncle Kallron," her voice softened, "I need you. I need your wisdom, your strength."

"Tarador needs me," Kallron protested, thinking the princess sought a tutor, or an ally in her recent personal struggles against her mother.

"Yes, Tarador does need you. Tarador needs you to serve me directly, and not my mother." Before the man could open his mouth to protest, she pressed her point. "What have you accomplished by serving my mother, Kallron? Nothing. *Nothing.* It is not any fault of your own; you have accomplished nothing, because my mother is determined to do nothing. You may give the Regent advice every moment of every day, and in the end, she will do nothing. Chancellor Kallron, your service of my mother has greatly displeased us. You are dismissed from office, effective immediately."

"Highness, I do not know what to say," he answered with complete honesty. When he woke that morning, the possibility of being dismissed from office had been the furthest thing from his mind.

"My decision will be officially entered into the royal archives this very day," Ariana pointed to a scroll on her desk. She dipped a pen into ink, and signed it with a flourish. Dripping hot wax onto the bottom of the scroll, she pressed her royal seal into the wax to make it official.

"Very well," the now unemployed Gustov Kallron said in a low voice. "Your Highness, I must say that I am disappointed. You will be queen soon. You must not allow your personal squabbles with your mother affect-"

"This is not personal. I will be queen soon. I will not be queen soon *enough*. Not soon enough for Tarador. Tell me, Mister Kallron, what will be left for me to inherit upon my sixteenth birthday? Will there be a Tarador then? Answer me," she demanded angrily. "You no longer serve my mother; you no longer serve anyone but yourself. Speak your mind, please. Speak as yourself."

Kallron let out a long breath. A breath he realized, right then, that he had been holding since the day Ariana's father had died. The day that he began to fear Tarador would not survive. "No. If the situation does not change, I fear there will not be a Tarador by then."

"Then help me," Ariana pleaded. "Help me ascend the throne, soon, now. Help me lead Tarador to victory." Or survival, if that is all they could accomplish.

"Your Highness-" Kallron's voice trailed off. Again, he was struck speechless. "The law-"

"No one knows the law better than you. If there is a way for me to become queen, to take power for my mother. To take action. To save our nation."

"You ask much, Your Highness. I am an old man," Kallron admitted. This would be the fight of his life. The past few years, the past decade, he had felt his years weighing on him. Every day, it became more difficult to rise from bed each morning.

"Don't do it for me, then. Do it for your family."

Kallron had to smile. "Do not try to manipulate me, young lady," he waggled a finger at his future ruler. "I taught you how to do that."

"And you taught me well," she replied with a sad smile. "Will you join me? I cannot pay you as much as my mother does; she has access to the royal treasury. As you know, I do have my own funds. And more useless jewelry that I can sell." She waved her right hand, on which she wore three rings.

Kallron walked over to the window and looked down into the courtyard. Guards were marching toward the training grounds. Servants were carrying things. People were going on about their lives. Lives that would not be possible if the enemy were to conquer Tarador. He found himself having to dab away a tear from his cheek. "Money, I do not need. I have my own funds; I have invested well. Highness," his voice choked up, "I am an old man. All my wife and I care about now is that our children and grandchildren are safe. Yes, I will do what I can to help you." Tears welled up in his eyes, and he wiped them away with his sleeve, not caring about the condition of his robes. The official robes of an office he no longer held. "Highness, you can pay me with the most precious currency of all. You can give me *hope*."

"Thank you-"

Kallron turned away from the window, mentally preparing himself for the upcoming struggle. "I feel that I must warn you; from what I know of the law, I do not know of any way for you to assume the throne before your sixteenth birthday. You can be assured that I will do my utmost. And, Your Highness, it is I who need to thank you. You have given an old man hope. Until this morning, I did not realize how I had been living without it."

Ariana had tears in her eyes, she blinked and dabbed away the tears with a handkerchief. "Can you begin searching the royal archives today?" She asked hopefully.

"Highness, I believe that my first task as your advisor, will be to inform your mother of my new situation. Unless," he asked with a straight face, "you wish to do so?"

"Oh, no," Ariana gritted her teeth. "You should do that." Then she clapped her hands in delight. "Though I do wish that I could see mother's face when you tell her."

Ariana might have enjoyed seeing her mother's face when Gustov Kallron told Carlana Trehayme that he had been dismissed from service by her daughter. When he showed the Regent the official declaration, signed by the crown princess. And when he explained that Ariana was entirely correct; that there was nothing the Regent could do about it. Ariana probably would have especially enjoyed seeing the enraged expression on Carlana's face after the Regent suggested with a smile that the former chancellor could continue serving as Carlana's advisor, with another title. Gustov Kallron had declined that opportunity, telling the Regent of Tarador that he had already accepted another position. He had to decline, because he had already accepted a position as chief advisor to the crown princess.

Before being angrily banished from the Regent's presence, Kallron had presented her with a list names; people who would be good candidates to replace him as royal chancellor. They were all good people, they would all serve the Regent well. None of them had the experience or the talent of Gustov Kallron.

What Ariana certainly did not like was her mother's reaction. Seeing that her daughter intended to cause trouble in the royal palace, Carlana decreed that for the safety of the crown princess, her daughter would be moving to the Trehayme's traditional summer palace.

"Can she really do that?" Ariana sputtered. It was her turn to be enraged.

"Your mother is not stupid, Highness," Kallron explained. "Yes, she can do that. This is one of the consequences I warned you about. Your mother has great power, even over you. As Regent, she is responsible for the safety of the royal family; which is you. She has the authority to move you to a location that she deems to be safe. Highness, your mother wanted to send you away to stay with your uncle Duke Yarron in LeVanne province."

"What? But that is so far away!" The princess protested.

"Too far, I agree. The law also agrees, and I have already intervened for you with your mother. The law states that, in time of war, the head of state must remain in a secure location that is controlled by the royal family. That is why she is sending you to the summer palace in the mountains, and not to far-off LeVanne."

"Ohhh!" Ariana felt like smashing something. "This is *so* unfair! Uncle Kallron, this is exactly why I must become queen, as soon as possible."

"Yes, Your Highness," Kallron agreed coolly, knowing he needed to let the young lady express her frustration.

"Mother wants me away from Linden, so I can't cause more trouble for her?"

"For that reason, yes. Also to punish you, I suspect. But the most important reason, because I know how your mother thinks, is that while you are at the summer palace, your personal guard will need to be with you."

Ariana tilted her head. There was a lesson for her in his words; she knew the way Kallron spoke when he wanted her to learn something. "Why is that important?"

"Because, Your Highness, while your personal guard force is with you in the mountains, they are not here. In the palace. At the seat of power."

Ariana paused to think before she responded. Of course, her guards could not be both here and with her at the same time. If her guards were here at the palace in Linden- She sucked in a sharp breath. "Mother is afraid that I might use my guards to overthrow her?" Had relations between mother and daughter fallen so far that her mother was afraid for her own safety?

"Your mother is simply being cautious."

"Mother is *always* cautious," Ariana said almost to herself. "That is her problem. Is she truly afraid of me?" As much as Ariana disdained her mother's leadership of the country, she felt a pang of guilt that her own mother might fear her.

"She is, I think, concerned that you may be influenced by the wrong sort of people. People such as myself, now that relations between your mother and I are broken." He had never seen the Regent so furious, so personally hurt. "She believes that my leaving her service and becoming your chief advisor was my own idea; that I am using you for my own purposes."

"That is preposterous! She must know- No, no, she doesn't." Ariana mused. Of course, her mother would assume the crown princess was being used by sinister forces. "I should speak with my mother."

"No, Your Highness, you should not," Kallron said firmly.

"But-"

"Highness, you assured me that your motivation for taking power away from Carlana Trehayme is a matter of state, for the survival of our nation. You told me this is not a personal spat between you and your mother. In your roles, you are the crown princess and she is the Regent. You need to treat her that way, and think of her as Regent, and not as your mother. Ariana," he added softly, "this is going to get much worse, if you are determined to take the throne as soon as possible. How will your mother feel when she learns that you are acting to strip her of her power?"

"She will be terribly hurt," Ariana said in a whisper. She straightened in her chair. This was a matter of state, a matter of national survival. Carlana Trehayme was in the way. There would be time for apologies and reconciliation after Ariana wore the crown, and sat on the throne of Tarador. "Very well. How soon do I have to leave?"

Kallron breathed a sigh of relief. His young student was learning quickly. "I am hoping not for two weeks, perhaps a bit more. The Royal Army needs to assure that the summer palace is secure, and that the roads to the palace are clear. Even with messages traveling by telegraph, that takes considerable time. Particularly because the Royal Army does not wish the additional burden of protecting you and your mother in two different locations. I might be able to stretch your departure possibly to three weeks, but certainly not longer. Until then, we must be careful that your personal guard force does nothing unusual or in any way threatening."

"I should plan for two weeks," Ariana mused. "Do you have to go with me?"

"Yes," Kallron said with a look that was a combination of defeat and defiance. "Your mother fears that, if I remain here, I may be plotting against her." That remark drew a brief smile. He certainly was plotting against her, but not in any way Carlana Trehayme could imagine. "Also, she is rather angry with me, and wished me out of her sight. I will take with me such books from the royal library that I think will be useful." There was no denying that not having access to the full library, would hamper his efforts to find a legal means of making Ariana queen before her sixteenth birthday.

"Confound that woman," Paedris said angrily, slapping down on his workbench a scroll he had just received from the Regent.

"That woman?" Shomas Feany mumbled over a mouthful of honeycake. "Carlana?"

"Who else vexes me so?" Paedris sighed. "Yesterday I wrote to her, expressing my concern that the crown princess needs to remain here in Linden, so that I am able to continue to advise her on wizardly matters regarding actions of the enemy. And also my concern that, at the summer palace, Ariana will not have my protection. I must remain here." Unless the entire government of Tarador decamped for the summer palace, Paedris needed to remain in Linden, at the center of power. "Now that, woman," Paedris gritted his teeth to choke down a bad word, "has refused me.

She says," he unrolled the scroll and read it in disbelief. "She says that she agrees with my concern for the safety of the crown princess, and therefore she is requesting that we send a wizard with Ariana. That woman thinks wizards grow on trees!" While it was true that the enemy's action against Paedris in the village of Longshire had brought many wizards to the defense of Tarador, most of them were now in the field with the Royal Army at the desperate request of Grand General Magrane. In Tarador were only Paedris, Shomas, Lord Mwazo and several minor and young wizards. Even Madame Chu had gone to the front lines after her exhausting journey from Indus. Paedris' heart ached when he thought of the wizard from Ching-Do putting herself in danger every day.

"I'll go," Shomas said with a burp. "Oh, that was a good honeycake."

"You?" Paedris was surprised at his jolly friend volunteering for a strenuous trip up into the mountains. Shomas would be traveling in a coach, but the roads were bad once they reached the foothills of the mountains. The journey would be long days being bounced and jolted in a coach, with nights in rough country inns, or tents. Then Paedris realized how Shomas, a friend of many years, might have perceived what Paedris said. Shomas was a powerful wizard in his own way, but not in ways that typically lent themselves to protecting a future queen.

"Certainly," Shomas said as he reached for another honeycake. "You know how I hate the summer heat here in Linden, Paedris. The summer palace will have plenty of fat fish in the streams, and game abundant in the woods. I will feast like a king!" He patted his belly. "The princess will have her personal guard, and a full century of Royal Army soldiers with her. You and Mwazo stay here and wrestle with the mind of the enemy, Paedris. I could use a fine summer holiday."

"Oh," Paedris didn't know what else to say. "Good, then." He did feel better knowing that Ariana would have a wizard with her.

"I will take Olivia with me. It will be a good experience for her. You certainly have not had time to instruct the girl properly," Shomas observed. "Unless you can't do without a young wizard to clean up after you for a few months?" He added with a raised eyebrow.

Shomas was taking Olivia away? Paedris tried to hide his dismay. He did have to admit; Olivia's instruction had been lacking since she came to work for the court wizard. "No, she should go with you. You are right, it will be good for her."

The *Lady Hildegard* fairly flew across the wavetops, racing north at her best speed. Before she left the island of Antigura, her crew had scraped her bottom clean, made any repairs needed to timbers or sails or rigging, and carefully loaded the valuable cargo of spices and fruits that were common in the South Isles, but considered exotic in the north. As he spliced a rope on deck, Koren thought that pirates could find the ship simply by following the tantalizing scent of dried spices and a delicious fruit called 'pine-apples'.

With the crew anxiously scanning the horizon for sails that could be a pirate ship, neither captain nor first mate needed to raise their voices to rouse the crew to action in trimming sails. If anyone saw a sail not so filled with wind so that it was stiff as iron, it was the crew cupping their hands and shouting to the officers for permission to adjust the sails. And add more sail, for every-one aboard had butterflies in their stomachs, anxious for the first sight of land. While the ship would normally seek to avoid squalls that could tear away precious sails and damage the rigging, in this case squalls were sought out and steered for. Squall winds could push the ship along rapidly, and the clouds and sudden, drenching rains served to conceal the *Lady Hildegard* from any searching eyes within the horizon. As a squall approached, sailors needed no urging to reef sails, in order that the strong winds not carry away spars and snap mast poles.

Koren was aboard, as were Alfonze, and even Renten. Only seven of the crew left the ship to avoid the prospect of being killed or captured by pirates, and three new men had signed on. Renten had grudgingly remained aboard, telling anyone who would listen that while it would not do his family any good for him to fall victim to piracy, neither would it do them any good for him to sit idle in the South Isles. When the ship reached Istandol, Renten had declared, he was going to take his share of the profits, set foot on land, and never go to sea again.

Alfonze had laughed privately, telling Koren that Renten had been a sailor since he was Koren's age. "He'll be back. If not this ship, then another. The sea is in his blood now, he doesn't know any other life. That happens to a lot of men, Kedrun," Alfonze said as a warning or merely an observa-tion, Koren couldn't tell which. "They come aboard a ship, to work for a couple years, they say. Earn some coin, then go back on land, buy a piece of land, and be a farmer for the rest of their lives. It happens," the big man shrugged, "but not often. You get used to a life like this," Alfonze looked up at billowing canvas against the bright blue sky, then down at the waves that raced along the ship's hull. "And after being on land for a week or two, you begin to miss it."

Koren wondered if that would happen to him. He had not intended to become a sailor; he had sought only to escape from Tarador. To save his own life. He had not expected to become a sailor. He had not expected to enjoy the life of a sailor; the feeling of being part of a crew, of seeing ex-otic foreign lands, of seeing something different most mornings when he came on deck. He had intended to go someplace where his jinx curse could not harm anyone he cared about, but here nothing had happened. Nothing bad, or alarming or in any way unusual had happened to him or around him at all. He had begun to hope, or begun to *hope* that he might someday dare hope, that he had left his curse behind when he went to sea. "Will you ever leave the sea, Alfonze?" He asked.

"Someday, I suppose," Alfonze said with a frown. "When I'm too old, maybe. I'd like to be cap-tain of my own ship someday. That takes not just experience, it takes money, and I'll need to save." Captain Reed was part owner of the *Lady Hildegard*; the ship was named after his mother. "Or have someone stake me the coins. That's not likely to happen with the war on, and commerce so bad." He scratched his beard thoughtfully. "If business doesn't pick up, some of us might find our-selves back on land, whether we intend to or not. Or, taking service in the Navy." Tarador's Royal Navy had been neglected in recent years, as the demands of the army on the realm's finances drained funds away from the sea service. The Royal Navy was frantically rebuilding, but it would be several years before it reached adequate strength.

"Would you do that?" Koren asked anxiously. He would hate to see Alfonze leave, but Koren himself could never risk daily contact with Tarador's military. Surely the navy had orders to look for Koren Bladewell, and he had heard that navy ships often transported army soldiers. No, Koren would steer well clear of Tarador's navy.

"Not unless I had to. It's a hard life in the navy, and pay is poor. I'd do it, if I had no other option. Or, if I thought my signing up would make a difference in the war, I guess." Despite his earlier disdain for the long-running war between Tarador and Acedor, Alfonze had more recently expressed concern when news arrived that the war was not going well for Tarador. If Tarador were to fall, Alfonze fretted, then not even the distant South Isles would be safe from the enemy. "As it is, Tarador's navy is so weak, nothing much they do can matter in the war. They can't even keep pirates away from their own coast." Word had reached Antigura that pirates were preying on ships in the coastal waters off Tarador; that pirates had been seen taking ships in broad daylight, within view of the coastline. Cargo that once would have traveled by ship along Tarador's coast now had to go by wagon on slow roads inland, and that had strangled commerce. The decline in shipping had reduced the targets available to pirate, but Alfonze remarked the pirates did not much care; they were paid by Acedor to disrupt seagoing commerce, and any ships they captured were merely a bonus. The pirates needed slaves to row their ships more than they needed booty for their crew to waste; many pirate captains and officers were under magical compulsion, and had no desire for anything other than destruction on behalf of their dark master. Alfonze looked up at the sails, which were beginning to flap as the breeze slackened. "I don't trust this wind to continue," Alfonze observed sourly, "we've had too much good luck with the weather on this trip. It's time for the weather to turn on us."

Fergus the blacksmith inspected the work of his helper, and grunted. "That's good. Strong, Not fine, but plenty strong."

"I told you," Bjorn said, "I've done field smithing before. Repairing parts of wagon, shield, armor. Just enough to hold things together until we could get to a real blacksmith."

"You have potential. Have you considered becoming a smith? You might be able to learn, after a while." Fergus held back the true measure of praise, not wanting Bjorn to know his true value. Fergus was hoping to sign the man as a full apprentice, and to do it for cheap.

"No, I haven't. I'm not staying here. Thank you, but I've regained much of my strength, and you pay fairly, so I have coins in my pocket. In another fortnight, perhaps a month, I'll be moving on."

"To do what?" Fergus was curious. The broken down, shaking man who had approached him was now strong, and had shown no sign of touching drinks such as whiskey. From what Fergus could tell, Bjorn had not spent a single coin of his pay, content to sleep in the shed behind the shop, and to eat the food cooked by Fergus' wife.

"I was a king's guard," Bjorn explained. He had told Fergus that before, but the blacksmith likely had not believed him at the time. "Then I became lost, for a while. I lost myself in drink, and I lost my family. I'd like to see them again. My wife has remarried, I'm told, but I'd like my children to see me as I once was. Before weakness and drink took everything away from me."

The blacksmith's helper was so sincere in his words, so hurt, that Fergus only nodded. It would do no good to try asking Bjorn to stay; he needed to go. He needed to find something that he had lost. Fergus had two children; both too young to help in the shop, but he reflected how he would feel if his own children could not look at him with respect. Fergus could not bear that. "A fortnight? We'd best get this order done before then, eh?"

Ariana's mother insisted the princess depart for the summer palace as soon as possible, so all Kallron's efforts to delay the journey came to nothing. Twelve days after the Regent announced the crown princess would be leaving Linden, the carriages were ready, and Ariana glumly went out through the west gate of the castle. The journey to the summer palace was not long; only three days traveling by swift carriage. While at first Ariana fumed at being away from Linden, and mostly fuming at her mother having outmaneuvered her, Ariana decided to force herself to enjoy being at the summer palace. She owed it to her servants and guards, who had all worked very hard to prepare for the journey and had all been tremendously inconvenienced, to put on a smile and pretend that the whole affair was a delightful holiday. She did enjoy the summer palace, perched high on a hill to the northwest of Linden. As a little girl, she remembered many wonderful summers there, when her family escaped the heat of the city. And gained a respite from the constant demand of courtiers, foreign dignitaries, envoys from the seven provinces, and everyone else who demanded the precious time and attention of the royal family.

Then, after her father had died, she had only been to the summer palace three times, as her mother feared to be away from Linden. Feared not only for the safety of her daughter and herself; Carlana also feared those who might be tempted to seize power in Linden during the Regent's absence. As the royal carriage wound its way up the long driveway toward the summer palace, Ariana hung out the window, letting the warm breeze caress her face. In days past, she remembered the drive being lined with flowers on both sides; now it was mostly low-growing bushes and wildflowers. With the royal family not in residence, the summer palace had been neglected. And, Ariana considered, the increasing financial demands of defending Tarador had likely caused her mother to cut the budget for permanent staff at the summer palace.

When the carriage went around a curve in the drive, the palace came into view. Being set atop the hill allowed for cooling breezes to blow through the building, a welcome respite from the still, hot summer air in Linden. Ariana could see servants, even guards, working to remove weeds from the flowerbeds and plant new flowers from the gardens. Ariana smiled. Gardening was something she could do to keep herself busy, and take her mind off the fact that she had effectively been banished from her own palace. Until Kallron found a way for her to assume power, Ariana had to swallow the fact that she would have to suffer enforced idleness at the summer palace, far from the seat of power.

She turned to look at the carriage behind her, where the young wizard Olivia Dupres was also hanging out the window. Having Olivia along would make the summer so much better for Ariana. In many ways, Ariana envied the young wizard, and not only envied her magical power. Olivia had power of her own; power and respect and a future of unlimited prospects. Ariana's prospects were vast but narrow, constricted by the role of the monarch. Ariana envied that freedom.

She also envied that Olivia knew what it was like to be a wizard. When Ariana allowed herself to daydream about Koren Bladewell, she often thought of how wonderful it would be for Koren to learn about his own magical powers. Ariana could share his joy, but she could never truly understand it. She could never share that part of Koren's life with him; his power would always be a barrier between them.

Perhaps Paedris was right when he cautioned Ariana not to dream too seriously of a life with Koren Bladewell. Wizards were different, that was the truth of it. Relationships between wizards and ordinary people rarely worked. And Ariana had crushing responsibilities of her own to occupy all of her attention.

As she considered the reality that Koren would be a powerful wizard able to go and do as he wished, and she would be trapped by crown and throne, her smile faded. Behind her, Olivia caught her eye and waved with pure delight, pointing to a cluster of butterflies on the wildflowers that lined the drive. Ariana forced a smile back on her face and waved back. She would make the best of her enforced exile from Linden, and she would not be a burden to the servants and guards who had no choice but to join her. She did not, however, expect to be truly happy.

CHAPTER FOUR

Four days after arriving at the summer palace, with life having already settled into a routine, Ariana decided that an outing to the lake would be a nice change of scene, to break her out of her developing dark mood. Although she had done her best effort to smile and enjoy being in the hills, most, people could see that she was deeply unhappy. Even Olivia doing magical 'tricks' had failed to cheer up Ariana.

Lord Feany was all in favor of an outing to the lake. He was certain there were many fat fish waiting to be caught in those pristine waters; indeed he had been talking about the lake since they arrived. Shomas Feany had been enjoying the hard work of the summer palace kitchen staff, so much so that he had not yet found time to continue Olivia's instruction on wizardry. Gustov Kall-ron declined the invitation to join the outing; he was much engrossed in studying the ancient law books from the royal library, and much discouraged by what he had found so far.

On the ride down to the lake, Olivia rode her horse next to Shomas. "Sir, could you help me to work with fireballs? I can't keep them stable, they go fuzzy and disappear," she added, her face red with embarrassment. 'Fuzzy?' That was not the way a wizard should speak. "Lord Salva was teach-ing me, and then he got too busy, and, I haven't been making progress."

Shomas tried not to be insulted; the young wizard was not aware that Shomas could barely cre-ate a fireball, about which he was still sensitive. "Creating an impressive fireball is not the true mark of wizard," he said defensively. "There are powers far greater than playing with tricks to im-press the common folk, Olivia." That came out more grumpily than he intended. "Show me what you can do. Be careful, don't hurt anyone."

"I will be careful, sir." She let go of the reins so she could concentrate, the road was fairly wide and flat, and her horse gentle. With her right hand, she made a flame flicker, and tried to follow Lord Salva's direction to make it spin, and feeding power into it. Her connection to the power was tenuous, and kept slipping from her grasp.

"That is quite good," Shomas was impressed. At her age, she was already more powerful than he was, in that arcane art of pulling raw power from the spirit world. "It looks like you are doing very well."

Olivia took the praise with a dose of frustration. Knowing that she was not using approved technique, she used the fingers of her left hand to draw the flame higher, and the fireball surged to the size of a small apple. It held stable, increasing in brightness. Then her concentration slipped when her horse stumbled, and the flame winked out.

Shomas was so startled, he nearly fell off his horse, having to hold onto the horse's mane with both hands. The animal only looked back at him briefly, being used to the sometimes clumsiness of its master. "What?" He exclaimed. "What did you do there?"

Olivia's face reddened again. "Oh, sir, I know it is not the way I should be doing it, I'm developing bad habits. But I grow so frustrated," she shook her fists in the air, "when I can't make it work the proper way."

"No! No, don't be ashamed. Girl, that is *brilliant*! Where did you learn that?" He had never seen that technique used before. He had never read about it, in all the hundreds of books and scrolls on wizardry that he had studied over many years. Had Paedris been withholding important knowledge from him? He could not believe it.

"No one taught it to me, sir. I, I figured it out. I tried it one time, and it worked. Only a little at first. After I kept doing it, trying different things, it worked."

"Do it again, please," Shomas pleaded, astonished.

This time, Olivia got the fireball spinning right from the start. "I kind of reach into it, like this," she demonstrated, "and you pull up. Stretching it, kind of," she struggled to explain what she herself did not understand. "When you stretch it out, it, sort of, pulls more power into it?" She shrugged. "I don't know how it works."

Fearing that he would appear weak, Shomas screwed up his courage and opened a hand. A flame then glimmered, barely holding its form. With his other hand, he reached toward the flame, concentrating on stretching it as Olivia had told him. It worked! He was startled again when the flame surged into a ball of fire the size of his fist, and he yelped in fear before the fire could singe his eyebrows. The flame snapped out of existence as quickly as it had appeared. "Miss Dupres," Shomas said, shaken. "You discovered this yourself?"

"I know I'm not supposed to-"

"No! No, you didn't do anything wrong not anything wrong at all, child," Shomas reassured her. "It is remarkable that you discovered this by yourself! Yes, it can be dangerous to experiment with magic, but," he lowered his voice to a conspiratorial whisper. "For everything we have learned about how to use magic, there was a wizard who tried something new. You have seen the experiments Paedris conducts in his laboratory?"

"Yes," Olivia stuck out her tongue. "I'm always cleaning up afterwards. Last week, he nearly burned a hole in the floor. If we hadn't stopped it, I think it would have burned all the way down into the ground beneath the tower."

"See? Most of Lord Salva's experiments are from old books of wizardry; he is trying to figure out how spells work, or to improve on them. This!" He created another fireball, teasing it upward with his fingers. Shomas laughed in delight as he soon had a very respectable fireball perfectly controlled. How many years had he tried and failed to create anything more than a pitiful flicker of a flame? "This is remarkable! *Brilliant*! Oh, I can't wait until you show this to Paedris."

When they reached the lake, it was time for lunch, then Shomas sat under a tree with Olivia and taught her healing techniques. Healing was one of the most difficult magics for a wizard to learn; many never mastered it. The trick was to control the flow of power from the spirit world, and direct it to where it could be used by the body of the injured person or animal to promote healing. Or used destructively to burn out an infection. Too much power, even if intended for healing, could harm or even kill. Most importantly, a wizard needed to understand how to *feel* what was wrong inside the body of the subject. That was what Shomas helped Olivia with, working on his own horse. The animal was used to wizardry; even clumsy, inexperienced wizardry. It bore Olivia's unskilled attempts to feel the energy flowing within the horse, although it expected to be rewarded with treats constantly, to the point where Olivia ate very little of her own lunch! She ate a roast chicken leg; but the apple tart, the bread and the honeycake all went into the horse's mouth. And still the animal nuzzled her hair, seeking more. "That's all I have," Olivia laughed, as the horse's insistent actions knocked her from sitting to rolling on the grass. "You greedy animal!" She held onto the horse's mane to pull herself up.

"Oh, yes," Shomas patted his horse affectionately, "he will eat everything you can give him, and more. That is enough for now," he cautioned. "You should rest." He looked along the lake shore to a cliff, where the princess and most of the party were taking lunch under the shade of a gazebo. "Let's go see what else our princess has to offer in the way of food," he looked at his empty plate. Too much of his own lunch was also now inside the horse. "And then, time for me to try fishing!" He clapped his hands. "That is enough wizardry for today. We will have to walk up that blasted hill. Well, there's nothing for it, then."

By the time Shomas got up the hill to the gazebo, he needed a rest. A cool drink and a seat under the shade of the gazebo refreshed him enough that he was able to eat a proper lunch, and Olivia also was able to enjoy lunch without having to feed most of the food to a horse. The horses were gathered on the far side of the field, contentedly munching the tall grass.

When his hunger was temporarily sated, Shomas sat back and talked with Olivia about the fundamentals of magic, all thoughts of catching fish that afternoon forgotten. He concentrated on helping the young wizard to feel her connection to the spirit world, and the two were so engrossed in conversation that Shomas didn't realize the sun had moved so he was no longer in the shade of the gazebo. "Ooh, I am thirsty," Lord Feany announced, and looked around. Most of the outing party was relaxing, even the dozen guards were sitting on the ground, taking a respite. The princess was relaxing in the sunshine, reading something, and she did not appear to be happy. Her brow was furrowed, she was muttering something to herself, and when a servant offered her a cool drink, she waved the man away in irritation. She tossed the book aside and left the gazebo to walk along the cliff, looking down at the lake.

"Our princess came to this beautiful lake, on this beautiful day," Shomas observed, "and she is not happy. She is far too serious for her age," he said, completely oblivious that he was speaking to a young wizard who had been studying intensely since she was a little girl. "We should do something to," he looked around, then clapped his hands softly. "Olivia, I will show you something."

Across the field, near the horses, butterflies flitted about wildflowers. Shomas intended to bring the butterflies up to the clifftop to fly around the princess. That might improve the young woman's mood, and demonstrate to Olivia a type of magic that she had not been taught yet.

"Hmm," Shomas frowned. He was having difficulty contacting the butterflies, they kept nervously slipping away from him. "Perhaps I am weary from this hot sun," he said with a yawn. Closing his eyes, he reached out gently and- And nothing.

"Lord Feany?" Olivia tugged at his arm. She pointed across the field. "What is wrong with the horses?"

Shomas opened his eyes. The horses were indeed acting strangely; trotting to and fro nervously, flicking their tails rapidly, their ears high and alert. Now he saw why he had trouble connecting with the butterflies; they, too, were disturbed by something. The butterflies had flown away from the wildflowers, soaring higher into the air, moving in a group toward the lake.

Then, the butterflies zoomed upward as if taken by an unseen gust of wind, for leaves on the trees at the edge of the field were unmoving. The horses all snorted and galloped away toward the lake. "What the-" Shomas rose to his feet, alarmed. The guards were now all their feet also, hands on the hilts of their swords. Everyone saw the horses had been startled by something. An animal? Was there a bear or a pack of wolves in the grove of trees beyond the field? Or something worse? Horses would be startled by wolves, but butterflies cared nothing about land predators. Shomas gestured for Oliva to be quiet, as the guards ran toward the princess. She was in a very bad place if her guards had to defend her; behind her was a sheer cliff down to the lake, and the cliff extended to the east also. As a site for a pleasant gazebo overlooking the lake, the cliff was ideal. As a spot for a mere dozen guards to protect the future queen of Tarador, it hardly could have been worse.

Striding as quickly as he could down the hill toward the trees on the far side of the field, Shomas almost closed his eyes, sending out his senses. He fell backward with a shock and lay momentarily stunned. "The enemy!" He cried out, and behind him, soldiers who had been hurrying the princess down the hill stopped and surrounded her, swords drawn. Before Shomas could get to his feet, a fireball burst out of the grove of trees, arcing through the air toward the princess. Shomas fell to the ground again as he used both hands to deflect the deadly ball of magical fire; it splashed to the ground to the right of the guards around the princess and set the grass aflame.

"Lord Feany," Olivia's voice cracked as she helped the wizard to his feet.

Shomas shook his head. "Stay behind me, girl. I've been a fool! We were so engrossed is talking about magic, I forgot to use magic. We are here to protect the princess, and I have been acting as if we were on a holiday," he was disgusted by himself. As he spoke, an enemy wizard in dark robes and a hideous skull mask stepped out of the woods, followed by several dozen soldiers who were also wearing the garish facepaint and helmets of Acedor. The enemy was spread out around the base of the field, trapping the princess against the top of the cliff.

The enemy wizard shook his fist at Shomas, then gathered another fireball and threw it at the princess. This time, Shomas was more prepared and he was able, barely able, to catch the glowing ball of flame on the air. He struggled to hold it, then his strength failed and the fire was flung to the ground. It splashed when it hit; burning specks of magic fire flying through the air to bounce off the shields held by Ariana's guards. Some of the guards were not so fortunate, suffering minor injuries as their arms or legs were scorched by fire. To their credit, they did not waver, only shaking their shields for the magical fire to drip onto the ground at their feet.

"Step aside, fool!" The enemy warned Shomas, his magic-enhanced voice booming out across the field. "Your pitiful powers cannot stop me. Step aside, and you may yet live for another day."

Shomas wavered on his feet, his knees weak. Olivia did her best to hold him up, and Shomas leaned into her for support. He gathered his strength and added magic to his own voice, so it was heard clearly by everyone within sight. "Pitiful? You say I am pitiful, though your greatest effort has been turned aside!" His voice cracked with the strain. "There are other magics known to true wizards, far stronger than the simple act of throwing fire!"

"Ha ha ha," the enemy laughed. "Wizards? You name yourself among us? Gardener I name you, not wizard. You play with your flowers and bees, and you insult us all by pretending to be a wizard. Step aside, master gardener, that a wizard may show you the form of real power!" The enemy wizard used both hands above his head to conjure a truly powerful fireball; its heat was felt upon Olivia's face, and she looked to Shomas for guidance. The older wizard's eyes were barely open, and his lips quavered. Olivia debated whether she should release Lord Feany in order to attempt throwing a fireball of her own. It would be weak, barely worth the effort, but it might distract the enemy for a moment.

While the enemy had been boasting, Shomas had his hands behind his back, fingers moving in intricate patterns; his eyes almost closed as he concentrated, his lips whispering incantations. When he was ready, his eyes opened fully, and he stood up straight and tall. "Evil one, you mock the power of flowers and bees, yet nature is the greatest power of all. You hate nature, for your kind hates all life and goodness. Mock all you wish, for it is your doom."

With an enraged screech, the enemy gathered the brightly burning fireball in one hand, and drew back to throw it. Olivia pulled her arm away from Shomas and held up both hands to knock the fireball aside, knowing it to be a futile gesture for one so young and untrained against such power.

But the fireball was never thrown, instead it winked out of existence as the enemy wizard lost all concentration, and the power was pulled back into the spirit world. The enemy cried out in fear and anger as the branches of trees and the looping strands of vine enveloped the dark wizard; roots erupted from the ground to entangle his legs. In the blink of an eye, he was torn asunder, ripped apart by a natural power that can crack stone. Not only the wizard met that terrible fate, any others of the enemy ranks who stood within reach of that grove of trees found themselves grasped by roots and tree limbs that wrapped themselves around arms, legs and necks. Frantic hacking with sword blades did little, and weapons were soon torn from the enemy's grip to fly across the field; soon followed by pieces of those who had served the evil one. One enemy soldier who had only been trapped by a single tree limb wrapped around his ankles, found himself flung one way then the other through the air, the tree swaying back and forth violently as it slammed the enemy to the ground over and over until the body lay limp and broken. Another most unfortunate soldier, at the very edge of the grove of trees, managed to break loose from the thin root which encircled his leg, by wriggling out of his boot. He thought he had escaped, but as he ran he was tripped by a bush that whirled at his legs. When he fell, he soon found a single rose vine around his neck, thorns tearing at his skin as the vine tightened and tightened.

When the trees stilled, their branches twisted horribly in the air, roots sagging back down to the soil, only a dozen of the enemy remained alive. Any other soldiers, no matter how brave, might have been overcome by good sense and retreated, having lost all chance of accomplishing their mission. These enemy soldiers, being under magical compulsion, screamed as one and charged across the field and up the hill toward the crown princess.

Ariana's guard, which until then had not struck a blow at the enemy, held firm, absorbing the enemy's undisciplined initial attack. Then it was small groups of soldiers pitted one against another, in a desperate battle. Ariana was forced back toward the edge of the bluff, her heels scraping the ground to stop herself from being flung over the edge. Her skilled soldiers were gaining the upper hand, but the enemy were fanatical, desperate to get at her and cared nothing for the swords that hacked at them.

Olivia shook Lord Feany's head; the wizard had collapsed after engaging his powerful spell. "Lord Feany! Shomas!" She cried, but the wizard lay on the ground, unaware what was happening around him. Olivia sprang to her feet, trying to draw a fireball, but in her confusion, the flame flickered and snuffed out. Two of the enemy, injured but undeterred, had broken through the line of guards, and one was poised to strike Ariana, his blood-dripping sword raised. Olivia pulled a dagger from her belt and threw it without thinking what she was doing. The small blade sliced through the air, flipping over and over from her hasty throw, and the handle struck the enemy just below his right eye. It was enough, it knocked the man off balance; his sword came down on empty air as the princess ducked aside. Then his mouth opened in surprise, as Ariana's own dagger plunged into the enemy's chest. The princess danced away and rolled to the ground as the stricken soldier fell to his knees, then died as one of Ariana's guards ran him through with a sword.

And then it was, suddenly and shockingly as it began, over. There was a stunned silence on the unintended battlefield, broken only by the gasps of soldiers raggedly breathing, and the agonized cries of the wounded. Not one of the enemy were alive, having all fanatically fought to their deaths. Five of Ariana's escort had been cut badly, and two lay dead. Only five were unharmed.

Unharmed physically; they were all in shock. Shock from the wholly unexpected attack at the royal summer playground, and shock at the carnage they had witnessed when nature itself had risen and destroyed the enemy.

Ariana rushed to help treat the wounded, ignoring the protests of the guards who were concerned more about her. Olivia helped Shomas, who was regaining his wits, to sit up although the wizard could not yet stand. "Lord Feany?" Olivia asked gently. "Can you help? We have people who need healing."

"Aye, lass," Shomas said with terrible weariness. "Let me rest a moment, I'm seeing spots swimming before my eyes." He shook his head, blinked, and gazed toward where the enemy wizard had been standing. "Ah," he said, a tear rolling down his cheek. "I'm sorry. I'm so very sorry. I had to do it, you understand?"

A soldier, who had been sent by the princess to attend to the wizard, heard Shomas and dropped to one knee. Seeing that Lord Feany was unharmed, the soldier spoke in reaction to the words of the wizard. "The death of any wizard is a grievance to all those with such power? I should not be surprised that you are sorry for killing him."

"Eh?" Shomas looked up, startled, just then noticing the soldier. "Sorry for the death of that filth? What in blazes are you talking about, man?"

"I, I meant no offense, Lord Feany," the soldier stammered. "You expressed sorrow at your actions. You wizards are different from us common folk, it is no shame to mourn the death of one blessed with magical power."

"Oh," Shomas laughed bitterly. "No. You do not understand. I was not apologizing to the enemy for having killed him; he deserved a thousand deaths for serving the evil one. I begged forgiveness from the *trees*. I asked them, I made them, act against their nature. They create life, and I made them end a life. What I did was a sin against nature, and I asked forgiveness and understanding for what I had to do."

The soldier's eyes grew wide, and he contemplated the cool, dark treeline. "The trees? They can hear us?" He was thinking fearfully of how many trees he had cut down in his life.

"Yes, man," Shomas said wearily, "though they do not often *listen*, for our affairs are of no interest to them. Their world is the cycle of nature, and we are but passing through, in their eyes."

"The trees?" The soldier swallowed, his throat dry. "They are dangerous?"

Shomas laughed. "If one were to fall on you, yes. Or if you are foolish enough to stand under a tree during a lightning storm. You need not fear them. Now, help me up," he held out a hand. "There are many here who could use the healing power of a wizard."

"Lord Salva," Carlana said with all the haughtiness she could muster, "I require your services. The enemy attacked the crown princess," she emphasized Ariana's official position rather than her relation to Carlana, "very shortly after she arrived at the summer palace. Such a plan could not have been put together so quickly; the enemy surely had advanced notice that Ariana would be there. There must be a spy in the royal palace; your unique skills as a wizard are needed to root out this danger."

Paedris was taken aback. "A spy? You think the enemy needed a spy to learn that Ariana would be going to the summer palace? Woman, news of the crown princess' movements was all over Linden within hours of your decision to banish your daughter. Preparations had to be made; the marketplaces in the city were busy as a beehive supplying goods for the journey. The roads to the summer palace were choked with courtiers traveling to their own summer homes near that palace, so the hangers-on could curry favor with Ariana. Did you think the movement of a future monarch could be a secret? Even if the enemy was unable to break the codes of army telegraph messages, I am certain many other messages were sent uncoded." He shook his head. "The enemy did not need a *spy* within these walls to learn that Ariana would be at the summer palace."

Carlana's eyes flashed with anger. "How then was the enemy so prepared? How did they arrive so quickly?"

"Because, you foolish-" Paedris caught himself. Carlana Trehayme was the Regent to whom he officially owed loyalty. And, until she was replaced by her daughter, Paedris might still need Carlana, even as useless as she mostly was. "Because, I suspect the enemy was already in the area for another purpose. Hearing that Ariana would not be safely within the walls of the royal palace must have seemed a great gift to the enemy, so they changed their plans. I suspect that enemy wizard was on his way here to Linden, to cause mischief of one sort or another. The enemy is within our borders, Regent. They have breached our borders and captured our territory, and you do nothing but pull the Royal Army back farther. Search for spies all you wish; all you will accomplish is to sow suspicion and discord within our ranks, to the delight of the enemy. I will not participate." Paedris set down his glass of wine untouched, stood up, bowed, and left the room without another word. He did not trust himself to speak at that moment, so great was his anger.

Ariana could not take power soon enough for Paedris Don Salva.

After the attack at the lake, Ariana's guards rushed her back to the summer palace, and insisted she remain in the strong tower at the southeast corner of the palace. That tower was the only part of the palace that had been built with protection of the royal family in mind; the remainder of the palace had been built for comfort. As soon as word of the attack had reached the summer palace from the lake, the telegraph on the roof of the palace had signaled for reinforcements from the Royal Army. Until a column of cavalry rode up the drive in a cloud of dust, the guards ringed the tower day and night, with the wizard and his young trainee on the roof searching for trouble. No trouble came, and as soon as the cavalry were able to rest and water their horses, they escorted the princess back to Linden. Shomas was not able to truly rest until the towers of the royal castle were in sight. Then he fell into an exhausted sleep for a full day.

CHAPTER FIVE

By midday, the wind had died completely, and the *Lady Hildegard* drifted on the calm water. Sails hung slack, and ropes slapped listlessly against the spars as the ship rolled slowly side to side in the long swells. Instead of the sound of waves splashing along the sides of the hull as the ship bobbed forward over the swells, there was only a faint rippling sound. Koren was used to hearing waves crashing against the side of ship, and hissing as they slid backward along the hull. Now, the low swells made only a desultory 'shploop' sound as they gently slapped the wood timbers of the hull, and there was no hissing, only the drip, drip, drip of water droplets falling.

It was odd to hear the ominous sounds of the ship's timbers while they were not at anchor. Koren was used to the unsettling creaking and groaning when the ship was in port; here on the open sea he found it unnerving. "Has this happened to you before?" Koren asked Alfonze. "Being on the open sea, with absolutely no wind?" Koren had experienced light winds, but never had his ship been totally dead in the water.

"Oh, sure, plenty of times." The big man squinted up at the sun to judge its position. "It's worse further south. There, we get what we call the Doldrums. It can stay dead calm like this for days, weeks even." Despite the heat, Alfonze's shoulders shuddered.

Old Jofer leaned over the rail and spat into the water. "Oh, it can get bad, young Kedrun. In days gone by, I was aboard a ship that was becalmed for twenty three days, in the Doldrums. In that heat and without waves soaking the upper timber of the hull, the wood dried out, seams opened. We took to using the pumps to spray seawater on dry timbers, because we ran low on caulk to seal the seams. Tar from the rigging dripped onto the deck. Fresh water in the casks grew foul, and there was no rain to replenish our supply. Food was running out; we took to fishing over the side to fill our bellies." Jofer's voice faded. "Some of the crew began to go mad after two weeks. We had to lock them in the hold. They screamed and moaned all day and night. I almost went mad with thirst myself."

Koren paused to give the old sailor time to consider the terrible events. "How did it end?"

Jofer shook himself back to the present. "A line of squalls, and then a long, hard blow behind it. We had to run before it, on almost bare poles; hardly any sails set. Those winds pushed us so far off course, it took a week, beating back and forth, to get back to where we started. I tell you, young Kedrun, I don't ever want to go through something like that ever again."

Koren looked up at the sun. "Could that happen to us?"

To his surprise, Jofer, who almost always was the very voice of gloom and doom, laughed and slapped Koren on the back. "Never you worry! We're not at the latitudes of the Doldrums; the wind will come back later today, or tomorrow. For sure. In all my long years, I've never seen a ship get stuck here, at this time of year, for more than a day. The Captain built time in the delivery schedule, we'll make it on time."

Koren had heard Jofer tell so many tall tales, he didn't know whether to trust the old man.

"Here's a treat, Kedrun," Alfonze nudged him with an elbow. "Looks like the Captain will let us go swimming today. Do you fancy a swim in the deep blue sea?"

Koren looked over the side, where swells barely half a foot high were languidly rolling against the hull, with the waves almost too lazy to make any sort of splash against the old wood. As he watched, a dark shadow came out from under the ship, and he followed the black shape as it came toward the surface, and then a fin broke the surface. He now knew the difference between the playful fin of a dolphin and the dangerous fin of a shark. This was a shark. And it wasn't the only one. Sharks followed the ship, they always did. Whenever the cook threw scraps overboard, there were mouths in the wake of the ship to gobble up the scraps. Mouths ringed with rows of large, sharp teeth. "I would not like to swim today, thank you," Koren looked up with a smile. He figured Alfonze had been joking, or testing him again.

"No," the man answered, pointing toward where the captain was standing at the rail, looking over the side. "I'm serious. Look see that spar," he pointed aft. "We attach another spar to it, and another here, forward," he pointed to the mizzen mast. "Then we lower a sail into the water, let it fill. We swim inside the sail, it keeps the sharks out. You'll see."

Koren soon saw that Alfonze was right, as the captain ordered a 'pool' to be rigged. The master of the ship had studied the sky and the clouds, and judged that the ship would lay becalmed for hours, at least. With no other sails in sight, he took the opportunity to give the crew a rest and a bit of fun that would be good for morale. If the ship became stuck without wind for an extended time, the crew would be grateful for a chance to splash around in the cool water. It was as Alfonze described; the crew rigged extra spars on the east side of the ship, where the sea was partly shaded by the limply hanging sails, and lowered a large sail into the water. The sail soon filled with seawater, and formed a pool that was secure from the circling sharks.

To Koren's surprise, old Jofer was the first to jump in; he climbed the mainmast to the first spar, walked out, and jumped overboard with a whoop. There was a tremendous splash that came up to the rail and got Koren's hair wet. Soon, half the crew was jumping off the ship or splashing around in the water. It was delightfully cool; just a touch too cool when Koren first got in, but then he was grateful for the soothing temperature.

"Eh?" Alfonze asked, laying almost flat on his back in the water. "Fun, eh?"

"Yes!" Koren laughed. "This is great, thank you!"

"Thank the captain. Ahh, we'll appreciate this tonight, if we're still becalmed. Hot as it is, it will be stifling in the hold without a breeze down there."

"Ooh," Koren hadn't thought about that. When in port, the crew didn't like to sleep in their cramped hammocks below decks, for even with the portholes open, the air in the hold was hot and stifling. "Maybe the captain will let us sleep on deck tonight?"

"Maybe," Alfonze agreed.

Later, it was Koren's turn to climb all the way up to the 'crow's nest'; the little platform at the top of the tallest mast. It was little more than a fabric basket atop a wood platform, with a thick rope railing around the rim. The captain wanted Koren's young eyes to sweep the horizon. Mostly, lookouts kept watch for other sails. Sails that might be pirate ships. This day, the captain had instructed 'Kedrun' to keep lookout also for ripples on the surface of the water; ripples that could indicate an area where a breeze was blowing. Distant ripples were, the captain explained, often seen as a darker area of the ocean surface, where there was no cloud. If Koren was unsure, he should ask the other lookout.

The climb was not as difficult as it usually was, for with the ship becalmed, the lines were not swaying back and forth as Koren pulled himself hand over hand. From the start, Koren had hated having to go all the way to the top of the mast, for any motion of the ship was greatly exaggerated up so high above the surface of the water. Unlike most of the crew, Koren had never suffered from seasickness more than a little, during his first week. The crew had grumbled that their new crewmate 'Kedrun' was very lucky. Koren suspected his seeming immunity to seasickness was part of the spell Paedris had cast on him. It also meant that Koren had been sent to the top mast only a few days after he had joined the crew. Whether the first mate had sent Koren aloft as an expression of confidence in the new shipmate, or to test Koren's abilities, or in the hope that Koren would embarrass himself and spew all over the deck, Koren still wasn't sure. He was sure that this day, he was grateful for the easy action of the slow rolling swells, for the motion of even the upper mast was no more than a gentle rocking.

When Koren reached the top of the mast, with his hands no longer cramping in fear as they did when he first became a sailor, he avoided the 'lubber's hole' in the bottom of the crow's nest. His first time, really his first dozen times climbing to the crow's nest, he had hugged tightly onto the rough wood pole of the mast and inched his way through the hole in the bottom of the crow's nest. Other sailors had laughed at him good-naturedly, assuring him that all land-lubbers like Koren used the hole before they gained experience.

This day, as he had done every time beyond his first fortnight aboard the ship, he climbed the lines at the side of the crow's nest, and swung himself over the railing. "Hello, Tom," he greeted the sailor already there.

"Ho there, Kedrun," Tom replied with a yawn. "Nothing to report. Ain't seen a darn thing the whole time I've been up here."

Koren nodded. "Captain wants us to watch for ripples on the surface, see if there's a breeze out there somewhere."

"Aye," Tom nodded, "I've been looking. Do you know what to look for?"

Koren shook his head.

"That's all right," Tom slapped the new sailor on the shoulder. "I'll show you. With your younger eyes," Tom scratched his beard, which had grown itchy in the heat, "you'll likely see it before I do. Let's scan the horizon first."

Koren pulled the precious glass from inside his vest. It was a narrow tube with polished glass at both ends; sailors called such devices a 'spyglass' and soldiers called them 'telescopes'. Whatever they were called, they were expensive, delicate and precious. The one Koren was using belonged to the first mate, and Koren had promised to guard the device with his life. Hooking an arm around a line for security, Koren extended the spyglass and pointed to the horizon, moving all the way around until he came back to the bow of the ship. "Nothing," he reported.

"Aye, that's what I have also," Tom agreed. "I did see some ripples; not enough to tell the Captain about. I'll show you." Tom pointed to the west, where a tall puffy white cloud towered in the sky. The cloud had been hanging there, dominating the sky since the Noon hour. It cast a dark shadow on the surface of the sea, and Tom pointed out that between the ship and the cloud's shadow was an area slightly darker that the surrounding water. "See how the sunlight reflects off it different?" Tom asked.

"Yes, I do," Koren replied excitedly. Since he had embraced his new life as a sailor, Koren was eager to learn all the skills of his new trade. In the circle of the spyglass, the light twinkling off the sea in the area Tom pointed to was more jittery; as if the light was scattered by numerous small waves rather than the larger slow-rolling swells. "Shall we tell the Captain?"

"No," Tom shook his head. "There's no point getting his hopes up. That area has been popping up ripples all day. It's cool air coming off the sides of that cloud as it builds, you see? That wind is too weak to do us any good."

"We're stuck here, then?" Koren asked with disappointment. At first, being becalmed was a novelty, but now it was worrying him. Mostly because the experienced sailors all seemed to be worried about it.

"No, I wouldn't worry about it. This ain't the Doldrums. I been there, this ain't it. It's unusual at these latitudes to be in this dead calm for more than a day. That cloud," Tom pointed again, "has been building since this morning, you been watching it?"

Koren nodded. Of course he had, now that he knew such things were important to the life of a sailor.

"Good," Tom said. "In my experience, that has a good chance to turn into a squall before nightfall. It may give us only a short, hard blow, but it will cool things off, and wash the salt off the decks. Give us a chance to refill the casks with fresh water, too, we could use that," he observed. The whole crew had been grumbling about how the drinking water had been tasting stale from sitting in barrels the past week.

After that, Tom and Koren sat quietly, backs to each other. Koren lifted his glass and scanned the northern and western horizon periodically; Tom watched his half of the sea. Neither of them saw anything worth reporting. Below on the deck, a bell rang for the hour, and Tom tucked away his spyglass. "That's my signal for relief," Tom said with a yawn, and below, they could see another sailor beginning to climb the mast to replace Tom. "Hopefully, I can get a nice cool swim before they pull in the pool," he pointed over the side, where sailors were still floating in the cool water. "I'm about burnt from being up here, my skin feels like sandpaper."

"Good luck to you," Koren grinned. Another dip in the cool water would feel good; it was likely the pool would be stowed away by the time Koren's turn in the crow's nest was done. He lifted his glass to scan the horizon in Tom's direction. "When do you think- Whoa!"

"What?" Tom froze.

"Sail!" Koren said in a harsh whisper.

"What? Where?" Tom swung himself back into the crow's nest.

"There," Koren tried to point to the northeast while looking through the spyglass; he found that didn't work. Lowering the glass, he pointed and gave directions to Tom. Even without the glass, Koren could see the ship as a smudge, it was already on their side of the horizon; Koren could see the other ship's hull as a dark line.

"I don't see it," Tom said skeptically.

"It's just over-"

"Ah! I see, something, oh." Tom looked with his bare eye, then back with the spyglass. "Is that a ship? Ah, blast!" he groaned. "It is! How could I have missed it?"

"I could barely see it at first," Koren admitted.

Tom snorted with disgust. "With your young eyes, you can barely see it? Kedrun, can you tell anything about that ship? I can only see a sail."

"It is," Koren concentrated on the image in the spyglass, "hmm. Two masts, both rigged fore and aft." Alfonze had explained to Koren that their ship had square-rigged sails, which were slower and more clumsy but more sturdy in the open ocean. Ships with sails rigged fore and aft were faster and could maneuver more quickly, but such ships generally could not carry heavy cargo. "That's a schooner?"

"It could be."

"They have one sail set out to starboard, the other to port. The ship is almost facing us." Koren set the spyglass aside and looked at Tom. "It has a narrow hull."

Tom shook his head, knowing what they were both thinking. It was a pirate ship; narrow and light and built for speed. "We need to tell the Captain." He leaned over the railing of the crow's nest and cupped his hands around his mouth. "Sail ho! Four points off the port bow!"

The Captain tried looking for the other ship from the deck, but with the humidity and salt haze in the air, he couldn't see anything. Tom climbed down to make room for the Captain, as the ship's master climbed the ratlines up to the top of the main mast. Koren was surprised to see the Captain climbing quickly, he had thought that the older man would not be so spry. Koren reminded himself that the Captain had been aboard ships since he was apprenticed at the age of twelve; the man was as at home in the rigging as Koren was on the ground. "Another sail, Sir!" Koren called out as he felt the crow's nest sway from the Captain's weight pulled on the lines. No lubber's hole for the Captain, he swung up over the side and dropped lightly as a feather. "There, Sir. I just spotted the second ship, her hull is not yet over the horizon."

The Captain studied the two ships with his glass for long minutes, sitting silently. Then he leaned over the railing and ordered the pool to be brought back in, and sails to be furled.

"We're lowering sails, Captain?" Koren asked, confused. The ship's rigging was suddenly alive with sailors, climbing the lines, walking out along the spars, and slowly rolling up the huge white sails. The utter lack of wind helped speed the process along; Koren knew what it was like to try furling sails when the sails were billowed out by a stiff wind. The canvas became like iron, and fought every attempt to control it.

"Aye," the Captain said, not taking his eye off his spyglass. "With us becalmed like this, the sails only make us more visible. I'm hoping that if we furl the sails, those other ships won't see us. I can barely see them with my glass." He looked at Koren. "Kedrun, you have excellent vision, even for one with your young eyes."

"Yes, Sir."

"Tell me, are those ships drawing closer?"

Koren studied the nearest ship for a long while, then shifted his gaze to the more distant ship. The second ship was now above the horizon; he could see the upper part of its hull. "Yes. Slowly. Their sails are slack, Sir."

"Aye," the Captain agreed. "The current is carrying us both, and those ships are not heavily-laden as us. They're drifting faster than we are."

With the sails furled, the Captain called down for the crew to be fed, several hours early. They were worried grumbling on the deck below; the crew knew the Captain was concerned that soon they might not have time for dinner. Food was brought up to the crow's nest; the Captain wanted 'Kedrun' with his outstanding eyesight to remain aloft.

Koren's eyesight was outstanding, so good, in fact, that he did not tell the Captain everything he could see. His vision had always been remarkable; even when he was a young boy, people in his village of Crebb's Ford had said he could see like an eagle. Now Koren was concerned that his eyesight might be too good; that his vision had been enhanced by whatever spell Paedris had cast upon him to make him fast and strong with a sword. So, he waited to tell the Captain that the two other ships were striking their sails, until the white canvas was gone. "Captain, I think they have furled their sails also."

"Eh?" The Captain had been resting his eyes; too much staring through the glass could make the eyes lose focus. "I see it. They're on bare poles. And they've gotten closer. Still, they're about side-on to us." He scratched his neck around the shirt collar; white salt of seawater from his swim in the pool had dried on his skin, and was now itching. "Keep watching, I'm going to sweep the horizon."

Koren kept watch, and over the next quarter hour, the closest other ship swung listlessly until it was pointed toward him. He adjusted the glass and squinted, then rubbed his own neck. What was that? There was a lighter-colored blur on each side of the other ship, like the foam a ship threw aside as it sailed through the water. But surely the faint white foam could not be a wake; the other ship still had its sails furled. He glanced toward the Captain, who was studying the clouds to the west. That one cloud had now built to cover half the sky, and its top had flattened into an anvil shape that loomed toward the ship. The cloud could, the Captain had explained, bring a squall before nightfall. Not soon enough for the Captain.

Should he tell the captain what he had seen? It was probably nothing; Koren was so inexperienced a sailor that he would be wasting the man's time.

Then Koren thought back to that fateful morning in Longshire, when he had noticed sheep alone in the fields, and his uncertainty had caused him to delay telling Lord Salva. A delay that might have cost lives. "Captain, could you look at this, please? I'm sure it's nothing."

"Eh? What?"

Koren explained about the light color in the sea closely around the other ship, and how it was now pointed directly toward them.

The Captain swore and pounded his fist on the railing. "Damn! And here we are, fat, heavily laden, and becalmed!" He leaned over the side and bellowed down to the deck "Man the sweeps!" Then he tucked his own spyglass away. "Kedrun, you do have good eyes. That there is a pirate ship, and so is the other one, is my guess. That color you saw is a wake, they've got their oars out, and they're pulling straight for us. They saw us! And now we've a long hard pull ahead of us, if we can get away at all." He looked up at the position of the sun, then at a cloud to the west. "Come down with me, we'll give your eyes a rest."

Koren's eyes did get a rest, they were the only part of his body that was not soon aching and weary. Not even his ears were spared, for a drum pounded rhythmically to keep the crew in time with each other, and the first mate bellowed and shouted for the crew to pull harder. The sweeps were long, clumsy oars that stuck out both sides of the ship from a lower deck near the waterline. Each sweep was handled by three men, who wrestled the awkward pole until the paddle was in the water, then they hauled on the pole while straining to walk backwards. The first mate tried to balance the crew across the sweeps so equal effort was made on both sides of the ship, and the ship was not turning in a circle.

Twenty minutes of pulling on the sweeps, then a break for five minutes. After each set on the sweeps, one man on each team was replaced with a fresh man. Koren, being so young, was the first to be replaced. He thought that he could rest his aching legs, back and shoulders but it was not to be. The first mate assigned him to carry around a bucket of drinking water, and his job was to ladle water into the mouths of the men at the end of a sweep. Others on the crew were working the pumps, with two men carrying around a hose to spray cool seawater on the overheated teams manning the sweeps.

It went on for an hour, then two hours. Koren took his turns at the sweeps until his arms were trembling even when serving water to the sweepers; he had to use two hands on the ladle to keep from spilling more water on the deck than the men got to drink. He went below to refill the water bucket, when the first mate called him. "Kedrun! Cap'n wants you in the crow's nest!"

"Yes, Sir!" Koren responded. He filled the water bucket and brought it up on deck, before scrambling up the ladder. This time, his shaky arms and trembling fingers made for a slower climb; he had no wish to slip and fall to the water. Or to the deck, for that would be the death of him. He paused at the second spar to rest his cramping fingers, and looked down. He was shocked to see how slowly the ship was moving through the water, despite the tremendous effort of the entire crew. The sweeps swung forward, dipped into the water, then were laboriously pulled back; the clumsy oars flexing and wobbling through the water as they attempted to propel the ship onward. As soon as the sweeps lifted, the pitifully weak wake disappeared, and the ship slid almost to a halt. All of the work the crew had done, over several hours, had given the ship almost no momentum. The ship was too big, too heavy. Its hull, built for stability in the often-heavy weather of the Southern Ocean and for hauling cargo, was too broad to slip easily through the water.

Mindful that when the captain of a ship gave an order, he expected it to be obeyed immediately, Koren resumed his climb. Sooner than he expected, he swung himself into the crow's nest. The Captain merely grunted. Koren didn't need a spyglass to see the other ships. Nor to see the large black pennant hanging from the upper spar of the closest ship. Pirates. They were pirates, and in these waters, that meant they served Acedor.

"They're so close!" Koren gasped. The first ship had come so far down from the horizon that he could see details of the masts with his naked eye. He even, if he squinted and looked slightly to the side as Alfonze had taught, imagined he could see the tiny dark shapes of pirates striding about the deck.

"They are close," the Captain said quietly. "If nothing changes, I expect that ship will catch us just after nightfall."

"Could we lighten ship by dumping part of our cargo?" Koren cringed as the words came out of his mouth. The Captain had not ordered him to the crow's nest to get Koren's suggestions. Surely the man had already forgotten more about seamanship that Koren would ever know.

"If we had done that as soon as we sighted them, that might have helped to buy us a few hours, perhaps. Although if we lost the cargo, I would lose the ship." He looked at Koren. "To get this cargo, I had to guarantee delivery. Without delivery, I lose the ship, and there's no money to pay the crew. We won't dump the cargo, not while there is still a chance to get away."

Koren looked to the pirate ship, then down at the pitifully slow progress their own ship was making, then back to the Captain.

"Fear not, young Kedrun," the Captain managed a hoarse laugh. "Look yonder to the west."

Koren turned, and noticed for the first time that the cloud that had been building all day, was now a solid bank of clouds stretched across the sky. Tall enough that the sun would soon duck behind the cloud tops. Then he looked down, and saw what gave the Captain hope. The surface of the sea between the clouds and their ship was rough; more than ripples, these were waves. Koren sucked in a breath. "Squall's coming," he exclaimed.

"Aye," the Captain chuckled. "I've been up here watching and praying. Maybe being up this high, my prayers got heard. We're in for a blow, and the wind will hit us before it hits those pirates," he pointed toward the two pirate ships.

"But," Koren was confused, "the wind is from the west, and will push us to east. Toward the pirates."

"You're catching on, Kedrun. Those ships are also faster, and they can hold closer to the wind than we can. When the wind arrives, we will run to the north, as close to the wind as can. When the wind reaches the pirates, we'll turn east. With our square-rigged sails, we can run before the wind better than they can."

Koren nodded agreement; Alfonze had taught him that much about ship-handling. He also knew that their ship's taller masts would better catch the wind if the seas grew rough; the smaller pirate ships' sails would fall into a wind shadow while in the trough of large waves. "We could-" he felt it on his face, and saw the blue pennant at the very top of the mast flutter. A breeze! The crew below felt it also, for a hearty cheer rose from the deck.

The Captain winked. "It's not much, the real wind won't reach us for a while yet." He leaned over the railing to shout down to the first mate. "Mister Scanton! Stow the sweeps and set all plain sail, if you please!"

The reply came joyfully from the deck. "Oh, yes, Sir, it would please me greatly."

The crew set all the sails the ship used in normal cruising, with Koren helping on the main mast. Then, with the ship ghosting along on the lightest zephyr of a breeze and the crew collectively wishing for stronger wind, the captain ordered more canvas to be added. Back up into the rigging the crew climbed, this time to rig additional spars to the ends of the yardarms, so that spars stuck out to each side of both masts. Attached to the extra spars were sails Koren had heard of, but never seen taken out of storage. Alfonze called them studding sails, or stuns'ls. Looking up, Koren had never imagined the ship carrying so much canvas, but the additional sails billowed and filled with the light breeze, adding to the ship's speed. That still was not enough for the captain; after talking with the first mate, he ordered the pumps manned, and soon seawater was being sprayed onto the sails. A wet sail was heavier, but it held the breeze better. Koren had thought that spraying water onto the sails would be the last of their labors, but he was wrong. Under the direction of the first mate, the crew went into the hold to shift cargo; the Captain wanted more weight aft to give the ship just that tiny extra bit of speed.

Exhausted from their labor, the crew greedily drank water and stood by the windward rail, peering at the still-becalmed pirate ships and guessing at their own ship's rate of progress. Looking down over the railing, Koren was disappointed to see the water only slowly gliding along the side of the hull. To his surprise, Jofer clapped him on the shoulder. "Ah, don't you worry, young Kedrun. We're only poking along yet, but the breeze is picking up, and those pirates are still rowing their hearts out to catch us. It won't be long before Mister Scanton orders us back up, climbing in the rigging like monkeys, to take down those stuns'ls." Jofer looked up to the enormous spread of canvas above their heads, then he pointed to the west, where the base of the approaching cloud was shrouded in rain falling on the sea surface. "We can't have every scrap of canvas aloft when that wind hits us; it would knock the ship on her side."

Sure enough, Jofer was right, for it was not more than ten minutes before the Captain ordered sails reduced, and the already weary crew hauled down the studding sails and removed the extra spars. While wrestling with the canvas that had grown lively as the wind picked up and became gusty, Koren glanced at the two pirate ships. The closest one was now setting its sails as the breeze reached it; with his keen eyesight, Koren could see the enemy sailors scrambling about in their rigging.

Then the rain squall hit his ship, and Koren was too busy adjusting sails to pay constant attention to the pirate ships. He only was able to catch glances at the enemy ships in between going aloft to wrestle with sails. Once the closest pirate ship filled its sails with wind, it steadily if slowly closed the distance to Koren's ship. But when the squall hit, Koren's ship turned and fairly flew before the wind. The pirate ships, with sails set to each side, were not able to use the wind as efficiently, and began to fall behind. Then the wind truly began to howl, and all three ships had to reduce sail. High in the rigging, with wind-driven rain stinging his skin and forcing him to almost close his eyes, Koren felt the ship plunging up and down across the waves. Rain fell like a heavy curtain, and he lost sight of the pirate ships. The last he saw of them, they had both reduced sail and had turned to avoid being blown over by the shrieking wind. One pirate ship turned north and one south, and then they were lost in the rain and spray.

The initial heavy squall quickly gave way to a steady storm with driving rain and gusty winds. Koren's ship staggered under the unpredictable winds; he and the rest of the crew were constantly up to the rigging to adjust sails. The Captain was determined to squeeze every bit of speed from his ship while they had the wind. As night fell, they could only see the pirate ship to the north; it had fallen behind, and could not run as easily with the wind behind it. Once the sun set and the night was utter blackness, the Captain changed course to the east-southeast, hoping to lose the pirates during the night.

Around midnight, the storm settled down to a steady wind out of the west, and stars shone through gaps in the clouds. Koren climbed the rigging again to furl the topmost sails; the Captain did not want that tall white canvas visible to the pursuing pirates. After midnight, the ship ran easily before the wind, with the crew being called up only three times to adjust sails. They had to turn and run due north to avoid a reef the Captain saw on his charts, and the crew worried that going north might mean sailing closer to the pirates. Some of the crew said aloud they hoped the pirates did not know about the reef, and that the pirate ship would wreck in those treacherous waters during the night. The rest of the crew was silently hoping the same, Koren among them. Koren slept fitfully in his swinging hammock that night, wedged in with so many others. He did not bother to change out of his wet clothes to sleep, for he knew it would not be long before the crew would be called up on deck to trim sails. As badly as Koren felt from being roused from slumber several times, he felt worse for the Captain and first mate. Every time Koren's sleep-addled head came up the ladder, he saw those two men, standing aft by the wheel, keeping constant watch throughout the night. There was no sleep for them that night.

CHAPTER SIX

The coming sun was not yet even a faint glimmer on the eastern horizon when Koren was roused yet again, this time ordered to go aloft into the crow's nest and keep lookout. The first mate handed Koren a hard biscuit to eat, before helping the inexperienced sailor get a firm grip on the rigging. "If you see anything, give us a shout," Scanton instructed, "but no false alarms." He did not want the ship dodging ghosts in the darkness, when dodging away from a ghost might draw them closer to a danger that was real.

"Aye, Sir," Koren replied. When he reached the crow's nest, at first all he could do was huddle out of the wind behind the canvas screen, and shake with fear. The last thirty feet of his climb, Koren had been almost paralyzed by fear twice, clutching the ropes tightly and closing his eyes. He had been forced to open his eyes, for the ship was bobbing front to back and rocking side to side, and the exaggerated motion so high above the waves had Koren swinging wildly back and forth.

When he gathered his wits, he knelt and stuck his head up above the railing. There was as yet nothing to see, other than glimpses of faint starlight above as clouds scudded low over his head. It had started raining again; a light rain but the drops were driven by the wind and stung his eyes. Knowing it was very likely useless, Koren pulled the spyglass from inside his jacket, and slowly scanned the horizon. There was nothing to see, nothing at all more than a hundred steps from the ship, so black was the early morning. Even the white foam of wavetops curling by the speeding ship were hard to see from the top of the mast. Koren sat back down, braced himself from the gyrating mast, and slowly ate the hard biscuit. Hopefully, he could come down to the deck when the cook had breakfast ready. After a day and night of hard labor, the cook might have a good, hot breakfast for the crew, with biscuits that were not tough as iron. Breaking the biscuit with his teeth, and then holding the bits in his hand to be soaked by the rain was the only way he could manage to chew the wretched thing.

When he finished the biscuit, his jaw was sore, but there was the barest glow of light to the east. Clouds lay heavily on the eastern horizon, blanking out direct light of the coming sun; all Koren could see was a very faint dark gray in the surrounding inky blackness. The rain had decreased to a light drizzle, and a few stars were visible overhead as the solid cloud cover began to break up. Where there were brief gaps in the clouds above, the sky was tinged with blue, and only the brightest of stars could be seen. He swept the horizon again, first with the naked eye, then with the spyglass. Rain droplets on the glass made it hard to see anything; he kept having to wipe the glass with a dry cloth, then tuck the cloth back inside his jacket. Nothing, again. This time, he could see whitecaps on large gray rolling waves, up to perhaps a mile from the ship. From the deck below, he heard a bell signaling the change of watch, and saw the cook bring a hot pot of coffee and something to eat to the Captain and the crewmen by the wheel. Seeing the covered dishes made Koren hungry, and he imagined he could smell bacon sizzling. If he was right, that scent would wake the crew more surely than any bell or shouting by the first mate.

His stomach growled, whether more from hunger or from the heavy biscuit he could not tell, but he was hungry. And sore; his muscles ached from the hard labor of the previous day. Even at the top of the tallest mast, he could hear men grumbling as they struggled to make sore, stubborn muscles work after a night of much-interrupted sleep. Guiltily, he realized he had been focused more on breakfast than on keeping watch. The entire crew depending on him to watch for pirate ships, uncharted reefs and rocks and any other hazard that they, down below on the deck with their sight obscured by salt spray blowing off the wavetops, could not see. It was still too dark to see much, still, he swept the horizon again. Once with his keen eyes, again with the spyglass. There was nothing- Wait!

He swung the glass back to the west, where he thought he had glimpsed something during a brief rent in the low clouds that scudded barely above the masts. A particularly large whitecap, from a high cresting wave? Looking down at the deck, he was unsure what to do. Should he call a warning? No, the first mate had cautioned him against false alarms. He needed to be certain, not to waste the Captain's time and possibly have the ship alter course in the wrong direction.

Hunger forgotten for the moment, he braced himself in the cramped crow's nest, and swept the glass slowly back and forth across the spot where he had seen, whatever he had seen. If he had seen anything. He was now not sure. The sky above was becoming light, the sea now a dark gray rather than black. Quickly, he dried the spray-spattered glass with a dry cloth, scanned the horizon to the north, then dried the glass again. Had he seen only a reflection in raindrops on the glass? Yes, he decided, that must be it. Clouds to the north were rent by wind, with gaps now becoming regular, and still he did not see anything. They had given the pirates the slip during the night! And he had overheard the Captain talking with the first mate when he first came on deck; running from the pirates had only added a day, maybe less, to their voyage. They would need to come about, and tack back and forth most of the day, to clear the long and dangerous reef system that lay to the east of the ship. Otherwise, they were still well within the time the captain had contracted to deliver the cargo; no penalties would need to be paid. The crew would be pleased, both to have escaped the scourge of piracy, and to fill their pockets with coins when they reached port at Istandol.

Koren was well pleased with himself also, anticipat- What was that? He swung the glass back. There *was* something out there, now hidden again behind low-laying clouds! What he had seen was not merely a breaking wave, it was a white patch of sail. And there it was again.

The pirate ship.

"Sail to port!" Koren shouted down to the deck, pointing to the west. In his excitement, he had forgotten how to properly report a sighting. It did not matter, for the Captain and others trained their spyglasses to the west, and after a tense few minute of no one seeing anything, and the first mate repeatedly calling Koren to verify what he'd seen from atop the mast, others spotted the pirate ship. The clouds were parting, as the sun rose above the horizon and the air warmed; a shaft of sunlight falling on Koren's face felt hot already.

Not a few of the crew on deck shook their fists up at Koren and cursed him for having delivered the bad news; it was a superstition that he well understood. The first mate gestured for Koren to come down on deck to report; as Koren climbed down, another sailor was slowly making his way up the rigging without enthusiasm.

Knowing time was pressing, Koren swung off the shrouds and onto a line that dropped directly to the deck. Squeezing his tough canvas shoes together and sliding hand over hand, he descended rapidly to the deck, and strode quickly over to the first mate. "Mister Scanton, sir, I saw only the one ship. I estimate the distance at seven miles."

"Aye, lad. That makes my numbers." The first mate looked to the sails, which were already slackening as the wind eased. "We'll have a long day of it, I think."

Somehow, during the utter blackness of night, in a storm, the pirate had stayed with them. That was either incredibly good luck for the pirates, or something sinister was at work. "Sir, how could this happen? How did they know where we are, all night?"

Scanton looked again at the pirate ship through his own spyglass. "It could be partly luck, Kedrun," he said in the same tone of voice he used when lecturing inexperienced sailors on the finer points of seamanship. "And partly that they know we can't go further east because of the reefs and shoals between us and the mainland in these parts. If they sent one ship north and one south, they had at least some chance of us being in view when morning arrived. As to how they came to be so close," he frowned. From the deck, the pirate ship was partly over the horizon, its hull not being visible. From the crow's nest, high above, Koren had been able to see the pirate's hull, and estimate the distance. "The enemy has been known to use wizardry to help their pirates find prey. If there's a minor wizard on that ship, or they have some device of dark magic, we'll never be able to give them the slip. We'll have to outrun them."

"Mister Scanton!" The Captain called out. "Make more sail, if you please."

No longer needed as a lookout high above, for the pirate ship was now plainly visible from the deck, Koren joined the crew in taking a reef out of the sails, and later in climbing to the tops again to set the topgallant sails; that uppermost rank of square sails. Those white squares of canvas made the ships visible from long distances, and so they had been ordered stowed overnight while the ship attempted to evade the pirates. Now that escape rather than evasion was the goal, they needed the extra canvas, with the wind slackening off. "Alfonze," Koren said after securing a line to the spar, "what will happen if they capture us?" He hung onto the spar, and dug his heels into the line below them. With seven men stepping on the line, it swayed alarmingly. Other sailors were nonchalantly holding onto the spar only a finger, but Koren maintained a firm grip with both arms.

"Capture us?" Alfonze asked sourly. "They'll take us for slaves, most likely, those of us they need. It depends. You know those poor souls heaving on their oars yesterday are slaves, don't you? Pirates don't row their own ships," he grimaced. "If they need replacements for slaves who have died, and they die regularly on a foul ship like that," Alfonze made a rude gesture toward the pirate ship, "they will select some of us to come aboard their ship. We'll be clapped in irons, until we die, or they no longer need us. I've seen pirates dump slaves overboard to escape pursuit. The rest, ah, if they like our cargo, they'll keep some of us to run this ship for them, until the ship gets into port, then we'll be sold. And you can be sure that, however many of us survive the coming battle, they'll kill a handful of survivors as a warning. Or because they enjoy killing."

Koren shuddered despite the warm breeze. "The battle, what will it be like?" Then they were interrupted as the first mate called them back down to the deck. They clustered along the windward rail, their weight helping to keep the ship from heeling over too far.

Alfonze answered. "What will the battle be like? Mind you, I've only been in one sea battle, and we were fortunate." As he spoke, other sailors crowded closer to hear. "The pirates broke away from our ship because they spotted a fatter prize."

"Oh. Did your ship and the other fight the pirate?"

Alfonze shook his head. "No, lad. We hauled on every scrap of canvas we could carry, and got over the horizon as quick as we could. You have to understand; there's not much a merchant ship can do against a pirate. Pirate ships carry large crews, to overwhelm their prey when boarding. And they have weapons that we don't."

Koren was disturbed that Alfonze's ship had not even tried to help a fellow merchant ship; it made him realize that his youthful idealized view of the world may not match how the world actually worked. "What weapons?"

"They call it a ballista, or I've also heard it called a windlass." Gesturing with his hands, he explained. "There's a large spring, and a cable attached to it, you wind the windlass to crank the spring back. There's a rail through the center of the spring, and the enemy shoots bolts through it. They can be large arrows, or a cluster of metal balls with spikes; one of those can knock out a whole group of men. These pirates will have something even more nasty; a bomb. It's a metal tube with flammable oil in it, and the nose of the tube is glass. Inside the glass is more oil, and flint and steel. When the bomb hits something, the glass breaks and ignites the oil."

All the men around Alfonze shuddered. Fire at sea, in a wooden ship, was every sailor's nightmare. A fire caused by oil could not be fought with water; throwing water on the fire would only make the burning oil spread across the deck. That explained to Koren why the first mate had ordered buckets of sand to be brought up on deck. Normally, sand was used to scrub the decks clean in the mornings, and to prevent feet from slipping on wet decks. If the pirates attacked, the sand would be used to smother burning oil.

Koren still did not understand. "If they want to take this ship, why would they burn it?"

"They won't," Alfonze said without a smile. "Not the ship." He looked upward. "The sails. They'll set fire to our sails. Without the sails, we'll be dead in the water. Their ship will come alongside, grapple onto us, and their crew will climb over the rails and take our ship."

"You said that your ship escaped," Jofer asked, "how do you know what the pirates do?"

"Because," Alfonze looked down at the water, "that's what the pirates did to that other ship. They caught it, and took it. Our ship fled, but not fast enough to avoid seeing what happened. It made all of us glad that we hadn't stayed to try fighting. We would have been dead, or slaves, also."

The pirate ship pursued them throughout the morning, as the wind slackened. Koren helped the crew set more sail, until it seemed like he could identify tablecloths and one of his shirts hanging from the upper spars. It was a stern chase, and the fickle, gusty, unpredictable winds kept Koren's ship ahead of the pirates past the Noon hour. But the pirate ship was creeping closer, and the winds were dying. At times, the wind was barely a zephyr, and the sails hung limp, only to fill again, and the ship heeled over and moved forward with a lurch. When the winds died, the pirate ship's oars swung outboard, and the water alongside the pirate ship churned furiously.

"Should we man the sweeps?" Koren quietly asked Alfonze, as they checked, sharpened and laid out sword and pikes for the coming battle.

"No," Alfonze snorted. "This tub weighs so much, we'd be wasting our energy. As long as the wind blows at all, we're better relying on the sails. We're carrying twice as much canvas, and our masts are taller."

"How much longer until they catch us?" Koren asked.

"Hard to say. Depends on the wind. They don't have to catch us to hit us. They're probably almost in range now." Alfonze used the spyglass he had borrowed from the third mate, and pointed it aft. "Kedrun, there, you can see the ballistas. There are two of them, in the bow. The pirates are setting them up. I don't see that either of them is wound up yet. Here," he handed the spyglass to Koren. "See for yourself."

Looking through the spyglass, Koren could clearly see the pirates winding the two ballistas in the bow of the enemy ship. On each side of a ballista were wheels, almost as large as the wheel that steered his own ship. Three pirates worked each wheel, putting their weight into turning it. Koren could see they were straining to wind the windlass. He couldn't see much of the other parts of the ballista mechanism; there was a wood screen in front of it; Koren figured that screen was there to protect the ballista crew from arrows. Although no arrow could reach across the current distance between the ships.

The ballista crew members he could see, and the other pirates who lined the rail and were gesturing and shouting at Koren's ship, had their faces painted in gruesome designs. Or they wore hideous masks. They looked like the Acedoran soldiers he had seen during the battle of Longshire. He shuddered involuntarily. Koren knew the enemy made their faces that way in order to scare him, and that he should ignore it. His head knew that. His gut was shaking. Then he reminded himself that the enemy died just as easily as soldiers from Tarador. He had seen the enemy falling when hit by arrows, or struck with swords or spears. When the enemy came over the rail to board Koren's ship, many of them would die.

The question was whether there were enough pirates aboard the enemy ship to take his own ship. There were a lot of pirates crowded on the other ship's deck, even though their ship was smaller.

"Koren," Alfonze nudged him and took the spyglass back. "Let's go, we have work to do." He gestured over to a hatchway near the bow, where other crewmen were bringing up canvas bags containing swords and pikes. Koren's task was to take weapons out of the bag, then he rotated a stone wheel while Alfonze sharpened swords. When the blades had a fine edge, Koren wiped the blades down and laid them out on the deck. While they were preparing weapons to defend their ship, Koren kept glancing aft to check on the progress of the enemy ship. It was growing close; during periods when the wind died to nothing, Koren imagined he could hear the enemy jeering and shouting curses. Some of the crew shouted back, until the first mate told them to be quiet. "Save your strength, you'll need it later. And don't give them the satisfaction of thinking they've rattled you, boys. They've underestimated this crew!" The first mate said with bravado that convinced none of the *Lady Hildegard's* crew.

When the weapons were ready, the first mate handed out swords and pikes to the crew; Koren was given a pike. He couldn't tell anyone about his long practice and skill with a sword; he was supposed to be a farm boy, and farmers did not commonly use swords. He hefted the pike, and looked longingly at a basket of bows and arrows on the aft deck. Perhaps he should tell the first mate or Captain about his extraordinary skill with a bow; that could be explained by the hunting that every farmer did to provide food on the table.

Before Koren could walk aft, an alarm bell was sounded. The enemy was firing on them! The first shot arced out from the pirate ship; Koren heard the shouting of the crew and turned to see a pointy black tube fly through the air and splash into the sea behind his ship. Almost instantly, the surface of the water was on fire, and the languid waves only stirred up the oil. A second bomb followed the first, with the second also falling short, but ten feet closer to the ship.

After the first two bombs, the pirates switched to shooting blanks; the first one bounced off the stern. The second crashed into a railing on the port side, splintering it. Shards of wood flew in all directions, striking two of the crew.

After firing four shots at the merchant ship, the pirate ship veered slightly to the west, to run parallel to Koren's ship. "Ha!" Koren exulted. "They're keeping their distance," he shook his pike at the enemy. "You stay away, if you know what is good for you." He grinned at Alfonze. "They couldn't hit us!"

"Kedrun," Alfonze chided him. "They're not keeping away from us, they're maneuvering into position. Those blank shots they fired were only to test the range of their ballistas."

"Only one of their shots struck us," Koren said unhappily.

"They were only shooting to set up the aim of their ballistas; they weren't trying to damage us yet."

"Then why did the first two burst into flames?"

"That was to scare us, to show us what will happen when those bombs are fired at our sails."

"Oh," Koren said sheepishly. He pointed his pike at the pirates. "Why did they turn aside?"

"Kedrun," think about it, Alfonze sounded disappointed.

Koren thought hard, but he thought as a landsman, not as an experienced sailor. "Because from the side, our ship is a larger target for their ballistas?"

"That's true, but that's not why. If their ship approached us from behind, then their bow would be alongside our stern when the ships make contact. That would not give the enemy much chance to come aboard; we can easily defend just our stern." He pointed at the pirate ship, which was drawing even with the merchant ship, perhaps two hundred yards away. "This way, they can close with us, and lay alongside our full length. We will have to defend the entire rail, bow to stern. They can concentrate their strength in one spot, come over the railing, and once they get a foothold on our deck," he shook his head.

"Oh," Koren nodded. That made sense.

"Also, they have the weather gage now. You know what that means?"

Koren grinned, pleased that he knew something about seamanship. "They are upwind from us, so their sails steal the wind from ours. And they can decide when to close with us; they choose when to engage."

"Good!" Alfonze patted Koren on the back. "You're learning. Yes, they have the advantage. With their slaves manning the oars, we can't escape from them in these light winds."

"We can turn away from them," Koren suggested.

Alfonse shook his head. "There's a reef to the east; we can't sail in that direction for long, or we'd wreck. Because we can't trust these winds, we don't dare get close to the reef; the current would pull us in and we'd be struck aground. And we can't go west because our sails can't point as close to the wind as the pirates can. No, the captain knows what he's doing. Our best chance is to fight off the pirates when they try to board us. If we stay together and don't panic, we have a decent chance to keep the pirates from taking the deck. We fight off their initial attack, sometimes pirates will break off, and look for a softer target."

"If they can't take us, they won't try to sink us?" Koren asked, just before Alfonze kicked his leg sharply.

Alfonze glared at him as a warning. The crew was frightened already, they didn't need anyone asking stupid questions. "No," Alfonze lied, and everyone knew he was lying. "They won't waste the effort."

Slavery or death, Koren thought silently. Those were his options. This was not the future he had hoped for when he fled Linden, and took passage aboard a ship. No, that was not true. When he fled the castle, he had no hopes for his future. He had not begun to hope for his future until the ship had reach the South Isles. Then he had realized that, not only did he enjoy being at sea, nothing bad had happened around him. His jinx curse had not caused any disasters since he had caused the gargoyle to fall on Princess Ariana. Until, he thought with a sudden shock, a pirate ship had appeared close to his ship, after somehow tracking them all night. Was that his jinx? Had he caused the pirates to locate his ship, in the vastness of the ocean?

"How did the pirates find us?" Koren asked aloud.

"What?" Alfonze turned to look at the young sailor. "It happens, Kedrun. Pirate ships lurk along the sea-lanes, waiting for fat merchants to sail by. We were to the east of the sea-lane between the South Isles and Istandol, but we can't go any further to the east, because of the reef. The pirates know that."

"Yes," Koren pressed for an answer, "but how was that pirate ship so close to us this morning? How did it track us all night?"

"Captain explained that," Alfonze said worriedly. The Kedrun he knew was not this shaky. "The enemy may be using a magical device to locate us. Or it could be bad luck. With the wind out of the west last night, and the reef to the east, there was only so far we could have gone. Bad luck, is what it is. We always had a chance to be attacked by pirates on this trip; that's why we were offered bonuses when we get to Istandol."

Koren was not convinced that he had not jinxed the ship. Jinxed the ship, and doomed the entire crew to death or slavery. Or slavery, then death. Either way, death was almost certain. Without a miracle, they were all going to die in battle, or be captured and suffer a slow death. "Bad luck?"

"Bad luck, yes. Why?" Alfonze was concerned for his young friend.

"Alfonze, I think that I brought this upon us. I'm sorry."

"You?" Alfonze laughed nervously. "What, were you holding a candle in the crow's nest all night for the pirates to see?"

"No, it's," Koren glanced around. Even on the crowded deck, there was no one else immediately near them. "I am bad luck. Bad luck for everyone around me. I always have been. When I was a little boy, people were afraid of me."

"Oh, is this some nonsense that old idiot Jofer put in your head?" Alfonze asked angrily. Sailors were a superstitious lot on their own; they didn't need a shipmate putting dangerous thoughts in their heads.

"No, this is me. I've always been, sort of, a, a jinx. I cause disasters for everyone around me." At that moment, Koren wished the sea would swallow him, and end his misery.

Alfonze grabbed his shoulders roughly and spun him to face the pirate ship. "You see that ship, you young fool? Those are bloodthirsty pirates. And their leaders are under the spell of Acedor. They don't need any luck to find merchant ships out here; they spend all day tacking back and forth across the sea-lanes. Lying in wait, like snakes in the grass. If it wasn't us they found, another ship would have fallen victim to them. I don't believe in luck, good or bad. You make your own luck in life, by your sweat and your brains," he released Koren and tapped his own head. "Right here, is the enemy's best weapon. Fear. They want us to be paralyzed by fear, and to doubt ourselves, and to fight amongst ourselves. What we can do, more importantly than sharpening these blades, is to trust ourselves, and each other. This is our ship; we only need to defend the deck. Our deck is higher; the enemy will need to climb ladders to get aboard. They will come across, carrying steel, and we will meet with our own steel." He plunged the tip of his sword into the wooden deck, and it stuck there, vibrating. "You want to help? Then stop talking childish nonsense, and prepare yourself to repel the enemy.

"Yes," Koren said gratefully. He did still think that he was a jinx, and dangerous, and that if the ship fell to the pirates, it would be mostly his fault. But right then, he could not do anything about the pirates having found the *Lady Hildegard* again in the morning. What he could do was pray, and fight. Pray for a miracle. He looked to the west, where only a few clouds dotted the sky. No miraculous squall would be rescuing them that afternoon. They needed to fight. Koren set the pike down, and walked aft toward the first mate. "Mister Scanton, you gave me a pike."

"Eh?" The first mate responded, distracted. "A young fellow like you will do best with a pike. A sword is too-"

"No. I'd be best with a bow."

"A bow?" Scanton scoffed, annoyed at the interruption. "Why? Because you shot fat deer on a farm, boy? Go back to-"

"No. I have been trained to use the bow. I. Never. Miss. *Never.* Not ever," he said vehemently, leaning toward the first mate aggressively.

Scanton reached for the handle of the knife he kept on his belt. "Kedrun, you get back to-"

"Why not give him a chance?" Asked Alfonze, who had followed Koren. He looked at the pirate ship. "They'll be in arrow range before long. If Kedrun here can pick off one or two before they tie onto us, that will make them keep their heads down. Sir," he added softly in response to Scanton's angry look. "It can't hurt, can it? Give the young lad a chance."

Alfonze was well respected by the crew; he would be a first mate on his own someday, or even a captain. Scanton was new to the ship, having joined the crew only a month before Koren. With disgust, he pointed to the barrel that held bows and arrows. "Have at it, Kedrun. But if you've fired three arrows and not hit anyone, you go back to your pike, and I'll not hear any more nonsense from you," the first mate said while waving a finger in Koren's face.

Koren knew not to be insulted. "Yes, Mister Scanton," he made a short bow and hurried over to the barrel to select a bow. He groaned when he saw the selection. Compared to the bows he had used at the castle, or the standard bow of the Royal Army, the weapons in the barrel were of poor quality. And the arrows were old, bent and their feathers ragged or missing entirely. "Oh, Alfonze, this is terrible."

"Why?" The big man asked. "The enemy will be directly alongside; you won't have to shoot far." He picked up and arrow and sighted along it, it was warped.

"No, I want to hit them well before they are alongside." Koren hefted what looked like the sturdiest bow, rejected it, and picked up another.

"No, you don't want a bow like that," Alfonze advised. "A bow like that takes too much effort, you won't be able to control it. You won't be able to hit anything with a heavy bow like that. Try this one," he held up a shorter bow made of a springier wood.

"No," Koren shook his head. "I can aim fine. With a bow like that one you have, I couldn't get an arrow halfway to the pirate ship."

"It's your choice," Alfonze said, unconvinced. Glancing at the pirate ship, he added "Choose quickly. The pirates are even with us; they'll start shooting soon." He could see the pirates had moved the two ballistas to the middle of the ship, and were jostling them into position. Soon, they would begin cranking the windlasses, and bringing bombs up from the hold.

Koren checked a third bow, which looked crude and well-worn but *felt* right. He didn't know why, it simply felt right in his hand. It would take a strong effort to draw back the string, but it was powerful, and he was confident it could propel an arrow across the gap between the ships. The arrows were the real problem, so many of them were warped and splintered that they would fly in a circle, or shatter when he released the bowstring. What he needed, he decided, was a half dozen good arrows; arrows that would fly straight and true to their targets. "This bow", he handed it to Alfonze. "I'll take these arrows apart to make some I can use." Ignoring the fletching, he pulled one arrow after another out of the barrel, rejecting most of them. The good ones he laid carefully on the deck, and when he had seven, he began removing the feathers from warped arrows. Even the first mate glanced over as Koren expertly pulled feathers from bad arrows and set them carefully to properly provide fletching for his seven chosen arrows. Finally, he stood up.

"Seven arrows?" Alfonze asked skeptically.

"Seven arrows," Koren declared simply while he struggled to fit a string to the bow. He looked at Alfonze with a face devoid of expression. "I was not exaggerating when I said that I never miss."

This was a Kedrun that Alfonze did not know. Where was the uncertain young man who had come aboard the ship, not knowing anything about seamanship? "Let me do that," he offered, and used his weight and strength to bend the stiff bow.

"Thank you," Koren whispered. He didn't know if he had the strength to get the bow strung correctly by himself.

"Now?" Alfonze suggested impatiently as he stood by the rail next to 'Kedrun'.

"No," Koren responded with a grunt. Holding the bowstring drawn back was a tremendous effort, his arm shook.

"They're about to fire that forward ballista," Alfonze warned in a harsh whisper.

"I know, it's not. It's not right yet," Koren gritted his teeth from the effort. "I have to wait until the time is right, until I know it's right."

"How do you know?" Alfonze asked, and shared an anxious look with the first mate, who was walking by.

"I don't know how I know; I just *know*. I feel it," Koren answered. "I have to wait until-" he released the arrow. The arrow flew high in the air between the ships, wavering in the unpredictable breezes, then arced downward. A cry went up from the deck of the pirate ship, and figures attempted to dodge out of the way, but they got in each other's way. The arrow found its mark, plunging into the chest of the pirate in command of the forward ballista. The man staggered forward against the railing, slumped over, and fell into the water with a splash.

Both crews were shouting; Koren's crew exulted with hope, and the pirates screamed threats and insults across the water. Alfonze pounded Koren on the back so hard, the young man could barely breathe. "You did it! You did it!" Alfonze grinned, and shook his sword at the pirates. "You waited to time the roll of both ships?"

"I wait until, it's hard to explain. Until it feels right, until I know that I will hit the target." Koren didn't know why he had such skill with a bow, he simply did, and always had.

On the pirate ship, the stricken man had been quickly replaced by another, and the pirates were cheering as the ballista crews put their backs into winding up the pair of weapons. Most of the pirates, surprised that an arrow had been accurate at such a distance, were warily crouched down behind wood screens along the railing. "Can we do anything?" Koren asked.

Alfonze looked up at the sails, which were listlessly half filled in the light breeze. "Nay, not much. If we had more wind, we could back the mizzen sails," he meant the sails on the rear of the ship's two masts, "and slow suddenly to throw off their aim. Or turn to starboard, away from them, to present a smaller target."

"They're behind those screens now," Koren expressed his frustration. "I can't hit them if they don't show themselves."

"Can you hit one of the men winding a ballista?" Alfonze pointed. The men had to stand up, exposed, as they strained to crank the wheel.

"Maybe," Koren pondered doubtfully. Even if he could, what good would that do? Any man he hit with an arrow would be quickly replaced by another. "Is there a-"

"Down!" Alfonze hauled on Koren's shirt and pulled the young man to the deck, as both ballistas fired. One of the bombs fell short, crashing into the *Hildegard* near the waterline. A few droplets of burning oil splattered up onto the deck, to be quickly rendered harmless by handfuls of sand dumped on them.

The other bombs did more damage, hitting the lower sail on the mizzen mast. Oil rained down on the aft deck, causing even the Captain to run for cover, and in an instant, the white canvas was on fire. That lowest sail was rigged fore and aft, so men had to scramble out along the upper spar to cut away the burning canvas, before the flames could spread to other sails. Beating back flames with their gloved hands, two brave sailors succeeded in hacking away the ropes that held the burning sail to the upper spar, while below them, other men worked to swing the sail to hang overboard. The now-loosened sail crashed down, partly on the aft deck, and men threw sand on the flames and sliced the sail with their sharp knives. Other sailors used their pikes to heave the flaming canvas over the rail, and in less than a minute, the sail was in the water and the danger to the ship had passed.

Except that, as Alfonze reminded Koren, they now had less sail area aloft, and the *Hildegard* had slowed even more. Across the water, the pirates were cranking their ballistas again. Koren could see two men carrying the 'bombs' up from a hold, then fitting the bombs to a rail on the ballistas. "Aye," Alfonze remarked sourly, "here it comes again. They'll keep shooting until we're running on bare poles, then they'll have us. It will be our steel against their steel then," he said grimly, holding up his sword.

The Captain, having run out of most options, ordered a sharp turn to starboard just as the pirates fired their ballistas again. The forward ballista, which had struck the mizzen sail on its first shot, missed this time, with the bomb passing through the air just forward of the mizzen mast. That bomb soared through the air, to splash harmlessly in the water on the far side of the ship.

The other ballista, whose bomb had fallen short the first time, again threw its bomb less high. The black metal object arced low across the water, headed straight for Alfonze and Koren. It flew too fast for them to safely duck out of the way, and as he fell to the deck, Koren held up his free hand in a futile gesture to ward off the deadly weapon.

Except it was not a futile gesture. The bomb staggered in the air, as if it had struck something invisible ten feet from the *Hildegard*, and burst before it hit the ship. Flaming oil cascaded up and to both sides, with some burning drops flying above Koren's head to splash onto the deck. Most of the oil fell into the water alongside the ship.

Koren got to his knees, retrieving the bow that he had flung away, and peeked above the railing. He had expected to die in a pillar of flame. And now he expected that his crew would be cheering, but they were mostly silent. Or murmuring to themselves, looking at him warily, and some were making gestures to ward off evil. "What?" Koren asked innocently.

Even Alfonze was looking at Koren differently, standing apart. "How did you do that?" Alfonze asked in a hoarse voice.

"What? I didn't do anything," he protested. "Their bomb must have burst too early. Or it, hit a bird or something," he added, now not sure of himself. Seeing that Alfonze's eyes were wide, that the big man feared him, Koren held up his hands. "I didn't do anything. You saw!"

"Aye," Alfonze muttered, keeping a distance between him and the young man.

Partly to distract himself, Koren selected an arrow, and fit it to the bowstring. "Who should I aim at?"

Alfonze shook his head. "Unless you can hit one of the men carrying bombs up from their hold, you're best to save your arrows until they are closing with us."

"That's an impossible shot," old Jofer scoffed, having shuffled across the deck to stand at the railing beside Koren. Whether Jofer was curious about the young man he knew as 'Kedrun', or simply figured that standing near Kedrun was the safest place aboard the ship, he didn't say.

It was an impossible shot, Koren agreed silently. Still, he asked himself what else could he do that was useful, as he watched the pirates shaking their fists at him. The pirate ship had turned to match the *Hildegard*'s eastward course, and once again was running parallel to the merchant ship on its port side. Pirates were working the wheels of the two ballistas, cranking them for another shot. A man came up from the hold, carrying a bomb. Koren saw the man's head first, and as the man was walking very slowly and carefully, Koren was able to draw back the bowstring. But he felt strongly that the timing was not right, and he relaxed the string slightly. The man crossed the deck to the forward ballista, and disappeared from view behind the wood screen. Koren could see the heads and hats of pirates working behind the screen to load the ballista; it would not be long before another bomb was on its way across the water to hit the *Hildegard*.

Shifting his focus from the ballistas to the hatchway where the pirates brought bombs up from the hold, he once again drew back the bowstring and held it there, his arm shaking from the strain. Closing his eyes, he said a silent prayer. When he opened his eyes again, he could see a man coming up from the hold. Only the man's head and shoulders were visible above the hatchway when Koren released the arrow.

The arrow flew almost flat across the water, propelled by the great force of the heavy bow. Its target had not yet fully emerged from the hatchway when the arrow struck his left arm, and with a strangled cry, he fell backwards down the steps into the hold, dropping the bomb out of his hands. The dangerous weapon bounced down the steps into the pirate ship's hold.

"Incredible!" Jofer whispered, astonished. "How did-"

"Look!" Alfonze shouted and pointed at the pirate ship. Flames licked up from the hatchway, followed by more flames. Then there was a great gout of flame leaping high above the hatchway, setting the sails on fire and catching many pirates in its grasp. The bomb must have exploded below the deck, and its burning oil had set off other bombs stowed there. Within seconds, the deck of the pirate ship was a mass of flames, and pirates were leaping into the water to escape, discarding their weapons and masks as they fell toward the waves.

"Hard to starboard!" The *Hildegard*'s captain ordered, and the merchant ship veered away from the stricken pirate vessel. Burning oil now surrounded the pirate ship, scorching men in the water who flailed their arms and slipped beneath the surface.

Koren held onto Alfonze's right arm in horror at what he had done. The screams of the dying were terrible to hear, and worse than the desperate cries of the pirates were the unseen slaves trapped below deck. "Can we do anything to help them? They're dying!"

"Aye, they are," Alfonze nodded grimly. "And better off they are, than to be slaves of the enemy. Kedrun, no, there is nothing we can do. The pirates chain their slaves below decks, we couldn't get to them in time." Already, the pirate ship was listing to port, showing the underside of its hull to the *Hildegard*. The hull shook as more bombs within its hold exploded, and more burning oil spread upon the surface of the water. The pirates must have had flammable oil stored in casks that had now burst, dooming them and their ship.

"I didn't mean to," Koren was unable to finish his thought. "I didn't mean to-"

"Aye, yes you did," Alfonze said quietly. "You meant to save us all, and you did."

"I didn't mean," Koren could not look at the men dying in the water as floating oil burst into flames around them. Only a few pirates were able to swim away strongly enough to escape the flames. As Koren watched, one pirate who had escaped turned to shake a fist at the *Hildegard*. The man's grotesquely painted face became even more shocking as his mouth suddenly flew open, and he was jerked under the surface. A triangular fin briefly appeared, then there was a violent ripple in the water, and the pirate was seen no more.

Other survivors recognized their new danger, and began crying out for help and frantically thrashing around in the water. Their actions did them no good, serving only to attract the sharks. The sharks, who had been maddeningly frustrated while following one or the other ship, having to satisfy themselves with scraps of garbage, saw their chance to finally feast. The water boiled as fins appeared, racing toward the survivors, and sleek gray shapes flashed at the surface as they fought over their prey. Alfonze took hold of Koren's shoulders and turned the young man away from the rail so that Koren would not see the pirate ship turn upside down and slip beneath the waves with a mass of bubbles.

The entire crew was silent, staring at the awful scene of destruction. Nothing but debris bobbed on the surface, in between scattered flames as the floating oil burned itself out. No one could speak, for they were all thinking that could have been their fate; to burn to death, to drown, or to be torn apart by horrible sharks.

Finally, Alfonze spoke to break the silence. "That was an incredible shot," Alfonze shook his head in wonder.

"An impossible shot," Jofer protested. "An *impossible* shot," he glared in fear at Kedrun, and backed slowly away from the young man who he realized he knew little about.

"It wasn't impossible. I did it," Koren said, but he knew what Jofer meant. He shrugged. "I've always been good with a bow."

"No one is *that* good," the first mate declared. "Captain wants to see you aft, Kedrun. I'll take the bow, and the arrows."

CHAPTER SEVEN

Koren went below to meet Captain Reed in the man's cabin. It was at the back of the ship, with several large windows to let in fresh air, light and gave a view of the ship's wake. The man was standing beside his desk with his back to Koren.

Koren knocked on the door frame. "You wanted to see me, Captain?"

"Yes, come in, and close the door."

Koren closed the door behind him, noting that the skylight above was also closed. Curious sailors, and all sailors were curious, would no doubt try to listen to the conversation, but they would have a difficult time making out words drifting out the half-open rear windows.

"Sit," Reed indicated a chair in front of the desk, and the captain pushed items around the desk, as if he planned to sit on the corner rather than in his own chair. Uncharacteristically, the desk was cluttered, Reed usually kept his cabin neat and clean. The wood serving platter from breakfast was still on the desk, although Koren saw that the dishes and cutlery were piled on a sideboard. As Koren moved to sit, Reed suddenly stabbed at Koren's face with a dagger. Quicker than the blink of an eye and even without Koren realizing what he was doing, he picked up the serving platter and held it up to block the blade, then knocked the captain off the desk to sprawl on the floor.

Koren sprung to his feet, holding the platter like a weapon. "Ah! Hold, Kedrun! I was testing you. Ah, that hurts. I should have known better." Reed flexed his sore wrist and pointed to the dagger that had gone flying off into a corner of the cabin.

Koren could see the dagger was still encased in a leather sheath. Captain Reed had not meant to harm him at all. He set the platter back on the desk, and sat down heavily in the chair.

Reed, nursing his sore wrist, went to the sidebar and poured himself a small measure of rum. He tilted his head back and swallowed it quickly, then walked over to sit across the desk from Koren. "Kedrun, no one is that fast. *No one.* Except for wizards. Are you a wizard?"

"Me? A wizard?" Koren asked, astonished. "No!"

"Your speed, and your skill with a bow, are not natural," Reed said in an unfriendly manner. A person like Kedrun could represent a threat to his ship and crew; Captain Reed could not stand for that. Even if Kedrun had just that day saved the *Lady Hildegard* from a ship of bloodthirsty pirates. "And that bomb exploded before it hit you, though you were not touched. How did you survive that? The bomb should have covered you in burning oil."

Koren's mind flashed to when he was with Paedris in the ruined keep, and an enemy wizard had thrown a fireball at him. The ball of magical fire had washed *around* Koren as if he had worn an invisible suit of armor, and he had not been harmed. That time, Koren was certain, Lord Salva had acted to protect him; Paedris had knocked the fireball aside.

Paedris was not aboard the *Lady Hildegard*, nor were any other wizards that Koren knew of. If there were a wizard aboard the ship, surely that wizard would have acted against the pirates. But without wizardry, Koren had no explanation for how or why the bomb had not harmed him. Even if the bomb had exploded prematurely, or struck something in the air, the burning oil should have continued to fall forward onto Koren and Alfonze. Now even Alfonze had looked at Koren with fear and suspicion. "I don't know how I survived, sir. I can only tell you that I didn't *do* anything."

"Aye," the captain considered. "If you were a wizard, you'd not have needed an arrow to set that pirate ship on fire. Yet, no one could make a shot like that, *two* shots, at such distance."

"I was lucky," Koren protested lamely.

"Mister Scanton tells me you release the arrow when you *feel* it is time," the captain leaned across the desk. "Archers that I know do not rely on a feeling."

"I can't explain it, sir. It's been like that ever since I was little, and I was hunting on my parent's farm," he said truthfully. "When I wait until I know it's the right time, I never miss."

Captain Reed leaned back in his chair. "Kedrun, the bomb missing you and Alfonze; I could have thought that merely strange. Taken together; the bomb missing you, your incredible skill with a bow, and your reflexes, I cannot ignore my suspicions. You are no mere landsman who joined my crew. Explain yourself."

Koren had been fearing this day. Ever since he had fled the castle, he had expected the skill Paedris had cast on him to fade away or suddenly disappear, but it had not. When the crew had drilled with wooden blades, Koren always had to force himself to slow down, until it was almost painful to watch the slow and clumsy actions of whatever man he was sparring with. He had feared this day, when his unnatural skill was discovered. And he had been preparing for this day. He had prepared a story that contained enough truth to be believable. "I was servant to a gentle-man from Estada," Koren explained at least half-truthfully.

"Ah," the captain said with a raised eyebrow. "That's why you know how to cook exotic foods, then."

"Ur, yes." That also was close enough to the truth. "This gentleman wished me to be able to act as a guard for him, and for such, I needed more speed and skill than I had. So my master caused a wizard to cast a spell on me, giving me unnatural abilities." He looked at the captain to judge whether the man was believing his story. As it appeared so, Koren continued. "It must have hap-pened while I was asleep; I did not know about it." That part was entirely true.

"You ran away, then?" The captain asked. Servants and apprentices running away from their masters did not bother him; new crewmates for merchant ships sometimes came from such cir-cumstances.

"Yes. I feared for my life. If that spell had been cast on me, I feared what could be next. And I thought, that once I was gone from my master, my abilities would disappear. I have been surprised to see they have not. I can't explain it."

The captain let out a long breath. "Magic like that is not natural. It can burn you out from inside, if not removed. You need to consult a wizard."

"A wizard? How? It was a wizard who did this to me, against my will. All wizards belong to the same Council, I think. One wizard would not likely help me, by undoing the work of another," he said bitterly. "They would be more likely to capture me, and bring me back to my master."

The captain sat back in his chair and considered for a moment. Above them on deck, Koren could hear footsteps on the wood planks, shouts, the creaking of timbers and ropes being tightened. The normal sounds of a ship, the crew going on about the business of sailing the *Hildegard*, as if nothing unusual had happened that day. They had to, for the sea was indifferent to the cares of men. "Aye. Wizards can be good or bad, but they can't be trusted to respect the lives of simple folk like us. Wizards live in their own world, and regular people such as you and me don't matter to them." Kedrun's problem was not the responsibility of Captain Reed or the crew of the *Lady Hildegard*. Still, Reed felt sympathy for the young man. Kedrun had come aboard the ship, concealing an important secret, but how many of the crew had carried their own secrets with them? Reed himself had been running from something he would rather forget when he first went to sea. "When I was a younger man," Reed reminisced, "I traveled north, to the dwarf lands. One of our party was injured in a fall down a mountain, and a dwarf wizard healed her. Maybe you could seek out a wizard of the dwarves. They have their own council."

"I could do that?" Koren asked, his eyes wide. He thought back to Hedurmur in Linden, a dwarf who had sold him a magic-spelled blade. The sword had been made by dwarves, he knew that; and by reputation, dwarves were the premier metalsmiths in all the world. But it had never occurred to him that the wizard who had put a magic spell into the blade had been a dwarf. It was not that he had thought dwarves incapable of being wizards; he had simply not mentally connected 'dwarves' and 'wizards' before. "They would help me?"

"There are good dwarves and bad dwarves, like any other people," Reed cautioned. "All I can say is, although we have an alliance with the dwarves against Acedor, dwarves are not beholden to anyone."

"I will think about it, Sir," Koren responded, his head spinning with possibilities. When he had fled Linden, all he had in his mind was to get far away. To get away from the reach of the Royal Army, for his own safety. And to get a safe distance away from anyone he cared about, so his jinx curse could not harm anyone. Except, everywhere he went, he found people to care about, like the crew of the *Hildegard*. He had never thought of seeking someone to help him. It had never occurred to him that anyone *could* help him. Despite the harsh words of the priest in the royal chapel that God himself had cursed Koren, could his curse be lifted by a wizard? Did dwarf wizards know magic that even Paedris did not? It was certainly worth a chance, Koren decided.

"Whatever you decide to do, you need to leave the ship," the captain declared, looking Koren directly in the eye. "We'll be docking at Istandol, I don't know if you've ever been there?"

Koren shook his head.

The captain reached into his desk, shuffled rolled-up papers around, and pulled out a map. He spread it on the table. "It's a busy port, you can surely find another ship there, if that's what you wish."

"No. I want to do as you suggested, and find a dwarf wizard. I'll go north." He knew where Istandol was, having seen it on maps back when he and Princess Ariana had loved to spend a lovely afternoon looking at maps from the royal library, and imagining what those distant lands were like. That memory was now bitter, he pushed it to the back of his mind. He touched the map, his finger tracing a route. Istandol lay where the broad mouth of a large river met the sea. The ridge-line of the hills to the west of the river valley formed much of Tarador's eastern border, so he could remain safely out of that realm's territory for much of his intended journey. He would take passage on a ship going upriver, but at some point, he would need to turn west and cross into Tarador to reach the dwarf lands. How he would do that, he could decide later. And he would need money, more money than he possessed. That, also, he could figure out later.

Bjorn was ready to leave the blacksmith shop. He had stayed there longer than a fortnight in order to help Fergus work with a new apprentice, an awkward boy who could barely make his way around the shop without burning himself. "That's it, then," Bjorn announced, setting down his tools after cleaning them and wiping them with oil.

"Yes," Fergus replied. "I guess that's it. Oh," he acted like he had just remembered something. "Here," he held out canvas sack. "My wife prepared food for your journey. It's hard bread, some cheese, dried beef, and a couple of those meat pies you like." The blacksmith was embarrassed.

"You didn't have to do that," Bjorn said gratefully.

"Please," Fergus said with a dismissive wave of a hand, "it will make her happy for you to take it. Here's your last pay," he tossed a small pouch to his former, and best, helper.

Bjorn caught it, felt the weight of it in his hand, then opened it. "This is too much," he protested.

"No it isn't." Fergus waved a hand to indicate all the finished pieces around the now clean and well-organized shop. "I'd not have completed all these orders on time without you, nor gotten these new orders," he held up a sheaf of papers. "You've earned it. Good luck to you, Bjorn Jihns-son. And good luck to your family, when you see them."

Every morning, Ariana woke up wishing to ask Chief Advisor Kallron what progress he had made in finding a way around the law of coronation, so she could take the throne immediately. Instead, she waited patiently. Actually, she waited impatiently, frustrated, knowing that as soon as Kallron had news, he would tell her. Before they both left for the summer palace, he had not found any legal means for her to become queen before the sixteenth birthday. At the summer palace he had remained in his suite of rooms except for during the evening meal, studying the ancient scrolls and books he had brought from the royal library. And much to his disappointment, he had not found anything useful. As soon as they returned to Linden, he had buried himself in the royal library again. So when he requested to meet with the crown princess as soon as possible, she was fairly trembling with excitement. Until she saw the gloomy expression on his face. "Highness, it is as I feared," Kallron reported sadly. "I have searched the royal archives; I have also made discrete, very discrete searches of other legal libraries throughout Tarador. The law is clear, it is well documented, and it is as strong as iron. You cannot take the throne until your sixteenth birthday. The Regency Council," consisting of the dukes and duchesses of Tarador's seven provinces, "guards its power carefully. They wrote the law to prevent a young crown princess, or prince, from taking the throne as long as possible. To sustain their influence as long as possible."

Ariana bit her lip in anger and frustration. "The Regency Council made the law. Surely they can change it."

"That is a good question. The law can be changed, yes. According to the law, the process for changing the rules of coronation for a sovereign begins with five of seven provinces approving a revised law."

"*Five* of seven?" Ariana asked, surprised. Four of seven was a majority. She could count on the votes of three provinces; two for sure. Four would require negotiation, but it could be managed, somehow. Five? Five was very difficult, with the Falcos controlling their own province and having strong influence over two others.

"Five, Highness. Five of seven is referred to in the law as a 'super majority'. That is not the real problem. After the law is approved by the Council, it must be approved by the sovereign."

"What?" The princess sputtered. "But the law of coronation is only in effect when there is no sovereign on the throne!"

"Exactly, Highness. The law was written specifically to prevent the Regency Council from making a deal with potential inheritors of the throne, and choosing their own sovereign. For example, were you to have a younger sister, she could make a deal with the Falcos to take the throne instead of you. That is why the law of coronation cannot be changed without a king or queen on the throne. It is, Your Highness, a wise law."

"Oh," Ariana sighed. "I suppose it is." She would not like the idea of a younger sibling passing over her to wear the crown. Especially not if she had been passed over because the throne had been sold to the Falcos. "There is truly no way, then?"

"Short of using the Royal Army to seize the throne by force, there is no way for you to become queen short of your sixteenth birthday. I would not recommend we attempt such an extreme act, in case you were wondering."

"No, of course not." Ariana hastened to say. She had been wondering exactly that; whether the Royal Army would follow her. Whether she could convince Grand General Magrane to support her. The problem was that not all of the Royal Army would likely join her cause, and then there would be strife within the Royal Army. The combined Ducal armies of the seven provinces were three times the size of the total royal force; against a united Regency Council, Ariana could not prevail. "There is truly no way?"

"Highness, I am truly sorry. There is no possibility of you becoming queen until you are sixteen years of age," Kallron looked down at the floor, as if accepting blame for his failure. "There is, however," he looked up with a twinkle in his eyes, "a wrinkle I have discovered."

"A wrinkle?"

"Yes. In my research of the royal archives, I came across a very curious, a most curious fact. I was reading about the history of the Regency, and, here is something odd; the only requirement to be Regent is for the person to have been born a Taradoran citizen."

"Why is that odd?" That requirement made sense to Ariana.

"My point," Kallron said with a broad grin, "is that, as you were born a citizen of Tarador, there is no reason *you* could not become Regent."

"That makes no sen-" Recognition dawned on the princess, and she gasped. "I could become *my own Regent*? Hold power for myself?"

"Yes. The law may, as you were going to say, make no sense," he said with a wink. "There is no law preventing *you* from holding power as Regent, until some girl named 'Ariana Trehayme' comes of age and takes the throne."

"Oh. Oh!" She stood up and playfully pounded the man's chest with her fists. "Uncle Kallron," she used the name she had called the man when she was a child, "you made me wait and worry!"

"A lesson in patience, Your Highness." He kissed the top of her head, as he had done when little Ariana had sat on his knee. "And a lesson in how convoluted our laws can be."

Ariana fairly danced across the room to pour a cup of tea for herself, and red wine for her advisor. Then she looked sharply at her advisor. "This is not a game you are playing on me? I truly can become my own Regent?"

Kallron nodded slowly, seriously. "I would never joke about such a subject, Your Highness. What I said is true."

"The law absolutely makes no sense," she crinkled her forehead in puzzlement, spooning sugar into her tea. "The law says that I am too young to take the throne, but I can hold the power of the throne through the Regency?"

"Highness, it is not that the law makes no sense; the law simply did not consider such a possibility. While you must be sixteen to be crowned queen or king, the office of the Regency has no age requirement. Because the law does not state that a future monarch is ineligible to be Regent, the Regency Council may elect anyone they wish. It is certain that the Falcos, perhaps others, will argue that you becoming Regent goes against the intent of the law, and such an argument may well be entirely correct. Such as argument is also entirely irrelevant; the law stands as written.

Authority for interpretation of the law rests with the sovereign, and as you mentioned, we have no sovereign."

"I know the law for appointing a Regent," Ariana said while carefully carrying a too-full goblet of wine to her new advisor. "We still need, what did you call it? A supermajority?" She pronounced the unfamiliar word slowly. "Appointing a new Regent also take five votes on the Council, for me to replace my mother."

"Five votes," Kallron nodded in agreement. "You can count on only two for certain," he warned, holding a finger in the air for emphasis.

"Rellanon and LeVanne." Ariana recited the names of the provinces closely allied to the Trehayme family. "Dukes Magnico and Yarron."

"Friends you can count on, now and when you take the throne," Kallron agreed. "Then there are Duchess Portiss of Anschulz Province, and Duke Romero of Winterthur. They likely would agree to you assuming the Regency, given certain assurances. Romero, as his lands border Acedor, would require a commitment that the Royal Army would assist in securing his border against the enemy."

"I have maintained my personal guard in the Thrallren Woods of LeVanne province, to bolster our defenses there. The Thrallren extends up into Winterthur." Ariana reminded the former chancellor. "Uncle Yar-" she slipped into speaking of the man as she had known him since she was a little girl. Yarron was her uncle because he was related to Ariana by marriage. "Duke Yarron knows that I will protect him. Romero surely can see the same."

"Romero knows you sympathize with him. He may fear that your guards are in the Thrallren to spite your mother, and that once you hold the reins of power, you will find better uses for those skilled soldiers. Romero will seek formal, written assurances."

"He will receive such assurances. And he will receive Royal Army soldiers to secure his western border. We must hold the Thrallren Woods. If we cannot prevent the enemy from invading through such difficult territory, we cannot hold our borders anywhere. What of Duchess Portiss?" Ariana asked fearfully. Portiss had a second son, in his early twenties now. In years past, Portiss had hinted that her son would be a good match for Ariana, but as the boy had grown into a man, Portiss had not mentioned the possibility of a union for quite some time. There were rumors that her son had been about to announce his engagement to a wealthy princess of Indus, until the outbreak of war had put a halt to any such celebrations.

"Duchess Portiss will, I think, offer her support in the sincere belief that our nation is doomed so long as your mother remains in power." Ballana Portiss and Carlana Trehayme had never liked each other; the rift between the two women had grown wider since Carlana had become Regent. Or, rather, since Carlana had shown herself to be a completely ineffective leader of Tarador. "Duchess Portiss is happy with the matches her sons have made," her oldest son and heir was married to Duke Magnico's oldest daughter, "and she has given up designs on you marrying one of her family."

"Four votes," Ariana's face brightened. "That is four votes, certain or likely! All we need is one more. Thank you, Uncle Kallron!" She refrained from flinging her arms around the man. He was her advisor now, and she the future ruler of Tarador. "We must begin to look at which-"

"Before we discuss details, are you certain you are ready for this, Your Highness?" Kallron asked cautiously. "The first action will be one of the provinces, such as LeVanne, posting a motion in the Council to declare no confidence in your mother, and putting forward your name as a candidate to replace her. Posting that motion will be declaring open warfare between your mother and yourself. That may not be as easy for you as you think now."

"I am ready," Ariana said firmly, her jaw set. She had considered the emotional toll the upcoming fight would take on her, and on her mother. Her mother was not a bad person; she was only unsuited to leading the nation in a time of war. Ariana would tell her mother that; tell her that as a daughter, she loved her mother. As the crown princess, she could no longer have Carlana serve as her Regent.

"There are more than familial feelings to take into consideration," Kallron warned, although he was greatly worried about how Carlana would react. The woman held power, and she could use it against those she perceived as her enemies. Gustov Kallron would most assuredly become Carlana's bitter enemy, the moment the motion to replace Carlana was filed in the Council. "A motion to remove your mother throws the Regency into open competition. Regin Falco will do his utmost to seize the Regency for himself or one of his lackeys; and the Falcos are masters of intrigue."

"We hold four votes to his three, or two," Ariana said thoughtfully. Duke Bargann of Farlane Province had been chafing at his forced alliance with the Falcos recently; Regin Falco might not automatically be able to count on support from Bargann. Not without Bargann extracting a substantial price for his support; a price the Falco family might not be willing or able to pay. "Is there anything the Falcos could do, within the law? Could he," she gasped, "get the Council to change the law of the Regency?"

"No," Kallron said with a curt shake of his head. "The Regency law, like the law of majority, requires approval of a sovereign to change. There are legal technicalities Falco could put up as roadblocks, if he knows of such technicalities. They are very obscure," Kallron said with confidence, "I do not think Regin Falco has a deep enough knowledge of the law to interfere with us. With you, Your Highness."

"With us, Uncle Kallron," Ariana stood, took the man's hands on her own, and kissed his cheek affectionately. "I can't do this without you. And I can't serve as Regent without you as my chancellor."

"Thank you, Your Highness. I most sincerely hope that your faith in me is justified. Before we can begin to draw up documents to submit to the Council, we need to consider how we could split away from the Falcos the vote of either Duke Bargann of Farlane, or Duchess Rochambeau of Demarche. Neither will be easy. Highness, I do have sources of information, I can begin to search for a way to, encourage, either one to vote with you. This will take time, and it will be expensive to acquire-"

"No need, Uncle Kallron," Ariana said with a mischievous smile. "I know of a way."

"You do?" Kallron asked, truly surprised again that extraordinary morning. "What is it?"

"It is best that you do not know, Chief Advisor."

"But how can I-"

"Uncle Kallron, if things do not go as planned, the Regency Council can call you to testify; they could even have you questioned by a wizard, so you would be compelled to tell the truth. You cannot reveal secrets that you do not know. The Council has no power to summon *me*," Ariana said with a haughty toss of her hair. "What I need is a man, or actually," she thought for a moment. "No, a dwarf. A dwarf who can do certain things; things that need to be done discretely."

"Ah." Kallron felt a chill of fear at what dangerous game the crown princess might plan to play. To play without his knowledge, or his experienced guidance. Could he trust her to- He stopped his own thoughts. He was working toward Ariana becoming Regent, and then queen. Once she held the reins of power, he would have to trust her with the very survival of the nation. This was not a time to question her. She would prove herself, or she would fail. The test was for her alone. "A dwarf, willing to do certain things discretely. Highness, I do know of such a person; he is willing to work for gold. He sells his services to the highest bidder, but once he has been bought, he gets the task done, and he tells no one."

"Good," Ariana sat back slightly in her chair, daring to relax for the first time since Koren fled. She spun one of the gold rings she wore, wondering if it would be enough to buy the service of the dwarf. "Arrange for him to contact me, directly and discretely. Can you do it soon?"

"Highness. Ariana," Kallron said, speaking as an uncle who cared for her. "I feel that I should warn you; this dwarf is not a pleasant person to deal with."

"Uncle, when I sit on the throne, I will very likely be forced to deal with all manner of unpleasant people. I shall consider this a lesson," she winked.

"There is something else we must consider," Kallron cautioned. "Assuming that you are successful in, whatever it is you plan to do- You will not give me a hint?"

"No, Uncle Kallron," she shook her head, "it would be too dangerous, for you."

"Very well," his voice expressed disappointment, wondering to himself, what could she be planning without me? "If you are successful, and either Duke Bargann or Duchess Rochambeau could be persuaded to vote in favor of you becoming Regent, the matter of timing will be delicate. The entire Regency Council must be present here to vote, yet only the Regent, or three members of the Council, may call for the Council to assemble. Your mother certainly would not call that pack of scheming wolves to come to Linden; it would be too dangerous for her. The law states that she must assemble the Council once per year; she accomplished that when all the dukes and duchesses were here for the Cornerstone celebration. In order to approach three members of the Council and ask them to request the Council to assemble, we would have to reveal our plans far in advance. That would be much too dangerous; such a secret could not be kept for long."

"But you have a suggestion, Uncle Kallron?" Ariana asked with a smile. She knew the man all too well; of course he would have a plan.

"According to the law, a Council of *War* may be called by a single member, in times of national crisis. Your mother formally declared a national crisis when she mobilized the army reserves, so that legal step is out of the way."

"Oh," Ariana slumped in her chair. There was so much she did not know of the law; the law that would constrain her every move, her entire life once she became queen. "Could we ask Uncle Yarron to call a War Council? He can keep a secret," she said hopefully.

"It is easier to keep secrets you do not know. My suggestion is that you ask Lord Salva to send a message to Yarron, requesting a Council of War."

"Paedris?" Ariana feigned innocence.

"Young lady," Kallron tilted his head. "Perhaps you and the wizard think you have kept your alliance secret. And it may be that most people are not aware of, whatever support you have from Lord Salva. But I am not so easily fooled."

"Oh," Ariana was alarmed. She had told her servants that during her meetings with the court wizard, he was explaining to her how magic worked; what wizards could and could not do. Until that moment, she thought their secret was safe. "Does mother know?"

"I would say that she suspects something is going on. She may not suspect that Lord Salva is willing to actively intervene on your behalf; the custom of wizards remaining above politics is so ingrained in our culture, that your mother likely does not think you or Lord Salva would go that far." He held up a hand to forestall the protests of the princess. "No, whatever you and the wizard have arranged, it is better that I not know. Going back to my original point, my advice is that you ask Lord Salva to send a message to Duke Yarron, requesting that Yarron call a Council of War. Your mother will not be happy; she also will not be able to prevent the Council from assembling. If she does learn that Lord Salva was behind calling a War Council, she may not imagine your involvement. The court wizard is widely known to be unhappy with the Regent's actions in defense of Tarador."

"Or lack of action," Ariana complained bitterly.

"Precisely. You should speak with Lord Salva as soon as possible."

Ariana looked down at her informal dress, now dotted with ink stains because she had been writing letters. "Oh," she breathed in exasperation. "I need to change my clothes. *Again.*"

"Regent?" The court wizard nearly choked on a raspberry tart. "How can you become your own *Regent*? That makes no sense whatsoever."

"It does not make any sense," Ariana laughed. "Uncle Kallron tells me that doesn't matter; the law is the law, as written. Nothing in the law prevents me from becoming Regent. All I need is five votes on the Regency Council."

"Five?" Paedris asked with raised eyebrows. "How will you ever get five votes? The Falcos have three votes on their side."

"In most cases, the Falcos can count on three votes, yes. In this case, I have an idea. But I will need your help, Lord Salva. It may be somewhat," she sought the best word, "unsavory."

It was the wizard's turn to smile. "Our enemy is purely evil. Anything that is merely unsavory I can most likely accept. What do you need?"

CHAPTER EIGHT

Duston was used to the crown princess doing things that a proper crown princess should not be doing; things that would scandalize the royal court. He had been with her as she splashed around dank tunnels under the castle with the wizard's servant, as those two young people searched for the legendary Cornerstone. Although the princess was not supposed to be alone with a boy, Duston had thought it harmless fun for the future queen to get away from her formal role for a time, and simply enjoy being a young person. And her searching for the Cornerstone had certainly been worth the effort, for she had found it! Or so was the official story, Duston privately thought someone else had allowed Ariana to take credit for finding the Cornerstone, for the good of the realm.

Duston had accompanied the crown princess as she knelt in muddy grass to tend her garden, he had helped her plant bushes to create a maze in the garden; bushes with thorns that had torn her dresses. He had frantically followed her as she raced across the landscape on horseback. None of that had bothered him.

But this night, this was not right. "Highness, this is extremely dangerous. You should–"

"Duston," she put a finger to his lips, "hush, please. I know what I am doing. I am not a silly girl having an adventure. This is serious business, and if you feel you can't accompany me, I will go on alone. We are safe here."

"I–"

"Please, trust me. This is important," she whispered.

Important enough that she had risen in the middle of the night, used a secret passage from her study to sneak out of her private chambers, then left the castle in disguise, accompanied only by her trusted but elderly guard. It was raining and chilly; fog already collected in low areas of the countryside and alleyways of the sleeping city. They had ridden horses through the night on dark, lonely back roads, around the outskirts of the city of Linden, until they arrived at a very rough area of the town. An area that Duston occasionally visited when he was a young man, and did things that young and stupid men did. Now, he feared for the safety of the crown princess, and gripped his sword all the more tightly. "If you say so, Highness," Duston responded, unconvinced.

"I do. This is it," she pointed through the drizzle and nighttime fog to a dark building with a tattered flag hanging from an upper window, and three barrels stacked next to the door. Hugging the wall to remain out the flickering light of a fire down the street, she reached the alley beside the building, and waited. "Hello?" She called out softly, hopefully.

"Good evening," came a voice out of the alley, and a figure stepped out of the utter blackness.

"Master of weapons?" Ariana asked quietly.

The figure, shorter than Ariana but wide and powerful, strode forward. "Young miss," the dwarf replied, knowing that speaking the name of the princess at that time and place would be unwise for both of them.

"*Hedurmur?*" Duston asked, as the figure stepped forward and the firelight down the street illuminated the man's face.

"Yes," the dwarf acknowledged, and pulled aside his rain cloak to show the battleaxe looped to his belt. Even in the dim light, the sharp edge of the axe shone. "Young miss, this is a poor night to be out in the streets."

Ariana looked up at the rain, which had lessened from a steady drizzle to a mist. It only made the fog more thick, and her skin under the cloak more chilled. "A poor night for anything, I think." Leading the way, she crossed the alley to the side door of the building and knocked twice, then three times, then twice again.

The thick wooden door was dirty and battered but it opened silently; the hinges were apparently well-oiled. Inside was a dwarf standing in a narrow, dark hallway; a place Duston recognized as having been designed to provide excellent defense for those inside, and peril for any who tried to force entry. Knots in the thick walls were likely not natural; the false knots could be opened to shoot arrows, crossbow bolts and poisoned darts at those people trapped in the hallway. Duston rapped a fist on the door; the dead sound told him that the inner surface of the door was clad with iron. Once inside, he and the princess would be well and truly trapped. He could be responsible for the death of his nation's queen, and if Ariana died, Tarador would be torn apart by factions fighting for the throne. The enemy could walk into Linden unopposed.

Duston was compelled to protest. "Highness, no. I will not let you–"

"Duston," Ariana said more harshly than she wished to speak to the man who had been her personal guard for as long as she could remember. She spoke only as harshly as she felt needed, for she had great need to enter the building. "I told you that I am not a silly girl chasing adventure. This is a matter of state, and I have urgent business here. I am the crown princess of Tarador and your future queen. Obey me in this, or leave my service, now. I will not return to the palace until my business here is concluded."

The man still hesitated from long training and hard-won experience. Lightly, she grasped his forearm which held his sword half drawn from it scabbard. Standing on tiptoe, she whispered in his ear. "We are safe here."

"Aye," Hedurmur grunted, and swung his cloak aside so that his battleaxe was ready for use.

Though Duston did not relax the grip on his sword, he did nod slowly. Ariana peered into the dark hallway. "I am here to see Grimla," she said quietly. Her confidence did not extend so far as to allow her to pull aside the hood of her rain cloak; she did not wish anyone to see her face clearly until she met with the dwarf she sought.

The dwarf in the hallway, who was dressed in rough clothing and a wool cap, gestured them inside. "Grimla is waiting. No one followed you?"

"On this night?" Duston snorted. "No. I'm not doing this for the first time. Lead the way, and keep your hands in sight."

The dwarf was not surprised at the command. "Yes, sir," he said mockingly, and held his hands at his side. Once Ariana was inside the hallway, the dwarf pulled open the shutter on the lantern he held, and the gloomy darkness was lessened somewhat. "Close the door behind you," the dwarf said. He turned and smiled with crooked teeth, the whites of his eyes shining without humor. "Please."

Despite his common sense telling him not to, Duston closed the door behind him, trying to see if there was a way to keep it unlatched. There was not, but only a simple bar held it shut. Easy enough to remove if they needed to escape, Duston thought. Although if they did need to escape, they would never make it as far as the door.

The dwarf led the way down a series of hallways into a large back room with a high ceiling. The ceiling itself was dark, soot-stained beams that were almost lost in the gloom; the whole room smelled of old wood smoke and dust. In the center of the far wall was a fireplace in which the logs had burned down to red embers, casting an eerie glow around the room. There was furniture scattered about, some of it stacked against the walls, and much of it covered with dusty sheets. Arranged in a rough semicircle around the fireplace were chairs. Only one of the chairs was occupied; a dwarf sat looking away from the fire, smoking a pipe. "Telen," the seated dwarf said to the fellow who had opened the door, "guard the door. Young miss," he addressed Ariana, "your guard should join Telen."

"I will not-" Duston began to protest.

"Duston," Ariana explained, "there will be things said here tonight that you should not hear. You cannot be later compelled to tell, what you do not hear."

"Oh," Duston understood suddenly. The princess had told him this night was a matter of state. "Very well, Your Highness, Master Hedurmur, I will be at the door if you need me."

Grimla waited until the two guards had gone around the corner. Then he stood and bowed graciously to the crown princess. "Please, sit down. Forgive my earlier rudeness, Your Highness. I am Grimla of the Ironstone clan, as my name is rendered in the common tongue."

Ariana was taken aback. Without changing his appearance in any way, the dwarf's appearance had completely changed. His clothes were still rough and well-worn; threadbare in places. His hair still fell in lank curls around his face, and copper rings still were woven into his beard. But now his eyes twinkled, and his smile was genuine.

"Master Ironstone," Hedurmur explained with a glance toward the hallway to assure no one was listening, "is one of our agents here in Tarador."

"Agent?" Ariana asked, confused.

"Grimla is here as, an unofficial representative of our leadership," Hedurmur said.

"Unofficial?" Ariana asked, surprised. "You mean you are a *spy*?"

"Your chancellor, your advisor Kallron, how did he describe me?" Grimla had an amused smile.

"He told me you are a, a sort of mercenary," she supposed that was the polite term.

"I am that, and more. People consider me to be a criminal. In my profession, that is a useful reputation to have. I do, things which need to be done; things which need to be done in an unofficial manner. Mostly, I work for my own people, but occasionally, I will take on tasks for others, if the action will benefit my people. Kallron is not a fool; he may suspect that I am something more than a common mercenary. The guise of my profession is useful to us both, which is why we maintain the ruse. Over the years, I have performed tasks for your former chancellor, and for your father. He was a good man, your father."

"Thank you," Ariana replied simply. Her father had used a dwarf spy? For what hidden task? Inwardly, she chided herself for being surprised. Her father had been a king at war. He must have had great need for certain things to be done, and done unofficially.

"You are welcome." Grimla leaned forward. "Kallron tells me you have need of my services? Highness, I must warn you; I will not agree to help you, if such action would not be approved by my leadership."

"I understand," Ariana said nervously. This had all seemed much easier when she had been rehearsing what to say in her private chambers of the royal palace. "I seek to prevent Tarador from falling to the enemy; I believe your people would not wish for the enemy's banners to fly above Linden?"

"No," Grimla agreed. "How do you wish me to help you?"

And Ariana told him. Grimla then spoke privately with Hedurmur for a short time, and Grimla agreed to help the crown princess. He agreed enthusiastically, to the point of refusing the diamond ring she offered as payment. In the end he took the ring, because the princess insisted that Grimla might have substantial expenses in the task set for him, and because Ariana wished to make a gesture of respect for the dwarf lords who Grimla worked for.

By the time Duston and Hedurmur escorted Ariana back to the palace and she crawled wearily into bed, there was less than two hours remaining before dawn. When her maids awakened her at the usual time, she rose as normal although she desperately wanted to stay in bed until noon, at the earliest. Responsibility, she told herself, was easier to contemplate after a full night of sleep.

Grimla Ironstone, under the name of Heldur Ironstone, arrived at the gold mine, bearing expertly forged letters of recommendation extolling his experience as a mining engineer. He smiled to himself as he patted the pouch of papers inside his pocket; the mere fact that he was a dwarf would make ignorant people at the mine assume that he knew how to work the stone deep underground. In truth, he knew little of the art and craft of deep mining, having only worked at it for a few months when he was much younger. Every mountain was different, his uncle the miner had told young Grimla. You need to learn the bones of each mountain, and let them tell you how to extract the secrets deep beneath the surface. But, Grimla knew enough to fake it, and he also knew the mine needed an experienced mining engineer. One of the previous engineers had been forced to leave due to a serious family emergency. Grimla knew the 'emergency' had been that dwarf being offered a large sum of money to leave the mine and go elsewhere. Grimla knew this, because he had been the one making the offer, using gold he had gotten from selling the diamond ring given to him by the crown princess. Seeing the look of pure delight on the former engineer's face, when he contemplated the large stack of gold coins offered to him, had been payment enough for Grimla.

The interview for the job took less than two hours, during which Grimla descended into the depths with the mine supervisor. The basket was slowly lowered into the darkness, illuminated only by baskets of a special glowing fungus supplied by the dwarves, and by magical lights that had been purchased at great cost from wizards. For every three miners, there was also a lantern that burned oil; more lanterns would have fouled the air even worse than it already was. Grimla counted as they descended, to keep his bearings on where they were. When the basket reached the fourth level, the supervisor pulled a chain, and the basket stopped. They walked around the mine shafts, with the supervisor, a man with very short hair and a bushy red beard, sounding like he wanted to impress a dwarf with how much he knew about mining. Grimla mostly nodded and agreed with whatever the supervisor was saying, until they reached a point where the tunnel split into three directions. Grimla stopped and looked at the rock column that separated the tunnel straight ahead from the one on the left. He tapped the rock with a small hammer, frowned, touched the rock with a finger and tasted in, then got on hands and knees to inspect that base of the column. "You need to shore up this column," Grimla concluded. "It's weak. I suspect the rock is undercut by water." In truth, he had tasted salt, and the base of the column was slightly damp. That exhausted his knowledge of mine engineering.

The supervisor seemed impressed. "That's what our last engineer said. He was a dwarf also." The man tapped the rock with his own hammer, and listened intently. "Maybe you're right."

Grimla nodded wisely, although he had absolutely no idea if the rock column was sturdy enough to hold up the weight of the ceiling. What Grimla did know was what he had been told by the previous engineer, when Grimla had asked him if the mine had any weak areas. That column, where the tunnel on the fourth level split into three, was one place that Grimla had memorized. Grimla had learned many other important and useful things about the mine, and he had not had to pay for the information. Not pay directly, that is. He had paid for many the drinks consumed, and he had paid with his time while the real engineer vented his grievances about the mine managers. And Grimla had paid with an aching head the next morning, for he had to drink along with the engineer or it would have looked suspicious.

His one little nugget of knowledge, learned from the real engineer, was enough to convince the mine supervisor to hire Grimla. "When can you start?" The man asked rather anxiously. He had recently lost one of his engineers to a family emergency, and Duke Bargann was demanding ever more gold to be extracted from the mine. The mine supervisor had crews working around the clock, and still the duke was not happy. Rumor had it that Duke Bargann was deeply in debt, due to his rivalry with Duke Falco and his vain attempts to keep up with his wealthier rival.

"Tomorrow," Grimla said with satisfaction. "I'll need a few days to familiarize myself with the mine, of course."

"Of course," the supervisor agreed.

Those few days were all Grimla would need. He could go anywhere in the mine, without raising suspicion, and he could deflect any engineering questions that he could not answer. The mine could survive a short time without a real engineer.

After two days, Grimla knew enough about the mine to perform his real job. Early on the morning of the third day, he descended to the fourth level and walked around pretending to be inspecting the posts that shored up the ceiling, waiting until there were no miners in sight. He worked quickly, and when he was done, he joined a group going down to work the newest seams of gold on the fifth level. Here, an engineer was truly needed, for they were cutting a new tunnel, and there was water seeping from the ceiling. Even Grimla's untrained eye thought the mine was being dug too deep, too close to an underground river or some other source of water under high pressure. But Duke Bargann demanded that the miners follow the seams of gold, and the gold led ever downward. In addition to the pumps that brought fresh air down from the surface to all levels, the fifth level had pumps that constantly pulled water up from the lowest depth of the mine. If the water pumps failed, the fifth level would slowly fill up with water. Then it would take weeks to drain the water so mining could continue. Unless more pumps were brought in to speed the work. With the duke needing every ounce of gold the mine could produce, he would surely bring in more pumps. "Good morning," Grimla said to a group of miners who were carefully chipping away at tough rock that covered a seam of gold. He could see a thin line of gold gleaming in the dim light of the magical lamps. Grimla brought his own lantern up close to the seam, and stared longingly at the gold. Pure, raw gold that had never been touched. It was so tempting. But no, he had work to do that morning.

Walking further into the tunnel, Grimla found his boots squishing on mud. Water dripped continually from the ceiling, and ran down the walls in rivulets. Trenches had been dug into the floor to channel the water, and it was collected in a deep pit, from there it was pulled up to the surface by powerful pumps. Grimla had seen the pumps on his first day at the mine; a team of oxen walked continuously in a circle to power the water pump, day and night, keeping the mine from slowly flooding.

Slowly was not good enough.

The engineer who Grimla had replaced had expressed great concerns about the fifth level of the mine. Perhaps the engineer's fears about the lowest level of the mine had been one reason why he had eagerly taken the gold coins to go away. There was one particular area of the fifth level where the former engineer had banned crews from digging, even though a moderately-sized seam of gold led in that direction. The engineer had not only banned further excavation in that direction, he also had crews cover the rock in a thick plaster to contain the water seepage. In that direction also lay water under high pressure, water that had seeped down from the top of the mountain that towered above their heads. There were natural fractures in the rock; fractures that would inexorably grow wider over time, with the weight of an entire mountain pressing down on them. The cracks had been there for millennia, and they grew very slowly. Grimla could speed the process along.

First, he scraped with a sharp chisel to quietly make cracks in the tough plaster. Then, out of sight around a corner, he crouched down and filled a leather water sack from the flowing trench, then dumped it at the base of the plaster-covered rock at the end of the tunnel. After repeating the process four times, there was now a large puddle of water at the base of the plaster.

Walking back to the group of miners he had spoken to earlier, he asked them to come with him. Pointing to the alarming amount of water and the cracks in the plaster, he asked "Is this amount of seepage normal here?"

The miners, eyes wide, told him no, there wasn't supposed to be any water there. And there had not been any cracks in the plaster the previous day! One of the miners put a finger into a crack in the plaster, when he pulled back, a section of the plaster came away, and a trickle of water became a steady stream. Then another piece of plaster popped loose.

Grimla did not have to fake his reaction; he felt genuine fear. Perhaps he should not have been tampering with things he knew little about, so deep underground. "I think it would be best," he said while backing away from the stream of water, "if we went back to the surface, so I can bring down equipment to deal with this development."

The miners needed no additional urging to run toward the basket; they shouted a warning to others, and soon the basket was full. It took three trips for the basket to remove all the miners from the fifth level, and Grimla was the last aboard the last basket, making sure none of the precious magical lanterns had been left behind. He had been busy while the miners anxiously waited for baskets to be lowered down to them, and miners gratefully slapped him on the back for remaining behind to monitor the widening cracks. That was not what Grimla had been doing, but he accepted their thanks, and he assured them that when he was able to bring down the proper equipment, the fifth level would be open for work again. Miners were paid only for the gold they extracted; a mine that was closed even temporarily lost money for the hard-working miners. And for the duke.

As the basket climbed to the fourth level, Grimla jumped off, and found a shift supervisor directing a work crew. "We should evacuate this level," Grimla advised, "until I can get the flooding below contained."

The shift supervisor looked scornfully at the new mining engineer. Pulling himself up to his full height so his head almost scraped the ceiling, he towered over the dwarf. "Unless you can show me that there is a problem on this level also, we will continue working."

Grimla stood on his toes and glared at the man. "You are questioning the judgement of your engineer?"

The workers stopped hammering and looked anxiously at the shift supervisor. The man was responsible only for extracting the maximum amount of gold from the mine during his assigned shift; he cared nothing about safety. The engineer was responsible for assuring the entire mine didn't collapse down on their heads.

"You have been here less than a week, and you're already shutting down the mine?" The shift supervisor scoffed. "The duke had best find another-"

The floor shook, and dust and pebbles rained down from the ceiling. "The mountain is shifting!" Grimla shouted, grateful for the metal helmet he wore. Pebbles and flakes of rock pinged off the metal. The shift supervisor, without further protest, was the first to spin on his heels and run for the basket. Grimla appealed for calm, and for the men to take the magical lanterns with them. By himself, he hugged one side of the tunnel as men ran past, going further into the mine. He asked men running past whether everyone had gotten the word to evacuate, and told them that he personally would assure than no one was left behind.

When he was on his own, he checked the item that Lord Salva had given him in Linden; it was still exactly where he had hidden it. As he checked the condition of the item and put it back into hiding, he suddenly was unsure of himself, and a thought sent a chill up his spine. Perhaps the court wizard of Tarador had thought it would be a bonus to get rid of Grimla Ironstone, to remove any link between the incident at Duke Bargann's gold mine and the crown princess. With his hands shaking, Grimla hurried toward the basket, and force himself to remain outwardly calm while waiting for an empty basket to be lowered. There were only a half dozen miners with him, and Grimla was wracked with guilt that he had put the lives of these people at risk. His plan had seemed much more secure when he was on the surface; now he felt the massive weight of the mountain looming over his head.

The floor shook slightly; shocks as the cracks on the fifth level opened wider. Grimla feared the shaking was caused by something more than the small cracks he had created; that he might have unintentionally caused faults deep within the mountain to slip against each other. He thought to himself that this is where some actual knowledge of mining engineering would have been useful! Without any insight into what might be happening within the rock around him, Grimla could only stand uncomfortably, trying to keep the men calm, until the basket creaked to a stop at the fourth level. Then, as the basket ascended with an agonizing lack of urgency, Grimla attempted to mentally estimate how long it had been since he hid on the fourth level the device given to him by Lord Salva. The device he had used on the fifth level had done its work within a quarter hour after he twisted the top of the bottle as the wizard had instructed. Lord Salva had told him to expect the larger device on the fourth level to remain dormant for one full hour. Although, the wizard had cautioned, the larger the device, the less accurate its timing could be. And the device on the fourth level was indeed large; big enough that Grimla had trouble concealing it.

No matter now. The basket reached the surface and Grimla stepped off with a sigh of relief, looking at the morning sun now peeking over the ridge of the mountain above him. To his surprise, waiting for him was the mine supervisor, who had a cart full of equipment with him. "How bad is it?" The supervisor asked, waving his people to begin loading the equipment into the basket.

To his horror, Grimla realized the supervisor had the equipment that would be needed to pump out water, seal cracks and shore up ceilings on the fifth level! And he expected Grimla to go straight back down and get working on fixing the problem. Grimla stared at the equipment, having no idea what most of it was used for. "We should wait," he heard himself saying in a shaky voice.

"Wait? What for?" The supervisor demanded of his new engineer. "The longer we wait, the more water we'll have to deal with."

Grimla tried to think of an excuse. He should have thought of this before, made it part of his plan. And he could not risk other people's lives; if anyone had go back into the mine now, it had to be him. "The mountain is shifting," Grimla said as a way of stalling. "If we go now, we will only-"

He was thrown off his feet as the mountain rumbled again beneath his feet. As he regained his footing, a dense cloud of smoke and dust came billowing out of the mine shaft, covering everyone and everything in choking soot. Grimla ran away with everyone else, stopping to help those who had been overcome by the thick dust in air. Whatever the nature of the magical devices he received from Lord Salva, they had tremendous explosive power for their size. Looking back, he could barely make out that not only had the explosion sent a fountain of dust and ash up the mine shaft, the lip of the shaft had sagged and partially collapsed in.

It was not until the next morning that the mine supervisor was able to send a man down in a small basket; a man who had been offered a large sum of money to report on conditions within the mine. Despite the substantial amount offered, there were only three people willing to descend into the depths, and they drew straws to decide which of them would go first. The supervisor was fervently hoping that whatever accident had befallen the mine only affected the fifth level. That would be bad enough, as the gold seams on the levels above had been almost exhausted. But if the fourth level was intact, it could be used as a staging area for pumping out and restoring access to the fifth level. And the mine could produce at least some gold as repairs were made.

The supervisor's hopes were dashed when the man in the basket came back up after descending only slightly below the third level. The rope had been jerked twice to stop the basket, then only a few minutes later, three pulls on the rope indicated the man wished to come back up. His report was not good; the vertical access shaft to the surface had partly collapsed in above the third level, requiring the man to wriggle the small basket around obstructions. The worst news was that, just below the third level, the mine shaft was flooded and the water was still rising.

"This is a disaster," the supervisor groaned. He turned to his expert, the dwarf mining engineer. "What should we do first?"

Grimla took off his hat and rubbed the back of his neck, as if he were actually pondering how best to bring the mine back to operation. What he was really doing was wondering what his favorite tavern in the town would be serving for lunch. Roast chicken would be nice; he was quite hungry. "The first thing you should do is hire a different engineer. I intend to seek a job in another mine."

"What?!" The supervisor exploded angrily.

Grimla held up his hands. "I know how to extract metals from rock, that's my training. A big mess like this," he pointed to the mine shaft, "you need experts. A team of them. If the mine will soon be flooded to the third level, it could take a year or more, before you can dig an ounce of gold from under this mountain."

CHAPTER NINE

Koren lifted his bag onto a shoulder, and stepped down off the carriage. This was as far north as he could go along the river; from here he needed to turn west, and over land. From Istandol, he had taken passage on a boat that was going up the river; near its mouth, the river was wide enough that a boat could use the prevailing westerly winds to sail north, and then the river opened into a vast inland sea. It took the boat most of a week, beating back and forth against contrary winds, to reach the other side. That was as far as that boat could go, for there were waterfalls and rapids on the river north of the freshwater sea. A carriage took him past the rapids, then he boarded another boat to cross a large lake that was almost a sea by itself. From one side of that lake, he couldn't see the other shore, and it would take the boat three days get to across. He stowed his single small bag of gear in a cubbyhole and stood by the railing, relaxing and watching the boat's crew go about the business of getting the single-masted boat ready to depart. He knew enough about sailing to study the way the mast and sails were rigged. Everything on the boat looked old and tired; the sails were frequently patched, and ropes had been spliced again and again. Still, to his inexperienced eye, the boat was well cared for by the crew, and he was confident it could handle any storm they might encounter out on the lake. He thought. He'd never before seen a lake so big that the other side was over the horizon. Shouldn't a body of water that large be called a 'sea', rather than a mere 'lake', he asked himself? The question reminded Koren of how little he knew about the world, a world he had seen more of in the past two years than in all his previous life. A life that had been confined to Crebbs Ford, and a few miles around that tiny village.

Koren resisted the temptation to tie knots in extra pieces of rope that were laying around; knots that only a sailor would use. Instead, he relaxed, leaning over the rail as a landsman would do. As he himself did, when he first came aboard the *Lady Hildegard*, before the real sailors trained him properly. He dangled over the railing, casually watching fish swimming around the mussel-encrusted pilings of the pier, and people on the dock. His attention was drawn to a coach rapidly making its way along the dock, with the driver cursing people to get out of the way. Where was the coach going, Koren asked himself? The dock ended shortly after the ship he was on; past his ship, the only thing on the dock was a beat-up fishing boat that was having a new mast fitted. That, and stacked barrels that were waiting to be packed with dried and salted fish. Koren watched the coach rocking and lurching its way along the dock with a mixture of curiosity and amusement; part of him was hoping the foolish coach driver did not realize the dock soon ended, and the coach would go splashing into the water. Although, he would feel bad for the horses, and he would feel obligated to jump into the chilly water with a knife to cut the horses loose, so his amusement faded and he was frowning when the coach braked to a stop opposite the ship he was on. Then he became briefly amused as a well-dressed but queasy looking nobleman stepped unsteadily out of the coach, swaying on the dock like he was going to be sick. "Damn fool driver!" The man exclaimed. "Ahoy the ship!" He waved toward Koren. "Hold! Hold the ship! I am coming aboard!" Then, to Koren's consternation, the man pointed toward Koren. "Boy! You there, boy! Come here, I need help with my luggage."

Koren looked to both sides, then behind him. Was the man speaking to him?

"You! Idiot boy, come here!" The man demanded.

Koren realized that the man thought he was part of the ship's crew. And Koren had gotten his fill of serving noblemen while he was in the royal castle. If he helped the nobleman with his luggage, the man would of course not offer to pay him; royalty rarely did. And the man would expect Koren to be at his beck and call throughout the three-day voyage. Pointing to himself, Koren replied "I'm not part of the crew. I'm a passenger," and he held up his pouch of coins and rattled it.

However many coins he had in the small leather pouch, and the amount was not insubstantial, it did not compare to the enjoyment he got from seeing the expression on the man's face. Seeing that was beyond any price. As the man stood fuming, red-faced, Koren casually strolled along the ship's railing, away from the gangway.

His amusement was not to last, for as two sailors from the ship hustled down the gangway to assist the man with the luggage that was piled high atop the coach, two other men came around from the far side of the coach. On their jackets, they wore the castle-and-sword symbol of the Royal Army of Tarador.

Koren was trapped. He could not now get off the ship, having already paid for passage and stowed his meager possessions. It would look terribly suspicious, and attract unwanted attention, for him to get off the ship now. Instead, as he watched the two Royal Army soldiers help the sailors get the heavy luggage down off the coach, he retreated toward the stern of the ship, out of the way and hopefully out of mind.

Koren was able to keep away from the nobleman, who he learned was Baron Wicksfeld of Rellanon, for the first two days. Rather than taking his meals with the other dozen passengers, Koren had made friends with the ship's crew, having told them that he was a sailor himself. He enjoyed eating meals with the common sailors, swapping stories of voyages, although Koren did not mention the encounter with pirates. And because he quickly learned that sailors on the lake assumed that salt-water sailors looked down on them, Koren had expressed admiration for the excellent condition of their little ship, and how finely it sailed across lake waters that he found to be surprisingly rough. The crew found Koren to be an eager listener to the stories they had all told a hundred times, and they regaled him with tales of terrible storms on the lake, of ships being out on the lake too late in the season and becoming trapped in ice, and of strange monsters that supposedly lived under the cold, deep and dark waters of the lake. Listening to the sailors, and paying attention as they showed him the finer points of handling their little ship on the vast lake, was a pleasant way to pass the time during the otherwise dull voyage.

Then, the second afternoon, a violent thunderstorm swept across the lake toward them, and Koren was obliged to go below with the other passengers. In the cramped wardroom, he was unable to avoid meeting the two Royal Army soldiers. One of them handed Koren a hunk of rough bread with sausage and cheese.

"Oh, no, thank you." Koren protested, but the man insisted.

"Go ahead, take it. We owe you," he said with a grin at the other soldier.

"Um, thank you," Koren mumbled.

The soldier poured himself a mug of wine, and waved the bottle toward Koren, but Koren shook his head. The man laughed. "We've been stuck babysitting Baron Wicksfeld for the past four months, and we're heartily sick of it. He was on a diplomatic mission to Krakendale," one of the minor kingdoms that lay between Tarador and the rugged mountains that led toward the Indus Empire. "You, young man, took His Lordship down a notch, and I'd give a week's pay to see that again!"

"Same here!" The other soldier laughed. "His Lordship has been confined to his cabin, sick as a dog and mewling like a baby since we left the dock. And I think half of what has made him sick, was a cheeky young man who refused His Lordship's most urgent request."

The first soldier offered a hand to shake. "John Devero," he said.

Koren shook the man's hand, and also the other soldier, named Steve Nygard. Koren had known a family named Nygard in tiny Crebbs Ford, and he almost blurted out the fact, before reminding himself that he was no longer Koren Bladewell of Crebbs Ford. "Kedrun Dartenon," he lied, using the name of a soldier who had died during the battle of Longshire. A soldier who had died to protect Koren.

"Where are you from, Kedrun?" Devero asked.

This was a question Koren had feared, and a question he had prepared for. He could not say he was from Winterthur province, for he might encounter someone also from that area of Tarador. With his northern accent, he could not claim to be from any southern province, so he had decided to say he was from LeVanne. He had walked through LeVanne, although in his time there, he had tried his best to avoid meeting or being seen by people. "Durstwell, in LeVanne," Koren said, and hoped that would be the end of it. Durstwell was a town large enough that, if he met someone who also claimed to be from there, Koren could reasonably claim not to be familiar with that family. Durstwell was also where major east-west and north-south roads crossed, so if he was pressed by a skeptical inquisitor, he could claim that his family were roving merchants, who only used Durstwell as a home base.

"Durstwell!" Nygard said excitedly. "I have a cousin from near there. Tell me," he looked at his companion and reached for the wine bottle.

Koren tensed. If either of the soldiers caught him in a lie, he could be in great trouble. He was still dressed in sailor fashion, his hair was longer, his skin tanned by long days at sea under the bright tropical sun of the South Isles, and he tried to act older than his few years. So he hoped that his appearance, and the passage of time, would not have the Royal Army wondering if the young man in front of them could be the Koren Bladewell they had been ordered to find. There was no reason for the two Royal Army soldiers to even imagine that the young sailor they were talking with might be the dangerous, traitorous jinx who almost killed the crown princess.

He needed a lie, a good one, and he had chosen the best lie he had been able to think of. Still, he tensed, waiting for Nygard's question.

The soldier did not seem to be in any hurry, for he took his time pouring wine, bracing himself against the table, lest he spill wine due to the ship's rocking in the storm. "Tell me, what have you heard about this hell wolf?"

Koren inwardly sighed with great relief. Although he had never been to Durstwell, never been near the place, had never even met anyone from that town, he did know much about the area and its history. For that, he could thank the royal library in Linden, and the pleasant afternoons he had spent quietly reading with the crown princess. Ariana Trehayme had probably thought indulging his love of books was a good way to improve a peasant boy's poor reading skills, but Koren had only cared that he could read about exotic places he had never been. To Koren Bladewell, who had spent most of his life within twenty miles of his home, even Durstwell was exotic. The reason he knew anything at all about Durstwell was because of a story he had read, an old legend of a horrible monster wolf that terrorized the countryside. The account Koren had read stated that the legend went back over a hundred years, but people in the area still reported seeing the ghostly wolf on the night of a full moon. Koren laughed. "My father told me that he heard that story from his father, and his father from his. Everyone in Durstwell knows someone who claims to have seen the hell wolf, but no one claims to have seen it themselves. Or, at least, no one that anyone believes."

"You never saw it?" Devero asked with a wry smile.

"No. I went out one time with friends, because someone said they saw the hell wolf up by a pond, and there were giant claw marks on a tree, and clumps of black fur there." Koren pulled that directly from the book he had read. In the book, one of the boys almost drowned in the pond; Koren left out that part of the story.

Nygard took a sip of wine. "And? What did you find?"

"We found it exactly as it was described-"

"A giant hell wolf?" Nygard was surprised.

"No," Koren winked. "A bear. Nothing more than a black bear had clawed the tree. But, at night, and after too much beer or spirits, it could have looked like a giant wolf."

"Ha!" Devero slapped his companion on the back. "Was it a *bear*, or was it a *beer*?"

Nygard laughed also.

"What is Krakendale like?" Koren hastened to change the subject. The three of them discussed their travels while the storm outside blew itself out. The two soldiers, who had never been to sea, wanted to know everything Koren could tell them about the South Isles, and he regaled them with tales of endless sunshine, clear water and palm trees swaying in warm tropical breezes. By the time the storm had moved on and they were allowed back on deck, the Royal Army soldiers were no longer curious about where 'Kedrun Dartenon' came from.

Koren once again took his dinner with the ship's crew, and the soldiers were grumblingly forced to dine with His Lordship once again, so he did not see the two men until the middle of the next morning as the ship approached the shore. They stood by the railing, eating scraps of biscuit left over from breakfast, and talking about future plans. To the dismay of Devero and Nygard, Baron Wicksfeld had a private coach waiting to take him and his escorts further up the river. North of the lake, the river was too narrow and fast-flowing for boats to go north; all passengers and cargo headed north needed to use roads rather than water. Koren would not be traveling by private coach. He would be purchasing passage on one of the slow carriages that plied the road beside the river, and hoping his backside would not get too sore from sitting in a lurching carriage on a bumpy road, day after day.

He said goodbye to the pair of friendly soldiers, and even helped them with His Lordship's heavy luggage, then they were gone, and Koren hefted his one bag of meager possessions. He needed to bargain with the line of carriage drivers waiting by the dock; not because he lacked money, but because it would seem odd if he did not.

Ariana's chief advisor requested an immediate audience with the crown princess, who was busily engaged in sorting her closets. She had too many dresses, far too many, and far too many that she did not like and would never wear. That morning, while rejecting all three of the outfits her maids had brought for her to choose from, she decided that she would take all the clothes she never intended to wear, and donate them to charity. It was, she declared, the least she could do for the war effort. And, she told herself with a smile, there would be that much more room in her closets for new clothes in the future. Someday. Someday when the royal treasury was not stretched so thin; someday when the war was over.

Gustov Kallron was ushered into the private rooms of the crown princess, and instructed to wait at the table by the window that served as Ariana's study. He had barely sat down when a door opened, and the princess walked in, wearing a very plain dress and with her hair still slightly damp. She waved for her maids to depart and shut the door behind them. "You have new information, Chief Advisor?" Her eyes twinkled.

"I have questions, Your Highness. The *information*, I suspect, is yours."

"Oh?" She asked as innocently as she could manage.

"Yes," Kallron continued. "It seems that Duke Bargann has suffered a calamity; his main gold mine has collapsed and flooded. The damage is severe enough that it may take a year to dig down far enough to reach the gold seams."

"That is extremely unfortunate," Ariana said with an exaggerated frown. "For Duke Bargann."

"It is extremely unfortunate. Bargann is heavily in debt; the loss of the mine could cause him to default on his debts. Including his substantial debts to the Falcos. That was stupid of Bargann; the Falcos are also overextended, and cannot provide any additional loans to Bargann at this time. If Bargann cannot pay, the Falcos could take action, of some form or another." Including, Kallron suspected, assassinating the current Duke of Farlane, and replacing him with someone more suitable to the Falcos.

"Oh my!" Ariana popped a sweetcake into her mouth. "That is terrible, just terrible. Whatever will poor Bargann do?" She shook her head with a smile.

"He will seek new allies, Your Highness. Allies with deep pockets, who can bail him out of his predicament."

"Interesting. Well, this shows the foolishness of getting one's self too deeply in debt, I suppose."

"Highness," Kallron asked with an admiring smile, "you would not have had anything to do with the unfortunate collapse of that mine, would you?"

"Me?" Ariana laughed. "Why, I have been here in Linden the whole time, and before that, as everyone knows I was at the summer palace. I would not know the first thing about how to make a mine collapse. Although, I was very gratified to hear that no one was injured." That had been her greatest fear; not that her plot would fail, but that innocent, hard-working miners would suffer. They had already been forced to seek work elsewhere, and she felt bad about that.

"Mmm hmmm," Kallron did not sound entirely convinced of her innocence. "Speaking hypothetically, if you were to have been involved, what would have given you the idea to block Bargann's access to his gold mine?"

Ariana poured herself a cup of tea, and Kallron indicated he did not want any for himself. "Speaking hypothetically, a wise man once told me," the princess said while staring her chief advisor in the eye, "that most questions of power in this world are about money. And this wise man told me that I should pay attention to the finances of the dukes and duchesses, if I wished to understand them. That is how I knew that Duke Bargann is deeply in debt, and he relies on gold from that mine to keep himself afloat." Her smile turned to a frown. "Is that river truly so important to Bargann?"

What she referred to was the source of the latest dispute between the Barganns and the Falcos. Twenty one years ago, shortly before Rills Bargann inherited the ducal throne of Farlane, the Rhane river had flooded a wide area of the valley that lay between the territories of the Barganns and the Falcos. When the flood receded, the channel through which the river flowed had changed, and a half-mile strip of territory that formerly belonged to the Barganns now lay within the Falco's Burwyck province. Before his death, Rills Bargann's father had attempted to regain the land from the Falcos by negotiation, but had been rebuffed by Regin Falco. Rebuffed rudely, in the eyes of the Barganns; the two provinces had almost come to war, with their ducal armies mobilized along their common border. Ariana's father had been forced to send the Royal Army to intervene, and Rills Bargann still fumed quietly about the insult. That was why he had spent so much money to increase the size of his ducal army, to build defenses, and in an attempt to gain allies in his dispute with the Falcos. Twice, he had brought petitions before the Regency Council for the original border to be restored between Farlane and Burwyck, and twice his requests had been rejected. Rejected in humiliating fashion.

Ironically, much of the money Rills Bargann had borrowed to build up his military strength had come in the form of loans from the Falcos. Regin Falco was not only supremely confident in the strength of his own ducal army, he also understood an important truth: money is power. Burwyck had always been wealthier than Farlane. More of Farlane province was unproductive swampland and craggy mountains. Farlane had no broad rivers inside its borders, so all goods had to move by wagon, increasing costs. The northern border of Farlane was also the northern border of Tarador, and Duke Bargann was forced to keep much of his military strength in the north, to defend against orcs. To the east of Farlane were many small, bickering kingdoms which occasionally became adventurous and raided into Farlane, creating another constant drain on Farlane's military forces. Farlane had a very large and rich gold mine, but only the one, while Burwyck had several mines which produced gold, silver, iron and other valuable metals.

"It's not the river that is important," Kallron explained. "It's a symbol. The Barganns have always felt the Falcos looked down upon them, because Burwyck traditionally has more wealth and power. Rills swore to change that when he took the throne; he was outraged over the insult to his father, when his father was already weak and dying."

"Then why have the Barganns always supported the Falcos in the Council?" It did not happen always, but certainly when Duke Bargann voted against the Falcos, it was a notable event. Kallron had told Ariana that he suspected the Falcos sometimes wanted the Barganns to vote against them, for one scheme or another.

"Because they have to. Farlane has been beholden to Burwyck's generous purse for centuries. And the Barganns in particular have owed their throne to the Falcos from the beginning," Kallron explained.

Ariana knew what her chief advisor meant. One hundred and forty years ago, the Tolstead family had ruled Farlane province, but the last Duchess Tolstead had died without an heir, and her only sibling had fled Tarador to avoid paying creditors. Several distant relatives of Duchess Tolstead had vied for the throne, and the Falcos had supported Ilsa Bargann, first cousin to the duchess. After a short but bloody war within Farlane, Ilsa had become the first of the Bargann family on the ducal throne of Farlane province. And the Barganns had been partly under the control of the Falcos ever since. Ariana sighed. "It is all about money, then."

"Not entirely, Your Highness. Particularly where pride is involved. Rills Bargann knows that strip of land along the river would never be worth the price he would pay to retake it. But every time he looks at a map showing that land belonging to Burwyck, it reminds him that he is not truly his own man. And, worse, he knows that everyone knows that. It wounds his pride."

Pride. And money. Two great motivators of the Regency Council. "Losing that gold mine will hurt Bargann's pride and his purse," Ariana considered. She had been aiming only at the man's purse. She should have included stubborn pride in her plans. Could Bargann's wounded pride cause all of her plans to go awry? "How did *you* learn of the gold mine?"

Kallron was not at all convinced of Ariana's innocence in the collapse of the gold mine. He was, however, convinced enough; if the Regency Council called him in for questioning, he would have nothing to tell them. "The reason I know about it, Your Highness, is because apparently Duke Bargann himself learned about the disaster at his mine late last night. This very morning Bargann sought your mother's assistance; pleaded with her to use the royal treasury as backing so the Duke could cover his debts temporarily. The Regent refused his entreaties, and Bargann is now reported to be quite desperate."

"Hmm," Ariana mumbled over another mouthful of sweetcake. "The *current* Regent refused to assist Bargann. I wonder, Chief Advisor, if the Duke of Farlane province would be interested in seeing a different person holding the Regency."

"I believe," Kallron said with great satisfaction and taking a sweetcake for himself, "that he would indeed. Very much so. The dukes and duchesses of the seven provinces will all soon be here in Linden for the war council. That makes it rather convenient for certain important items to be brought before the Regency Council." He ate the sweetcake quickly, then wiped his fingers on a napkin. "Now, Your Highness, if you will excuse me, I should approach certain representatives of Duke Bargann, and begin discussing- What shall I call it? Possibilities. I will begin discussing possibilities."

"Please do," Ariana responded with a mischievous twinkle in her eyes. "Make a *bargain* with *Bargann*."

"Your Highness?"

"Yes, Chief Advisor?"

"My advice, young lady, is not to do this sort of thing again. Not until you have the Regency, and I can, *advise*, you fully."

"I have no idea what you mean," she said with a wink. "Yes, Uncle Kallron."

"However," Kallron continued with a wink. "I am *very* proud to be your advisor right now. You will be a most formidable queen."

The boats and carriages had been expensive to Koren's purse; with the war in Tarador, prices of pretty much everything had gone up. Fortunately, before he left the *Lady Hildegard*, the crew had voted an extra share of the profit for 'Kedrun'. Whether he'd been granted an extra share out of gratitude for him saving the ship from pirates, or because the crew were happy to get a frightening source of dark magic off their ship, Koren did not know. The reason did not matter, all that mattered was that his pockets were full of coins, and he had plenty of money to pay for his journey north. He had spent what seemed to him too much money for a sword that had seen better days, a serviceable bow and a quiver of arrows that he could work with to bring into acceptable condition.

The carriage he had been riding was going further north, but the road north along the river went into lands broken up into small kingdoms that were constantly squabbling with each other, when they were not banding together to fight off orc incursions. Travel through such lands were slow, with travelers needing to stop and pay tariffs at the border of every tiny 'kingdom'. North of those kingdoms lay the tall, forbidding mountains that were orc territory anyway, and Koren wanted to contact the dwarves. So he changed carriages to one going west. The road went west, first to the border of Tarador, then through Tarador.

There were only two bridges across the river into Tarador for a stretch of almost eighty miles. In days gone by, there were more bridges, but those others had fallen into disrepair, or had been damaged during Spring floods and never rebuilt. Both of the current bridges had Taradoran Royal Army garrisons on their side of the river, and soldiers were checking every wagon, carriage and person who wished to enter Tarador. Koren could not take the risk that he could successfully pass as 'Kedrun Dartenon from Durstwell'. There were several ferries that regularly ran back and forth across the river, but those were also met on the far side by soldiers of Tarador.

What Koren needed was to hire a boat; a boat that would take him across the river at night, and land him at a place where no soldiers would be waiting for him. Standing at the shore, he looked along the riverbank at the town. There were rough-looking wharves and warehouses, and clusters of fishing boats. It all looked run down and shabby; a town that existed for the purposes of people and goods passing through, and a town that did not waste money or effort on appearances. Around those wharves, in a warehouse or a tavern or where racks of fish were salted and dried, he would likely find the sort of man he sought. A man who would look at the coins Koren offered, and not ask any questions.

Regin Falco was enraged; Niles Forne had never seen his liege lord so enraged, and Regin Falco was frequently angry at someone or something. "You knew nothing of this beforehand? What else do I pay you exorbitant sums for?" Duke Falco demanded of his advisor. The duke had arrived in Linden only the day before, to attend what he thought was a Council of War. It was maddening and tedious for him to travel all the way to Linden, especially for a council meeting that could only, according to the law, 'provide guidance to the monarch or Regent on conduct during time of national crisis'. Regin had considered allowing his eldest son Kyre attend in his place, rather than making the long and tiring journey from Burwyck province to Linden. It felt like he had only just returned to his home from the Cornerstone festival, when the summons for a Council of War arrived.

To Regin's enormous shock, the meeting of the War Council that morning had barely opened when, of all people, Duke Bargann had called for a vote of no confidence in Carlana Trehayme as Regent. Before Regin could recover his shock, the dukes and duchesses of Rellanon, LeVanne, Anschulz and Winterthur provinces had quickly seconded the motion. Regin had been forced to call for a brief recess to confer with Duchess Rochambeau of Demarche, and to give his head time to stop spinning.

Regin himself had planned to call for a Council of War soon, so he could call for a vote of no confidence in the Lady Carlana, and so he could propose his own candidate to be Regent. But Regin had planned to wait until Carlana's lack of leadership led to a major military defeat; when a no confidence vote would be certain to pass. When Duke Bargann struck first, Regin had been caught completely unprepared. Following a quick discussion with Duchess Rochambeau, the two of them had voted no confidence in Carlana, making it unanimous. It had been a thoroughly obvious decision; the Falcos could not vote in favor of Carlana, and then propose a candidate to replace her.

After the vote had been declared official, a thoroughly shaken Lady Carlana had left the council chambers. Until a new Regent was chosen, she would retain the title of Regent, but she no longer had any effective power.

Just when Regin, quickly recovering from the shock, had been about to propose his candidate for the regency, Duchess Portiss of Anschulz spoke up. And Regin received perhaps the greatest shock since he had become Duke of Burwyck. Portiss proposed the crown princess Ariana Trehayme to become Regent! And four other provinces had voted in favor, including Duke Bargann of Farlane. Clearly, the entire affair had been arranged in advance. Regin had forestalled Ariana assuming her own regency by calling for a formal declaration of legality; that bought him perhaps a day as the royal magistrates investigated the intricacies of the law.

That the leaders of Rellanon and LeVanne had voted together was no surprise at all; those two families had strong ties together, and strong ties to the Trehaymes. Such familial ties did not apparently extend to Carlana, who had married into the royal family of Tarador. That Anschulz and Winterthur had voted with Rellanon and LeVanne was also no great shock, although Regin wondered what deals had been cut behind the scenes to bring in those two votes.

But Farlane! For Duke Bargann of Farlane to vote with the other four, and against the Falcos, was unprecedented. And shocking; it had stunned Duke Falco. Whatever machinations had happened before the War Council opened, it had happened completely without Regin Falco's notice, and that shook him to his core. What else had gone on behind his back?

And what else had his senior advisor in Linden missed completely?

Niles Forne struggled to outwardly remain calm in the face of his duke's fury, a fury directed at him. Forne knew that not only his position, income and family status was at stake; his very life was in great danger. If Duke Falco decided to fire Niles Forne, the duke would surely understand that Forne knew a great many secrets of the Falco family, and having such a man forced to seek employment elsewhere would be extremely dangerous. The Falcos could offer Niles Forne a pension, to live somewhere remote, existing on half pay and with no status or connections. But Regin Falco would live every day in fear that his former trusted advisor would betray his oath of secrecy. No, it would be better for Duke Falco to have Niles Forne meet an unfortunate accident. Perhaps Forne would be attacked and killed by bandits on a lonely road. It was, after all, a dangerous world. Niles Forne had to admit he himself had advised his duke to take such action against people who could no longer be trusted; Forne had even arranged for such 'accidents' to occur.

"No, Sire, I did not know anything about this beforehand. It is to my great shame. I have failed you," he admitted. Forne had learned over his years of service to the Falcos that taking complete responsibility for setbacks, and making no attempt at excuses, was the only way to have even a chance of survival. "It was wise for you to call for a formal declaration of legality, Sire," Forne said, even though that had been Forne's hasty and desperate suggestion at the time. "Although I am almost certain that the result will be the magistrates declaring that, strange as it may seem, Ariana is eligible to become her own Regent. I must say, that is an absolutely brilliant use of gaps in the law. Gustov Kallron has outmaneuvered me, badly."

"Kallron," Regin said the word as if spitting something distasteful. As chancellor of the realm, Gustov Kallron had been a thorn in Regin's side; blocking almost every move the Falcos made. It had gotten to the point, some years ago, that Regin considered attempting to assassinate Kallron, to remove an obstacle in the most brutal fashion. At the time, Niles Forne, Regin's wife and others had persuaded him not to make such a rash move. He now regretted that he did not act earlier. "I do hate that man. My hope was, when Carlana dismissed him as chancellor, that he would be out of the game. It appears I was mistaken."

"We were all greatly mistaken," Forne agreed, even though he had warned his duke not to ignore Kallron. "I now believe that Kallron orchestrated his dismissal as chancellor, in order to serve the princess directly," which is exactly what Forne had told Regin Falco at the time, and Falco had ignored him. "Kallron saw the Lady Carlana was a sinking ship, and he sought to attach himself to the future power. Now he has manipulated the situation so that he will become chancellor once again. He is a brilliant and subtle man." That was high praise for Niles Forne, who rarely thought of anyone as his equal in the game of power. "Kallron has manipulated the entire situation to suit himself."

"You think *Kallron* persuaded Bargann to vote with the princess?" Falco asked, surprised. The Barganns hated the Trehaymes almost as much as the Falcos did, and Kallron had served the Trehaymes all his life.

"Sire, I now think it is no coincidence that, just as the crown princess needed to find a fifth vote to assume the regency, Duke Bargann's gold mine collapsed and flooded," Forne hinted darkly.

"Kallron is that clever?" Regin asked with admiration. If the chief advisor to the crown princess had indeed caused the disaster at the gold mine in Farlane province, then it had been a master stroke. With one blow, he had crippled Duke Bargann, and also hurt the Falcos financially. Without a steady income from that gold mine, Bargann was unable to keep up repayments on loans extended by the Falcos, and that in turn had caused a severe crisis in the Falco family finances. His own financial position was now so weakened, that Regin was unable to respond to Council politics the way he usually did. It was as if he were fighting with one hand tied behind his back. He did not like that at all.

"He is most certainly that clever," Forne said gravely. What he did not do was remind his duke that Forne had, many times, warned against getting deeply financially entangled with the Bargann family. Warned against extending more and more credit to a ducal family that was less and less a reliable ally. An ally which grew weaker as they borrowed more money for unwise purposes; purposes that in some cases worked directly against the interests of the Falcos. Niles Forne's strong sense of self-preservation made him not say any of that. "Whether Kallron was behind the disaster at the mine, I do not know for certain. It could be merely that the disaster happened, and Kallron saw an opportunity to act now."

"Damn it," Regin could not help admiring his enemy's skilled maneuver. "But the Council of War was called before the mine collapsed," he pointed out.

"Yes," Forne nodded. "That is another reason why I suspect the disaster was no accident."

"How could a mine be made to collapse and flood like that?" Duke Falco asked, alarmed. The mine supervisor was a trusted cousin to Duke Bargann.

"There is, my lord, only one possibility, I fear," Forne paused for effect. "Kallron had help from wizardry. A powerful wizard."

"A wizard?" Now Regin was truly fearful. "Lord Salva would surely not-"

"He surely *would*, Sire," Forne said gently. "The court wizard has made no secret of his disdain for the Lady Carlana as Regent. He has warned, in Council meetings, that her conduct of the war will lead us only to defeat and disaster. What keeps wizards out of the affairs of politics is law, and tradition. Wizards are a law unto themselves, and traditions may be broken, if the need is great. If Lord Salva foresaw Tarador headed toward ruin, I believe he would act. I believe he would feel *compelled* to act, regardless of the law. And the Council cannot force a wizard to answer questions. That also is the law."

"*Very* clever," Regin was beyond surprise, nearly numb with shock. He could see all his plans crumbling before him. He looked at his own advisor in disgust. "That is it, then? Ariana has the five votes she needs to become Regent? You have been completely outplayed?"

Forne noted that his duke said '*you* have been outplayed', indicating that Regin Falco would take none of the blame himself. "Outplayed, yes, Sire. Completely? No. Kallron thinks he has secured five votes in favor of Ariana, but he has not," he said with a tight smile.

"Eh? I counted five. Unless you have some plan to split one away, in our favor."

"Whatever deals Kallron made in secret to secure five votes, I am sure it is far too late for us to intervene now," Forne announced. Particularly since everyone knew of the recent financial setbacks suffered by the Falco family, and knew Regin Falco had severely limited options for inducing another province to vote with him. "No, Sire, it is too late for the political strategies of which you are a master," he continued without pausing for the flattery to sink in. "Kallron has used the law in his favor; we will now use the law to strike back. Sire, Duke Yarron is Ariana's uncle. His wife is sister to the late king. The Yarrons are related to Ariana by blood. Therefore, according to the law, he must abstain from voting on her candidacy."

For the first time that morning, Regin Falco saw a glimmer of hope. He took a deep breath and stared his advisor straight in the eye. "There is no question of this? You are certain?"

"Yes, my lord. Either Gustov Kallron does not know the law as well as I do, or he hopes that my own knowledge is deficient. I suspect the latter; Kallron has underestimated us in the past." Forne said 'my own knowledge' to remind his duke that Regin Falco relied on Niles Forne to know the subtleties of the law. And he said 'underestimated *us*' to allow his duke to take credit, for the many times Niles Forne had given the Falco family an advantage in the great game of power between the royal families of Tarador.

"Ariana is effectively blocked from the regency, then?" Duke Falco asked anxiously. Until he was certain, he did not dare to allow himself to hope.

"Most assuredly, Sire. In order to secure a fifth vote, she will need to come to you, or to Duchess Rochambeau."

"Ha!" Regin snorted. "Rochambeau would never vote in favor of that brat," he referred to the crown princess, "taking power one minute before her sixteenth birthday. Very well, Forne," he looked his advisor in the eye as an unsubtle way of letting Niles Forne know that his life still hung in the balance. "I will put forward Leese Trehayme as candidate for the regency."

"Yes, Sire, certainly. That was clever of you to bring the man to Burwyck, and now to Linden. However, there is another possibility that I believe you should consider."

"Oh?" Regin raised an eyebrow, only half listening. His mind was busy scheming how to get the worthless Leese Trehayme installed as Regent, and how to control the unpredictable man once he took power.

"Kallron has been quite bold in his plans. I wonder, Your Grace, if we should be equally bold in this unique opportunity." Niles Forne explained his plan.

And Regin Falco found himself listening with rapt attention.

CHAPTER TEN

"Can he *DO* that?" Ariana shouted as she fairly stormed into Kallron's office. "Shhhh," the man cautioned, and gestured for the princess to close the door behind her.

Ariana waved her guard and servant to wait outside, and flung the door closed. That was rude, she thought, ashamed. She would apologize to them later. "Uncle Kallron, can he do that?"

"I assume you mean, can Regin Falco block Duke Yarron from voting on your behalf?" He nodded sadly. "Yes, yes he can. Falco is correct about the law; I was hoping that he would not know about that rather particular, obscure statute. I certainly was not going to mention it. The Falcos must have a very skilled legal expert; I suspect Niles Forne." When he was chancellor of the realm, Kallron had often had to contend with the crafty advisor to the Falcos. Forne's presence in Linden was supposedly to guide the development of the Falco heir, but he also acted as the duke's personal agent and spy in the castle. "Damn that man," Kallron said bitterly, "he has caused us no end of trouble in the past."

Ariana flopped into a chair, and reminded herself not to sulk. She could indulge in a lengthy fit of sulking later, if she had time. Being the crown princess not only meant she was not supposed to act like a spoiled little girl, it also meant she rarely had time to herself. "What can we do, then?"

"Your Highness, at the moment, I truly do not know. Because Yarron is a blood relative to you, he can't simply renounce familial ties. He could not even divorce your aunt and renounce blood ties at this point; those ties are a matter of record. This puts Yarron in an impossible position. As much as he may care for you, Yarron will not give up his ancestral seat; no duke or duchess would."

Ariana understood, she could not have brought herself to ask Duke Yarron to resign for her anyway. "Then there are only six potential votes on the Regency Council, and we have four. Is that not enough?"

"No," Kallron said sourly. "The law requires five votes, regardless of the total number of votes available. Before you ask, the law can be changed only with five votes, and the approval of a sovereign."

"Argh!" Ariana ground her teeth in great frustration. "This is impossible! Chief Advisor, advise me. What can we do?"

Kallron was at a loss for advice. "Make a deal with Duchess Rochambeau for the fifth vote, or, somehow, deal with the Falcos."

"I will never agree to any arrangement with the Falcos," Ariana spat the distasteful words out.

"Your Highness, we are in a very difficult and dangerous position," Kallron warned. "The *nation* is in a difficult and dangerous position. The Council has declared no faith in your mother; she still officially has the title of Regent, but no real power. Tarador is leaderless, in a time of war. The enemy will not fail to take advantage of our weakness. Whatever you do, whatever *we* do, it must be done quickly. I am afraid, Highness, that you must begin to consider alternative candidates for the regency."

"Who?" She gasped.

"I do not know as yet, I will think on it. We are faced with the same problem that put your mother in the regency; the seven provinces cannot agree on a candidate. Your mother has the regency only because the Council could not agree on any other candidate, and they thought she could be controlled. Of the four votes you now have, you can count on Bargann only if you take the regency; your deal with Bargann will not hold with someone else as Regent. And I do not think that Duke Magnico, or even Duke Yarron, can be assured of voting for someone else you put forward as a candidate. Support for you as Regent is very much personal to yourself; it would not necessarily transfer to another person you nominate."

"Oh, why is this *so* complicated? I am only trying to do the right thing for Tarador! Why must I fight my own people, in order to defeat our common enemy?"

"It is complicated, young lady, because-"

"Uncle Kallron!" She huffed. "I know why it is complicated. I was not looking for an explanation." Sometimes, she felt like screaming. Perhaps she should visit the old caverns deep under the palace, where food and water were stored in case the castle suffered a siege. Down there, in private, she could scream away her frustrations. Perhaps later, if she had time.

"Would it help if I got you a sweetcake, patted your head and told you that everything will be all right?" He asked with a gentle smile.

"Uncle, that worked when I was six," she recalled the dark years shortly after her father died. The harried royal chancellor would find time to read stories to the young princess, to rub her back until she fell asleep, and to simply listen when she needed to cry. "Is there anything you can think of, that would get Duchess Rochambeau's vote?"

"Nothing that comes to mind at the moment, no." In some ways, the Rochambeaus hated the Trehaymes even more than the Falcos did. The enmity between the two families went back even further than the intense rivalry between the Falcos and the Trehaymes. "I shall think on that, Your Highness, as well as drawing up a list of candidates for the regency. Tarador must have a leader, soon. Highness, I must caution you, we are not the only people considering candidates for the regency. I am sure Regin Falco has a list of his own candidates."

"His candidates were rejected last time," Ariana remarked haughtily. "Which is why my mother became Regent."

"Yes, but this time, I fear that Falco has been more clever. Instead of candidates who are more or less openly beholden to the Falcos, he may be playing a more subtle hand. There have been rumors, credible rumors, that your father's brother Leese has been seen in Burwyck, as a guest of the Falcos." Kallron knew the rumors to be true, for he had spies within the capital city of Burwyck.

"Uncle Leese?" Ariana was incredulous. "He is-" She hesitated, choosing her words carefully. Leese Trehayme was a very close relative, even the crown princess had to be careful about speaking ill of the man.

"He is a drunkard, and worse, yes," Kallron finished her thought. "He is also a Trehayme, and your late father's brother. Many on the Council will think him a good compromise candidate, for the short time until you become queen."

"He would be worse than my mother!" Ariana gasped.

"Possibly," Kallron admitted. "I fear the Council will think of their own interests first, and the immediate need to fill the regency, over what is best for Tarador in the long run. Highness, I did warn you that once we started down this road, once the Council declared no confidence in your mother, that we may lose control of the process."

Regin Falco was enraged again that evening, when he invited Leese Trehayme to dine with him. Having Leese at the Falco table for dinner was an informal way of announcing the man's presence in Linden, and his almost forced alliance with the Falco family. Leese had been kept isolated while in Burwyck, and he had been practically smuggled into the Falco family estate in Linden. Regin was certain that once his invited guests saw Leese sitting at the table with the Falcos, word would soon spread throughout Linden and up to the royal palace.

So Regin was enraged that, despite his express orders to his servants and their best efforts to enforce their lord's commands, the man had somehow found alcohol during the afternoon. The servants reported that Leese had been sober and quietly reading when he took his mid-day meal, then Leese had said he was taking a nap to be fresh for dinner. When he did not rise in time to bathe and dress for dinner, and did not respond to servants frantically pounding on his locked door, guards had broken down the door to find him sleeping on the floor, drunk.

All of Regin's grand plans for dinner were dashed. "Damn that man!" The Duke of Burwyck shouted as he burst into Niles Forne's apartment in the Falco estate. Regin strode across the room to the cabinet where he knew Forne kept his best wine, poured himself a large goblet, then set it down in disgust. Drinking too much is what ruined Leese Trehayme's life, and no Falco was going to be that weak. For a moment, Regin considered smashing the goblet to the floor, but then he considered that it was his wine, and the fine rug on the floor also belonged to him. "Damn! Blast!" He satisfied himself with an angry tirade.

"He is a Trehayme, Sire," Forne said gently, saying what he knew his duke wished to hear. "And he is a true brother to our late king. The king lacked self-control and he was impulsive; that is why he married unwisely, and why he died foolishly in battle. Leese's weakness manifested itself in a passion for drink, and stronger substances."

"That is another reason why the Trehaymes should never hold the throne!" Regin slapped his palm on a table. "Forne, what am I to do? I cannot bring Leese to dinner drunk as he is. And to wait until the Council meeting tomorrow to announce his presence, would not allow time for the other Council members to become accustomed to the idea of him becoming Regent. Damn the man! I need him to be seen at dinner, sober, calm and rational. I need him to be seen as a responsible adult, to dispel the rumors about his, other activities. I need people to leave here tonight and spread the word that Leese Trehayme is ready to lead our nation."

"It shall be so, Your Grace," Niles Forne announced confidently.

"How? Do not jest with me, Forne. There is barely two hours before dinner time! If needs be, Leese could arrive only in time for coffee and dessert, but-"

"He will be ready in time for dinner to commence, Sire. Not much before dinner, perhaps, but he will be ready by the time you are ready to enter the hall, with Leese by your side."

Regin Falco was not pleased, thinking his advisor toyed with him. "You propose magic, Forne?"

"Exactly, sire. Years ago, I acquired several doses of a magical potion that wonderfully restores sobriety and sensibility to a person affected by alcohol. It is embarrassing to admit, I sought it for myself, in case I overindulged and needed to quickly regain my full faculties." Forne rose from the chair and walked over a cabinet, where he removed a heavy, dusty box. "Leese Trehayme will be sober at dinner, Sire. I cannot guarantee the man will be charming or in any way impressive, but he will be sober." He would also, Forne did not add, suffer a terrible headache about four hours after the dinner concluded. For that, and to assure Leese slept well and was refreshed for the Council meeting the next day, Forne had another potion.

There was no magic that could make Leese Trehayme a good choice as leader of Tarador. The man need only be a figurehead, with Regin Falco as the true power. And behind Regin, providing crucial guidance, would be the ever diligent, indispensable Niles Forne.

"Is there any potion in that box that will make Leese a capable leader?" Regin asked with dry humor.

"No, Sire," Forne forced himself to laugh at his Duke's joke. "I am afraid that would take a miracle, not mere magic. No matter, Leese only needs to be considered by the Council to be a better choice than the Lady Carlana, and that is no great feat."

Koren crouched by a large willow tree that leaned out over the river, near where the fisherman had told him to wait. The man and his boat were dirty and stank of fish; the man more so than his boat. But he had asked no questions, only looked greedily at the coins Koren had offered. Certainly, Koren Bladewell would not be the first person that fisherman had smuggled across the river.

As he waited, Koren studied the far shore. Torchlights illuminated a Royal Army patrol, and a boat manned by the Royal Army had passed by close to the far shore, looking for boats trying to land unseen. Koren was not concerned; the river shore was long and the Royal Army could not cover all of it, their patrols were only to discourage the foolish. He did not care where he landed, so if his original destination was near soldiers, he would go further down the river. The fisherman surely wished to avoid trouble with Tarador, and would steer away from being seen. It would be a longer row back up the river for the man, and Koren would offer him a few more copper coins to keep his end of the bargain.

It seemed odd to Koren that he had to sneak into his home country, and it saddened him. He was hunted, as far as he knew the Royal Army still had orders to capture or kill him; and some soldiers might think it easier and less trouble to kill than to capture.

There was a creaking sound, and faint splash. With clouds blocking out the moonlight, Koren's keen eyes had to use the dim light of torches on the far shore. The sounds he heard were a boat being rowed up the river toward him; the creaking and splashing of oars. The boat was hugging the shore, making its way toward where a creek ran down into the river; the spot where the fisherman had instructed Koren to wait. As the boat drew even with the creek, and turned toward the shore, Koren crept out from behind the tree and carefully picked his way through the bushes down to the creek.

Koren did not need Paedris to give him magical fighting skills or wizard senses to protect himself that night; the man behind him smelled as much of fish guts as the fisherman did, and his wheezing breath was loud. Rather than feeling fear, Koren smiled to himself in the dark; he had expected trouble, and now he knew it was nothing he couldn't handle. He stood still and raised his left arm to wave at the incoming boat, while his right hand held a dagger.

He felt rather than heard the man behind him, and when he felt the man lunge forward to stab him in the back, Koren ducked to the side and let the man stumble and fall forward. Then as the man sprawled in the dirt and scrambled to get up, Koren pounced onto the man's back with both knees, knocking the breath out of him. The man grunted in pain and lay flat; he became still when he felt Koren's dagger at his neck. "Thought you would find easy prey this night?" Koren hissed into the man's ear. Keeping the tip of his dagger at the man's neck, he took his knife, then patted his jacket and removed a leather purse. Shaking the coin-filled purse next to the thief's ear, he whispered "I will be taking this, and you may count yourself lucky tonight."

Having prepared for betrayal, Koren had a leather cord in a pocket; he tied the man's hands behind his back, then gagged him with a rag tied around the thief's head. Looking up, he saw the boat was almost at the shore, and the fisherman called out in a harsh whisper. "Neelan! You got him?"

"Aye," Koren grunted to mask his voice, and rose slowly, jingling the purse he'd taken off the thief. "He was a rich one, too." He fit an arrow to the bowstring, and as the boat glided into the creek, he let fly an arrow to thump into the bottom of the boat right between the fisherman's feet. "If you move without my saying so, the next one goes into your heart."

Sneed the fisherman held up both hands. "I heard you, I heard you. You were robbed? There are ruffians around here, a man needs to be careful-"

"*You* need to be careful," Koren spat. "Save your lies. Get out of the boat, slowly."

"I'll need my hands to get out, or I'll fall," Sneed protested.

"Then fall. Keep your hands up. And you'd best think about this; I have no reason to keep you alive. It would be easier for me to put an arrow in your gut, and be done with you."

"Take pity on an old man," Sneed pleaded as he struggled to get out of the boat while his hands were in the air. In truth, he had been working small fishing boats on the river since he was a little boy, and he could have gotten out of or into the boat on one foot, blindfolded.

"Pity? Did you and your friend here," Koren kicked Neelan in the leg and the thief grunted, "have pity on the others you robbed? I'm not the first, of that I'm sure."

Koren pulled hard on the oars, struggling to keep both oars working together so he didn't go in circles. As a sailor, he had rowed boats, but always as part of a crew where he was responsible for only one oar. And back then, he had not had to steer the boat, only to pull. This was more complicated. He headed slightly upstream at first, intending to get toward the middle of the river before turning downstream; from the shore that afternoon he had seen that the current flowed more swiftly in the middle of the river.

There were also a series of small islands in the middle of the river, and he intended to use their dark tree-covered shapes as cover while running downstream unseen. His only concerns were the torchlights on the far side of the river, and on the bridge he would need to pass under. For that, he would steer the boat along the near shore, where the torchlight was less bright, and many small boats were moored. Being seen while he went under the bridge was his greatest concern; but one small boat on the river at night was unlikely to be noticed.

A shout arose from the riverbank where he had launched the boat, and Koren ducked down in the boat. The two men he had tied up and gagged must have gotten themselves loose; Koren had left them a knife for that purpose. They had worked rather more quickly than he expected. He could not hear what they were shouting, but the fact that he had thrown Sneed's two knives into the river, and taken money purses from both men, likely was a topic of conversation. Also that he had stolen Sneed's boat, and intended to let it go floating on down the river by itself after he landed. Sneed and his friend would need to find another way to make living; they would need to buy another boat before they could rob any more travelers.

As Koren drifted downstream with the current, the shouting faded behind him; he did not see any reaction from the Taradoran side of the river. Five minutes later, he floated under the bridge, and even waved to a man who was fishing from the bridge. Koren was sitting upright in the boat, casually working the oars, with Sneed's fishing gear arrayed in the bottom of the boat, and he was wearing Sneed's rather fishy-smelling cap. He was merely an innocent fisherman, out late to set up traps in the river. After a few heart-stopping moments, he was past the bridge and the torchlight faded behind him. Breathing a sigh of relief, he allowed himself to shudder for the first time that night. Although he knew that he was younger and faster than the two men who had attempted to rob him, there had still been an element of danger that he had pushed to the back of his mind. Until now, when he had to put his head between his legs and breathe deeply.

He drifted for another quarter hour, when the clouds overhead began to break up, and patchy moonlight shone through to glitter silvery on the river's surface. The far side of the river had scattered houses and fishing docks, Koren steered the boat for a patch of dark trees, and brought the boat in silently as possible. When the boat reached the shore, he hung onto a low-lying branch and stilled his breathing to listen. All he could hear was the river lapping against the tree roots, and distant laughter from a house upriver. Stepping out of the boat, he removed his gear, stowed the oars, and waded out to his waist to push the boat out into the river. Too late, he realized that he could have chosen a better spot to land; the shoreline bent outward just downstream, and he had an anxious moment as the drifting boat almost became hung up on a tree that had fallen into the river. Then the boat spun, bounced along the submerged tree, and floated out into the river. Koren vaguely remembered rapids on this river from his study of maps, but he thought they were quite further south. Most likely, in the morning, someone would see a boat floating by itself and row out to get it. Sneed was never getting that boat back, and that made Koren smile.

Back on shore, he poured water out of his boots and began walking westward. He hoped to be hired as a caravan guard, or to take passage on yet another carriage, but he first needed to put some distance between himself and the border. There would be questions asked about a stranger in a border town; hopefully there would be less questions the further he was from the river. He walked most of the night, and found a dry spot in a thicket of bushes to sleep. When he awoke, he would start the next phase of his journey.

As he fell into dreamless sleep, he thought to himself that he was back inside Tarador. Home. It did not feel like home to him.

Ariana was nearly in tears when she and her chief advisor returned to her private apartment in the royal palace. Gustov Kallron was exhausted, not having time to sleep at all the previous night. Despite his best efforts going back and forth between the Linden estates of various dukes and duchesses, he had not been able to further delay the Council meeting. The magistrates had issued two declarations that morning. First, that Ariana was legally eligible to be a candidate for the regency, although the three magistrates were of the strongly-held opinion that was a glaring gap in the law that should someday be fixed. Second, at the request of Regin Falco, they ruled that Duke Yarron was not eligible to vote for Ariana, as he was related her by blood. After the sleep-deprived and grumpy magistrates left, Duke Falco called for a vote. To no one's surprise, Ariana only had four of the five votes she needed.

"How could *anyone* vote for that man?" Ariana angrily swept books and papers off a table, onto the floor. She sat down heavily in a chair, crossing her arms and sulking.

"The vote has not yet been held, Your Highness," Kallron reminded her.

"You told me that Leese likely has four votes already," Ariana said with her lower lip stuck out.

"That is my guess, yes. Duke Falco and Duchess Rochambeau will almost certainly vote together in favor of your father's brother," he avoided reminding Ariana that Leese Trehayme was her blood uncle. "Based on the brief discussions I was able to conduct, it is my belief that Duchess Portiss and Duke Romero might be persuaded to vote in favor of Leese. That means Regin Falco is likely also offering inducements to Duke Bargann, despite the recent bad blood between them."

Ariana said a very bad word, and she did not apologize for it. "Could we sweeten our offer to Bargann?"

"Certainly, Your Highness; it depends on how much of the royal treasury you wish to give away." Considering the precarious state of Tarador's finances, whatever promises Ariana made to Bargann would remain only that: promises. Actual financial support would need to wait until the royal treasury was healthy. And Bargann likely suspected that was the case, which limited Ariana's bargaining power. "You must understand that at this point, no one believes you will be able to get five votes. So the Council members are making other plans. You should not be offended if Portiss and Romero vote for Leese."

"But how? How could anyone vote for *him*?"

"Highness, the Council is desperate. Because of us, Tarador effectively has no leader, in a time of war. The enemy sees our weakness, and will not hesitate to strike soon. If you cannot be our Regent, someone must be. Leese is a Trehayme, and this morning, he was sober and serious." Kallron suspected Leese had been extensively coached on what to say; that had not mattered during the Council meeting. His presence in Linden was no secret; the man had been seen at dinner with the Falcos the previous night. Leese had been serious, sober, a bit sad and, Kallron hated to admit, rather charming. After Regin Falco nominated Leese for Regent, Leese had stood before the Council and made a brief speech. He had spoken of the urgent need to select a Regent quickly, of the need for national unity in the face of imminent threat of invasion, of his desire to end the centuries-old enmity between the Trehaymes and the Falcos. He had pledged to protect Ariana until she became queen. And he had closed his speech with an appeal to the Council members. "Most importantly, he told the Council that he would need their support and guidance to get our nation through the war. There is nothing our Council members desire more than influence; the idea that Leese wishes guidance from the Council makes him very tempting as a candidate."

Ariana forced herself to take a deep breath. She also uncrossed her arms, stopped pouting, and sat up straight. She was trying to become leader of her nation; she needed to act like someone who could be trusted to lead Tarador. "What can we do, uncle?" Regin Falco had called for a formal vote on Leese Trehayme the next morning. That gave Duke Falco time to line up two more votes; Kallron anticipated another sleepless night attempting to block Leese from taking the regency. "Should I speak directly with Duchess Portiss and Duke Romero?"

"Highness, no. You should not approach them unless you have a deal to propose, and you do not. I will be speaking with them today."

"There is nothing to be done, then?" Ariana kept her posture upright, refusing to admit defeat.

"I did not say that. Leese gave a fairly good speech this morning, but the most important thing he did was show up, sober." Kallron suspected that had involved more than strong coffee and willpower. Reports Kallron had received about Leese only a week ago stated the man was unsteady on his feet, and his hands shook. Such a rapid transformation might involve magic. "I wonder if he can manage to be sober two days in a row?" Before he met with any of the Council members, Gustov Kallron needed to speak with the court wizard. "Leave this to me."

"Kallron, this is going a bit far," Paedris turned in his chair uncomfortably. "We wizards are supposed to remain entirely out of political intrigue. I am not even a citizen of Tarador."

"Lord Salva, I would not ask if the situation were not extremely desperate," Kallron insisted. "Unless something is done, Leese Trehayme will become Regent of Tarador tomorrow morning."

"That cannot happen," Paedris declared. "Still, there is only so much I can do, without openly interfering."

"I suspect Leese is sober only with, shall we say, *super*natural help."

"Ah." Paedris stroked his beard. "There are potions that can temporarily suppress the effects of alcohol and other substances."

"Is there any means of counteracting such potions?"

"I will not drug the man, Kallron," Paedris said emphatically.

"Nor would I ask you too, Lord Salva. It is my belief that Leese will find a way to acquire certain substances; addicts always do. What I ask is this; if the Falcos seek to deceive the Regency Council about whether Leese is fit to hold the Regency, you prevent them from using magic to conceal his true condition."

"That," Paedris said with a smile, "I can do."

"What does he want?" Ariana asked her chief advisor. When Kallron handed her the note from Regin Falco, she had read it twice. Duke Falco requested an urgent private meeting with the crown princess, that very afternoon.

"I truly do not know," Kallron was bothered by Falco's move. Could the Falcos be coming to announce that they had sewn up enough votes to block Ariana from the Regency? That sort of gloating would be an emotional outburst that was unlike the Regin Falco he knew.

"I hope he doesn't expect me to support my Un-" She couldn't bring herself to call Leese Trehayme her uncle. "To support Leese as Regent."

That made Kallron smile. "I do not think so, Your Highness. He may attempt to appeal to your sense of patriotism, knowing that you understand the country cannot remain without a leader in this time of war."

"Does *he* know that?" Ariana asked in disgust.

"I am sure he does, Highness," Kallron replied soothingly. "Please consider that it does no harm to listen to what Duke Falco has to say."

"It wastes my time," Ariana huffed. "And tries my patience."

Duke Falco was ushered in by palace guards, and the first minutes were taken in exchanging the required pleasantries. Ariana found herself unable to contain her impatience. "As we are both busy, Duke Falco, could you get to the point of this meeting?"

Falco shot a glance at Kallron, a glance which meant Regin Falco disdained the young woman's lack of restraint. "Highness, I have been speaking with my peers; the dukes and duchesses of the provinces of Tarador. Tomorrow morning, I will ask for a vote in favor of making your uncle Leese Trehayme the next Regent."

"You would give a drunken weakling the power of the Regency?" Ariana fumed.

"Your uncle was sober at today's meeting. The Council was favorably impressed. Highness, you must appreciate that the Council is very eager to fill the vacuum of power while we face defeat in battle. Leese Trehayme may not be a good Regent, but the Council deems he may be good enough. I am very confident that tomorrow's vote will see Leese confirmed as Regent. As *your* Regent," he reminded the crown princess. Leese would hold power in her name. He would hold power over Ariana. And behind Leese would be Regin Falco.

"Do not be so confident," Kallron cautioned. "We are still working to secure votes for the princess."

Duke Falco lip curled in a dismissive smile. "You have four votes, of the five needed. I have the other two; I have confirmed with Duchess Rochambeau that she will not vote for you under any circumstance."

"You come here to boast, then?" Kallron demanded.

"No," Regin shook his head in a fair semblance of regret. "I will not boast; it is sad that our nation has come to this point. Your Highness, I propose an arrangement. I will provide your fifth vote."

Ariana looked to her chief advisor for guidance. "In exchange for?" Kallron broke the silence.

Regin took a deep breath. "On the morning of her sixteenth birthday, before her coronation as queen, Ariana marries my son Kyre."

"How could he ever *think* I would marry his son? Marry that, that, oooooh," Ariana shook her fists in the air. "I can't even think of a word bad enough to describe Kyre," she spat the name out. "I would sooner marry a frog! Or a, a," she tried to think of a creature even more slimy and disgusting than a frog. "A slug." She tilted her head, curious. "Why would Duke Falco even *ask* me? He had to know I would never marry a Falco." Why would the duke seek rejection?

"Because, Your Highness, the duke believes he is in a very strong position to negotiate. He has blocked you from getting the fifth vote you need, and he has a strong candidate for the Regency. I suspect this is Niles Forne's work." Forne likely thought himself a genius for developing a plan that could put a Falco on the throne of Tarador. "Duke Falco is correct that, for the moment, he has prevented you from assuming the Regency. Forne probably thought there is no harm in proposing a marriage between you and Kyre. If you say no, Falco will proceed with his plan to make deals to get five votes for Leese."

"Is he right that he can make Leese the Regent?" She asked anxiously.

Kallron allowed himself a brief smile. "Duke Falco has two votes for certain; his own and that of Duchess Rochambeau. Of the other five provinces, he needs only three, and he knows the Council is anxious to avoid our nation being leaderless in time of war. However, tomorrow morning," he winked, "

Regin Falco may find that things are not as certain as they seem."

Koren's first choice for going west through Tarador was to hire on as a guard for a merchant caravan that was going northwest. When he reached the town of Tunbridge in the early evening following his crossing of the river, he purchased clothes that were not so obviously the garb of a sailor, and cut his hair shorter, rather than wearing it long and tied back as most sailors did. Unfortunately, he found only two caravans that were going west within the week. One caravan was owned by a merchant from Indus, who used only his countrymen as guards. Koren approached the other caravan, a train of four heavily-laden wagons owned by two men from Tarador. He had heard, along the journey north, that with the war taking many men as soldiers or mercenaries, guards for merchant caravans were in high demand. Slinging his bow and arrow over one shoulder and attaching his now-sharpened sword prominently to his belt, he approached one of the merchants, but two guards quickly stepped in between Koren and the man.

"You? A guard?" The merchant looked him up and down. "If you have something to sell, we already have all we can carry. If you're buying," the man wrinkled his nose, "you'll need more coins than I judge you can afford."

"Please sir," Koren made a short bow, "I seek employment as a guard. If you wish, I can demonstrate my skills." He planned to hold back and not show anyone his true speed and skill; only enough to impress the merchant.

"That will not be necessary," the merchant did not smile, although the guards chuckled. "I am not such a fool as my brother believes," he looked toward the other well-dressed merchant. "But I would never hire a beardless boy to safeguard my life."

"But I am not-" Koren began to protest.

"Nor would I hire anyone who comes to me, unknown to me or my men, and without refer-ences. Tell me, boy, would you hire a guard you did not know?"

"No," Koren had to admit. To allow an armed man into the caravan, a man who may very well be working with bandits, would be idiocy. "Your point in well-founded, good sir," he bowed again. "As you are going west, might I purchase passage on one of your wagons?" He lifted the leather pouch of coins that hung around his neck and shook it. "I can pay."

"Ha!" That drew a laugh from the merchant, and the guards. "Since you seek to be a guard, you may do me a service and advise me on my security. If a stranger sought to be a guard and was de-nied, would you allow that stranger into our midst?"

"No," Koren had to agree again. Defeated, and knowing he had been foolish, he backed away from the merchant under the watchful eyes of the guards. "Very sorry to have troubled you today, good sir." Mentally, he kicked himself. What he should have done, he now knew, was to have gone into a tavern and befriended some of the guards. While that likely would not have gotten him hired either, it had a better chance than him walking up to a wealthy merchant and begging to be hired.

Clutching his limited store of coins, he walked toward the center of the town, where he hoped to buy passage on yet another cramped, uncomfortable carriage. This journey was all so much harder than it had sounded when he had discussed it with Captain Reed aboard the *Lady Hilde-gard*, not so long ago.

CHAPTER ELEVEN

Regin Falco rose early, hoping there would be a message waiting for him. A message from the crown princess, stating that she had reconsidered, and would agree to marry Kyre. He was disappointed when his servants told him no such message had been received. Hurrying down the hall, he found his advisor already up. Niles Forne had been up for hours, and was formally dressed for the Council meeting that morning. Annoyed, Regin saw the man had already taken breakfast. Partly out of spite, Regin ate the two pieces of bacon Forne had left on his plate. "Any news, Forne?"

"From the princess, Sire?" Forne shook his head. "No. I fear our crown princess cannot bring herself to consider the value to our nation, of your proposal for Leese to become Regent."

Regin split a sweet roll in half and ate it. "Would it help to give her more time?"

"Perhaps, Your Grace, but the Council vote must be this morning. We could delay the investiture of Leese for several days, to give the princess time to reconsider. Perhaps if she sees that her uncle will certainly become Regent, that will overcome her objections."

"How many days could we delay?" Regin thought about eating the other half of the sweet roll, then decided he wanted his own proper breakfast.

"Legally, no more than three days, Sire. More than three days would require a new vote, and anything can happen in three days."

"That is not ideal," Regin frowned. A short while ago, he would have felt triumphant to get Leese voted in as Regent. Now that Forne had dangled in front of him the prospect of Kyre marrying the crown princess, Regin was not satisfied to settle for what now appeared to be second best. "Is that damned Leese out of bed yet?"

"No, Sire. I am reluctant to wake him earlier than needed, so he will be fresh for the meeting." Forne knew those people who abused alcohol and stronger substances needed extra rest to be fresh. There were only two doses of magical potion left in his vial; he did not wish to use them until it was truly necessary.

"Wake him anyway," the duke of Burwyck ordered. "I wish no surprises this morning."

The duke's wish for no surprises was not to be fulfilled. Despite the best efforts of Duke Falco's servants, including Niles Forne, to search Leese's rooms for troublesome substances, the man had outwitted them all. Concealed in the heels of his boots was a grayish-white powder that was one of his favorites, and because he had not enjoyed that particular substance in weeks, Leese had indulged freely after the Falco household went to bed.

The servants who found Leese unconscious in his bed knew to call Forne before they informed the duke. If Forne could fix the problem, the duke would not ever need to know, and not ever need to be angry with the failure of his servants. Forne cursed himself, regretting that he had not posted a servant to remain in Leese Trehayme's room all night, to keep watch on that degenerate weakling.

And then Niles Forne panicked. His magical potion did not work, not nearly enough! Something had gone wrong with the magic! Leese was still unable to stand or to speak sensibly. The candidate for the Regency's eyes were glassy and unfocused, drool dribbled down his chin. And the Council meeting was in only three hours! Forne tried using another two drops of the precious magical potion, making sure Leese swallowed it all, despite the warning of the wizard who Forne had gotten the potion from. The wizard had warned that using the potion too often, or in too high a dose, could be dangerous.

Niles Forne panicked. His panic was not because all of his plans were about to be dashed. He panicked, because he now needed to inform Regin Falco that their chosen candidate for the Regency of Tarador was flopped on the bed, giggling to himself and drooling.

"Well?" demanded Duke Bargann, glancing around the table at the Regency Council meeting. "Is the man here, or not?"

"As I said," Regin struggled mightily to remain calm, "Leese Trehayme has taken ill, and is indisposed at the moment. He is receiving treatment for his-"

"What kind of treatment? What exactly is wrong with him?" Bargann pressed the point. He was angry. He had lost his gold mine, then the deal to make Ariana the Regent had been blocked by Falco. To add further insult, Falco had approached him with inducements to vote for Leese Trehayme; inducements so pitiful they could only be viewed as a slap in the face. Falco did not absolutely need Bargann's vote, and they both knew it.

"He is ill," Regin offered as explanation. "The rich food here may not-"

"His tummy is upset?" Bargann asked mockingly. "And because of that, he can't be here this morning? What do the experts in the hospital say? It is stomach trouble, or could it be some other issue? A recurrence of," he looked slowly around the table, "health issues he has had in the past? Self-inflicted medical problems?"

Regin looked pained. He was running out of answers. "He is not in the royal hospital; he is being cared for by my own physicians-"

Duchess Portiss raised her voice. "Then let the physicians of the royal hospital examine him, Falco. If necessary, we can bring the Council meeting to his sick bed."

Regin was caught. "Really, I think the man only needs rest. If we could delay the vote until-"

"There will be no delay," Carlana spoke for the first time since she formally opened the meeting. Even though the Council had voted no confidence in her leadership, she was still officially the Regent until there was someone to replace her. "The vote will be today. This morning." Carlana still had the power to schedule Council votes. "Duke Falco, can you produce your candidate, or not?"

Duke Falco wanted to strangle the Regent. "No." Regin knew that if the Council saw the drug addled state Leese was in, he could never win a vote. The entire Council now strongly suspected that Leese had once again fallen victim to his appetite for drink and more exotic substances. Regin tilted his head as his advisor Niles Forne whispered something to him. Then Falco's hateful look was focused on Forne instead of the Regent. "We wish to," Falco looked again at Forne, who nodded and stared down at the table. "We wish to withdraw Leese Trehayme as a candidate for Regent of Tarador."

"What is next?" Ariana asked, undoing the tight collar of her formal dress. She could hardly wait to get back to her apartments in the palace. Sitting next to her mother in the Council meeting, both of them stiff in their chairs, neither of them talking to each other or looking at each other, had been incredibly uncomfortable for everyone in the Council chamber.

"Highness, I truly do not know at the moment," Kallron admitted. "The only thing of which I am sure is that Leese Trehayme has lost his only chance to be Regent. Rumor has it that Regin Falco is going to banish Leese from the Falco estate tonight. Each member of the Council will put forward their own candidates, and scheme against each other to make deals in secret. It will be utter chaos, and we may not have a compromise on a candidate for weeks. Or more."

"We can't wait weeks," Ariana said in a near whisper. "The enemy is across our border. And Tarador has no leader."

Olivia looked in dismay at the pile of letters on the table next to the battered old chair where the wizard sat while taking a break from experiments on his workbench. She had cleaned off that table only the day before, and now it was completely covered again, to the point that the letters were in danger of sliding off onto the floor, or even into the fireplace. "Lord Salva, would you like me to sort those letters for you?"

"Hmm?" The wizard did not look up from the thick book he was studying. "No, I've looked at those. Nothing important in there."

"What about this one, Sir?" She held up a letter that the wizard had opened and apparently at least looked at, for it had a mustard stain on the first page. It did not appear he had bothered to even remove the other two pages from the envelope. She recognized the address on the front of the envelope. "It is from the people who farm your land."

"Hmm? No," Paedris waved a hand dismissively, annoyed at the continued interruption. "It is mostly facts and figures about this year's harvest." Carlana had finally granted the land to Paedris, and now that he owned it, he was even less interested in management of the farm. Although to his chagrin, he had discovered that owning the land meant he now needed to pay taxes on it. He had briefly glanced at the letter when it arrived a few days ago and quickly lost interest. The only letters he actually read was anything from a member of the Wizards Council. Or the royal family. Or any royalty, for that matter. Paedris often received letters from dukes, duchesses, barons and baronesses. Also from foreign royalty. Now that he thought about it, such messages made up most of his correspondence; and he had to read those and respond even though they were invariably tedious and took up far too much of his time. Which made any other letters even less important. "You can get rid of it. Oh, uh, put it in the fire, please. That whole stack of letters can go." Many of those letters Paedris had not even opened; he simply did not have time. It would not do to simply toss unopened letters into the trash; servants around the castle would notice and they would talk. And the people who had written the letters would be insulted.

Olivia swept the letters off the table and into her arms; there were quite a lot of them. "Yes, Sir. Would you like more tea?"

"Hmmm? Oh, not right now, thank you." Although the mention of tea reminded Paedris that he was hungry. Concentrating so intensely was tiring. "I would appreciate tea and, some little thing to eat, in a while."

Olivia carried the letters and the empty tea set out of the library and up to the wizard's common room, knowing that Lord Salva would not like to be further distracted. Most of the letters she placed into the fireplace, where logs were burning nicely. Other letters, she used to practice her skill at creating magical fireballs. On her own, she was able to make a faint, weak flame dance in the palm of her hand. The flame flickered and kept going out; Lord Salva said she did not lack power within her; she needed to concentrate on feeling the ephemeral connection with the spirit world that fed power into the flame. It was maddening to Olivia that sometimes when she could not sense a connection at all, the flame held steady, and other times when she felt the connection strongly, the flame sputtered and barely came to life.

She had found, on her own, a technique that helped build a tiny flame into something that might generously be called a fireball. Adult wizards would no doubt say that what she was doing was cheating, and bad form, and actually setting back her overall progress. But she liked seeing a fireball dance in her hand. Power from the spirit world, drawn into her hand, at her bidding! It was truly magical. She knew that not all wizards could create a fireball, and fireballs were no measure of a wizard's true power. Lord Mwazo openly admitted that he could not manage any sort of flame at all, yet Paedris considered Mwazo to be an immensely powerful wizard at the arcane and dangerous art of peering into the future, and into the mind of the enemy.

No matter what the adult wizards told her, Olivia liked creating a flame in her hand. At times when she was frustrated at other aspects of wizardry, and despaired of ever being able to do more than simple tricks, watching a ball of fire grow out of nothing always reassured her that she had magical power within her. And that she would someday be a wizard.

Olivia concentrated as she had been taught to do, and after a scary moment when nothing happened, a flicker appeared half-seen in her right palm. Holding her right palm open, she used the fingers of her left hand to pull the flame upward, stretching it. That was the technique she had invented on her own. Using her other hand to tease the flame higher somehow steadied it, and it grew from a faint, barely-seen glimmer into a yellow ball of fire. A ball of magical fire, dancing in her hand. Power from the spirit world, that had come into the world of the real because Olivia Dupres willed it to happen!

Concentrating on keeping the glowing ball of fire dancing above her palm, Olivia nudged a letter into the fireball. The letter crisped up, curled and blackened, then burst into a satisfying flame.

"Ow!" Olivia shouted, dropping the burning letter onto the floor, almost on the rug. She frantically stamped on the letter, putting out the fire, then kicked it into the fireplace. That had been foolish, she told herself. While the heat of magical fire could not harm the wizard who willed it into existence, a burning piece of paper was a burning piece of paper, no matter how the paper had been set aflame. She sucked at the red mark on her thumb where the flaming letter had almost burned her skin. If only she knew healing spells; those had not been part of education yet.

For the next letter, she set it on fire while holding it over the fireplace, so that once the letter was burning, she could release it before she scorched her own skin. A dozen letters she set aflame that way, testing her control of magical fire. Some letters were already open, and she glanced at the contents. None of the letters contained anything important. If these letters showed the daily correspondence of a powerful court wizard, then Olivia had no wish to ever seek such a position. It all seemed so frightfully *dull*. Avoiding a life of dullness was why she was so eager to become a wizard!

With the letters all gone and her beginning to feel tired from using magic, Olivia realized she had spent too much time getting rid of the letters. The wizard wants tea, which she could make in the tower, but he also wanted a snack, of which there was nothing in the tower, because Lord Feany had eaten everything. Everything! Even the crisp sugar cookies that she had hidden in a ceramic crock in the storeroom, behind a box of soap, and under a box of rags. She had placed a concealment spell on that crock of cookies; and concealment was her best magical talent, so far in her training. How had Shomas Feany found her secret stash of cookies, which were one of Lord Salva's favorite? Olivia had filled that crock with fresh-baked cookies, keeping them in the tower so she could bring them to the court wizard quickly. Now she needed to run over to the royal kitchen and hope they had something savory for a mid-afternoon snack. She groaned inwardly, thinking that she likely would have to perform a magic 'trick' for the kitchen staff, in exchange for a sweet treat. And she was already tired from creating fireballs.

But, no! First, she needed to get a bucket of soap and warm water, and scrub clean the floor where she had dropped the burning letter. There was a charred stain on the wood floor; it would simply not do to have the wizards come into the common room for wine after their dinner, and see a mark on the floor. Olivia briefly considered using a temporary concealment spell to hide the mark, but if Lord Feany had found her crock of cookies, the wizards would surely see through her amateur attempt to cover up her little accident. Glancing out the window at the position of the sun, she decided she needed to put on water for tea, rush over to the royal kitchens, and run back as fast as she could before the teapot boiled over. Then she could scrub the floor clean with hot water later.

How had Lord Salva's previous servant managed to do everything the court wizard needed? And Koren Bladewell had not even the advantage of being a wizard. Or maybe that is how he had been able to keep up with the workload. Unlike Olivia, who was expected to spend half of each day being trained by one wizard or another, or practicing and studying magic on her own, Koren Bladewell only had to serve the wizard.

At times like this, Olivia wished she was a simple, ordinary person like Koren, rather than a young wizard.

"Your tea is ready," Olivia announced, carrying the teapot set and a plate with a freshly baked berry tart for the wizard. She had run up the stairs, and paused outside the door to regain her breath.

"Hmm?" Paedris hadn't even noticed that Olivia had left, or why she had been there before. Now that he thought about it, he was hungry. How nice of the young wizard to think of bringing afternoon tea for him! "Oh, thank you very much, Olivia. That was very thoughtful of you."

"Yes, Lord Salva, you are welcome," Olivia replied with a smile, as she realized the master wizard had forgotten all about his request for tea and 'some little thing to eat'. She prepared a cup of tea the way Paedris liked it, and set the tea and berry tart on the table next to the wizard's favorite battered and disreputable chair. "You should rest, come away from the workbench, sir. Sitting for a long time like that is not good for you," she pointed out how Paedris had been perched hunched over a thick, ancient book for hours.

"I suppose you are right," Paedris admitted. He got up stiffly and walked over to window to look out, while stretching his back.

"I disposed of those letters," Olivia said, waiting for the court wizard to sit down and be comfortable, so she could race upstairs and scrub the floor in the common room.

"Letters? Oh, yes. Thank you," Paedris said. He had forgotten about that also. He sat down and took a bite of the tart. "Oh, that is good."

"It is a shame about that horse, sir. I hope it comes back."

"Mmm." Paedris responded, already lost in thought again as he sipped tea and stared into the fire. The dancing flames were mesmerizing.

Olivia took the opportunity to slip out of the room unnoticed. While heating up water for tea, she had put another pot of water on the fire so she could use it to scrub the floor in the common room. There was plenty of time to do that, and put more logs on the fire there, and get the table set for dinner. She was out the door, and had a foot on the first step of the stairs when Paedris spoke. "What horse?"

She popped her head back around the doorway. "Horse, sir?"

"You said something about a horse? You hoped it comes back? Did it run away?" Paedris had not had time to exercise his own horse, he had not even been to the royal stables in the past few days. Still, he expected that if something had happened to his horse, the stable master would have said something about it to him directly. "Is there a problem in the royal stables?"

"Not with your horse, Lord Salva," she explained. "I meant the horse you keep on your farm? That horse ran away."

Paedris jumped up from the chair, knocking the teacup onto the floor and breaking it. "Thunderbolt ran away?" He asked with great alarm.

"Oh, sir," Olivia rushed over to pick up the broken tea cup. "I'll clean it up," she said, but the wizard grasped her shoulders.

"Thunderbolt ran away? When? How do you know this?" Paedris demanded.

Olivia had not known the horse's name. "If Thunderbolt is the horse you keep on your farm, sir, it ran away. It was in the letter from the couple who work the farm for you."

"Letter?" Paedris mentally kicked himself. He had only glanced at the top of that letter's first page; it had been something about how many acres had been planted, and the Spring rainfall being either good or bad, he couldn't remember. "You have this letter? Show it to me," he demanded.

Olivia's eyes welled up with tears. "Oh, sir, no, I don't have it. You told me to burn all those letters."

"Ah!" Paedris slapped his forehead. "I did! Olivia, don't cry, this is not your fault. Not your fault at all." He steered the young wizard trainee to his battered chair and sat her down. "Tell me, what did the letter say about Thunderbolt? Tell me everything you remember."

"It said," she closed her eyes, trying to picture the letter in her mind. Real wizards could do that to recall memories; Olivia had not yet been taught how to do that. "I only glanced at the letter as it went into the fire, I didn't truly read it. I think all it said was that the horse jumped the fence and ran away, and the couple who manage your farm haven't seen it since. Oh!" She remembered something else. "They said they wanted to offer a reward for anyone who brings the horse back and they wanted your approval?" She shook her head. "That's all I remember."

"Nothing about what day it was, anything unusual that happened around the farm around that time?" Paedris pressed.

"No. It was only a short paragraph?" She answered uncertainly. "Most of the letter was about growing wheat, and something about clearing a woodlot?"

"Mmm, yes," Paedris groaned. The little he remembered from his own quick glance at the letter had been dry details about seeds and crops yields, and that is why he had set the letter aside. Why had the writers of the letter not put Thunderbolt's escape on top of the first page?! It was maddening. "Olivia, this is not your fault in any way. I should have tended to that letter when it arrived, instead of," he looked guiltily at the half-eaten berry tart. "Taking afternoon tea. The letter!" He gasped. "When did it arrive?"

"I don't know," Olivia answered honestly. When had she first noticed it? Paedris had received a bundle of letters from the royal post the day before, but that bundle was still sitting, tied with string and untouched on the desk by the door. The last bundle of letters before that had arrived more than a week previous, and Olivia didn't remember seeing that particular letter in that batch. She did not remember when she had first seen it, the court wizard received so many letters. "I don't sort your letters, sir," she pointed to the bundle by the door. "I just bring them in for you."

Paedris said a *very bad* word, then the court wizard blushed and apologized for cursing in front of a young lady. He walked across the room and pointed to the table beside his battered old chair. "That letter was here?" On the table that now held his tea set. When had he last looked through his correspondence? Really looked through it, and not only pushed the piles around various desks and tables? He had no idea. He did remember carrying a pile of letters to the table by the chair, but that had only been to make room on his workbench. That letter could have arrived weeks ago! And considering the typically slow delivery of the royal post, it could have been sent from his farm a full month before!

"It was in the big," she almost said 'mess', "collection of letters there, yes." Anticipating the wizard's next question, she added "Those letters were on your workbench until yesterday. You told me not to touch anything on your workbench, Sir."

"Oh, yes. Quite right," he looked in dismay at the cluttered workbench. He had spent many days recently studying ancient books of magic, looking for any hint of a way that he could locate Koren Bladewell. And he had missed a vital clue that had, at one point, been quite literally right in front of his nose! Striding over to the workbench, he swept books onto the floor, took out a fresh sheet of paper, and quickly scrawled out a message. While the ink dried, he held up the paper. "Olivia, can you read that?" Paedris knew his handwriting was often terrible; he had made a painstaking effort to be legible with this crucial message.

Olivia peered at the letter. "Yes, sir." She recognized the format of the message, the way it was addressed. "You wish this to be sent over the telegraph?"

"Yes, immediately. It is extremely urgent. Please go, now."

Lord Salva's words were not necessary; the terribly anxious expression on his face gave Olivia haste. She tucked the message into a pouch and ran out the door, down the stairs and across the courtyard. At the entrance to the palace, she pulled out the badge Paedris had given her and showed it to the guards there. "Official wizard business," she said, out of breath. The guards knew she was a wizard in her own right, and pulled the doors open for her. Inside the palace, she ran, her shoes slapping on the polished floor, ignoring the stares of palace officials.

Out the other door, for she had only used the corridors of the royal palace as a shortcut to running all the way around the courtyard, she ran across the uneven cobblestones to the telegraph tower that was built into the northeast wall of the castle. "Lord Salva has a message to send," she explained to the guard at the door, and the man stepped aside. By now, everyone around the castle knew the court wizard's newest servant, and knew that she was also a young wizard.

Getting into the telegraph station was easier than getting the message sent out. The captain in charge of the telegraph was already overwhelmed by a stack of messages to be sent, and urging his staff to decode incoming messages quickly. With the enemy across Tarador's border, the Royal Army was constantly sending messages back and forth to the capital. "Yes, we will get to this message in due time," the captain snapped in irritation. "The wizard will have to wait his turn, young lady. There are many high-priority messages ahead of him," he pointed to the stack on his desk. "Come back," he glanced out the window at the position of the sun to judge the time, "late this afternoon, and I will see what I can do."

"Of course," she said, ignoring the man. With the fingers of her left hand, she performed the trick of pulling the flickering magical flame above her right palm, until a small fireball spun there. "I was told, by the *most powerful wizard in the land*, that this message is extremely urgent. But, I shall inform Lord Salva that the royal telegraph service has better things to do. What shall I say your name is, sir?"

The man's face changed from angry red to the color of newly-fallen snow, and his lips moved without sound. He spun and stumbled out the door, bashing a knee on the door frame and taking the stairs two or three at a time. The man shouted at his underlings, and they shouted at theirs, and Olivia heard the shouts echoing through the tower up to the platform at the top.

The message that was in process of being sent was halted, the flag arms reset to indicate a new message would be coming, and that the message had the highest of priorities. The first part of the message was the code key for deciphering it, then the symbol for the telegraph station for which the message was intended, then the body of the message itself. From one tower to another, relayed from one hilltop to another, the message flew across Tarador, until it arrived at the telegraph station closest to Lord Salva's farm. Which was, in truth, not very close at all. The telegraph operator there was startled when she read the decoded message, not understanding how a runaway horse could rate the highest signal priority. Then she read the last part of the message; words that had been added by the chief telegraph agent in Linden. The chief telegraph agent there was a captain in the Royal Army. The last part of the message read *Take all measures to answer Lord Salva's questions, and reply without the loss of a moment.*

Without the loss of a moment. Every soldier in the Royal Army knew what that meant. More shouting followed that message being read, and within mere minutes, two Royal Army soldiers were on horseback, racing across the countryside as fast as their steeds could carry them. When they reached the first village, their horses lathered with sweat and unsteady on their legs, the soldiers rode to the only inn, where several horses were tied up outside. One of the soldiers hurriedly took the army saddles and bridles off their horses and, selecting the two other horses that looked fastest, saddled them. The other soldier went into the inn, showed her Royal Army badge, and announced that they would be temporarily requisitioning new horses, and that the owners would be compensated by the crown and the horses would be returned as soon as possible. It was not necessary for her to draw her sword, nor even for her to place her hand meaningfully on the pommel of her sword; the grim expression on her face told the villages that she and her companion would be taking horses one way or another. On her way out, she tossed coins to the innkeeper, with instructions that the exhausted army horses should be cared for.

The process was repeated at the next village, but the third place they stopped was a town with a Royal Army garrison, so they were able to borrow well-tended army horses, with a promise of fresh horses on their way back.

The same two soldiers came back through to the garrison in the early hours of the next morning, dead tired and on horses that could not manage more than a slow trot. Although the two soldiers wanted to change horses and press on back to the telegraph station, the garrison commander ordered them to rest, and sent two fresh soldiers on fresh horses to carry the message onward. The exhausted soldiers collapsed into bunks immediately, too tired to eat anything at all. Laying in their bunks, they expected to fall asleep immediately, but slumber was elusive as their minds raced. When they had arrived at the farm, they had been dismayed to find the farmhouse and barn empty, and the wagon also gone! Panicked, the soldiers considered that the couple who managed the farm could be anywhere, and all of their efforts to race across the countryside might have been for nothing. Then the soldiers went into the house and found a pot of stew bubbling gently on the stove. The farmers could not be far, so the soldiers climbed back on their horses and rode down the lane that separated the farm fields in half. Quickly, they found the elderly couple in the farm's woodlot, loading firewood into their wagon. Once the old man and woman recovered from the shock of seeing a pair of Royal Army soldiers racing across the wheat field toward them, they had answered the wizard's questions as best they could. Then, without pausing for stew even though their stomachs were growling with hunger, the soldiers turned and raced back the way they had come, satisfying their hunger with the hard biscuits and dried meat in their saddlebags. Laying in bunks at the garrison station, unable to sleep yet, they asked themselves once again, what could possibly be so important about a runaway horse?

Paedris and Olivia were sitting in the wizard's study after breakfast, across from each other at a small table. Lord Salva was quizzing the apprentice wizard about the proper use of herbs for spells when there was shouting in the courtyard, a furious knocking on the door there, and booted feet pounding on the stairs. A breathless telegraph courier handed a leather pouch to Paedris, gesturing for the wizard to read it. "Your, reply, Lor-, Lord Salva," the man gasped.

"Oh, thank you," the wizard replied casually, his mind still on herbs and spells. Opening the pouch, he read the brief message. Thunderbolt had run away in the morning, eleven days ago. The wind had been from the north-northeast that morning. Nothing unusual happened around the farm that morning or in the days prior, nor had anything unusual happened in the entire village. Thunderbolt had been his typical energetic self, until the horse had stuck his head up into the breeze that morning, sniffing intently. Then the horse had run straight across the corral, jumped the fence and disappeared toward the north-northeast.

Such dry words, Paedris thought, for such a momentous message. "Olivia, excuse me, I must speak with Shomas and Cecil," the wizard said, closing the spell book on the table. "Hmm?" he said, startled, as his servant kicked him under the table.

Olivia looked toward the telegraph courier, then back at Paedris, then the courier.

"Oh," Paedris said as he understood her meaning. Standing up, the wizard clapped a hand on the courier's shoulder. "Please convey to your fellows, and everyone involved, my sincere thanks. And my admiration. I did not expect a reply until tomorrow at the earliest! I do not know how it was managed to bring a reply to me so soon, but I can imagine the effort it must have taken. Rest assured," he waved the message in the air, "as frivolous as this message may seem, it is vital. Vital! In fact," he murmured almost to himself, "it would be best if everyone who read the decoded message forgot what they saw, eh?"

"Yes, Lord Salva," the man nodded vigorously. "I shall inform my captain."

"Good man, good man," Paedris said as he steered the man toward the door. The court wizard needed to speak with a fellow wizard, and there was not a moment to lose.

Shomas read the message again. He was still skeptical. "Certainly you know more about this than I do, Paedris, but how can you be sure this horse didn't just catch the scent of a female horse? Or a wolf? There are many reasons why," he checked the message again for the horse's name, "Thunderbolt might have jumped the fence." Shomas Feany was concerned about the strain Paedris was under; the powerful wizard hardly slept these days. His every waking moment was a concentrated effort to counter moves of the enemy.

"Shomas is correct," Lord Mwazo observed. "However, you do know this animal better than we do."

"It is more than a horse jumping a fence. It is *this* horse," Paedris responded vehemently. "Thunderbolt was Koren's horse, those two are tied to each other. When Koren left, Thunderbolt was frantic; if the walls of the royal stable corral were not so high, that horse might have jumped them back then. Looking back, I should have released Thunderbolt, and followed him if I could. Thunderbolt was brought to my farm in part because he was driving the royal stable master half mad. And in part because I was afraid Thunderbolt would injure himself if we kept him here. But mostly, I wanted Thunderbolt away from any sight or scent that would remind him of Koren. So, yes, I believe that the actions that morning; of Thunderbolt suddenly catching scent of something and running off, are significant. Particularly in light of, something else," Paedris struggled for words. "Cecil, I have had a, a *feeling*, for the past fortnight. I have dreamt several times of Koren, dreamt that he is nearby, and in my dream I reach for him, but he slips away. It is as if he is always just beyond my reach." Paedris avoided the eyes of his fellow wizards, embarrassed by talking about his feelings, of all things. "But he is close now. Closer than he has been."

Mwazo slapped the table in exasperation. "Paedris! You fool! How long have you had this feeling?"

"Uh," Lord Salva was taken aback. "Around a fortnight, I suppose." He searched his memory. When had he first had a dream about Koren? In that dream, the young man had keep walking along the edge of a cliff, seemingly unaware of the danger. Paedris had called to him, and reached out for him, but Koren had blithely walked right off the edge and plunged downward to his doom. "Yes, a fortnight."

Mwazo shook his head, joined by Shomas. "Paedris," Shomas sighed, "for a wise man, sometimes you act foolishly."

"You are a powerful wizard," Mwazo chided, "and you have experienced a compelling vision, yet you did not think to mention this to anyone? Paedris, you know better than that. Koren is tied to his horse, yes, he is also tied to you. You placed a blocking spell on him, you spent time working closely with him. He rescued you. You are tied together."

"I had not considered that," Paedris said truthfully.

"I'm convinced, Cecil," Shomas announced. "One of us should go after this horse. And it should be me. The two of you are too important here. No, no, don't bother telling me how important I am, save your breath. Paedris, the Royal Army needs you. And you, Mwazo, are the only one of us who can see into the mind of our enemy."

Mwazo almost blushed. "Not now I can't. My powers-"

"Your powers are far greater than any other of us," Shomas scoffed. "You may yet be able to glimpse inside that pit of evil," he shuddered. "The two of you stay here and wrestle with our enemy; I will go find this horse. How hard could that be for a wizard?" He laughed nervously.

"You should not go alone," Paedris said with relief. He had wanted Shomas to be the one to go after Thunderbolt, to find Koren, and Paedris had anticipated a long argument with Lord Feany. Without an argument, the court wizard had to mentally shift gears.

"Alone! Ha!" Shomas laughed. "I am certainly not going to carry all my provisions by myself. No, I will require at least a royal baggage train with me." Turning serious, he added "Paedris, the wind came from the north. If Koren is not within our borders, he could be with the dwarves. Or in orc strongholds. I will need soldiers with me."

"A small group," Cecil advised. "To move swiftly and unnoticed."

"That would be best." Shomas now looked distinctly unhappy, contemplating a long and possibly treacherous journey. "Paedris, if I do find Koren Bladewell, I am going to tell him the truth. Deception has led us to nothing but disaster."

"Agreed. We had our reasons," Paedris admitted. "*I* had my reasons," he added, taking full responsibility. It had been his decision initially to hide the truth from Koren. At the time, it was,

Paedris was still convinced, the right decision. Koren Bladewell was too inexperienced to control his unimaginable power. And too young to resist the temptation to use his power anyway. Now, Paedris was willing to reveal the truth to Koren. "We should tell him the truth. All of it."

"Why?" Lord Mwazo asked quietly.

"Are you daft, man?" Shomas asked in disbelief. "Haven't you seen the destruction caused by our deceiving the boy? Our entire society is on the brink of destruction, and you ask-"

"I only ask what has changed," Cecil explained, simply. "I agree that we should tell Koren the truth. I want to be sure that all of us understand and agree *why* that is the right course now, when we all agreed before to hide the truth. Koren Bladewell is still inexperienced, and still young. So, I ask again, if Koren has not changed, what changes our decision?"

Shomas knew he should not be annoyed; one of Cecil's roles on the Wizard's Council was to remind them all to be conscious of the reasons behind their decisions. "What has changed? It's simple for me. We tried deception, and it didn't work."

"Yes," Paedris agreed. "More than that, Koren *has* changed. He is not the frightened farm boy he was when I first met him. He risked his life and his good name to rescue me, by himself. If we find him, *when* we find him, I am going to trust him. I was wrong to deceive him; Koren is stronger in character than I anticipated."

"Koren has changed," Cecil said with a smile, happy that his fellows recognized their true motivations. "I believe we all can agree that he is still too young to control such power."

"*I* could not control that much power," Paedris admitted. "The three of us together could not control such power, not yet."

Mwazo rapped the table with his knuckles. "Exactly. Shomas, when you meet Koren, and reveal the truth to him, you must stress the danger his power poses to himself. Explain to him that we, not even all three of us, can control the power within him at this point."

"I will explain that to him," Lord Feany said with a frown. "Whether the young man will listen to me is a question I cannot answer."

"Koren trusts you, Shomas," Paedris assured his fellow wizard. "More than that, he likes you, I believe."

"He liked me enough when I was here before the winter," Shomas observed. "To him back then, I was a jolly fat wizard of no particular power. I didn't threaten him. When we meet again, I will be telling Koren that we lied to him. I will tell him that he is a wizard, and that we should have discovered his power when he was a mere boy. His parents should not have abandoned him; they should have been living in luxury while Koren trained properly as one of us. Instead, our lies and incompetence destroyed his life. He is going to be angry, Paedris. All the kind words I can offer will not change the harsh truth for him. If anyone has a suggestion for how I should handle an angry young wizard with unimaginable power, I would appreciate you speaking now."

Unsurprisingly, no one had a useful suggestion.

CHAPTER TWELVE

G rand General Magrane sat quietly, waiting patiently as the wizard from Ching-Do lay on a cot, her body twitching in motions that Magrane found uncomfortable to watch. Madam Chu's eyelids fluttered, and her fingers curled as if she were swimming, for in a way, she was swimming. Swimming through the air, in a world unseen. Her body was prone on a cot, in a tent surrounded by the Royal Army of Tarador, three miles east of the River Fasse in Anschulz province.

Her consciousness was in the spirit world, flying gently on the breeze on the other side of the river, above the vast enemy camp. With Magrane frantically rushing troops from other parts of Tarador to bolster the defensive line along the River Fasse in Anschulz, he needed information on the enemy's strength, intentions and timing. Magrane had sent spies across the river at night, but none of them had returned. Chu volunteered to investigate the enemy's preparation for an invasion, despite the risk that enemy wizards would intercept her in the spirit world, and sever her connection to her physical body. The other wizards had been divided about whether Chu should attempt the reconnaissance under such dangerous conditions. The risk to Chu Wing was substantial; so was the risk of remaining ignorant of when and how the enemy would attack. The only thing everyone could agree on was that the enemy would be coming across the River Fasse, and soon.

Her eyelids opened, and she blinked as her consciousness slowly returned to the real world.

"Madame Chu-" Magrane began to say.

"Shhh," the wizard from Indus cautioned. "Do not startle her, please."

"No, I am all right, Desai," Wing smiled, and stretched her arms above her head, then swung her legs over the side of the cot. "How long was I away?" One problem with being in the spirit world was the spirits had no sense of time; past, present and future were all the same to the spirits. It would be easy for an inexperienced or careless wizard to lose track of time in the spirit world, and be lost forever.

Magrane glanced at the hourglass on a table behind the cot. "Less than half a glass. Madame Chu, were you successful? What can you tell me?"

"Successful in spying on the enemy, without being detected? Yes, General, I was. The news I have for you, I am afraid, is not good. The enemy will cross the river, tomorrow or the next day, and their numbers are far greater than we can resist. Their commanders will send boats across the river in waves, until your defenses are overwhelmed, and they will gain a foothold on the eastern shore. The numbers of orcs and men they lose in securing a position on this side of the river is of no consequence to their commanders. I also can confirm that they have almost twice our number of wizards."

Her last remark did not surprise Magrane; it had long been known the enemy had more wizards than in the free world. The Wizards Council thought the demon at the heart of Acedor took people who showed even a hint of magical power, people who would never develop into true wizards elsewhere. The demon took people, and orcs, and fed his own essence into them, forcing them to contain magical power they were not capable of withstanding. The unnatural power twisted such unfortunates, burning them out from inside, but the demon cared nothing about what happened to his slaves. "We need Lord Salva here, with us," Magrane insisted.

"No," Chu disagreed. "Paedris must for now, remain in Linden, at the center of power. If the enemy were to strike there, we could lose everything. The enemy knows this. No, although Lord Salva's power could greatly help us here, he must remain in Linden at this time. You need to trust us about this, General."

"If, *when*, the enemy crosses the river here, we could also lose everything," Magrane declared. "Tomorrow or the next day, the enemy will cross the river? We are not ready. There are seven battalions still on their way to us. I must play for time. We will raid tonight." Magrane had been preparing a desperate plan for a surprise attack to disrupt the enemy's ability to cross the river. He was going to send a thousand soldiers across the river at night, to burn and otherwise destroy the boats the enemy had stacked close to the western shore of the river. Magrane had catapults and other siege devices throwing bombs filled with burning oil across the river, but the enemy's boats were stored just beyond the range of his most powerful weapons. The women and men of the raiding force were all volunteers, knowing most of them would not be returning safely to the eastern shore of the river. To the credit of the Royal Army, so many captains, lieutenants and sergeants had volunteered for the raid that Magrane had been forced to deny most of them the opportunity, pleading that he would need experienced leaders when the enemy inevitably did cross the river.

The raid would cost many lives, and would only delay, not stop, the enemy attack, but Magrane absolutely needed time to build up his defense force. If the Regent had not earlier denied his request to move troops down from LeVanne and to pull from army reserves deeper inside Tarador, he would be ready. He was not.

"No," Chu was emphatic in her response, cutting the air with a hand in a chopping gesture. "General, do not do that. Your raid will fail."

"The enemy will not be expecting *us* to cross the river in force," Magrane argued. "We can achieve strategic surprise, if we move tonight."

"You can get your people across the river, *if* we wizards are able to conceal them from the enemy long enough to get our boats in the river," Chu retorted. "Most of them will land on the opposite shore. They will die there, without accomplishing much to justify their sacrifice."

Magrane bit the inside of his lip to keep himself from harsh words he might later regret. Wizards sometimes could not appreciate how people living in what the general considered the 'real world' had to deal with situations. Situations that did not have a magical solution. Madame Chu was a foreigner, and Magrane knew little of Ching-Do. One thing he was sure of was that his counterpart in the army of Ching-Do could be just as frustrated in dealing with wizards as he was. "Madame Chu, we will lose people tonight. Good people, brave people. Their sacrifice will buy time for us to prepare for the invasion."

"General, I understand you need more time to build your strength here. I do not think sending a thousand soldiers on a raid is the best tactic."

"What do you have in mind?" Magrane asked skeptically.

"I will go, by myself, as soon as it is dark tonight. There will be heavy cloud cover tonight. If by midnight, I have not been successful, you may send your people across."

"What can one person do, alone?"

"One *wizard*, General. One wizard."

Madame Chu crossed the river by swimming, mostly letting the current carry her along. She wore leather outer garments to protect her from being chilled by the river water, which even in late summer was uncomfortably cool after a long exposure. She had ridden north along the east side of the river, going far enough to be above the enemy's camp, and went into the water after sunset. Two other wizards had enveloped her in a spell of concealment, although such spells did not work well, or long, in water. The spell worked well enough so that her gently swimming out into the current was not noticed by the enemy sentries on the far side of the river, and she had chosen a bend in the river where the strongest part of the current came close to the eastern shore. Her plan was to swim across the river, being careful not to splash the surface as she moved, and allow the current to carry her to another bend downriver, where the current came close to the western shore. In that regard, her plan had worked, although as she approached the bend in the river, she saw the land there was strongly garrisoned by orcs. The enemy knew that bend in the river, where the Fasse bent around a tall, rocky bluff, was a likely place for spies to come ashore. Chu was not overly alarmed, she swam close enough to the shore to be in the slack waters out of the center of the current, and floated slowly along, around the bend, coming ashore a quarter mile farther downriver from her original plan. It made no difference where she came ashore, so long as it was in the orc's sector of the enemy camp, and she was not seen.

Hiding behind a rock under an overhanging area of the bluff, where the river's spring floods had undercut the cliff above her, she stripped off the leather outer garments that had kept her warm in the water, and dressed in black clothes which she kept in a waterproof pouch. Before wrapping herself in a concealment spell, she warily sent out her senses, feeling for enemy wizards.

While enemy wizards often had considerable destructive power, their skills were often crude and their use of power easy to detect. Chu quickly found an enemy wizard, an orc, less than a mile from her. The orc was sending its senses across the river, attempting to see what General Magrane's army was doing. She smiled when she sensed the orc wizard's great frustration, for free wizards on the other side of the river were pushing back, blocking the orc wizard from seeing the raiding force that was gathered, awaiting orders to carry their flimsy assault boats forward.

Confident her use of magic would not be detected, Chu Wing drew a concealment around her, and headed off into the night, climbing the bluff. She only had two hours, she judged, before she needed to signal either success or failure. Failure would require Magrane to send nearly a thousand people to their deaths.

Madame Chu took a deep breath, and reached out to the spirit world to light the torches along the path. One after the other, the torches that had long burned out flared to life again, flickering with magical fire. When all the torches along the chosen route were alight, she reached out again, to snuff out the torches that lead the other way from the crossroads. As if one giant gust of wind had swept across the road, every one of those torches were snuffed out in the same instant.

Slowly, carefully, Wing removed her senses from the spirit world, standing still and calm to feel whether enemy wizards had noticed her use of magical power in their midst. No, none of the enemy reached out in alarm; their focus was across the river, trying to break the powerful concealment spell which enveloped the Royal Army camp.

Wing smiled to herself in the darkness. The concealment created by her fellow wizards on the east side of the river actually did not cloak anything important; its sole purpose was to draw the curiosity and focus of the enemy wizards. To the north of the camp, where the Royal Army raiding force awaited a signal to launch their boats into the river, there was only a weak concealment, but a concealment that not yet been detected by the enemy. With enemy wizards concentrating their power on penetrating the concealment that truly did not conceal anything, the raiding force had so far gone unnoticed.

Satisfied her presence on the west side of the river also had not been noticed, she turned her attention back to the crossroads. The road from the northwest split there, with one road going north into the heart of the camp that was set aside only for orcs. The other road lead south, crossing an area that had been designated as a buffer between the orcs and the men. The road to the south used to have a barrier across it, blocking passage in that direction. That barrier, consisting of tangled tree roots, thorns and sharpened spikes, had been rolled aside by Wing, and she had the cuts and scratches to prove it. Calling on the power of the spirits to help her move the heavy barrier had been her greatest risk that night; use of that power was the most likely to attract the attention of the enemy.

With the barrier out of the way, Wing used branches to sweep away remaining debris from the dirt road. Her last preparation was to weave an illusion to block view of the road to the north.

With the illusion securely in place, the crossroads was no longer a crossroads, it was merely an ordinary spot along the road which had been designated for use by orcs.

When Wing had overflown the enemy camp in the spirit world, one thing she had seen was a battalion of orcs marching down the road from the northwest. To prevent fighting between orcs and men, the enemy commanders had kept some of the orcs away from the river until they were needed. Seeing that battalion of orcs on the march toward the riverbank had been one piece of evidence telling Wing the enemy would soon cross the river.

The orcs were now close, the front ranks of the battalion less than a mile from her. She hid behind a gnarled and stunted tree as the torches of the orcs drew near. The enemy commanders had placed four orcs at the crossroads, to guide the incoming battalion and make certain they did not mistakenly wander off course to the south. Those four orcs were now sleeping, having been ensorcelled by Wing, and dragged into a ditch away from the road.

As the orcs reached the crossroads, Madame Chu had to concentrate to maintain the illusion that blocked sight of the road to the north. This was the critical moment; once the orcs in the lead were past, the rest of the column would follow without question. The orcs in the column were weary, she knew; they had been on the march almost the entire day, with little rest. Most of the orcs trudged along, heads down, following the rank in front of them.

Wing unconsciously held her breath as the battalion leaders reached her; orcs mounted on dirty and rough-looking horses. Not one of them even hesitated, nor looked around them. There was no reason to question where they were. The leaders had been told to follow torches on the road, until they reached a crossroads, where guides would direct them to the battalion's designated part of the orc camp. They saw no crossroads, what they did see was a line of torches glowing brightly in front of them, a chain of torchlight leading toward the fires and tents of a camp in the distance.

The column of orcs continued past her, tramping in bad humor through the night. All the orcs wanted was to reach their destination, set up camp, and sleep. They cared nothing about larger issues of strategy; all they knew was that they would soon be crossing the river, and many of them would die in the attempt. Many more would die fighting inside Tarador, pushing into the heart of that country, until they surrounded the capital and laid siege to it. Victory was inevitable.

Wing was careful to maintain her concentration, yet she risked peeking around the tree, looking toward the south. There were signs of movement in the camp of men the orcs were unwittingly marching toward. No doubt the men were alarmed by the large force bearing down on them from the north, from the direction of orc camp.

An alarm rang in the men's camp. Orcs! Orcs were approaching, orcs were attacking! Men scrambled to gather weapons.

What should have happened was scouts riding out, to determine why the orcs were approaching, along a road that was supposed to be blocked. The scouts should have contacted the orc commanders, and warned them away from the camp of men.

What happened instead, because the men of Acedor hated and feared orcs far more than they hated and feared Tarador, was a volley of arrows flying through the air.

The leaders of the orc battalion had slowed their march, beginning to nervously talk among themselves, wondering whether they had somehow gotten off course. Some of them had noticed they were marching south, not north, and the camp ahead of them smelled distinctly of men, not the sour yet familiar stink of their fellow orcs. The leaders were considering calling a halt to their march, when arrows began raining down on the leaders and the front rank of the column.

Madame Chu did only one more thing against the enemy that night. She reached out to send a wave of fear through the men in the camp, making them terrified that the orcs were attacking. To the orcs, she washed over them a mixture of anger and betrayal. Without any orders, for their leaders now had no control of the soldiers on either side, a battle soon raged in the enemy army. Orcs at the rear of the column rushed forward when they heard their fellows up front were being slaughtered by men. Horns sounded, attracting the attention of orcs in their camp to the north, and soon several disorganized companies of orcs were crossing the zone toward the camp of men. All the orcs involved were seeking to protect their own kind and get revenge on men for their cowardly betrayal. In truth, that was merely an excuse, for orcs hated all of mankind. They did not need an excuse to kill men, only opportunity.

For their part, the men of the enemy rushed forward to stop the sneak attack by orcs, and more and more men joined the battle, pulling in units from deep inside the encampment. In less than half an hour, a full-scale battle raged within the enemy camp, involving thousands. No amount of effort by commanders and wizards could stop the fighting. It was not until mid-morning of the following day that the fighting came under control, with only small groups that found themselves outside of their designated camp areas still actively fighting. The damage had been done; thousands of the enemy lay dead, with more injured, and all the effort their commanders had put into organizing units for the invasion was squandered. It would take several days simply to get men and orcs back with their own units. In the confusion of the battle, many of the collapsible boats had been damaged or burned; boats would need to be constructed to replace the ones lost, requiring materials to be brought in from elsewhere inside Acedor. Because the invasion could not be delayed long enough to replace all the boats, Acedor would cross the river with far less men and orcs than had been planned. This smaller force would leave their flanks open for counterattack by the Royal Army of Tarador, but there was no choice. The demon at the heart of Acedor would allow no significant delay.

For her part, Madame Chu sent a message of success through the spirit world to the other side of the river, to prevent Magrane from launching his planned raid. She then slipped back through the warring camp unseen, down to the river. Once there, the sounds of the battle provided cover as she donned her outer leather clothing again and dove into the water, swimming strongly, no longer caring much that she might be seen.

She was eating the finest breakfast General Magrane's cooks could provide, when the general himself came in to congratulate her. Magrane had spent the last hour atop a hill, observing with elated amazement the utter chaos on the enemy's side through a spyglass, and enjoying himself immensely. "Madame Chu," he bowed deeply in respect. Then, a twinkle in his eyes, he plopped himself in a chair across from the wizard of Ching-Do, and plucked a crisp piece of bacon from her plate. "Would you care to tell me how *one* wizard, who I believe I could lift with one arm," he referenced Chu Wing's willowy frame, "destroyed a good portion of the enemy's army?"

"It was," Wing pulled her plate into her lap protectively, "a wizard trick," she winked in good nature.

"Ah," Magrane nodded. "You will tell me, someday?"

"Someday," Wing winked back, a twinkle of mirth in her own eyes. "It is not difficult to get two poisonous snakes to fight each other; you only need to put them together."

"How much time have you gained for us, do you think?" Magrane asked, while holding up a mug for coffee. "I know I am asking you to make an educated guess."

"A few days, no more," She replied. Seeing the look of disappointment that flashed across the general's face, she hastened to reassure him. "The enemy commanders know their demon lord will not accept excuses for a delay. They will come across the river, within four days at the most, I judge. They will come across with far fewer numbers, and far less ability to reinforce their gains after they land."

Magrane stroked his beard. "Madame Chu, I am greatly in your debt. That is a better result, a result far more advantageous to us than a longer delay. A weak enemy force coming across the river soon is better for us than a strong force later." He stood up and bowed deeply again. "Forgive my abruptness, Madame Chu, I must discuss this development with my captains." Already, possibilities were swirling in his head. Possibilities of victory. The greatest difficulty facing him was not the weakness or unreadiness of his army, nor the power of the vast host across the river.

The greatest obstacle to victory was the current Regent of Tarador. Grand General Magrane could not let this incredible opportunity pass by. He might need to do something about his nation's leadership. Something desperate.

Even if such action could be considered treason.

Walking through the woods was indeed a good idea, at first. It wasn't the first time Koren had been on his own, making his way through a trackless wilderness, and this time he had with him everything needed to assure his survival. Skills acquired as a boy around Crebbs Ford had not faded, and he now had experience to guide him. As he had done the first time, he sought to avoid contact with any other people. The first time he had walked alone, he skirted farm fields and villages, and his purpose in avoiding people was his fear that they would recognize him as a dangerous jinx. Now he was in a wilderness that had no farms, no villages; no areas of peaceable habitation he could easily find and walk around. Here, the only inhabitants of the forest would be wild animals, bandits and perhaps roving bands of orcs. Bandits and orcs would seek to conceal their presence, making it difficult for Koren to avoid what he could not see. He carefully chose places to sleep each night; well-hidden but with escape routes so he would not be trapped. He ate his food cold, because he could not afford to light a fire and have drifting wood smoke attract unwanted attention. And he paused often to listen for unnatural sounds in the deep, quiet woods. Twice, he saw signs that small groups had camped in the wilderness; old firepits, flattened underbrush, bones of animals that had been cooked and eaten. And, next to a log near one of the campsites, he found a small gold ring. Bandits, he thought with unexpected relief. While bandits were trouble, they were much to be preferred to orcs. A gang of bandits could be discouraged by a few well-aimed arrows; they would decide that attempting to rob a well-armed lone traveler was not worth risking their lives. Orcs, on the other hand, would likely be enraged if Koren hit a couple of their band with arrows. If he encountered orcs, he would need to run for his life; they would not give up their pursuit until they were certain they had lost his trail. Seeing that the old campsite belonged to mere bandits made Koren shudder with relief.

Bandits in the area had robbed travelers, and a sleepy or drunk or simply careless bandit had likely dropped a stolen ring. Koren examined the ring, it had no markings to identify the previous owner. He put the ring in his pocket; it did no good to anyone buried under a pile of decaying leaves in the wilderness, and he could use the money he could get from selling it. His journey to and through the dwarf lands might use up all the coins in his pouch. He might even need to pay a dwarf wizard to remove the spells Paedris had cast on him. And, whether he received help from the dwarves or not, he would later need to-

To what? What was he going to do after he left the dwarves? Where was he going to go? He could not stay there in the forbidding mountains of the north; not without permission from the dwarves, and they guarded their borders dearly. The realization that he had not given any thought to what he should do after visiting the dwarves saddened him, and he sat on a log by the old firepit for a long time. Nothing had changed, really. He still did not belong anywhere. He was still hunted by the Royal Army. He was still a dangerous jinx; the pirate ship finding the *Lady Hildegard* after a stormy night had proven that.

Then, he heard his father's voice in his head, chiding him, and he got to his feet. There was no point to feeling sorry for himself, he needed to move on. Not having future plans at the time was not a problem; he could not make plans until he knew whether a dwarf wizard could or would help him. If a dwarf wizard could remove his jinx curse, then he could seek to live a normal life among people, somewhere. He would have a future, and make plans for it. Maybe he would go back to sea, to the South Islands. He left the old bandit campsite behind and resumed walking northwest.

For a short time, he resumed walking northwest. The trouble with deciding to walk through an uninhabited, trackless wilderness is that there was a good reason those woods had few roads, and no farms or villages. And a reason why the people of Tunbridge had advised him against what he was doing. The woods ahead of him were becoming a marsh or swamp. At first, he had carefully picked his way through, trying to stay on the patchy high ground, but then the ground became more water than land. The trees became a mass of tangled branches, with many fallen trees block-ing his path. After two frustrating hours, he gave up, and turned back, cursing his own arrogance. The people in Tunbridge had known that the old royal road was the only route to the west from their village; yet he had foolishly assumed he was such a skilled backwoodsman that he could find a way through.

He followed the eastern edge of the swamp south, wary of encountering bandits. The area was not, in fact, entirely trackless; he found many paths created by deer or other wild inhabitants, and even though some of them led in the direction he wanted to go, he avoided walking along them. Bandits walking in the area were likely to choose the easiest path, so Koren must find his own way through the woods. Which became increasingly difficult; the trees were becoming gnarled and grew thickly together, their low-growing branches tangled together so that he had to bend them aside, or hack at them with his sword. Walking though the damp ground was so slow that the sun had nearly set when he saw the road ahead of him. At first, the road was merely a faint line of spotty gaps in the dense tree canopy. Cautiously, he stepped out into the road, which he saw was more of an overgrown farm track than the well-maintained royal roads he was accustomed to. Grass, weeds and even small sapling grew where the road had been cut; only two muddy lines of flattened grass marked where wagon wheels had passed by. From the eroded edges of the wheel marks, Koren guessed no wagon had traveled the road in a week, perhaps more if rain had fallen recently. Seeing the neglected condition of the road made Koren fear that he was truly alone in the wilderness, and that no guards from the Duke, nor sheriff of the local baron were providing any trace of security for travelers in the lonely woods. But seeing signs that few wagons dared use the road gave Koren hope that the road ahead was unlikely to be closely watched by bandits. Thieves who lurked by roads relied on a steady traffic of cargo and travelers they could rob; no bandits were going to wait long in an area that was devoid of targets for their predations.

Satisfied, Koren walked across the road to check whether the forest there was easier to walk through, but it was just as tangled as the woods to the north. He found a reasonable dry place, and settled in for the night, chewing on hard cheese and bread that was tough as leather. He had eaten worse.

In the morning, what he had hoped would look better in the light of day was not. The previous evening, the road had appeared forbidding, with dark, gnarled trees overhanging the grassy track. It appeared even worse that morning, for the direct light of the morning sun showed details he had not seen at sunset. Here along the road, not only did entangled tree branches weave a thick barrier on both sides, but also vines seeking sunlight surrounded the gap created by the road cut. Vines that had thorns, or that Koren recognized as having sap that could raise itchy blisters on the skin of anyone who touched the vine or its leaves. He needed to be careful, for if bandits did attack, he would not have the option of dashing off quickly to one side of the road or the other. Fortunately, the woodsman in him recognized that the impassibly thick underbrush also meant bandits could not simply hide behind trees next to the road; they would have needed to cut a path into the woods. He would look for curled or discolored leaves where cut vegetation was being used as concealment.

Before setting out, he took time to sharpen the sword that had become dull from hacking away branches the day before. And he tucked away his money pouch in a boot, and once again checked his arrows. He would leave the sword on his belt, and carry the bow with an arrow at the ready. Then there was nothing else to do but begin walking. "Aye, Koren," he mumbled to himself. "If Alfonze could see me now, he'd name me a fool, and be right of it."

The morning was lonely walking, which suited Koren just fine. After an hour or so, he began to get numb to his fear, and slightly relaxed his grip on the bow. Then the road became worse; going through a swampy area where parts of the road were submerged up to his ankles in black, stinking, chilly water. When the royal engineers had built the road, ages ago, they had built up the surface, and provided culverts for drainage. Over time, the stone and soil under the road had become compacted, and the formerly neat edges eroded away. Culverts collapsed or were clogged with debris, or choked with the greedy roots of trees. Now parts of the road were barely above the surrounding swamp, and Koren's boots slipped in the muck. This, he knew, would be an excellent place for bandits to stage an ambush, for heavily-laden wagons would be especially slow and clumsy. Horses pulling wagons could not get firm traction in the mud beneath their hooves, and wagon wheels would sink into the mire, making the wagon difficult to pull. He could see signs that wagons had become stuck at that part of the road; stacked next to the road were trees cut and split into planks, to be placed under the sinking wheels of wagons.

And, worse, he found arrowheads embedded in trees. There had been a battle here, likely more than one over the years. None of the arrowheads was fresh; the scars they'd made in the trees had healed, bark had grown partly over the offending once-sharp and now rusted steel. His grip on the bow tightened nonetheless when he saw signs of battles with bandits. And his grip tightened again when he saw the broken piece of an orc blade embedded in a tree stump. The crude orc-made metal was rusted, dented and old, but seeing it chilled him. If he were ambushed by orcs here, he did not know where he could flee, other than into the inhospitable swamp.

The swamp went on for two miles, during which Koren's shoes became thoroughly soaked through with filthy water, then the land rose, and boulders appeared scattered amongst the trees. Some of the rocks were gigantic, large enough that the formerly mostly straight road began to weave back and forth to avoid them. The long-ago team of royal engineers had decided not to waste tremendous effort to move rocks that could weigh more than any team of oxen could move.

Wizards could have split the rocks, but with so many of them littering the landscape, that effort would also have been wasted.

Ahead of him, the road went between two particularly large rocks, and Koren could not see a practical way around. Rocks, large and small, choked the land, and trees grew thickly and tangled over and between them

This, he thought as he looked at the gap between rocks, was an excellent place for an ambush! Partly to still his shaking hands, he fitted an arrow to the bow, and held it ready. Taking a moment to calm himself with deep breaths, he listened in between breaths. It would be best, he told himself, to run straight through the gap, hopefully catch any bandits unready for a lone traveler on foot. Koren tensed himself to run, and-

Froze in place. There was a slow, rhythmic sound. A horse. There was a horse ahead of him, coming toward him. There was only one horse, moving at a trot. Another lone traveler, although one fortunate to have a horse?

Or bandits, only one of whom rode? Looking behind him, Koren did not see a good place to hide, so he turned and ran back to hide as best he could behind a rock to the north of the road. He had to kneel in muddy water to crouch down enough, and as the unseen horse neared the two rocks ahead, he could hear the hoofbeats slow to a walk. Then stop, then resume a slow walk.

Knowing he was being foolhardy, Koren could not resist sticking his head up over the rock to see who was coming along the road. He set the bow down and yanked a small bush out of the ground, using it as a screen to cover his face. There was a shadow of a horse on one of the rocks, a shadow of a riderless horse, and-

"*Thunderbolt?*" Koren exclaimed, so surprised that he lost his grip on the rock and fell backwards to sit in the chilly mud.

Thunderbolt was the last thing he expected to see, in the middle of nowhere, so far from Linden. As Koren slipped trying to get up from the mud, the horse snorted with delight, and darted around the rock to nuzzle Koren's face. "All right! All right!" Koren laughed. "Let me get up, you crazy horse!" As he got to his knees in the mud, Thunderbolt's uncontained enthusiasm caused the horse's muzzle to hit Koren under the chin, and he fell backwards. "You crazy horse!" Koren found that he could not be mad at Thunderbolt. The delighted horse was scampering with joy. To forestall being knocked to the ground again, Koren reached up and grabbed hold of the horse's mane, using it to pull himself up. He hugged the horse fiercely, thumping his great back over and over. Finally, he stepped back and looked at what he still could barely believe; his horse. Thunderbolt's mane and tail were tangled, with burrs and leaves stuck deeply into the black strands. His coat was dirty, with scratches on his head, chest and flanks; Koren found three rose thorns embedded, and carefully worked them out. And the great horse's ribs were showing; he had not been fed properly. From his pack, Koren took out the rough travel bread, broke it into pieces and fed it to the hungry animal. "Where have you been?" He asked as the horse gobbled up the last of the bread and stuck his nose in Koren's pocket. "How did you get here?"

Koren walked into the middle of the road to peer between the two huge boulders to the west, while Thunderbolt happily ate grass that grew in the roadway. Holding onto the hilt of his sword, he walked between the two giant rocks, and saw that the road beyond was empty. "How did you get here?" He asked again, amazed. When he first saw Thunderbolt, he had assumed the horse was with soldiers. But there was no one in sight, and considering the horse's condition, no one had cared for Thunderbolt along the journey from, from where? Had the horse come all the way from Linden? On his own? That did not seem possible.

And, Koren considered, sitting on a rock as Thunderbolt tore clumps of grass out of the roadway, how had Thunderbolt found him? In the middle of nowhere? Found Koren, in a place that Koren himself had not intended to be. Something very strange was going on, something Koren could not imagine an explanation for. He walked back and carefully inspected the horse's legs for injury; other than scratches and mud, Thunderbolt's legs seemed fine, and the horse walked without a limp. Not willing to take a risk with the horse's health, Koren decided he would walk, until he could be sure the horse could bear his weight.

Thunderbolt had other ideas. Koren walked beside the horse, until Thunderbolt annoyed him so much by bumping Koren with his great head that Koren walked ahead. And then Thunderbolt nipped Koren's butt. "Ow!" Koren shouted, rubbing his pants. "That hurt! What do you want?"

Thunderbolt stood in the road and snorted, then knelt with his front legs.

"You want me to ride you?" Koren asked.

The horse tossed its head and whinnied happily.

"All right, you win, we'll try this. Get back up, you look ridiculous on your knees." With the horse standing again, Koren took firm hold of its mane, and swung onto its back. "Easy, easy," he pulled on the mane as Thunderbolt broke into happy, bouncing gallop. "Let's try walking first. You do that, and I'll get these tangles out of your mane." The horse looked back at him with one eye, and Koren swore the horse was saying that it did not care about whether his mane was properly groomed. With a heavy snort, he fell into an easy trot, and Koren settled comfortably on the horse's back, picking at the burrs embedded in Thunderbolt's once glossy mane. "Oh, forget it," he exclaimed after getting one burr loose. "This is a mess."

Riding Thunderbolt had the advantage of speed and being able to cover more ground in a day; in the wilderness Koren found himself in it had the disadvantage that any bandits or orcs could hear the horse coming. On foot, Koren could have walked very quietly, and had the possibility of hacking away the underbrush and dodging off the road if he were attacked. On the horse, Thunderbolt presented a large target for an arrow, and so Koren held his bow and kept an arrow nocked. Roughly every half mile, he halted Thunderbolt and listened carefully, while the horse lifted its great head and sniffed the air. Koren startled at every sound, and flinched at every strange shadow. Twice that day, they came across old, broken-down wagons that had been attacked by bandits. Or, judging by the crude arrowheads embedded in the wood, by orcs.

Wherever the bandits or packs of orcs were, Koren did not see them. By late afternoon, his nerves were so rattled, he imagined that he was seeing and hearing dangers that did not exist. He didn't fear for his own life; Koren was supremely confident in his wizard-spelled speed and skill with weapons. He was afraid for Thunderbolt. The big horse would be an easy target for arrows, and Koren could not be sure to protect the animal. When they came to a clearing and Koren saw the roof of a barn, he breathed a sigh of relief.

Then he caught his breath again. What he had at first thought was a farm field had been a farm field, long ago. Now it was a meadow, overgrown with shrubs and saplings. The barn's roof had partly fallen in, and as they rode up the weed-choked lane, he saw the farmhouse had burned to the ground. No one had lived there in a long time.

They came across four other farms like the first one. Thunderbolt found tasty hay to eat, and Koren collected a hat full of juicy berries. Just beyond the farms was the north-south royal road that was Koren's destination, and he was disappointed. The north-south road was reasonably well maintained, certainly better than the grass-covered almost abandoned east-west lane he had been following. At the crossroads there had once been an inn and a stable, both burned to ashes years before. Trees grew up through the ruins of the inn; Koren poked around the ruins near the stone fireplace, finding only broken crockery and rusted metal. As it was growing dark, he led the horse back to one of the abandoned farms, and they settled into the corner of barn that still had half of its roof intact. His sleep was restless, and every time he opened his eyes, he looked at the contentedly sleeping horse. How had Thunderbolt found him, in the trackless wilderness? And why was the horse alone?

CHAPTER THIRTEEN

As the crown princess, Ariana had few official duties. Mostly her role was to avoid dying, until she became queen and had actual power. Sitting idle or spending all day with tutors did not provide an outlet for her energies, and did not prepare her for the daily responsibilities she would fulfill once she wore the crown of the monarch. Ariana had made her own duties that she attended to regularly; one of those activities was an almost daily visit to the royal hospital. There were times when her mother kept her busy with tasks the princess deemed of less importance so that she was not able to get to the hospital. And there were times when the physicians of the hospital requested she stay away; when an infection was raging uncontained and the hospital staff feared the crown princess becoming ill. Other than those times, Ariana tried to visit the hospital every day.

Some of the physicians welcomed the arrival of their princess, saying that her mere presence and attention helped sick people to heal faster. Other physicians, although polite, clearly thought royalty walking through the halls was a distraction, and took time away from actual medical treatment.

On that day, Ariana made her rounds, stopping to talk with the sick and the injured, offering words of encouragement. She remembered almost everyone's name, and tried to remember whatever they told her; names of family members, where they were from. Anything to offer good cheer and alleviate pain, even for a moment. The royal hospital was especially busy that week, having to absorb overflow from the Royal Army hospital that was outside the walls of the castle. She visited that hospital several times a month, but the royal hospital now had many more soldiers than she had ever seen there. There were beds set up even in hallways, with people awaiting care. "Excuse me," she whispered to a harried nurse. "Are we able to care for all these people?"

"As best we can, Your Highness," the nurse answered as she edged away with an armful of clean linen. "The physicians are working too many hours, but the real problem is we lack wizards with the power to heal."

"I understand," Ariana said sadly. There were not enough wizards in the realm to begin with, and now many of them were at the western border with the Royal Army. Shomas Feany was a skilled healer, unfortunately Paedris had sent Lord Feany on some urgent errand up north. Paedris himself did what he could at the hospital, and his pleas for help had brought in three wizards. None of the three new wizards had any particular skill with the healing arts. "Is there anything I can do?"

Annoyance flashed across the nurse's face, before she remembered who she was speaking with. No one wished the crown princess to actually do anything around the hospital; carrying laundry, washing floors. And certainly none of the nurses or physicians wanted Ariana touching the patients. Mostly, they wanted her to cheer up any patients she could, see how hard the hospital staff were working, and go away quickly. "No, Your Highness, we have plenty of help," she pointed to the volunteers, mostly drawn from the ranks of Royal Army families.

Ariana took the hint. "Very well. I shall walk the halls, and let you go back to your duties." She ducked her head in the various side halls, checking whether it would be all right for her to enter. In many halls, she saw the physicians were busy, or the patients were all resting. In other halls, the patients welcomed their future queen; many of them were used to seeing her every day.

A soldier, new to the hospital, tried to rise from his bed and stand when he saw the princess. He stumbled and nearly fell on the floor; Ariana had to help him back in bed, and nurses rushed over to politely shoo her away. The soldier was not letting them. "Highness," he said in a voice so strained it was barely a whisper, "we did our best."

"I know," Ariana assured the man, kneeling by the bed as the nurses adjusted the dressing on his wounds. He apparently had suffered injuries to his left leg, left arm, shoulder and there was a bandage around his throat and the left side of his face. "Shh, shh, don't try to talk."

"It was orcs," the man explained, and Ariana had to lean toward him to hear his words. "There were too many of them, we couldn't hold. The general wanted us to hit them first, before they built up their strength, but we were not allowed to attack." His voice faded, and he jerked, as if he'd fallen briefly asleep and awakened suddenly. "Oh, princess. Your Highness," he seemed startled to see her. "We should have attacked. In Winterthur. The orcs were encamped just across the border. We could have hit them at night, and scattered them to the winds, but the general said we were not allowed to attack. When they came across at us, they were too many."

"You did well," Ariana murmured, as the man's eyes closed again, his head rolled to the side and he fell asleep. She knew of that battle in Winterthur, and she knew the man was right. The Royal Army should have been free to raid across the border into Acedor, while the orcs were assembling to launch a raid. Instead, the local Royal Army commander had been forced to wait, because the Regent of Tarador forbade any crossing of the border. The Regent of Tarador. Ariana's mother.

"How is he?" Ariana quietly asked a nurse.

"Well, Your Highness. Lord Salva was here last night, he is hopeful for a full recovery." The nurse looked sadly down the ranks of beds. "I wish I could say that about all of them."

Ariana completed her visit in that hall, and was in the corridor, when there was a wailing and crying that attracted her attention. A young girl, perhaps five or six years of age, burst from a doorway, sobbing. She ran right at the princess, and clutched her arms around Ariana's legs. Her two guards moved forward, and Ariana waved them back. Dropping to her knees, Ariana hugged the girl. "What is wrong, little one?"

Between sobs, the girl managed to say that her father, a soldier had just died. As the girl cried and Ariana held her, two nurses came through the door into the corridor, carrying a stretcher with a sheet covering the body. Behind them was a woman carrying a baby, her eyes red from crying. When the girl saw her mother, she released the princess and ran to her mother.

"I am sorry for your loss," Ariana said simply. The words sounded hollow to her. "Your husband was a soldier?"

"Yes," the woman held her baby close to her. "Thank you, Your Highness." And she walked slowly away, following the body of her husband.

A soldier, on crutches because of a broken leg, came to the doorway. "Arlan was a good one, Your Highness," he said of the dead man. "Took an orc arrow in Winterthur, and he never recovered. The orcs poison their arrows, or they are just covered in filth. Saved my life, Arlan did, before he went down with two arrows in him."

"An honorable man."

The soldier straightened up, and for a moment, the look on his face was anything but friendly. "Honor. Aye, he was honorable. Much more so than our Regent. I'd like to-" As Ariana's guards stepped forward, hands on the hilt of their swords, the soldier remembered who he was speaking with. On crutches, he managed a short bow. "Forgive me, Your Highness. I am tired, is all."

"You have no need to apologize," Ariana assured him. "Is there anything I can do for you?"

Her words restored the soldier's resolve. He lowered his voice to a whisper. "If you could talk sense into your mother's head, yes. Otherwise," he looked back at the ranks of injured laying on beds, "there will be many more of us here, and no gain for it."

The telegraph message was in code, but everyone in Linden could tell it was of extreme importance, based on the flags indicating the urgency assigned to the incoming message. The message was also quite lengthy, taking nearly half an hour to be received. The initial message was followed by others, and all other messages were halted. Despite the secrecy intended, news of the enemy's victory in forcing a crossing of the River Fasse had reached the farthest corners of Linden within two hours. Captain Earwood of the Royal Army requested a meeting with the Regent; he was forced to wait, growing ever more anxious. Finally, as night was falling, the Lady Carlana consented to speak with him.

Earwood bowed properly to his nation's leader, or a near to a leader as Tarador had at the moment. "Your Highness."

Carlana waved him in, and Earwood quickly unrolled a map, showing that the enemy forces were now across the River Fasse, and had now begun to push eastward in force. General Magrane had pulled back the Royal Army toward the north and south along the Fasse, leaving only a thin force in the center to face the enemy. "Highness, the enemy is still consolidating their position east of the Fasse. They are yet vulnerable, and General Magrane's plan is to allow the enemy to send more troops across the Fasse for another day. Then," Earwood used his hands to show the imaginary action on the map, "we will strike against the enemy, along the river. Our counterattack will cut the enemy force in two pieces, one on each side of the river. Then, we will only have to fight the enemy that are trapped on our side of the border. We can-"

"No." Carlana turned away from the table, ignoring the map. "Tell me, Captain Earwood, for this counterattack, General Magrane will need to throw his entire force into the battle? He will need to attack north and south along the Fasse, and support a blocking force to the east?"

"Yes, Your Highness." Earwood thought the tactics of a counterattack were fairly obvious. "The enemy will be blocked from marching farther east, while the army will strike along the Fasse. With the River Fasse at their backs, the enemy will be trapped, unless they can manage to get part of their force back across the river. It is unlikely they could manage to save more than a small part of their force; they do not have enough boats."

"And if the counterattack fails, what force will be available to prevent the enemy from marching east, crossing the Tormel and into the heart of Tarador?"

"Very little, Your Highness," Earwood had to admit. "But-"

"It took the enemy over three years to cross the River Fasse, after they established a substantial force there," Carlana observed with disdain. "Surely General Magrane could hold the enemy at our second defensive line along the Tormel river until winter? A mere few months, rather than three years? Holding the Tormel will give us time to strengthen our defenses there by springtime."

Earwood winced. "Ma'am, our defenses along the Tormel cannot be compared to those of the Fasse. It is not certain the enemy will halt their offensive until after the winter. General Magrane believes, strongly believes, that a counterattack now, here," he stabbed an index finger at the map, "now, is our best chance to-"

"No." The Regent ended further discussion with a gesture, sweeping the edge of the map, and it rolled back up. "Captain Earwood, there will be no foolish adventures which risk our army. No dubious tactics that squander our remaining strength. I am certain that General Magrane would prefer to lead a glorious charge, rather than garrison his forces in dull defensive duty along the Tormel. General Magrane failed to hold the enemy at the Fasse, despite my giving him all the resources he requested, and more."

Earwood held his tongue. It was true that the Regent had provided troops and supplies to the Royal Army at the Fasse; what she had not done was allow Magrane freedom to use his army in the best manner. Knowing anything he said would only anger the Regent, he remained silent.

Carlana made a cutting motion with one hand. "I will order General Magrane to pull back across the Tormel river. We shall see whether he fails again."

Ariana did not sleep well that night, or sleep much at all. Her sleep had been interrupted by thoughts of the soldier who had died in the hospital, and his grieving family. She wanted to do something for that family, and in the middle of the night she had gone through her jewelry to find a gem to give. In the cold light of morning, she considered that it would be unfair to help the family of one soldier, when there were so many families in need. That was why she arose even before her maids came in to wake her, and why she had gathered much of her jewelry in a leather sack. That day, she was going to give the jewelry to Kallron, for him to sell as discretely as possible. The money would be given to the families of Royal Army soldiers who had died in battle. How that would work, she was not exactly sure; Kallron would surely know how to distribute the money.

It was frustrating to Ariana that only a small part of the fancy jewels she wore every day were actually her property. Most of the jewels were legally property of the state; as a princess Ariana had no right to sell them, or give them away. That is something she intended to change when she became queen. If she lived that long. If there was still a Tarador on her sixteenth birthday. The blunt words of the soldier on crutches had been absolutely correct; Ariana's mother was leading Tarador to ruin, and the sacrifices of brave soldiers were for nothing.

The present situation could not continue. Ariana needed to do something.

She picked at her breakfast in the study by the window, eating it more because she did not want to insult the cooks who prepared the food, or the maids who brought it to her. When she was about to push the plate away because she couldn't stomach the thought of another bite, her maid Nurelka came into the room and curtsied. "Your Highness, there is an army captain here to see you. I told him to make an appointment through Master Kallron, but this captain insisted it is extremely urgent."

Ariana looked down in dismay at her clothes; she was not dressed to receive visitors. If an army captain said a matter was urgent, she could not delay. "Send him in, Nurry."

The army captain strode into the room and dropped to one knee. "Thank you for receiving me, Your Highness."

"Captain," she struggled to remember the man's name. He was a rugged man with long black hair and an angry scar on the forearm of his sword arm; the old injury did not lessen his skill with sword nor bow. He was trusted by Grand General Magrane to act as the general's liaison when Magrane was away from Linden. As a captain, he could move around the castle with less notice than one of the army's generals could. She remembered the man's name. "Captain Earwood, rise, please. Sit down. Have you eaten this morning?" As she said it, Ariana mentally kicked herself for asking such a silly question. Of course the army rose early and took their breakfast early.

Earwood sat hesitantly, perched on the edge of the chair. "Yes, Highness, I ate in the barracks. Could we," he looked meaningfully at Nurelka and the two other maids. "Speak in confidence?"

As the crown princess, Ariana was supposed to avoid being alone with men, to keep up appearances. "Nurry, would you select an outfit for me to wear today?"

"Yes, ma'am," Nurelka knew from long experience that meant the princess wished to speak privately. She gestured for the other two maids to leave the study and close the door; Nurelka went into the back of the room-sized closet where she was far enough away not to overhear what was being said.

"Captain Earwood," Ariana said in a low voice, "what news from the border?" She had heard rumors the previous night.

The captain shook his head slowly. "It is not good, Highness. It is a disaster. The army has regrouped, and General Magrane was preparing a counterattack on the enemy's flanks along the River Fasse; to hit them before they have the bulk of their forces across the river. Yesterday, when Magrane requested permission to strike, your mother ordered him instead to pull the defensive line back forty miles, to the east bank of the Tormel river." Earwood took a deep breath. "As I am sure you are aware, the land in that part of Anschulz is flat and open, mostly farmland. There are few natural barriers to the enemy's advance, and a rearguard action while our forces pull back would be costly. And achieve little. The River Fasse is deep and wide, with bluffs on both sides. The Tormel is shallow; this time of year there are places where horses can wade across. That river is not suitable to a strong defensive line, and we have not invested in fortifications there as we did along the east bank of the Fasse. Your mother, I mean, the Regent, ordered General Magrane to hold at the Tormel until winter. Her hope is that winter will halt the enemy's advance." His face was bleak, his eyes searching her face to see her reaction. "General Magrane believes the winter conditions in central Tarador cannot be relied upon to halt the enemy's advance. If, when, the enemy crosses the Tormel, they will be in mostly flat, open country all the way here to Linden."

"You wish me to speak to my mother for you?" Ariana asked skeptically. Her mother had not listened to Ariana's advice in the past, and they were not speaking at all now. The princess was not even sure her mother would respond to a request for a meeting.

Captain Earwood shook his head. "I fear the time for that is past, Highness. General Magrane was able to persuade the Regent to transfer part of the army reserves from Rellanon; they will be on the march toward the Tormel line today or tomorrow. In order to," Earwood hesitated, "avoid clogging roads across Anschulz, some of the reserves will be passing through Linden within the next three days." He looked her directly in the eyes and lowered his voice further. "At that time, there will be almost a thousand Royal Army soldiers close to the capital."

Ariana felt like she could not breathe. What General Magrane had planned was a coup; to use the army reserves to seize Linden and lay siege to the royal castle. Ariana thought it very unlikely the coup attempt could succeed; the royal guards who controlled the castle would be on high alert when the army passed through Linden. Magrane must be truly desperate to plan such a treasonous action. And desperate to send a trusted captain to reveal his plans to the crown princess. "I see," she said in a voice that could barely be heard. "Does General Magrane wish me to, to review the troops as they pass by?"

Earwood's shoulders relaxed almost imperceptibly. The moment when the crown princess could have denounced him for treason had passed. "Highness, it would be helpful for you to be outside the castle walls when the Royal Army reserves come through Linden. My suggestion would be for you to leave the castle within the next day, two at the most. If you need assistance to remove yourself from the castle," he lowered his voice, "please contact me. I cannot promise this will be without risk to your person. Your mother has people watching you."

The army needed Ariana outside the castle; beyond the control of the royal guards. Because then the army could surround the castle with Ariana leading them. The guards inside the castle would be loyal to the legal leader of Tarador, the Regent Carlana. While the army would have an underage princess.

It would tear the country apart. The dukes and duchesses of the seven provinces were in Linden for the War Council, inside their own walled and heavily fortified estates. With their own provincial army soldiers, who would be drawn into the desperate fight for control of Tarador. "Captain Earwood," she rose from her chair and the army man stood up. "Please signal General Magrane to-" To what? To wait? For what? "Would it be possible to move some of our forces back toward the Tormel line for now, while still being ready for a counterattack?"

"It would be possible, for a short time, Highness," Earwood responded hopefully. "Should I also-"

"Captain, I must make preparations," Ariana felt her own throat was choking her. "Please await my word."

The crown princess wanted to go to the royal chapel, to seek guidance from Mother Furliss, but she did not have time. In her private study, she knelt by the window and prayed silently, then sent for her chief advisor. Kallron found Ariana garbed in a formal but rather somber dress, and he was surprised to see her crown on the table. Ariana rarely wore the crown she was accorded as the future queen; she often said that she preferred to wait until the crown of a monarch sat upon her head. And her chief advisor could tell she had been crying, despite the makeup her maids had applied. "Kallron," she said simply, "send for Duke Falco."

"Your Highness," Duke Falco said with a short bow, no lower than was required for the occasion. "You wished to speak with me?" The note from the crown princess had given no indication what she wanted to discuss. Regin, and Niles Forne, guessed she intended to appeal for Falco's support, now that the forces of Acedor were across the River Fasse. Regin was ready to resist calls to his patriotism. If the princess cared so much about Tarador, she could work with Falco to agree on a compromise candidate for the Regency. With the Council in total disarray and every province putting forward their own candidate, even the princess and Regin Falco grudgingly coming together might not hasten the process of selecting a new leader for the nation. What Duke Falco could not understand was the expression on the face of Gustov Kallron. The man's face was pale and his jaw set. Whatever the princess was going to say, it had greatly upset her chief advisor.

"I do," Ariana said stiffly. She was wearing her official crown, and had received Falco in her formal parlor, rather than in the more comfortable study. It was warm and stuffy in the parlor, but there she sat on a raised throne, while Falco stood below her. "The forces of the enemy have crossed into Anschulz. General Magrane reports there is little between the enemy and the Wendurn Hills, and he is not confident he could hold them there, if they move their entire army across the Fasse." She spoke in a stilted fashion, reciting a speech she had rehearsed. "We must be unified, if we are to defeat the enemy. If Tarador is to survive." She took a breath to continue.

Falco interjected. "Your Highness, we are unfortunately more divided than ever. There are many candidates for the Regency, and none has enough-"

"I will marry your son," Ariana said quickly, before she could change her mind.

At first, Regin Falco was so stunned, he could not believe his own ears. "I am sorry, Your Highness. You agree to marry my heir?"

"I do. Tarador will not survive without strong leadership, now. We will draw up a betrothal contract; I will marry Kyre on the morning of my sixteenth birthday, before my coronation ceremony. In exchange, you will vote for me as Regent, this very afternoon. And you will support me fully in this war, once I am Regent."

Duke Falco was still so surprised, that he had to pause to collect his thoughts before he could reply. "This afternoon, a vote, yes. I am sure that our advisors," he looked at Forne and then Kallron. "can create an acceptable betrothal agreement quickly. Highness, might I suggest that I speak with Duchess Rochambeau, so that your selection as Regent be six out of six votes? To show that we are unanimous in the face of the enemy?" Rochambeau would choke just thinking of voting for Ariana, but Regin was confident he could persuade her to vote with him.

"No," Ariana said emphatically, shocking everyone in the parlor. "I wish Duchess Rochambeau of Demarche to vote against me."

Niles Forne walked all the way through the long, echoing corridors of the place, down the steps, across the courtyard and into the carriage with his duke, without saying a single word. He remained silent as the carriage was driven out through the gates of the castle, because Duke Falco was lost in thought. The carriage bumped over the bridge on its way into the city of Linden before the duke spoke. "Forne, that was interesting."

"Interesting, Sire? It was a triumph! And absolute triumph for you! That silly little girl challenged you, and you beat her at her own game," Forne gloated.

"Careful, Forne," Regin's expression was displeasure, not exultation. "You speak of my future daughter-in-law. The future mother of my grandchild."

I will marry your son. Regin heard the words in his head again, and still he almost did not dare to believe it. What he found most surprising were his own feelings. Instead of feeling triumphant, what he felt was admiration for the princess. What an extraordinary young woman, he told himself. What a brave young woman. She was sacrificing her future happiness, perhaps her entire future, for the good of the nation.

My future daughter-in-law. The mother of my future grandchild. A child who would unite the Falcos and the Trehaymes.

Irritated with himself, Regin tried to push emotions from his mind. There would be a Regency Council meeting that day, then he and the entire Council needed to focus all their energies to supporting Ariana. To save Tarador. If they could.

Koren awoke to find Thunderbolt missing, but as soon as he scrambled to his feet, he saw the horse nearby in the meadow, happily eating hay. Eager to get going, Koren practically had to drag the horse away from the overgrown field. "I promise, we'll get to a village soon, and you will have all the grain you can eat," he laughed as the horse nuzzled his ear. Surely, a village had to be close by. On royal roads, inns and stables were typically located one day's journey apart, and villages often sprung up around the inns. With the inn at the crossroads burned, surely there must be another within a day's ride, Koren told himself. Although, as they rode all morning without seeing any signs of civilization, perhaps the north country of Tarador was more thinly inhabited than Koren expected.

Around noon, Koren halted the horse by a stream by the road, intending to rest and eat the meager food left in his pack. All he had left was jerky and hard cheese, having given everything else to the hungry horse. As he knelt down to drink from the stream, a distant sound caught his attention, and Thunderbolt's ear pricked up also. The great horse began breathing deeply, nostrils flared. "Shh, shh," Koren patted his flank to calm the horse's breathing.

Shouting. Someone was shouting, more than one person. It was coming from the north, the direction they had been riding all morning. Koren pulled the sword from its scabbard; the blade was not the best quality, but he had smoothed out the chips in the edge and kept it sharp. Of his quiver of arrows, there were only four that he trusted to fly straight and true; he moved them to the side where they could be easy to reach. "Thunderbolt, I think there is a fight ahead. I know, it isn't our fight, but I can't stand here and do nothing."

Thunderbolt tossed his head and stamped his feet eagerly.

"Don't you be so eager," Koren warned, already feeling guilty. What right did he have to bring the horse into a battle? Thunderbolt had been in battle, but he had not been trained as a war horse. "We will see what it is, and if is trouble we can't handle, we turn and run, you understand?" He tugged on the horse's mane to look Thunderbolt in the eye, but the horse was practically shaking with excitement, and danced away from him.

As the horse raced up the road, hooves kicking up dust, Koren had a brief moment to realize that he did not know why he was riding into danger. Whatever was happening ahead was not his problem, and- He pushed the thought from his mind. If he thought about it, he might not do what he knew was right. Then, in a moment, the time for thought was past.

The royal road passed through meadows and forests; Koren had thought the woods would be the most likely spot for an attack by bandits, but the bandits had other ideas. Knowing guards would think as Koren did, the bandits had concealed themselves in the tall grass and bushes of a meadow. As a train of two wagons passed by, the bandits had hauled up a stout iron chain that had been concealed in the dirt of the road, and fastened it around a tree. With the chain blocking the road to the north and ditches along both sides, the wagons could not go forward and could not turn around without their wheels becoming stuck in a ditch. More than a dozen bandits had attacked from both sides, against six guards and four wagon drivers. Two of the drivers had fallen in the first volley of arrows, and as Koren pulled Thunderbolt to a halt, the fighting was concentrated around the rear of the first of the two wagons. From what little he could see, some people were taking shelter under the wagon, and guards were using shields to fend off arrow, but two of the guards were down, and the bandits had drawn swords to end the fight.

Koren did not need to dig his heels in to spur the horse onward, Thunderbolt kicked up clods of dirt in his headlong flight. Holding onto the tangled mane with one hand, Koren gripped the bow and an arrow with the other. They kept to the center of the road, with Koren hoping the wagon in the rear would conceal their approach. The bandits charged as Thunderbolt sped toward the fight, and no one had time to look to the south. As they neared the wagons, Koren directed Thunderbolt to the right with his knees, releasing hold of the mane so he could draw back the bowstring.

Two of the enemy fell before they realized they faced a new threat; a third was struck by an arrow as he shouted a warning. The arrow thudding into his chest cut off his cry, and he was flung backward into the ditch. Koren had no time to nock a fourth arrow, they were already in the fight. Tossing the bow away, he drew his sword and swung a leg over to slide off the horse's back. Koren skidded and stumbled in the dirt and desperately thrust the sword up to block a sword coming down toward him; the bandit's sword was deflected but Koren momentarily lost his grip and his sword slipped from his hand. As he reached for the sword that was still spinning in the air and the enemy draw back to strike him, there was a dark flash to Koren's right, and Thunderbolt's front hooves thudded into the bandit's face, sending the man into the spirit world. Koren caught his sword in the air and slapped the flat of it against the horse's flank. "Go!"

Startled, the horse leaped the ditch and bounded across the field, nearly falling prey to a pair of arrows that barely missed. With the horse running away, the stunned bandits turned their attention to the newcomer, and charged at him with a blood-curdling cry.

Koren stood his ground, back to the wagon. He moved by instinct, as he had done in the sparring ground at the castle in Linden. Three of the bandits charged him in unison; Koren's mind flashed an observation that the three likely had military training and were not merely thugs. His sword began to move on its own, almost faster than Koren could follow. Then, he could follow his sword's arcing movements, because time slowed for him. Exactly as time had done when he sparred with the weapons master in Linden. And exactly as time had done when he killed an enemy wizard, to save Lord Salva. Koren heard the gruff voice of the weapons master in his head, instructing him to pay attention to the movements of the three bandits. The way they moved was important, as were their clothes, the way they held their swords, everything he could see could be important. And the fact that they moved together did suggest prior military training, which could be trouble for Koren. It could also be an advantage for him, because it made them somewhat predictable. The wisdom of the weapons master flashed through Koren's mind; it was all good and true and useful. And it meant nothing, for Koren's blade was lightning, flashing through the air in the blink of an eye. The skill and strength and coordination of the three bandits did them absolutely no good; two of them fell back to sprawl on the road, while the third suffered merely the loss of his sword and two fingers. A fourth bandit came up behind Koren, dagger poised to strike, when the man came up short, paralyzed, as the sharp tip of Koren's sword swung around to be poised at his throat.

"I yield! Yield!" The man said in a strangled voice, his dagger thumping to the ground.

Before Koren could speak, the bandit dropped to his knees, a knife sticking out of his belly. One of the guards had thrown the knife, and the man shouted a warning that another bandit was readying an arrow. Koren spun, facing the bandit archer, poised to cut the arrow out of the air.

And the moment was gone. Koren's surprise attack had changed the balance in the fight, and the bandits who were still able to move decided the wagons were no longer easy targets. They broke and ran, scattering across the meadow on both sides of the road. "You! Boy!" A guard exclaimed, picking up Koren's discarded bow and tossing it to him. "You are deadly with that bow, whoever you are. Those two are getting away." The guard pointed across the meadow to the frantically fleeing bandits.

Koren nodded, pulled an arrow from the quiver he still wore on his back, nocked it, and aimed. And lowered the bow. "I won't do it," he said quietly.

"They'll only attack another wagon, boy," the guard growled.

"That may be," Koren said as he put the arrow back in the quiver. "If you wish to shoot men in the back, you can do it yourself."

"Ah," the guard spat in the road, disgusted. "Who are-"

"You?" Another guard, coming from the other side of the wagon, said in an astonished voice. "You!"

Koren turned. At first, he did not recognize the man. Blood streaked the guard's face, and his leather jacket had a slash across the chest. The man had put on weight, healthy muscle. But mostly, he did not recognize the man because he was standing upright, proud and tall, in decent clothing. And because his breath did not stink of whiskey. "You!" It was Koren's turn to be surprised.

"You young pup!" The man had to hold onto the wagon, so great was his shock. "I thought you were headed to the South Isles, last time I saw you."

Koren managed a smile, despite the post-combat reaction that had his hands and knees shaking. "I did. I did go to the South Isles. They were as beautiful as you," he remembered the man telling him that he had never actually been to the South Isles. "As you had heard they were."

"What happened?"

"I had to come back," Koren searched for an explanation that was not an explanation. "Unfinished business."

"I know all about unfinished business," the man nodded slowly. He set his sword back in its scabbard and offered a hand. "Bjorn Jihnsson. Formerly with the king's guard of Tarador, and now, I'm here, with this lot."

Koren shook Jihnsson's hand, and had to catch himself before he blurted out his true name. "Kedrun Dartenon. Formerly of, I don't know-"

"Formerly of a warehouse on a dark night," Jihnsson laughed heartily. "Aye, and before you, I should say I was formerly at the bottom of a whiskey bottle."

With the bandits on the run, Jihnsson vouched for 'Kedrun', not that any of the surviving guards had any question about the stranger's value in a fight. They buried the two dead guards in the meadow, and buried the dead bandits together in a shallow pit; no one felt like digging deep into the rocky soil to properly bury thieves and killers. The wounded on both sides were treated as best they could, perhaps the injured bandits were not given the gentlest of treatment. That hardly mattered, as the bandits knew they would be taken to prison, or worse. The chain was removed from the roadway, dragged into the meadow and dumped into a pond where it would not be used to cause mischief in the future.

As the wagons rolled along at the best pace the tired horses could manage, Koren rode alongside on Thunderbolt, conversing with Jihnsson while the man sat atop a wagon. "This," Jihnsson said, pulling a coin from a leather pouch that hung around his neck, "is the very coin you gave me, on that dark night." The man held onto the coin tightly between thumb and two fingers, so tightly that the skin of his thumb was white.

Koren was surprised. "I thought you would have spent it by now."

"Spent it on drink, likely," Jihnsson remarked with bitterness. "Aye, I would have. But this," he held the coin up and inspected it closely, "changed my life that night, Kedrun. *You* changed my life. Whether you meant to or not, I don't know. But I haven't touched a drop of whiskey or any other hard drink since you gave me this coin. I won't spend this coin, I will not part with it. But," he hesitated, "if you want it back, it is yours."

"No! No, you keep it," Koren responded to the look of fervent devotion in the man's eyes. The eyes of a man who had lost hope, and now found it again. Such a man would do anything to keep that new-found hope. The coin was a symbol that had changed the man's life for the better; Koren did not remember himself fervently *wishing* the coin would bring the man good fortune. That night, he had been caught up in his own concerns.

Jihnsson put the coin back in its pouch and tucked it into his shirt. "Where are you going from here, Kedrun? We're headed to a village up the road a bit, we'll stop there for the night at least. Then we're going on into Winterthur, up north there."

Koren concentrated on picking another burr out of Thunderbolt's mane, giving himself time to think. Winterthur was one of Tarador's northernmost provinces, and it lead to the dwarf lands. He could either go through Farlane, where they were, or through Winterthur. "I am headed north, into the dwarf lands," he said in a near whisper.

Jihnsson raised an eyebrow. "The dwarves? You have business there? Ah, forget I asked. Your business is your own. Kedrun, I am not ashamed to say that you saved my life that night. I was headed for ruin, and now," he thought a moment. He had been a member of the king's guard. Now he was an ill-paid guard for a stingy merchant. "Now I have hope. The mountains up north can be dangerous, even if the dwarves allow you past their borders."

Koren was startled. He had never considered that the dwarves would not allow travelers into their homeland. "They have closed their borders, Mr. Jihnsson?"

"Since Acedor moved forces to Tarador's border, word is the dwarves are protecting their own lands. You'll need permission to cross into the mountains. And don't call me Mr. Jihnsson, call me Bjorn, please."

"Mister-"

"Kedrun, you saved my life, twice. It's Bjorn. And if you mean to cross into the dwarf lands, I will go with you. Westerholm is no place to be traveling alone."

"You don't have to do that, Bjorn," he stumbled over the name.

"Yes," Bjorn said gravely, touching the coin inside his shirt. "I *do*."

Bjorn kept his word not to ask what business 'Kedrun' had with the dwarves, but his curiosity about another subject needed to be satisfied. "Where did you learn to fight like that?"

Koren had an answer ready; the same story he told to the crew of the *Lady Hildegard*. It had seemed to satisfy the curiosity of sailors. He shrugged. "With a bow, I never miss, I never have. Later, I was apprenticed to a weapons master. He said I had potential, if I could unlearn my bad habits and have the discipline to practice properly." That was exactly what the royal master of weapons in Linden had told Koren. Even at the end, after months of instruction and endless sparring practice that left Koren shaking with exhaustion, the weapons master had expressed despair that Koren's technique was raw and amateurish. It was only the speed and skill of the spell Paedris cast upon Koren that allowed him into the sparring ring. Aboard the *Lady Hildegard*, Koren had kept up practice with 'forms' as best he could, though painfully slowing down his motions so as not to draw unwanted attention to himself.

"What happened?"

"The weapons master was not pleased with me," Koren said with a grin that he hoped would end the conversation.

"Ah, hah!" Bjorn laughed. "Did his displeasure involve his daughter?"

"No!" Koren protested, startled by a question he hadn't anticipated.

"Oh, come now, Kedrun. With young men like you, if there is trouble, you can be sure there's a girl involved somewhere along the way."

"There was a girl," Koren thought wistfully of Ariana. "Not the weapons master's daughter. Another girl," he shook his head at Bjorn, indicating that discussion was closed.

"All right, then," Bjorn took the hint.

Koren nudged Thunderbolt, and the horse trotted ahead of the wagon, where Koren rode alone. He had not allowed himself to think about Ariana in a long time, although thoughts of her came to him unbidden every day. When that happened, he pushed her from his mind. It did him no good to think about the crown princess of Tarador, a young woman whose life he had put in danger because of his jinx curse. Even thinking about her, Koren feared, might bring harm to Ariana. There had been a time, a blissful all-too-brief stretch of weeks spent in a tropical paradise, when Koren hoped that he had left his curse well and truly behind. There had been no dangerous or strange incidents during his time aboard the *Lady Hildegard*, or in the South Isles in general. Somehow, Koren had dared hope, his jinx had not followed him past the shores of Tarador.

His hopes were dashed that fateful morning, when the sunrise revealed a pirate ship had found Koren's ship in the night. An ink-black, stormy night, when by all odds, the pirate ship should have lost track of its quarry. Instead, in all the broad sea, the pirate ship had not only been in sight of the *Lady Hildegard*, it had the advantage of being upwind.

After that harsh slap in the face, Koren was determined never again to dismiss the power and reach of the curse upon him. He was a danger to everyone around him, he always would be, and there was nothing he or anyone else could ever do about it.

For the remainder of the day, Koren rode alone, stone-faced, forcing himself not to think of princesses, or the future beyond the next day. Bjorn, too, was in danger from Koren's curse. Koren decided right then that he would accept the help of the former king's guard to get across the border into the dwarf homeland, but no farther. Bjorn Jihnsson now had hope, and Koren would not take that away from him.

CHAPTER FOURTEEN

Regin's new admiration for the crown princess did not extend to trusting her word on important matters of state. After Kallron and Forne wrestled with the wording of a betrothal agreement, Duke Falco came back to Ariana's apartments in the royal palace. Walking through the wide, opulent corridors of the palace, Regin realized that he would soon be spending much time in that ancient building. Hopefully. If the forces of Acedor had not captured Linden by then.

Falco and Forne arrived at Ariana's study, where he found the official royal scribe waiting, along with the princess and her chief advisor. Until he saw the scribe, Regin had feared the agreement would fall apart, that Ariana would change her mind when the reality of marrying Kyre Falco hit her.

"The document is ready," Ariana pointed to a scroll on the desk. The scroll was the heavy parchment of official state documents, held down by gold weights on the four corners. On a side table were ink bottles and pens, ready for signature. And the royal scribe had her official seal, to witness the signatures. "The royal scribe will first examine the contract for legitimacy. Then Duke Falco and I will sign, and the scribe will witness."

The royal scribe nodded formally, and approached the table, burning with curiosity. She had been summoned to the princess, without being told why. From where she had been standing, she was too far away from the table to read the fine script of the document, so she had no idea what type of agreement she would witness. When she read only the first paragraph, she gasped with shock.

"What?" Falco demanded.

The scribe looked stricken. Her face pale, she turned to the crown princess. "Your Highness, I fear that there is a complication. As the official scribe, I have already entered into the royal records a betrothal agreement for you."

"*What?*" Shouted Ariana, Falco, Kallron and Forne in unison.

The scribe, her hands shaking, bowed again. "I beg your pardon, Highness, but your mother-the Regent Carlana," she used the official title, "signed a state document agreeing to your betrothal to a prince of Indus, in exchange for financial guarantees and assistance for Tarador. And military aid from the Raj."

"My mother *sold* me?" Ariana screeched. She could not remember ever being so enraged. "Why wasn't I told of this?"

Before the scribe could answer, Regin turned to Kallron. "You were the woman's chancellor. What did you do?" Regin should have anticipated Kallron's treachery.

"I did not know," Kallron responded, shaken. He was not surprised that Ariana's mother would have hidden such an agreement from him, given his divided loyalties between the Regent and Ariana. "I would like to see this document. When was this agreement signed?"

"At the end of winter, Master Kallron," the scribe cringed under Kallron's withering glare. "I witnessed the signing of the agreement between the Regent and the Bey of Begal."

"Can mother *do* that?" Ariana was fairly shaking with rage.

"To give a short answer," Kallron said flatly, "yes, she can. As the Regent, she has authority to make binding agreements with foreign governments, on behalf of the state. In this case, Your Highness, you *are* the state."

Regin Falco regretted not being able to bring guards with him. And regretted that he was not allowed to carry a sword. "Kallron, I find it difficult to believe-"

"I did *not* know," Kallron declared. "Toward the end of my service as chancellor, the Regent became concerned that my loyalties were, by necessity, divided between her and the crown princess. I am not surprised that the Regent wished to hide this agreement from me. What does surprise me," he said with a glance at the still-cringing royal scribe, "is that I did not learn of it anyway." Were his skills slipping? Had he grown too old? The Bey of Begal had abruptly departed Linden in early spring. Kallron should have suspected something. At the time, he was dealing with too many crises to consider the possibility of yet another. "Highness, as Regent you can certainly void any agreement made by your predecessor. There may be a price to pay, with the Raj, for violating a signed agreement of state."

"The Council will fully support you overturning that betrothal agreement," Regin stated emphatically. No one on the Regency Council would approve the idea of the crown princess marrying a foreign prince; not even a prince of the powerful Indus Empire.

"That will be my first action as Regent," Ariana said through clenched teeth. "Then I will deal with my mother." She sighed. "My first act as Regent will be to break a treaty with our most powerful ally. Scribe, review the document, we must sign it quickly."

"Yes," Kallron agreed. "And then, I really must insist on seeing the agreement with the Raj." Hopefully, he could find a way out. If not, he could at least assess how much trouble Tarador would be in for breaking a signed treaty.

The meeting of the Regency Council was brief but dramatic. Duke Falco opened the proceedings by nominating Ariana for the Regency. Few people were surprised; Falco had spoken to Duchess Rochambeau before the meeting, and Kallron had sent messages to the other four provincial leaders who were eligible to vote. The person most surprised was Carlana Trehayme; she left the Council chambers immediately after the vote for her daughter to replace her. Mother and daughter did not speak, they barely looked at each other.

Ariana quickly thanked the members of the Council, except for Duchess Rochambeau, and the new Regent hurried away for a pre-arranged meeting with Captain Earwood. "Captain, oh, please get up," she said to the kneeling soldier, "we don't have time for such formality. Please signal Grand General Magrane that he may prepare for and conduct his counterattack, in whatever time and manner he thinks is best."

"Yes, Your Highness," said a greatly relieved Earwood.

She pointed to a map of western Tarador on the table. "I will also be ordering the Royal Army to pull back behind the Turmalane mountains in Demarche."

Earwood's face reflected his astonishment. The new Regent wished Magrane to push the enemy back across the border in Anschulz province, but she was abandoning the western third of Demarche province? "Your Highness?" Earwood didn't know what else to say.

"Duchess Rochambeau of Demarche voted against me as Regent. She will see there is a price for being stubborn."

The Royal Army captain could not believe what he was hearing. Were all of the army's hopes about the new Regent for nothing? Had the council replaced an indecisive Regent with a spiteful girl? "Highness, if the Royal Army were to pull back east of the Turmalane ridge, the enemy would surely strike across the border there. Between the border along the River Fasse and the Turmalanes, there is nothing but flat, rich farmland in Demarche. Acedor will soon be across the river in Demarche, and there will be nothing to stop them from forcing their way through passes in the mountains."

"Yes, I know," Ariana ran a finger along the mountains on the map. East of the Turmalane range was a broad valley, with only shallow rivers to act as barriers to the enemy horde. Beyond the tall ridge of the Turmalanes, the enemy could range freely throughout Tarador. The prospect of sending an army through passes in the Turmalane mountains would be very tempting to the enemy. "I am counting on it."

Ariana's next meeting as Regent was with the court wizard. He pondered the map, as she explained the problem. "It is *possible*," Paedris commented with concern. "Your Highness, this is an ambitious plan." He looked up at her. "Perhaps too ambitious?"

"We need ambition, Lord Salva," Ariana declared, stabbing a fingernail onto the map for emphasis. "What do you need from me?"

Paedris resisted the urge to stroke his beard while he was thinking. Pondering the distance from Linden to the Turmalane mountains, his eyes followed the roads. There was no road that led there directly; a detour to the south was necessary. "Time, Your Highness. Time is needed simply to get there, then to prepare. And, I think, we will need the services of Lord Mwazo to make this work at all."

"Mwazo?" Ariana asked in surprise.

Paedris nodded gravely. He knew Cecil Mwazo was not considered a great wizard by those without magical ability, because Mwazo's power did not manifest itself in fireballs or other shows that Paedris considered mostly frivolous. "Yes. Truthfully, if Cecil cannot help us, I do not see any chance of your plan working. The enemy has far too many spies, both here and in the spirit world. Your plan requires the utmost security to succeed."

Cecil Mwazo froze, a spoonful of soup halfway to his mouth. Carefully, he set the spoon back in the bowl, not trusting himself to keep the liquid from spilling on his clothes, the way his hand shook. "Paedris, could you repeat that, please?"

Paedris smiled gently, knowing he had delivered a terrible shock to his longtime friend. "Can it be done?" He knew Cecil had heard him correctly.

"I have long thought it possible," Mwazo had to admit he was as intrigued as he was frightened. "You understand the risks? I will need you to lend your power."

"You shall have it, gladly."

"I have never done this, you understand."

"I understand."

"Dirmell once tried-"

"Dirmell is dead," Paedris remarked with sadness at the passing of the dwarf master wizard. "Cecil, I trust you, and only you, to do this. These arcane arts are your specialty, I have neither the knowledge, the skill nor the power in this area of wizardry."

Mwazo let out a long breath. "Our new Regent wishes to start with no small plans, eh? She is jumping right into this with both feet." Or, perhaps a better analogy would be the young future queen diving headfirst off a cliff, and taking Tarador with her.

"Her Highness reminded me that Tarador has been cautious and idle for far too long, and only boldness can save us at this late hour."

Cecil pushed the bowl of soup away, his appetite gone. "It can be a fine line between boldness and recklessness, Paedris."

"True, and Ariana does have a touch of her father within her character, in that regard. If you think this is too difficult a-"

"No! I am willing to try it. I am eager to try this, Paedris. You know I have longed to expand our knowledge of the arcane arts. This is, I must admit, the perfect time to attempt that which has not been done before." He shook his head slowly. "It serves me right for discussing my ideas with you, Paedris."

"Who else can you tell your wild flights of fancy to?" Paedris patted his friend's shoulder with affection. "When can we start? And what do we need?"

"As to when, there is no time like the present. What we need," Mwazo pulled the soup bowl back toward him. "Is sustenance, for this will consume all of our energies."

"In that case," Paedris went to ring the bell for Olivia, before he remembered that she was busy with his laundry. "I shall send for a hearty lunch."

Grand General Magrane observed the enemy's advance through his spyglass, from atop a hill between the River Fasse and the Tormel river. In compliance with orders from Regent Carlana Trehayme, he was pulling back the Royal Army east of the Tormel, to establish a new defensive line there. In defiance of orders from Regent Carlana Trehayme, he was retreating as slowly as he possibly could. His fear had been the enemy, seeing the Royal Army of Tarador retreating on all three fronts, would strike quickly to the east, overrunning his thin screen of troops there, and crossing the Tormel ahead of him. To his great relief, when the enemy guessed what Magrane was doing, they slowed their advance to match his. No doubt the enemy judged they would have little trouble crossing the shallow Tormel river, so there was no great haste to go east, and rushing only exposed their flanks. Part of Magrane wished the enemy had made a headlong bid for the banks of the Tormel, because then their ranks would be in one long, thin column stretching between the two rivers. As it was, the enemy was now concentrating on bringing soldiers across the River Fasse as quickly as possible, so that their force could not be dislodged from Tarador by Magrane's overburdened army. As the enemy spread out north and south along the east bank of the Fasse, Magrane's ability to counterattack there was closing rapidly.

Only until recently, he had hopes that Ariana might become Regent using legal means, through the complicated machinations of court politics. Now that those hopes were dashed, Magrane had left secret instructions for Captain Earwood in Linden. Regardless of his orders, he intended to counterattack within three days, and even delaying that long might doom all of his plans. And doom Tarador. After the counterattack was launched, Magrane expected to be arrested, possibly hanged for disobeying orders. But after the counterattack was in progress, it would be impossible to stop, until either victory or defeat had resulted.

"General!" Wing Chu called out, as she raced her horse up the hill. Pulling her horse up beside his, she said breathlessly "We must speak, in private."

Magrane nodded silently, with a look to his personal guard force. From long experience, they knew to ride their horses a short distance away; far enough not to overhear a conversation yet close enough to protect the leader of Tarador's Royal Army. "What is it, Madame Chu?" He bowed slightly in the saddle.

"I bear good news, for once. Oooh," she laughed. "This feels good. I must try delivering good news more often."

"And I wish you every opportunity to do so," Magrane tried to smile, but found he could not.

Reading his mood, Wing got straight to the point. "Ariana Trehayme has been elected Regent of Tarador."

"She has?" He exulted. "When?" Magrane automatically looked at the portable telegraph tower that had been built on a hill just to the east. He had not seen the distinctive flags indicating a top priority message.

"Just within the hour. I received notice from Lord Salva; he judged such important news could not wait for the slow telegraph." Paedris had also explained there was a severe thunderstorm between Linden and Anschulz, so that the telegraphs in the area were temporarily unable to see one another in order to pass messages.

Magrane was stunned. "How did this happen? The last word we received was that she was not eligible to become Regent, because her Uncle Yarron could not vote for her."

"Apparently, she became eligible. The message did not provide many details."

Magrane ran a hand through his hair, and let out a long sigh. "I'll not argue with it! Oh, to not have to take another order from her mother, that is a blessing. I can only imagine the politics involved behind the scenes. Madame Chu, if I ever am tempted to dabble in politics, you have my permission to turn me into a frog."

Chu laughed, wondering why people always thought wizards chose frogs as punishment. Why not worms, or slugs? "I will consider it, General."

"Please do, whether I ask you or not. Politics is- Hmm." An unpleasant thought came unbidden to him. "How *did* she accomplish it? My understanding of the law is that she needed five out of six votes, and Duke Falco and Duchess Rochambeau would never vote in favor of Ariana as our Regent."

Chu looked around, to verify none of the general's guards could hear. She lowered her voice anyway. "What will not be in the official message, and is to remain secret for now, is that your crown princess cut a deal with Duke Falco to secure his support. She has pledged to marry the Duke's eldest son, before she becomes queen."

Magrane's eyebrows rose in shock. "No! She is to marry a *Falco*? They cannot be trusted! Is she-"

"I am sure Her Highness is aware of the danger to herself. General, she judged the danger to us all from Acedor to be greater than a future risk to her own safety."

"She is a remarkable young woman."

"Remarkable, and decisive. You have permission from the Regent to counterattack, at the time and in the manner of your own choosing. A confirmation will be sent by telegraph, if you need something more than the word of a foreign wizard?" She asked with a tilt of her head.

"Madame Chu, I trust you completely. In this case, our need is so desperate, I would accept such orders if a bird landed on my shoulder and whispered them in my ear." He raised his hand to signal for his guards.

"General, you have not heard the full message," Chu warned.

Magrane lowered his hand. "Is this more good news, I hope?"

Wing shrugged and smiled. "It could be, though it does not seem to me. Or it does not make sense to me."

CRAIG ALANSON

Magrane's composure slipped just a little, a sign of the great strain he had been under. "That means it is bad news."

"Duchess Rochambeau was the only one of your Regency Council to vote against princess Ariana," Chu explained. "You will soon be receiving orders that your new Regent is ordering the Royal Army to pull out of western Demarche province, behind the Turmalane mountains."

"*What?!*" Magrane exploded.

Chu waved her hands to calm the general. "Paedris instructed me to tell you not to worry, that this is a part of a plan the two of you discussed, some time ago?"

Magrane stared at her, open-mouthed in confusion. "I am quite certain I never discussed a plan to leave western Demarche defenseless," he said with sarcasm.

"Paedris also instructed me, to ask you to trust him."

"Hmmph. If this is some wizard trick-"

Madame Chu bristled at that remark. "Wizard 'tricks' have served you very well to date, General," she reminded him.

Magrane knew he had overstepped his bounds. "If Paedris asks me to trust him, I will do so. With reluctance, until he can explain further."

"He is on his way to meet you," Chu said with a wry smile. "You can ask him then."

Magrane bowed in the saddle to the powerful wizard from Ching-Do. "Will I be receiving confirmation of the reason for my new Regent's," he searched for the proper word, "*unusual* orders regarding Demarche?"

"No. This information is too important to be trusted to a telegraph. No matter what codes you use, there is the possibility an enemy wizard could read the message. You will need to trust me."

Magrane was aware that, as powerful wizard, Madame Chu could right then be manipulating his emotions to make him trust her. Against such a potential threat, he had no defense. What he did have was his memory of recent events. Chu Wing had traveled a great distance to help Magrane fight the enemy, and she had done so with a success Magrane could scarcely have hoped for. Like Paedris, she had pledged her life to fight Tarador's ancient enemy. Magrane had no reason not to trust her. Except for his instincts as a soldier. "What does Lord Salva need me to do?" He asked warily.

"When your army captains in Demarche send messages to you, questioning their orders to withdraw behind the mountains, you need to confirm the orders."

"That will not be easy," Magrane warned.

Despite the seriousness of the situation, Chu smiled. "You chose to be a soldier. Is any part of your life easy?"

"No," he grimaced. "Especially when Regents, princesses and wizards are involved."

A shaken Regin Falco strode into Niles Forne's study and went straight to the wine cabinet, pouring almost a full goblet of red wine. Tilting his head back, he downed half the wine in one gulp. Then he wiped his mouth on the sleeve of his expensive shirt, something the duke of Burwyck never did. His duke was extremely upset about something, and Niles Forne was fairly certain he knew why.

"A difficult conversation with your son and heir, Sire?" Forne asked, after closing the heavy door to his study.

"Does anything escape your notice, Forne?" Regin was irritated that his advisor seemed to know everything that went on around the Falco estate. "Did your spies tell you?"

"No, sire. I did know that Kyre came to speak with you, and I now see that you are drinking wine before midday." Forne had also seen the ducal heir stomping angrily across the estate's courtyard after meeting with his father; from that Forne could easily deduce the meeting had not gone well.

Regin looked at the wine goblet and set it down. "Am I that transparent?"

"Not at all, sire. You only reveal your feelings to select members of your household. And, you do pay me to be observant."

Regin decided not to mention that Forne had been completely blindsided by Gustov Kallron's plan to make Ariana her own Regent. Where had the man's observation skills been then? "Very well, if you are so observant, tell me what happened between me and my son."

Forne suppressed a smile. "You told your eldest son that he is now engaged to our future queen. Kyre is unhappy that you arranged his marriage to the crown princess without his involvement."

Regin gave Nile Forne a sharp look. Damn the man! Regin's private office in the Falco's Linden estate was supposed to be soundproof; Regin had tested it himself. Yet, too many times, Forne knew too much of what went on behind closed doors. "That was either a very good guess, Forne, or you have a way to hear my thoughts."

"It was a good guess, sire. If harsh words were exchanged, I beg you to remember that Kyre is at the age when he wishes to be independent from his parents; to become his own man. You have arranged a wonderful opportunity for him, but for now, he may see it as you restricting his path in life. He may resent that, though he will be prince consort and father of the heir of Tarador, that will always be your accomplishment, not his. He knows everyone will see it that way; that he will ever only be merely a means to an end for you. Putting a Falco on the throne of Tarador will be your triumph, not his. And his position in Linden will be as a figurehead. That might be a bitter pill for him to swallow, sire."

Regin sat down in a comfortable chair, swirled the wine in the goblet, and took a sip. "I had not considered how Kyre might look at this." He waved a hand dismissively in disgust. "It should not matter! My eldest son has a role to play in this great game we play. I am offering him the queen of Tarador! He should be happy. More than happy! Yes, I have had this dream all my life; all

Falcos have longed for this opportunity for centuries. Now Kyre has the chance to fulfill all out dreams, and he spits on it!"

"Sire, perhaps the boy needs time," Forne said softly. He referred to Kyre as 'boy' to remind the duke how young his eldest son still was. "This marriage arrangement must be a shock to him."

"If Kyre needed only time to adjust to the idea, Forne," Regin swirled the wine in the goblet, watching the dark red liquid spinning. "My son told me that if he married Ariana, he will protect the queen, and that if anything were to happen to her after a baby is born, he will raise their child as a," he choked on the words. "As a *Trehayme*. My son betrays me!" He slammed the goblet on a desk, and droplets of red wine flew up to splash on the duke's fine shirt. It was a measure of his anger that the duke did not move to blot away the stains. "Harsh words were exchanged. Some were words that cannot be taken back, I fear. Words by each of us. Forne, this may become a," Regin looked out the window, "problem."

It did not escape the attention of Niles Forne that his duke did not look at him as he spoke. Nor had he failed to notice the duke's red eyes, or the single tear that rolled down the duke's cheek. Regin angrily wiped it away, glancing guiltily toward Forne, who wisely pretended to be adjusting a shoe and therefore not witnessing a moment of weakness. "Ah, I must get these shoes fixed, they pinch me. Sire, if Kyre were to, become a problem, there is a solution. Your Grace, when I wrote the contract for marriage, I deliberately specified the marriage was to be between the crown princess of Tarador and the 'Falco family heir of Burwyck'. Kyre is *currently* your heir, but his brother Talen is, according to the marriage contract, also eligible to marry Ariana. If, for any reason, Kyre is unable to fulfill his duties as heir," Forne coughed. This was a conversation about which even he was uncomfortable. "Then Talen would marry Ariana."

Regin froze for a moment. Changing the heir to a province was not so simple as a duke or duchess naming one child over another. Regin could not merely disinherit Kyre. The laws of inheritance for royal privileges were strict. A new Falco heir such as Talen would need the approval of the Regency Council; four out of six votes; for Regin himself could not vote. Talen becoming the heir in place of Kyre could be easily blocked by the Council.

Unless Kyre was no longer eligible to be heir. That would require Kyre to be imprisoned for treason. Or for Kyre to be dead. Forne had likely written that into the betrothal contract to prevent the Trehaymes from killing Kyre before the wedding. Now Kyre might face a threat from his own family.

Regin sat up abruptly. "We will not speak of this again," he said in a numb, emotionless voice. He had come to his advisor's study to vent his feelings, not for the man to offer solutions. Regin had feared there was no solution, short of Kyre coming to his senses, which seemed unlikely. Then the damned Forne had offered a solution that Regin hated to contemplate. And even more, he hated himself for contemplating it. "You will particularly never mention this to Kyre's mother."

Forne bowed as the duke stood up. "Yes, Your Grace." Forne noted that Regin had referred to Britta Falco not as 'my wife' but as 'Kyre's mother'. Regin was already mentally distancing himself from both his wife and his eldest son.

Regin paused before opening the door. "While we are here in Linden, Forne, you should take the opportunity to instruct Talen."

"Certainly, Your Grace. Might I make a suggestion, Sire? You will be sending part of your ducal army to support the Royal Army in Anschulz. It might be good for Kyre to join your troops there. He will gain experience leading an army in battle, and more importantly, he will not be here, close to our new Regent."

Regin thought for a moment. "That is an excellent idea, Forne. In order for him to meet up with the force I sent, he should leave today, I think."

"Oh, certainly, Sire. It is a long journey."

After his duke departed, Forne walked over to his wine cabinet and poured a quarter glass for himself, savoring it while looking out the window. He had chosen that particular apartment in the Falco estate because it looked out over the rooftops of Linden, up to the royal castle and the palace within. The view of the rooftops was not scenic, the turret of an adjoining mansion partly blocked his view of the castle, and the south-facing nature of the windows could make the study hot during summers. It was seeing the royal palace that mattered; the upper story of the bright white walls were visible above the grey stone of the castle fortress that surrounded it. Seeing the castle reminded Niles Forne of why he was in Linden, why Duke Falco relied on him so greatly. Forne held his powerful position in the Falco household for one purpose: to help Regin Falco regain the throne of Tarador for the Falco family.

Toward that end, Forne had considered a plan even more bold than a deal for Ariana to marry Kyre. Forne had thought, in his dark and twisted mind, that if the Duchess Britta Falco were to suffer an unfortunate accident, then Duke Regin Falco himself would be available to marry the crown princess. As the royal prince consort, Regin Falco could not become king himself, but he could legally be guardian to any child he had with Ariana. And if Queen Ariana were to tragically die before her child and heir reached the age of sixteen, Regin Falco could become their child's Regent, and the true power within Tarador.

Niles Forne had discarded the idea of removing Britta Falco, not because he found the idea morally repugnant. Not because the Duke would never consider arranging for his own wife's death. Forne had discarded the idea simply because he judged that the Regency Council would never allow Regin Falco to become prince consort. And so, Britta Falco lived.

Whether Kyre Falco also lived would depend on that young man's actions, and his attitude.

Niles Forne was not optimistic about the young man's future.

As Madame Chu predicted, the message to pull out of western Demarche province was not received well by the Royal Army contingent there. Not received well, and not believed. While one set of telegraphs was busy requesting, almost demanding, confirmation from Linden, another telegraph message was on its way north, to Anschulz province. That second message requested orders directly from Grand General Magrane. The second message verged on insubordination, possibly skirting along the razor edge of treason. It implied that the Royal Army in Demarche might not obey orders from the new Regent in Linden, if General Magrane thought such orders were foolish or dangerous.

As the message was going north to Magrane, another message was traveling south, sent by Magrane himself. Only the message from Magrane did not travel by anything so crude as a telegraph; it flew through the air on magical wings. Madame Chu had reached out through the spirit world to a wizard serving with the Royal Army in Demarche, providing a message that could not be intercepted and decoded by the enemy. *Follow orders to pull back west of the Turmalanes*, the magical message stated, *all is not as it seems. Await further instructions from me. –Magrane.*

Exactly what that short and cryptic message was supposed to mean, the Royal Army general in Demarche could only guess, but he kept his thoughts to himself. Not knowing Magrane's full plan made it difficult to explain to Royal Army soldiers that they were ordered to abandon lands they had dedicated years to defending. Worse were the conversations with officers of Demarche's own ducal army, who rightfully felt betrayed. There was considerable bad blood on both sides, with fights breaking out, even after the Royal Army offered to assist in evacuating civilians from western Demarche as they pulled back.

That old warrior Magrane, thought the Royal Army general in Demarche, had better have a damned good plan. A brilliant plan.

Ariana kept Kyre Falco waiting for over an hour. As the new Regent, she was extremely busy, surprisingly busy. She would need to learn quickly to 'delegate', which Kallron explained meant losing a measure of control over what happened. It was overwhelming, and what dismayed her was how many little, seemingly mundane decisions a Regent needed to make, every single day!

Ariana also kept Kyre waiting because she wished to. She wanted the arrogant Falco heir to sit in the waiting room, as more important people were allowed in her office to speak with the Regent. Kallron strongly urged Ariana to rebuff Kyre's urgent request for a meeting, telling her that no good could come from it, and that an emotional discussion with her future husband could only be a distraction that she could not afford right then. Ariana disagreed; she knew herself better than her advisor did. Kyre Falco no doubt wanted to gloat about his victory over her, and Ariana simply wanted to get that out of the way. She knew that it was better to let Kyre boast now, so she could put it out of her mind. And, there were some things she wished to say to the Falco heir, to let Kyre know just how little he mattered, among the many important things that concerned her.

Finally, she allowed Kyre past the door. As he stomped into the official office of the Regent, Ariana was seated behind a large desk, signing documents under the guidance of Gustov Kallron.

Kyre bowed curtly, barely a bow at all. "Your Highness-"

"One moment, please." Ariana held up a finger, not even looking up at Kyre.

"Sign here," Kallron indicated on one document, "and here also, Your Highness."

"Oh, how many of these will I need to sign? And read?" Ariana said grumpily, and there she was not putting on an act for Kyre's benefit. "This is such a bother. There, done," she plopped the pen back into its inkwell, and swept the documents aside. Most of the desk was still covered with books and documents left by her mother; documents she and Kallron were still sorting through. The former Regent Carlana Trehayme was secluded in her royal apartments, and had sent a note to Ariana, stating that her mother intended to spend the next several months at the summer palace. Kallron heartily endorsed that idea; he wanted Carlana as far away from her daughter as was possible. "Chancellor," she addressed Kallron by his old, and now restored, title. "Ask Captain Earwood to join us as soon as possible, please."

"Yes, Highness," Kallron replied, and snapped his fingers to a servant, to relay the message to the Royal Army barracks.

Ariana sat back in the chair with a satisfied smile, which she quickly wiped off her face and replaced by a scowl. "Your Grace," she addressed Kyre in a voice dripping with sarcasm. "You wished to speak with me?"

"In private, Your Highness." Kyre's jaw clenched. "If you please."

Ariana looked to Kallron, who nodded. The chancellor waved for the remaining servants to depart. "My chancellor will remain."

"But-" Kyre began to protest.

"The relationship between you and I is *strictly* a matter of state," Ariana snapped, "and Chancellor Kallron advises me on matters of state." With a mocking smile, she added "Your Grace."

Kyre struggled to control his anger. "Your *Highness*," he said, thinking that term would apply to him after they were married. "I had nothing to do with our betrothal. My father informed me, only this morning, of the arrangement he made with you."

"No doubt you were greatly displeased," Ariana readied the insults she had planned.

"I am displeased!" Kyre insisted, much to the surprise of the crown princess. "I am not a stud horse. I am not my father's property, to be bargained like a prize, a prize, *cow*," he sputtered. "Your Highness, have you completely lost your mind?"

Ariana's eyes grew wide. The conversation was not at all going the way she had imagined it would. All of her carefully planned insults and retorts were forgotten. "Do you forget who you are speaking to?" Her anger was not feigned. "I am-"

"You are either a foolish little girl, or a truly desperate one." Kyre's anger was also real. "Highness, after a baby is born to us, a *Falco* baby, my father is going to kill you. Do you understand that? He may very well kill us both, so he could become both guardian to our child, and become Regent. You have no idea how dangerous my father is," he shook his head angrily. "Regaining the throne for the Falcos is all he can think about. He will do *anything* to put a Falco on the throne of Tarador."

So great was Ariana's shock that she could not speak. Could not think of anything to say.

"I will refuse to marry you," Kyre said emphatically, "whatever bargain you have made is not worth your life. My father is sending me away this very afternoon; before I leave, I will tell him that I refuse-"

"No!" Ariana shouted. "No," she repeated in a whisper, and Kallron took her hand and squeezed it. "Kyre," she began to say, then her voice failed her.

Kallron cleared his throat. "Your Grace, the crown princess made a bargain with your father, in order to save Tarador. She needed five votes to assume the Regency, to loosen the Royal Army's chains and allow General Magrane to strike at the enemy. The price your father demanded, in exchange for his vote, was for the crown princess to marry you, before her coronation as queen." Kallron squeezed her hand again, as Ariana stared down at the table. "Her Highness did not enter this bargain blindly; she is well aware of your father's intentions. It is a measure of her desire to save Tarador, and her desperation in the face of the enemy crossing our borders, that she entered his bargain. If there were any other choice, your father's offer would of course have been rejected."

"She is Regent now," Kyre protested, "I can tell my father that I refuse-"

"No!" Ariana looked up, her eyes red. Of all things she had expected, persuading Kyre Falco to go through with their forced marriage was the furthest from her mind. "Kyre, don't. *Don't.* Please. Your father could call for a vote of no confidence in me. We can't afford that. Not now. I have already had to-" She looked up at Kallron.

He nodded. "Her Highness, and I, learned recently that her mother secretly agreed to a betrothal between the crown princess and a prince of the Indus Empire."

"*What?*" Kyre was genuinely shocked.

Ariana managed a smile. "That was exactly what we said. Ky-" She could not bring herself to use his name again. "Your Grace," she said stiffly, "I have already been forced to break one betrothal contract, a contract with our most powerful ally. I cannot break another. Please, *please*, do not say anything to your father."

The conversation also had not at all gone the way Kyre expected. "But-"

"Your Grace," Kallron interrupted. "The betrothal contract specifies that the crown princess is to marry the Falco heir. The heir to the duchy of Burwyck is *not* necessarily yourself. You do have a younger brother. If your father became displeased with you-" Kallron left the rest to Kyre's imagination.

Kyre's face reddened. He had come to protect the crown princess, and instead found himself fearing for his own life. Impulsively, he dropped to one knee and stared at the floor. "Your Highness, I pledge with my life to protect you, and to serve Tarador in any way that I can. Including protecting you from my father, if needed."

Kallron and Ariana glanced at each other, neither of them knowing what to say. Then, Kallron silently gestured for Ariana to speak. "Thank you?" Ariana said uncertainly. Then, "Your Grace, we accept your," she had no idea what was the proper way to respond, "offer of fealty?" Damn it, she thought to herself. The one time in her life she needed Charl Fusting, the royal chief of protocol, and the annoying man was not there! "And we hope that you fare well, in, where are you going? You are leaving today?"

Kyre rose, and squared his shoulders. "I am to lead a battalion of my father's soldiers, to support the Royal Army in Anschulz," he said with a touch of pride. Then his shoulders slumped ever so slightly. "Likely, my father mostly wishes me away from Linden. And surrounded by troops loyal to him at all times."

"Be careful, Your Grace," Ariana surprised herself by saying.

Kyre bowed deeply. "And you also, Your Highness. Please remember, you have enemies everywhere, especially now that you have power as Regent."

When the door closed behind Kyre Falco, Ariana fell back in the chair. "Uncle Kallron, what just happened?"

Kallron shook his head slowly. "There are days when I think, with all my years, that nothing could ever surprise me. Whenever I begin to think that, life surprises me greatly. Highness, I urge you to be careful. Kyre is a Falco. Today, he may resent his father for setting the path of his life," Kallron unknowingly echoed the words of Niles Forne. "Kyre is young, and wants nothing so much as to be independent. Family ties are strong; Kyre may change his mind tomorrow, or the next day. Or next year. He will always be a Falco, I do not think he could ever be trusted."

"I don't plan to trust him. I don't trust him," Ariana declared. Words of fealty were only that; words. Emotions came and went, especially at Kyre's age. At her own age. Still, Kyre's lack of arrogance had astonished her. "Chancellor, if it is possible, perhaps the Royal Army could watch over Kyre, while he is in Anschulz?" The prospect of marrying Kyre Falco was disturbing, but at least she knew him. His younger brother Talen was unquestionably a Falco to his core; arrogant, ruthless and fiercely loyal to their father. The thought of marrying Kyre made Ariana sick to her stomach. The thought of marrying Talen filled her with fear.

Britta Falco, duchess of Burwyck and wife to Regin, stormed into her husband's private study and ordered all the servants out. They knew to comply so they did, without even a glance at the duke who was their liege lord. Whenever Britta and Regin had a row, it was epic, and no servant wished to be caught in the middle.

When the last servant closed the heavy door behind him, Regin asked wearily "How have I vexed you this time, my dear heart?" He reached for his wineglass and downed the last third of it in one gulp.

"How dare you?! How dare you put our eldest son's life at risk, without consulting me?"

"Please, my dearest love, lower your voice." Regin pleaded. Their marriage was not a particularly happy one, both having married for family advantage rather than love, yet they had reached a compromise over the years. More of a cease fire than a compromise, Regin considered. One of the ways they picked at each other was to use terms of endearment that neither truly felt. "Britta, my dear. Please, sit, so we may speak privately," Regin said softly, with a glance toward the door. The door was indeed heavy, and it was no ordinary door. Years ago, Regin had paid a large sum of money to a dwarf wizard, so that the door would be utterly soundproof. The same magical treatment had been given to the two sets of windows, which Regin now closed, despite the heat of the day.

Britta consented resentfully to sit down. "Have you considered, *my* dearest love, that Kyre's life will be in great danger every day after the wedding? Your agreement is only that Ariana marry Kyre, not that the marriage last a certain length of time to be effective."

"Be calm, my sweet," Regin poured himself a splash of wine. Now that he knew what his wife was upset about, he could sip the wine slowly and enjoy it. "A monarch cannot end a marriage without the votes of five members of the Council. Ariana will never get five votes."

"A marriage can easily be ended by a knife," Britta hissed. "Or a drop of poison," she looked meaningfully at her husband's wine glass.

Regin was suddenly not thirsty at all. He pushed the wine glass away. "Certainly, there will be a measure of danger shortly after the wedding. Once Kyre and Ariana have a baby, an heir to the throne, Kyre will be safe. No mother would harm the father of her children," Regin said with a questioning raised eyebrow.

"No," Britta responded, after a pause longer than Regin was comfortable with. "*Most* wives would never do such a thing. Kyre's future wife is not the only consideration. The queen will be surrounded by many people; many ruthless, unscrupulous people, who would gladly act behind the queen's back. People who may believe they are acting in the queen's best interest. Or acting purely in their own interests. Have you given thought to the notion that the Trehaymes might accept an heir to the throne who is a Falco by blood, but they would never accept an heir who had been raised as a Falco? With Kyre out of the way, any child of his would be raised as a Trehayme. Kyre would be an obstacle to the Trehaymes retaining the throne." His wife sat stiffly, unyielding. "What shall we speak of, dearest husband?"

Regin took a sip of wine, perceiving the danger had passed. It was good wine. "We shall speak of plans. My dear, you mentioned that a marriage may be ended by a knife, or a drop of poison. Or by many other means. After a baby is born, Kyre's life will not be the only one in danger. Consider this; if our future queen Ariana were to suffer a terrible fate, then her child could certainly not be left unprotected. I, with you by my side, would be forced to step in, *legally* forced to step in, to assume guardianship of the child. And Kyre would be the logical choice to act as Regent, until our grandchild is ready to become king, or queen, in their own right. If such a terrible thing were to happen to Ariana, our grandchild would be raised properly as a Falco."

"You propose to play a dangerous game, husband," Britta breathed, taken aback by the scope and boldness of Regin's plan. "With our son's life, and our lives, in the balance."

"Our lives are always at risk, dearest," Regin said dryly. "With the enemy at our borders, the game of power we play between the royal families of Tarador, may be the least of the dangers we face."

Britta pursed her lips. She was not a passive player in the game of power; she had often participated and even instigated her husband's schemes. Some of his decisions, such as lending far too much money to Duke Bargann in an attempt to make Farlane province an effective vassal of the Falcos, she had not agreed with. Most of Regin's machinations had worked in the favor of their family. That did not mean she always trusted his judgement. Especially his judgement regarding the Trehaymes. Regin was too often blinded by his overwhelming desire to see the throne of Tarador restored to the Falcos. That would be his legacy, and it seemed to be all he thought about most days. The quest to restore the throne to the Falco family consumed Regin; it motivated him, but it also could severely affect his judgement. "Love of my heart," she kept the sarcasm from her voice, "I, too, play this game that you obsess over." Britta Falco was a Falco by birth, she was a third cousin to Regin and a baroness in her own right. "You have sent Kyre into danger in Anschulz. I pray that you not risk our son's life unnecessarily. Or unwisely." The duchess left the room abruptly, without bothering to use a mocking term of endearment for her husband.

Regin Falco sat quietly by himself, contemplating his wife's words. The warm feelings he had toward his future daughter-in-law were quickly wearing off, and he rebuked himself for having been emotionally soft. Ariana was a Trehayme; there could never be good relations between her and the Falcos, regardless of the circumstances. Ariana was a means to an end, and Regin needed to be ruthless about attaining that end.

CHAPTER FIFTEEN

When Niles Forne told Kyre Falco that the heir to Burwyck province was ordered to leave Linden, for the supposed purpose of commanding the Falco battalion on their way to support the Royal Army in Anschulz, Kyre simply nodded. He did not ask any questions, he did not protest, and he did not complain. What he did do was go immediately to his apartment in the Falco estate, pack his weapons and a few personal belongings, and alert his personal guards that they would be departing in half a glass. His pair of personal guards were used to getting short notice of Kyre traveling, so they had bags already packed and ready. In less than an hour from receiving the news from Forne, Kyre and his two guards rode out through the stable gate, setting his horse at an easy gallop through the countryside that surrounded Linden. When they reached the main road north, he slowed his horse to a steady trot that would assure covering much ground before nightfall.

Only, when night was falling, his guards were surprised to find that Kyre did not stop at the village they were passing through. Looking back in dismay to see the inviting lights of the village fading behind them, his guard Terry Carter cleared his throat politely. "Your Grace, we will not be stopping for the night?" Carter was more concerned about his horse than himself. While riding throughout the night was not all that unusual in service to the demanding Falco family, he would have appreciated knowing that is what they would be doing. His supply of dried meat and fruit was inconveniently at the bottom of a saddlebag, and his stomach was beginning to growl with hunger.

"No, Carter, not yet. It is a fine night for a ride, eh?" He pointed to the clear summer night sky, where stars were beginning to twinkle. "We can get to Longbarrow, I think, before we stop. I fancy the food at the Black Bear."

"Yes, Your Grace," agreed the other guard, Gerry Falzon. The two guards exchanged a glance, and Falzon put a hand around his throat in a choking motion, almost making Carter laugh out loud. No one liked the food at the Black Bear tavern, travelers only stopped there when they couldn't reach the villages to the north or south. "It certainly is a fine night for a ride." The summer air was warm on his skin, and the moon was beginning to rise. This stretch of road was considered safe by most travelers, being regularly patrolled by the Royal Army, with neatly tended farms everywhere. As they rode, Falzon breathed in the scent of newly-mown hay, wildflowers growing in the ditches beside the road, and fruit ripening in the orchards.

Where the road crossed a stream, they let the horses drink their fill of water, and snack on wild grasses. "The Black Bear?" Falzon whispered. "He seeks food poisoning?"

Carter made sure they were out of Kyre's hearing. "I think His Grace wants to get away from his father as quickly as possible. If we ride to the Black Bear, we might be ahead of anyone his father sends in pursuit."

"Ah," Falzon grimaced. If Kyre were acting against his father, even if merely snubbing his nose at the duke, the two guards could incur the wrath of Duke Falco. Such was their lot in life, and they were used to it. "In that case, I hope the Black Bear has something better than that awful chicken pie we ate the last time we were there. That stringy chicken was older than I am."

"You are in luck, Falzon," Carter said with a hearty laugh. "I hear tell that because no one else ate that particular chicken pie, they still have a slice of it waiting for you."

"Kyre! That damned stubborn brat!" Regin slammed his fist on the table, after reading the note Kyre had left behind. When his eldest son had not come to dinner, Regin sent servants to look for him, and a maid found a letter on the bed in Kyre's apartment. The guards also reported that Kyre had ridden out of the estate's grounds earlier that day, and he had not returned. Duke Falco crumpled his son's letter and tossed it to Niles Forne.

Forne quickly scanned the letter. Kyre had stated simply that as he was ordered away from Linden, he was leaving immediately, to best comply with the wishes of his father. It was an unsubtle way of defying his father, while obeying him. "I would say determined rather than stubborn, Sire," Forne said with a straight face. "A trait that may serve him well someday."

Regin sighed heavily. "He *is* my son, isn't he? My father said I was far too stubborn and headstrong when I was Kyre's age. What think you, Forne," the duke held his wine glass up to the light, and took a sip. "Should I teach him a lesson, recall him to Linden before he gets the idea he can defy me like this?"

Forne pursed his lips and answered carefully. "If Kyre were your second son, that may indeed be the proper course of action, Sire. As Kyre is your eldest, and your *prospective*," he raised his eyebrows, "heir, I would advise it best for you to wait and let the young man demonstrate his capabilities. If Kyre is going to grow into being worthy of your trust, this may be an excellent opportunity to test his character. Some semblance of free rein for him, surrounded as he is by your own army, will allow him to either prove himself-"

"Or hang himself," the duke said as he gulped the glass of wine. "Very well, Forne, Kyre believes he has slipped the leash for now. I will be patient," he held up a finger, "for now. For now, only."

"Yes, Your Grace. A note from you, to Kyre, outlining your orders for the battalion he will command, and your expectations of him, would be useful."

Whether or not the Black Bear had saved a slice of very old chicken pie for him, Falzon had the great fortune of never knowing, for when the innkeeper learned that his very late-arriving guests included the heir to Burwyck, he roused his grumpy cook and laid out a feast. Grilled steaks that were thick and juicy and perfectly charred on an applewood fire, roasted potatoes, onions and carrots, and slabs of dark bread slathered with butter. "Your Grace, I apologize," the innkeeper stuttered, "the bread was baked this morning. We do not have anything more fresh, as we did not know you would honor us with your presence."

"No need to apologize," Kyre mumbled through a mouthful of the delicious and chewy bread. "It is good honest food, and no one should think less of it. My compliments to your inn, and to the cook."

"Thank you, Your Grace," the innkeeper bowed so low his head almost scraped the table, and both Carter and Falzon had to suppress laughter. "Will you be staying with us tonight?"

Kyre wiped his mouth on the back of his sleeve, something he would not have been able to do in Linden. He had been thinking of pressing on along the road after dinner, the horses having had time to rest and eat a bag of grain, but the food in his belly was making him sleepy. "Why, yes, that sounds like an excellent idea."

The innkeeper got a terribly pained look on his face. "All of our rooms are full at the moment, Your Grace. I will roust the customers from my two best rooms-"

Kyre frowned at that. "Nonsense. No, let your guests sleep."

"Then you may have my very own bed, Sire, my wife and I-"

"Your wife should get her rest. We have tents and bedrolls with us; if you could bring us fresh straw from your stable, we will make do with that."

The innkeeper's face reflected his great shock and shame, at the idea of a future duke sleeping on straw in his yard, but Kyre sent him away with a dismissive wave of a hand.

"It is a good idea to sleep on straw in our tents, rather than in one of this inn's beds," Carter said with a grin, his teeth gleaming in the firelight. "Less fleas."

Kyre exploded in genuine laughter, pounding on the table. "Yes, Carter, I suppose that is true. Ah, one more bite, then I'm for bed. We should rise early and ride. It is a long way to Teregen, and I wish to arrive there before Captain Jaques."

Koren had been anxious that the caravan's route through Winterthur might take him near his hometown where people might recognize him, but the map Bjorn showed him indicated they were comfortably to the north of Crickdon County already. The two-wagon caravan was headed toward the western border of Tarador, bringing supplies to the Royal Army garrison there. After he formally signed on as a guard, Koren escorted the pair of wagons for two days, then they joined a caravan of eight wagons, all going roughly northwest. While the western border was not where Koren wanted to go, their route would intersect several roads to the north. He would decide later when to leave the caravan and go north.

The caravan of ten wagons halted for the day at a substantial town, close to the border between Farlane and Winterthur. They would be crossing into Koren's home province the next day, and he realized that he felt no pang of homesickness at the prospect of coming back to the province where he had been born. Before the baron of Crickdon County had banished his family, Koren had never been more than fifteen miles from his home, and had never set foot outside of Crickdon. He and his family had no reason to travel farther, as there was always so much to be done around the farm.

Everyone in the caravan appreciated stopping in the town. Some of the wagons needed repairs that required a blacksmith. All of the horses, including Thunderbolt, needed proper grooming. Koren had bought a bridle and a beat-up old saddle in the first village they had come to; now he was able to sell the ill-fitting saddle and buy a new one. And he paid a few coins to the stable hands for Thunderbolt to eat his fill of corn and grain. Already, the horse was looking much better; being able to eat properly and have his coat brushed until it shone again made Thunderbolt look properly like a horse who belonged in the royal stables, even if Koren could not tell anyone where his horse had come from.

While the horses were attended to, and wagons and other gear repaired, the merchants bargained for supplies. And the guards and wagon drivers split up to sample the inns and taverns in the center of town. "What about here?" Koren asked in front of a rough-looking tavern. Several of the front windows were cracked, all were dirty, and the partly broken sign which hung at an angle was so old and faded that Koren could not read it. The tavern was just down the road from a bridge, so he guessed what the sign read. "Des Bridge?"

"Haha," the leader of their original band of guards chuckled. "Del Ray. It used to say 'Del Ray', not that anyone can read that sign now. You don't want to go in there, Kedrun; there are better places around the corner."

For some reason, the dilapidated tavern called out to Koren. That, or the scent of chops sizzling on the grill called out to his growling belly. He looked at Bjorn for guidance. "I want to try this place."

Their leader, a man named Robern, stopped to peer in the dirty windows. "Their beer is watered down, but they do serve good, thick chops." The scent was enticing him also.

"What place around here doesn't water down their beer?" Bjorn asked. The town was a crossroads that existed largely on caravans traveling through. Watering the beer down meant more beer could be sold, and the caravan leaders did not like their hired men to be drunk. "let's go," he clapped Kedrun on the shoulder, and they walked into the open front door.

Lunch was good; the chops were indeed thick and juicy and perfectly cooked on the outdoor grill. Koren sipped greedily at his goblet of water and looked around the smoky room. In the late summer heat, the tavern was too warm, even with the windows and doors open. Smoke drifted in the back door from the grill, and several men were smoking pipes as they relaxed with tankards of beer. Koren scraped up the last of the roasted potatoes from his plate, and relaxed as he listened to other guards telling stories. Despite the poor reputation of the tavern, there were few chairs empty at the noonday hour and-

Koren received a paralyzing shock.

The guards at his table had called for another round of beer, with Koren and Bjorn waving that they didn't want any. When the serving girl brought the platter of beer tankards, she set the platter down in front of Koren, and the pendant she wore around her neck caught his eye. The pendant swung in front of his eyes, shining dully in the smoky air. "Where did you get that?" He shouted, lunging across the table to grasp the pendant and knocking over his chair in the process. His feet became entangled with Bjorn's, and he sprawled on the table, missing the pendant.

The girl darted away, annoyed but not alarmed; she was used to drunken customers pawing at her and she knew how to deal with them. Koren's chair was against the wall, and he would have to squeeze by five or six people on either side of him along the long communal table. Instead, he surprised her by jumping onto the table, scattering crockery and tankards. The tavern was in an uproar as people grasped at his legs, laughing for most assumed he had drunk too much beer. The laughter halted when he wriggled his legs loose, hopped to the floor and put a hand to the hilt of his sword.

"Whoa! Whoa now, Kedrun!" Robern shouted across the table. "No reason to-"

Next to the serving girl who was now backing away in fear, a very large man stood up, grasping the hilt of his own sword. "Go back to your chair, young fool," the man growled. To the serving girl, he said "Mathilda, get behind me."

Koren did not back down. "I know that pendant. Where did you get it?" He demanded through gritted teeth, and drew his sword partly from its scabbard. Bjorn was coming around the table to back up Koren, his hand poised near his own sword.

The man next to Mathilda was more than a head taller than Koren and much heavier; he matched Koren's action, and people dove out of the way. "Wait! Hold!" Robern ordered. He addressed the man facing Koren. "You know me, Tom Resnick. We've traveled many a mile together. Don't you do this. This one," he pointed to Koren, "is a berserker. I don't know who he is, but I wouldn't pit my whole team against him."

Tom was not persuaded. "You are trying to frighten me, Robern?" Tom's friends moved their chairs aside, ready to back up their friend.

"I am trying to save your life, you stubborn fool," Robern growled. "Miss," he said to the serving girl, "it is a reasonable question. Where did you get that pendant?"

Tom Resnick looked from Robern who he knew, and Koren who he did not. The look in Koren's eye was more powerful than Robern's warning. "Mathilda," Tom said gently as he took his hand away from his sword, "perhaps you had best answer the question."

Still standing behind her protector, Mathilda protested weakly, looking around the tavern for support. "It's mine! It was given to me, and it's mine."

Koren took a deep breath. Beside him, Bjorn whispered "I'll support anything you do, Kedrun, but be sure it's worth the price."

"On the left side is a dent that continues on to the back. And an inscription on the back, it reads 'BB and AB' inside a heart," Koren tried to contain his anger.

No one needed to watch the serving girl turn the pendant, they could all see that she knew exactly what was on the back of the pendant. "How did you know?" She asked.

Koren slid his sword back in the scabbard. "Because it belonged to my mother."

"It belonged to your mother?" The girl asked contritely.

"It was a wedding gift from my father. My mother would not have sold it or given it away, so how did you get it?"

"It was given to me. It was! It was given to me, by a man," Mathilda's voice had an undertone of defeat. "I don't know where he got it."

"Who?" Koren demanded. "What man?"

"Lekerk. Simon Lekerk."

A loud mutter arose around the tavern. Even Bjorn cursed beside Koren. "Lekerk," he said the name like a swear word.

"Who is Lekerk?" Koren asked.

"A bandit," Mathilda replied in disgust. She pulled the necklace over her head and held it out to Koren, who took it with a shaking hand. Then Koren's knees would not support him, and Bjorn guided him to a chair.

"A bandit?" Koren whispered, holding the pendant in both hands.

"Aye," Bjorn patted Koren's back. "He's a bad one."

From Bjorn, Robern and others, Koren learned that Simon Lekerk had been a soldier in service to Duke Romero of Winterthur, until the man decided he preferred the easier life and better pay of a caravan guard. Only after a while, he was not content with a guard's pay either, and he began selling information about valuable caravans to bandits. Not content with that, Lekerk recruited a team of bandits to pose with him as guards, and they stole everything of value from the three wagons of a caravan they had been hired to protect. Since then, Lekerk and his gang had been plaguing Winterthur and Farlane provinces as bandits. It was known that Lekerk had a scar across the left side of his face, so he himself could not infiltrate caravans as a guard, but members of his bandit gang were thought to be working as guards, sending information back to their leader. The bandits were known to attack anyone they thought might have something of value; even single travelers had fallen victim to the gang.

Koren was sitting under a tree outside the tavern, where Bjorn had brought him. Bjorn had brought a large tankard of water and made Koren drink it. "Where is this Lekerk now?" Koren stared at the ground.

"You think he stole that pendant from your mother?" Bjorn asked. He did not mention the more awful possibility.

"My mother would never give up this pendant," Koren insisted, "nor sell it. Never."

"Your family, where are they now?"

"I don't know. I, I ran away. And then they moved away, I don't know where."

"All right," Bjorn did not know what do to next. "Do you want to go find your family?"

"I wouldn't know where to start," Koren admitted. And the last person his parents wanted to see was their cursed son. "Where is this Lekerk now?"

"Kedrun, if you are thinking of-"

"Where is he?" Koren drained the last of the water and stood up.

Bjorn followed, brushing dust off his pants. "Rumor has it, he has been operating in northern Farlane. North of here," Bjorn pointed to the crossroads in the center of the town. "Kedrun, if you're going after Lekerk, I am coming with you."

"I can't ask-"

"You can't stop me, either. I owe my life to you," Bjorn pushed to the back of his mind the goal of seeing his children again. He wanted his children to see an honorable man. He needed to help Kedrun to keep his honor. "You'll need help to do this."

Koren offered a hand and they shook. "Thank you."

"Thank me after we've found Lekerk. Now, to the stables. I'll need a horse."

"Kedrun, you need to tell me why you want to find Lekerk," Bjorn said as their horses trotted easily along the road. Thunderbolt had gotten over teasing Bjorn's horse; at first Koren kept having to rein in his powerful royal horse, who needed to demonstrate how much faster he was. Bjorn's horse had taken the wise course of ignoring Thunderbolt, except when Thunderbolt nipped at him, then Bjorn's horse nipped back hard enough to leave a mark. That had seemed to end the silent contest, and the horses got along well after that. Koren's purse was lighter after purchasing the horse for Bjorn; he counted that a good bargain, if Bjorn could help him find the bandit Lekerk.

"I want him to tell me where he got my mother's pendant," Koren declared simply.

"That's all?" Bjorn looked doubtfully at his young companion. "Lekerk is a bandit, and a cruel one, to be sure. That doesn't mean he didn't simply buy that pendant at a market-"

"My mother would never sell that pendant!" Koren protested.

"Kedrun, you are young-"

"Don't tell me I don't know my own parents!"

"I am telling you," Bjorn said patiently, "that you don't know everything that could have happened. Your father may have been injured or fallen ill, and your mother could have sold the pendant to pay for his medical care. Or your parents, you said you don't know where they are? They moved away from your village?"

"Yes." Koren didn't want to say any more. "I ran away, then they left."

"If they were traveling, their horse could have broken a leg, and they needed to buy a horse. My point, Koren, is there are many reasons why your mother may have sold her pendant. You also need to consider that successful bandits like Lekerk often act as a fence for other bandits-"

"A fence?" Koren asked, puzzled.

Bjorn chuckled. "A go-between. It's criminal slang. When bandits or burglars have something they can't immediately sell, they will sell it or trade it to a 'fence'. The fence pays a lot less than the item is worth, because the fence later expects to sell it for a higher price later. There was a case of a fence in Rellanon, she bought up gold jewelry that was burgled from royalty. Jewelry like that is distinctive, and only other royalty can afford to buy it. So, it's hard to sell. This fence bought up a lot of it, operated her own furnace, and melted it down into gold bars." The former king's guard chuckled again. "When she was finally caught, she got only a short time in jail, because she had discovered much of the supposedly gold jewelry bought by the quality folk was only partly gold. The royalty were glad to know which goldsmiths were cheating them. And the fence? When she sold the gold bars she'd made, she made sure they were pure gold. She knew what type of trouble not to get into. Sorry, I got away from my point there. Kedrun, it could be that your mother didn't sell her pendant. But it could also be that Lekerk and his men aren't the ones who stole it from her. You shouldn't go getting your hopes up that you will get the answer you want from Lekerk."

Koren had not thought of that. He hadn't thought beyond finding Lekerk, and somehow getting the man to tell him where he'd gotten the pendant. Koren got a terrible sinking feeling in the pit of his stomach. What if Lekerk said he had bought the pendant, or got it from another bandit? How would Koren know the man wasn't lying?

Thunderbolt sensed his master's reverie, and slowed to a walk. Bjorn reined his own horse in and dropped back. Koren covered his face with his hands for a moment.

"It's all right, lad," Bjorn reached over and patted Koren's back. "We find Lekerk, that's what we do first. We can figure out the rest later."

"I have to know," Koren whispered. "I *have* to. I have to try."

"That's the spirit!" Bjorn kneed his horse back into a trot, and Thunderbolt followed. "Besides, there's a reward for Lekerk. We could come out of this with a fat purse of coins-"

"You can keep the coins," Koren surprised Bjorn by saying, "I don't want them." Collecting a reward also risked drawing attention to himself and exposing his true identity. "After we find Lekerk, however it happens, I'm going north."

"Aye, Kedrun, and I'm going with you."

"Thank you," Koren said simply and honestly. They rode on for another mile, each in his own thoughts, then Koren asked a question that he had been mulling over. "Bjorn, how *will* we catch

Lekerk?" The infamous bandit had mercenaries after his head, to collect the reward money. And Duke Bargann had his own soldiers out searching for Lekerk, because the bandit lately had been preying on commerce within Farlane province. How were two people going to find, let alone capture, a skilled and ruthless bandit when so many others had failed?

"Aye," Bjorn smiled to himself. "I was wondering when you were going to ask that. It depends on what we find up north, but I have some ideas. Let me mull it over."

While Bjorn tried to think of a way to find the bandit leader who had eluded soldiers and mercenaries who had been seeking him for years, Koren thought about his other problem. In his mind, Koren imagined holding the point of his sword at Lekerk's throat, demanding the bandit tell him where he had gotten Amalie Bladewell's pendant. The thought of making the bandit fear for his life pleased Koren greatly. What bothered him was that, as Bjorn suggested, Lekerk could say that he had bought the pendant, or had traded another gang of bandits for it. Lekerk could tell Koren anything, and Koren would have no way of knowing whether the bandit was telling him the truth or not. "Bjorn, I know you're thinking of how to find Lekerk. I have another problem." He explained his dilemma.

Bjorn thought for a long while, considering and discarding ideas in his head. "Kedrun, I don't rightly know how to get Lekerk to tell the truth. Here is what I can tell you; if the man thinks telling the truth will get him further into trouble, he will either tell you nothing, or lie about it. You need a way for the man to think that telling you the truth costs him nothing. Or, better yet, that telling the truth will benefit him. I don't know how to do that, either, except, hmm, the one thing that motivates a bandit is the prospect of money."

"He could tell me anything, and I'd have no way to know he isn't lying," Koren complained.

Bjorn scratched his beard and thought. They covered a quarter mile before the former king's guard spoke again. "Unless you tell him you already know most of the story, you only need him to fill in the details? Kedrun, whatever story you cook up for Lekerk's benefit, he can't ever suspect that pendant belonged to your mother. If he thinks you believe that he harmed your parents, he will know anything he says to you will be at great risk to his life."

After many days of riding, Koren thought he had a way to get Lekerk to talk, and to assure the bandit told him the truth. He discussed the plan with Bjorn, and Bjorn congratulated him on coming up with a clever idea. Bjorn himself would not reveal his own plans for finding Lekerk. "Kedrun, it depends on what we learn when we get to Hellvik. There's a Farlane army garrison there; it's a safe bet they have been in the thick of the hunt for Lekerk. If the garrison commander has had no luck finding Lekerk, well, I'm expecting he'll be open to listening to some new ideas."

The village of Hellvik existed for two reasons. The duke of Farlane had established a garrison there for his army, where there was a substantial bridge over a river. While most villages were centered around farmland, the generally rocky and swampy soil of northern Farlane province did not encourage farming, other than hay to feed cattle and horses. The ducal army post was there to se-cure portions of the important east-west roads across Farlane into Winterthur, and the north-south road that came down from the dwarf lands. When Bjorn approached the army post, stating that he was a mercenary hunting bandits, the soldier told Bjorn that the commander was in the field and would not return until the following morning. Bjorn left with the impression that mer-cenaries were distinctly unwelcome in Hellvik.

The village had only one tavern, a rough, well-worn place with, according to the soldier, bitter beer and skimpy portions of beef stew and roast chicken. Bjorn took Koren in past the low front door to find the only late afternoon customers were four dwarves. By the empty tankards of beer on the table in front of them, Bjorn guessed the dwarves had started drinking early that day. They were also bored, and seeing newcomers perked up their interest. "I'm Barlen," one dwarf said as he stuck out a hand. Barlen was more than a head shorter than Koren but powerfully built. Like al-most all dwarf men Koren had seen, Barlen had a well-groomed, long beard, although Barlen's beard was not adorned with beads or any other ornamentation. Though there were streaks of gray in Barlen's blonde beard, Koren thought the dwarf looked youthful. Koren reminded himself that he knew little of dwarves.

Bjorn shook the dwarf's hand in a grip strong enough to generate respect but not inviting a contest. "I'm Bjorn, this one here is Kedrun. We hear tell the beer here is bitter, and the food por-tions small?"

"Small? Shameful is more like it," Barlen scoffed. In a low voice, he added "Slip the serving girl a few coins, and you'll find a reasonable amount on your plate. She also will tap the better cask of beer for you."

"I'm grateful," Bjorn nodded, and just then, a serving girl came through the doorway from the kitchen. Following Barlen's advice, Bjorn ordered one beef stew and one roast chicken dinner, and water for himself and Koren. He slipped two copper coins into the pocket of the girl's skirt, and she smiled knowingly.

"What's your business in this miserable part of the world?" Barlen asked as he propped his boots on a table, and took out a pipe.

"We're bounty hunters and we're looking for a bandit; Lekerk is his name. There's reward money in it," Bjorn explained.

That remark drew a laugh from all four of the dwarves. "Lekerk?" Barlen broke up with laugh-ter. "You two and a hundred others are seeking that reward money. The four of us," Barlen used his pipe to point to the other three dwarves, "having been looking for him more than two months. There were a dozen of us until last week; the others gave up and went home last week. We'll likely be following them soon. Our coins are running low, and our luck ran out before we got here. With only four of us, we dare not take on Lekerk's band."

"You've had no luck at all?" Koren asked anxiously.

Barlen frowned. "Does bad luck count? No, we haven't seen hide nor hair of Lekerk the whole time we've been here. And we have covered roads in every direction."

Bjorn lowered his voice. "Your bad luck had some help, I think?" He looked toward the door to the kitchen.

"Mmm," Barlen leaned forward across the table. "That's what I've been thinking. Our friendly local bandit has spies everywhere. Including," he glared at Bjorn, "people who say they are mercenaries hunting him."

"We're not spies," Koren said hotly, leaning toward the dwarf.

"Calm down, there, my young friend," Bjorn put out an arm to hold Koren back.

"He is young," Barlen observed. "You would have me believe the two of you plan to capture or kill Lekerk, by yourselves?" He laughed. "Your friend Kedrun here isn't old enough to enjoy drinking beer. How are the two of you going to find Lekerk, let alone take on him and his gang?"

Bjorn leaned forward again. "The two of us aren't." he looked around the table. "The six of us are."

"Ho!" Barlen slapped the table as he chuckled. "You have great ambitions, or you think me a fool. One is amusing, the other insulting."

"Ambition? Aye, that we are." Bjorn unbuttoned his shirt and pulled down his left sleeve to expose a tattoo. "I was a king's man. Those days are past, but I know how to fight. And Kedrun here, he's a berserker."

"Strong words," Barlen mused, but the dwarf had been clearly impressed by Bjorn's tattoo.

"Kedrun will best any of you with a sword," Bjorn boasted confidently. In the evenings, he had watched 'Kedrun' practice shooting arrows, setting up targets at impossible ranges and hitting the targets every time. "We have time before our food is ready, would you care for a wager?" He took a silver coin from a pocket and slapped it on the table.

Barlen's eyes grew wide from seeing the shiny silver coin. "What type of wager?"

"Bjorn, is this really necessary?" Koren whispered. Barlen had drawn a circle on a tree with white chalk; the bet was that Koren could put five out of five arrows in the circle. The circle was the size of Barlen's outstretched hand, that is, it was not big at all. The tree was uncomfortably far away, and there was an unpredictable, gusty wind that afternoon. Besides the four dwarves, a half dozen villagers and two Farlane Army soldiers had gathered to watch the show; none of them thought Koren had any chance to win the bet.

"It is. You can do this?" Bjorn asked nervously. Perhaps he should not have let Barlen pace off the distance, it was quite far.

"Yes," Koren hissed, annoyed. He had no doubt about hitting the target; the difficult part would be putting a couple arrows just inside the edge of the circle; to conceal his true uncanny skill. With the wind throwing off his aim, it took him five minutes to put all five arrows inside the target circle, because with each arrow he had to wait until it 'felt right' to release the bow-string.

"Mmm," Barlen grumbled. "Well, everyone gets lucky."

Koren did not bear the insult well. "Do you wish to see me do it again? For double the money? Or more?"

Barlen ignored the entreaties of his fellows, who were eager to get their precious money back. "No, you've shown your skill," he looked at Bjorn in an unfriendly manner. "Is this what you do? Pretend to be bounty hunters, and fleece unsuspecting honest folk out of their money?"

That remark angered Koren. "We are hunting for Lek-"

"Hold, Kedrun," Bjorn advised. "Barlen, you can keep your coin, if you'll hear us out. I'll even buy you a beer," he offered graciously.

Barlen made a sour face. "I've had enough beer for one day, but my fellows will be grateful for it. All right, you've proven me wrong once today, I'll listen while you spin your tale."

An hour later, Barlen was forced to admit that Bjorn had a plan, and it was as good a plan as any. "I'm willing to try it. You'll need the army here to cooperate."

"Aye," Bjorn grimaced. "The soldier I talked with was not welcoming to mercenaries and bounty hunters."

"Oh, ignore them. The soldiers here all want to get the reward money for themselves, and they'd be welcome to it, if they were willing to go more than a mile from their soft beds. The commander is a man named Cramer, he's a good one. He took over here from the previous commander two months ago, and he's had his men actually out escorting caravans, and patrolling the roads for bandits. He captured a gang of bandits in his first month, a small gang that was more of an annoyance than a threat. Since then, Lekerk must have gotten the word, and he's made himself scarce. We know Lekerk is still around here somewhere; at least once a week a group of wagons goes missing, or survivors straggle to Hellvik and report they were robbed by Lekerk."

"They know it is him, for sure?" Koren asked eagerly.

Barlen chuckled. "He makes no secret about it, Kedrun. The man boasts about how feared he is. He wants everyone to know he is the great Lekerk. He even has a name for himself. 'Scourge of the North Woods', he calls himself," Barlen said with disgust.

Bjorn nodded. "He thinks a lot of himself. A man like that needs to be taken down a peg or two. Does anyone have a rough idea where he is now?"

Barlen gestured with his pipe to the four corners of the compass. "North, south, east, west? No one knows, except Lekerk himself. Me and my band, we certainly searched all over. We'd be south of here, and come back to find he hit a caravan to the west. It's like chasing a ghost. He has too many spies everywhere, is what I think."

"Including in the Farlane Army?" Bjorn asked. "The local garrison here?"

"That's more than a bit possible," Barlen said morosely. "Likely that's why we weren't able to get even a single clue to help us find Lekerk. I can say this new commander, Cramer, he's cracked down on the garrison here. When he takes a patrol out, he doesn't tell anyone where he's going beforehand, and sometimes he doubles back and goes the opposite way after he's left Hellvik behind. He's had at least a measure of success, we know he disrupted Lekerk's operations; made him move his base once. Rumor has it, Lekerk is annoyed enough to put a price on Cramer's head. Our commander here surrounds himself with a chosen group of people, and trusts no one else. His life depends on it."

The next day, after Captain Cramer returned to the garrison, Barlen took Bjorn over to see the soldier, and introduced the two men to each other. Cramer was impressed that Bjorn was a former king's man. "Any luck?" Barlen asked, hoping Cramer had not already killed or captured Lekerk. Or, almost as bad, driven the bandit gang far away from Hellvik.

"No," Cramer answered with great weariness. "Two days out there, and nothing! All we found was an old campsite only big enough for a handful of men, and a firepit long gone cold. On our way back, we escorted a caravan that wasn't attacked, so there's that, I suppose." He took off his boots and rubbed his aching feet. "Duke Bargann is not going to be pleased with me."

"We may be able to do something about that," Bjorn offered. "You can only take your men in one direction, we can cover another."

"The six of you?" Cramer asked skeptically.

"No," Bjorn said with a smile. "We'll need more than six." He explained his plan.

It was a sign of Cramer's desperation for results that he did not immediately dismiss Bjorn's idea. "That's all you need?" He asked with sarcasm.

"No, Captain," Bjorn continued. "We'll need two of your wagons. And, paint. Some bright paint, several colors."

"Paint?" Cramer asked, intrigued. "Why?"

"Because," Bjorn pointed to the battered Farlane army wagons. "To catch a thief, you need bait. Anyone can see those two wagons do not belong to rich merchants."

CHAPTER SIXTEEN

Teregen was a fair-sized town, located at the junction of two rivers. One of the rivers flowed down from Burwyck, allowing the ducal army contingent to float swiftly down to Teregen aboard barges, rather than walking the entire way. Despite Kyre's determination to reach Teregen ahead of Captain Jaques, the ducal army commander already had his soldiers, horses and equipment unloaded from the barges and ready to march by the time Kyre arrived. Kyre's delay had been because a bridge to the south had been damaged in that spring's flood, and with the war taking priority of manpower and material in Tarador, the bridge had not yet been repaired. Kyre, Falzon and Carter had been forced to wait for a very slow ferry to carry them across, with Kyre fuming at the delay. His mood was not improved when he saw Captain Jaques was riding at the head of the army column, under a banner that bore the Falco family crest.

"Captain Jaques!" Kyre shouted, out of breath. "You made excellent time from Burwyck."

Jaques was not surprised to see his future duke, he had received a message from Duke Falco, stating that the Falco heir was to take command of the battalion. He was surprised to see Kyre so soon. Jaques bowed. "Yes, Your Grace. I was ordered to bring the battalion to Anschulz with all possible speed."

"Excellent. Then," Kyre couldn't think of anything useful to do that Jaques had not already done. "We ride."

"Hurry up, you laggards," shouted a sergeant from the rear of the column, as Kyre was riding past with Captain Jaques.

Kyre pulled his horse to a slow walk. "What is the problem, Sergeant?"

The sergeant snatched off his cap and bowed. "Begging your pardon, Your Grace, but these two aren't keeping up with the column's march," he slapped a rope across the backs of two soldiers in front of him.

"Hold!" Kyre ordered, and the men stopped walking. He had noticed they were both limping badly. "You can't walk?"

"Sire," one of the soldiers answered, not daring to look at Kyre. "That is, Your Grace, I twisted my ankle on the barge, tripped over ropes in the dark. Luren here," he pointed to the man beside him, "hurt his knee when a clumsy sailor dropped a sack of grain on it."

CRAIG ALANSON

"It's true, Your Grace," Luren added, staring at the road. "I'd be all right in a few days," he winced from the pain, "this marching is making it worse."

"Sergeant," Kyre asked, "have these two men been a problem before?" He noticed the two men were marching without packs, to lighten their load.

"No, Your Grace," the sergeant answered honestly.

"Captain Jaques, making men march when they are injured only leads to men who can't fight. Let these two ride in a wagon, until they can walk properly."

"Sire," Jaques cautioned his young leader in a low voice, "we don't have room, the wagons are full." The march was only scheduled to be for six days, over a range of hills. Once they reached the Tormel river, they would board barges for the ride down to near the western border of Tarador. Making use of river transport was the only practical way to move large armies within the borders of Tarador; there were not enough horses in the land for every soldier, and supplying horses would be too expensive. So, other than small groups of cavalry, most soldiers in Tarador marched, unless they were lucky to ride a barge or a wagon. "I only hired enough wagons to carry our gear." That was on the strict instructions of Duke Falco, who watched every expenditure by his army carefully.

"What is in that second wagon?" Kyre asked. "In the back?" He had not been able to see the wagons being loaded in Teregen.

"That is your campaign tent, Sire," Jaques explained. He referred to a large, luxurious white tent that Kyre would use as his headquarters while the army was stationed in the field.

"Dump it," Kyre ordered. "I don't need luxury, I need soldiers who can fight."

"But, Sire!" Jaques protested, shocked. "That tent belongs to the army of Burwyck," he added. Jaques had planned to use the tent as his headquarters also. It was, if nothing else, a symbol of his authority. For a Burwyck army captain to use a regular tent, or to set up a table under the shade of a tree, would be scandalous.

Kyre smiled with one side of his mouth. "If my father desires that tent so badly, he can come and get it. I will send him a note detailing where we left it."

"Your Grace," Jaques' face was turning white. Duke Falco would certainly blame Jaques for losing an expensive tent.

"Captain Jaques," Kyre raised his voice above the whisper they had been using. "I am the heir to Burwyck, and my father sent me here to take command. As long as I am here, you will obey my orders without question. Is that clear?"

Jaques winced at the sting of Kyre's remark. "Yes, Your Grace," he answered stiffly.

Kyre had not meant to hurt the man, who he knew to be a good soldier and a disciplined but fair leader of men. "Jaques, that does not mean that I do not value your experience and advice. I do things differently from my father, and we will both have to adjust to each other. For my part, I will follow proper Burwyck army protocol when I can. And," he smiled, "I expect you will do your best from keeping me from making the worst possible mistakes."

"Yes, Your Grace," Jaques responded, slightly mollified. Leading his army contingent alongside the Royal Army, in a foreign province, in a desperate battle to save Tarador from invasion by their ancient enemy, would be difficult on its own. Here, Captain Jaques also had to tolerate, adapt to, and educate a young heir to the duchy of Burwyck.

Perhaps, Jaques thought to himself, he would be lucky enough to fall victim to an orc arrow soon after arriving at the border. To die in combat would be a far better fate for a soldier, than to get drawn into the mess of politics.

An hour later, Kyre dropped back from the head of the column, holding his horse off to the side as the soldiers marched by, followed by the wagons. Captain Jaques followed Kyre, keeping silent. Kyre wanted to see the soldiers he would be fighting with, and he wanted them to see him. He wanted the army to see him on a horse, strong and confident, when in truth Kyre was anything but confident. He feared that at any moment, a message would arrive from his father, recalling him to Linden, or worse. Until then, he was determined to make the best of the situation.

When the second wagon rolled past, he saw the two men who had been limping were now sitting at the back of the wagon. Their feet hung over the back, and the two were looking completely miserable. They knew their fellow soldiers resented marching, while those two rode in a wagon. "Luren, is it?" Kyre asked.

"He is Luren, Your Grace," the man said quickly, taking off his cap and bending low in a seated bow. "I'm Tom Potosi."

"Well, Potosi," Kyre said with an exaggerated frown, "are your hands injured also?"

"No, Sire," Potosi expression showed surprise. He and Luren held up their hands. "Our hands work fine, Your Grace."

"Excellent. Sergeant Garner!" Kyre shouted, and a sergeant came running over to walk beside the wagon.

"Yes, Your Grace?" The sergeant asked.

"I am sure that we have gear or clothing that needs mending, or potatoes that need to be peeled for dinner. Idle hands," Kyre pointed to Luren and Potosi, "make for unhappy soldiers. And when we stop for the night, these two are on cooking duty. And whatever duty you can find for them, that does not require marching."

"Yes, Sire," the sergeant beamed happily, and Potosi and Luren smiled also. There was indeed gear that needed mending, work soldiers had to do at the end of a long day of marching; work that took away from what little leisure time the soldiers had.

"Giving those men work to do, Sire?" Jaques asked later in a quiet voice. "That is a good idea. Their fellows will not resent them as laggards quite so much."

"I might be capable of learning, Jaques?" Kyre asked with a grin.

"You might, Your Grace, you just might."

The battalion halted for the night at a farm just outside a village. With hundreds of soldiers, a half dozen wagons and dozens of horses, there was no place in the village to set up their encampment, and the local stable could not accommodate so many horses. The farmer was delighted to take Captain Jaques' coins in exchange for use of the farm and all the grain the battalion's horses needed. The farmer and his wife also did a brisk business selling canned fruit, jars of jam and honey to the soldiers.

As tents were being set up for the night's encampment, Kyre strode over to the wagon that served as the battalion's field kitchen. The cooks had gotten fires started in the ovens as soon as their wagon stopped, and something was beginning to bubble in the large kettles. "Your Grace?" One of the cooks asked anxiously. "You wish to inspect the kitchen?" The cook helpfully held out a pair of white cotton gloves for Kyre to use in checking the cleanliness of the kitchen utensils.

To the surprise of the cooks, Kyre shook his head. "No, I trust Captain Jaques inspects your equipment regularly." The field kitchen wagon, and the hospital wagon, were the only wagons that had made the long trip all the way from Burwyck; all the other wagons had been hired when the battalion got off the river barges. Kyre picked up a battered metal bowl. "I wish to taste what is for dinner."

The cooks froze as if they'd been shot with arrows. Officers never ate the food that was served to common soldiers. And royalty certainly never expressed any interest in knowing what the common soldiers were eating. With trembling hands, the chief cook lifted the lid of a kettle and ladled out a small portion into Kyre's bowl. Kyre sniffed at it suspiciously, then tasted it. "This is supposed to be beef stew?" The Falco heir asked.

"Yes, Your Grace," the cook bowed low, wringing his hands. "We have casks of salt beef-"

"And not enough of it," Kyre observed as he lifted the kettle's lid and stirred the stew with a ladle. "This is a vegetable stew, with salt beef for flavoring. I am not pleased. How do you expect soldiers to march all day, on stomachs filled with this?" He did not truly expect an answer from the cooks, who stared at the ground in shame. Kyre reached into his pocket and pulled out a coin purse. "Lieutenant Baines!" He called out, and the man ran over.

"Yes, Your Grace?"

"I will be dining with the troops tonight, as will all the officers," as Kyre spoke, he could see the shock and disappointment on the lieutenant's face. No doubt, the officers were arranging to buy chickens from the farmer, and have the cooks roast them for dinner. "Take these coins," he handed the silver pieces to Baines, "and bargain with our good farmer for a couple of his old cows," Kyre pointed to the pasture, where several fat cows were contentedly munching on hay. He winked at Baines. "We will put some beef into this beef stew."

Luren and Potosi, after a long evening of helping the cooks to prepare, cook, serve and then clean up, finally were able to sit down and enjoy their own dinner. Sergeant Garner joined them.

"Well, you two layabouts, did you enjoy your time in the wagon? Riding along like royalty, waving to the common folk as you went by, taking the air while your coach took you on a turn about the countryside?"

"Ah, Sergeant," Luren said as he wriggled on the ground to make his sore back as comfortable as he could. "That damned wagon bumps and lurches over every rut in the road, I swear the driver was aiming for every pothole."

"Aye," Potosi agreed. "The driver has springs under the seat for her comfort," he made a rude gesture toward where their wagon's driver was sitting. "In the back, we got the worst of it. My back and my backside are killing me."

"Tomorrow, I'd rather walk," Luren grumbled.

"Can you?" Sergeant Garner asked.

"I don't think so, not yet," Luren said as he flexed his sore knee. Changing the subject, he dug a spoon into his bowl of beef stew, and pulled out a piece of actual beef. "This is the best meal I've had from that kitchen."

"Thanks to His Grace," Potosi observed, not sure what to make of the ducal heir. Kyre was sitting on the ground against a fence, eating beef stew with the officers. "Holding court over there, looks like."

"He's a clever one," Garber announced. "he let you two ride-"

"Aye, and then gave us enough work for four men!" Luren protested.

Garner ignored the interruption. "And he will be sleeping in a regular tent with us tonight, rather than taking the best room in the village's inn. He buys us fresh beef, now he's talking with the officers. He's sounding them out, seeing who of them will be loyal to him, if it comes to that. And us," Garner ladled a spoonful of beef stew into his mouth, "he thinks to buy our loyalty with beef."

"Better that, than to try beating loyalty into us with the end of a rope," Luren said quietly, "Sergeant."

Garner took no offense. He knew Luren was a good soldier. "We will see how well this purchased loyalty works for His Grace, when it comes to fighting orcs."

"Maybe His Grace is different," Potosi mused, and pointed toward Kyre with his spoon. "he is eating our food. And making the officers eat it, too. If that keeps up, I have hopes my stomach will survive this campaign."

"We will see how long that lasts," Luren grimaced. "Sure, His Grace is eating with us now, when we have fresh beef. Wait until all we have is dried fish, or salted pork and mashed peas, and biscuits so hard you could kill an orc with one."

"I hear tell he gave up his tent for a sick soldier, earlier this year," Potosi said hopefully. "And he helped his guards set up and take down tents. Kyre may like to get his hands dirty, on occasion."

"All I can say is," Garner ate more of the delicious stew before it grew cold, "dirty hands will not be his biggest problem, when his father finds out the heir has been coddling the Duke's soldiers. Duke Falco doesn't hold with fraternizing between royalty and common folk."

Four days later, even Sergeant Garner had to admit that Kyre Falco was indeed different from his father the duke. The officers and Kyre ate only what the common soldiers ate. Even when the cooks were nearly in tears due to the poor selection of food supplies left, Kyre ate what the cooks were able to serve, and complained no more than anyone else. When they passed by farms, Kyre had his lieutenants bargain for chickens, and each evening a different group of soldiers were given chickens to roast on their own. When Kyre told his officers that their turn for a special dinner would come only after all the soldiers had enjoyed a special meal, his lieutenants somehow found the energy to range far and wide in search of chickens and anything else they could find. One especially eager party of three lieutenants and a sergeant returned one afternoon with two deer, four chickens and two fat geese, to the cheers of the entire battalion.

Even the officers ate well that night.

Koren, Bjorn and the four dwarves took their newly painted wagons north. They could have gone any direction; Koren wanted to go north because that 'felt right'. Bjorn thought going west was a better bet, but he agreed to follow his friend's lead on their first trip. He also did not tell the dwarves the reason he had decided to go north.

Bjorn and Koren rode ahead on horseback, with the dwarves driving the two wagons. Barlen was on the seat of the first wagon, feeling ridiculous and exposed. The wagons were bait and Barlen knew he was a target; any bandit wishing to capture the wagons would shoot at the drivers first. Two days had gone by, with the wagons stopping every few hours so Koren and Bjorn could ride ahead and look for signs of trouble. So far, all they had seen was wilderness, and to Koren's excitement, the snow-capped peaks of the mountains in the dwarf homeland. The mountains were only a faint line on the northern horizon; they still grabbed Koren's imagination. "Have you ever been there, Bjorn?"

"Aye, once. King Adric visited, early in his reign. He wished to show his respect to the dwarves, and forge an alliance with their leaders. That alliance stands today," Bjorn added with considerable pride.

"Why are the mountains covered with snow, this late in the year?" Koren could not understand that. It was late summer in Tarador; apples were ripening in the orchards. Mornings were already cool in the north of the land, soon there would be frost tinging the trees before sunrise.

"You are only seeing the very peaks of those mountains, Kedrun. Their lower slopes are free of snow now. And, unless you have been there, you can't imagine how tall those mountains are. The dwarves say those mountaintops hold up the sky, and I believe them."

"Will we be-"

Bjorn snapped his fingers twice softly, the signal for danger. "Kedrun, you see that tree up ahead on the right? Just past that great old oak."

Koren knew to keep his eyes staring straight ahead. "Which one?"

"I think it's an ash. It's dead, see, most of the leaves have fallen off it? But there are some leaves still clinging to it. That tree is recently dead; someone cut it. Up yonder on the right is another tree like it."

"Bandits?"

"Got to be. They'll drop that second tree ahead of us, then this one behind, and our wagons will be well and truly trapped on the road. That's good, it means they'll try to take the wagons without fighting, if they can." As he spoke, Bjorn tugged at the red bandana around his neck, as if were itching him. He tugged at the bandana until the tail of it spun around to hang over the back of his collar. The wagon drivers were watching; that was the signal to them. Barlen on the seat of the lead wagon pulled three times on a rope that went into the back of the wagon, alerting the Far-lane army archers there. One of the archers dropped a blue rag from the bottom of the lead wagon, giving the signal to the wagon behind. As Koren and Bjorn passed the first dead tree, everyone in the party was alert. The archers each had an arrow nocked and ready; others in the back of the wagons pulled the pins to lower the sides, holding the sides up by hand. Up on the seats of the two wagons, the dwarves used their boots to nudge their battleaxes and bows out from under the seats, where they were readily available.

Koren took deep, even breaths to keep himself calm, although he was anything but calm. Anything could go wrong. He was not afraid for his own life. His fear was that he might miss his only chance to answer the question of why his mother's pendant had come to be in the hands of a no-torious bandit. He feared that another gang of bandits may attack the wagons; that Lekerk may be far away. Or that these bandits were Lekerk's own, but the man himself was not with them, or staying far enough behind that he could escape easily. Or, worse, that the archers would kill Lek-erk. Koren and Bjorn had stressed to the archers the importance of keeping Lekerk alive, and the archers had nodded and agreed. But Koren had seen in the eyes of the archers that they knew the reward for Lekerk would be paid the same whether the bandit was alive or dead, and dead was much more simple to manage. An archer could kill Lekerk from afar, with little risk to the archer himself. Approaching Lekerk involved taking on risk, with no reward.

So, Koren did not trust the archers to discriminate between bandits. He and Bjorn had agreed they would go after Lekerk themselves. Go after Lekerk, and then- Then what? Koren did have an idea how he could capture the infamous bandit, and then how he would get the man to talk. His plan required Simon Lekerk to cooperate.

As he rode past the first dead tree, Koren almost had to laugh. Perhaps it was the keen senses that Paedris had given him, or perhaps the bandits had become overconfident and sloppy. He could see movement in the underbrush; the bandits too eager to get moving. He could see the outlines of people who had not concealed themselves well enough behind bushes. There were muddy tracks where the bandits had walked off the road; they had not taken any particular care in covering signs of their presence. Bjorn glanced to Koren out of the side of his eyes; Bjorn had seen them also. Koren could also hear the bandits whispering to another. One of them was complaining about insects biting as he lay behind a scrawny bush. Another bandit swore because the two wagons were moving too slowly. The bandits' lack of discipline annoyed Koren enough that he was tempted to turn and charge into the forest at them. He did nothing of the sort; instead he spoke to Bjorn, in a voice that he hoped was not so loud that the bandits would know he was playing for their benefit. "The inn ahead has good beer, you say?"

Bjorn gave an exaggerated shrug. "If it's still there. I haven't passed this way in many a year. I wouldn't trust a dwarf to know good beer," he said with a chuckle and a look back at the wagons. That glance assured him the wagons were ready, and that the second wagon was now past the first dead tree. The dwarves driving the wagons were cool under pressure; they were sitting back in their seats, holding the reins almost slack. One of the dwarves on the seat of the second wagon was filling a pipe, acting as if he didn't have a care in the world.

The bandits waited almost too long to drop the trees onto the road; Bjorn grew concerned that the tree in front would fall right on him, or fall behind him and cut him off from the wagons. He was about to rein in his horse to slow down, when there was a loud cracking sound, and with a groan, a tree crashed down across his path. The tree bounced once as Bjorn and Koren made a show of being startled and having trouble getting their mounts under control. Thunderbolt annoyed Koren by putting on a performance of dancing and bucking, almost throwing Koren off his back until Koren dug his heels in. Koren stood in the stirrups, arrow knocked and ready. Bjorn also had his own bow ready, although he had warned Koren that he had no great skill with a bow.

Bandits emerged from their poor concealment, some of them with bows of their own, although none of them had arrows ready. Koren tried to decide which bandit to target first; he saw that the dwarves were also selecting targets. No one was shooting just yet. The casual attitude of the bandits troubled Koren. Surely this could not possibly be the men of the ruthless Lekerk?

"Ho there, the wagons!" A voice rang out in a mocking tone, as a man stepped out onto a tree stump beside the road on the right, just beyond the fallen tree in front of Koren. "There is no need for violence," he laughed. "Please, friends, lower your bows."

"You go first," Barlen shouted from the seat of the first wagon. They had decided ahead of time that, as the wagons supposedly were owned by dwarves and Barlen was a dwarf, he should speak as the leader.

"I am unarmed," the man held up his hands and twirled around slowly, showing that he was unafraid. "Oh, except for my sword, of course, And a dagger. Maybe another dagger in my boot. You can't be too careful around these parts; I hear tell there are ruffians about."

The bandits all laughed at that remark.

Koren did not join in the laughter. Was this Lekerk? The man dressed like a dandy, with a colorful plume of feathers sticking out of his broad-brimmed hat. He wore a clean linen shirt and black pants, but no vest as the day was hot. His boots were polished and of fine leather, not the sort of footwear for walking long distances in the wilderness.

And across the left side of his face was a thin white scar.

It was Lekerk.

"Kedrun, not yet," Bjorn cautioned. "We don't know for sure that is him. And we are badly outnumbered. Not all of us have your speed and skill."

"Ruffians?" Barlen was also not laughing. "I see ruffians, and worse. We paid Sturlington for protection, you fool."

"Ah, Sturlington. Regrettably, Sturlington is no longer able to offer protection on this stretch of road, or any other. He ate something that disagreed with him," the bandits all roared with laughter at that remark. "The steel of my dagger did not agree with his belly, it seems. And so, this stretch of road belongs to me now. I would offer you a refund on the money you paid for protection," the man's teeth sparkled in the sunlight, "but my men would like to be paid, you see."

"And who are you?" Barlen demanded.

The man bowed deeply, flamboyantly, clearly having fun. "Simon Lekerk, at your service, master dwarf. "Yes, it is I, the famous and terrible bandit Lekerk. Why, you should be honored, for ones such as yourselves to come to my attention."

"This is an honor I would rather do without," Barlen growled.

"Not yet," Bjorn hissed, and Kedrun relaxed the bowstring. Lekerk could duck behind a tree in a flash; the man was being very careful.

"I am hurt, master dwarf," Lekerk placed a hand over his heart as if stricken. "We went through all this trouble, on your account. Now, please, lower your weapons. This is a fine day," he shaded his face with a hand and glanced up at the sun. "It would be a shame to spoil it with bloodshed."

"Your blood will be the first shed," Barlen warned, keeping his bow at the ready.

"Master dwarf, I count six of you, and there are over two dozen of us. I do not like your chances, if we resort to violence. Come now, you are a sensible man. All we wish is whatever is in your wagons. Possibly whatever you carrying in your coin purses. Surely all that is not worth your life."

Barlen thought the bandits would be suspicious if he gave up so quickly and easily. "My master will have my hide if I lose what is in these wagons."

"That could be," Lekerk answered with a laugh, "but you will still have your hide to give. And, what a story you will have to tell! You were ambushed by the terrible bandit Lekerk," as he had been speaking, his men had been inching closer to the pair of wagons, encircling them. Koren could see that Lekerk's boast about having more than two dozen men was not a lie. For the first time, Koren questioned whether he had put all their lives in danger. "What master could blame you for losing his goods, when confronted by my famously vicious band of ruffians?"

Barlen nodded slowly, and dropped his bow on the ground. "Drop your weapons," he ordered gruffly. "He speaks the truth, we're outnumbered." What Lekerk did not see was the second bow at the dwarf's feet, tucked under the footboard of the wagon.

Bjorn nodded, then he and Koren both tucked their arrows back in the quivers, and gently dropped their bows onto the road.

"You are a wise man, master dwarf. You and your drivers step down off the wagons. Your two men on horseback can stay right where they are," Lekerk ordered. He did not want Koren and Bjorn on the ground near their bows.

Without further word from their leader, the bandits broke into a run and approached the two wagons from both sides, eager to see their prize. The first half dozen stepped down into the weed-choked ditch beside the road, when Barlen pounded his fist twice on the side of the wagon.

After that, everything happened in a chaotic flash. The sides of both wagons fell away, exposing the Farlane ducal army archers. The bandits were caught completely by surprise, and nine of them fell in the initial volley of arrows. Then it was a pitched battle, with the skilled army archers taking time to choose their targets carefully, while the bandits either shot wildly or ran away. Koren and Bjorn yanked on the thin strings tied to their bows, so they didn't have to get off their horses to retrieve them. The first target Koren sighted on was Lekerk, but the bandit leader had ducked behind a tree by the time Koren had an arrow fitted to the bowstring. Koren hesitated, then let fly the arrow when he saw a patch of black beside the tree, and the arrowhead sliced through the bandit leader's pants. Lekerk yelped in pain and flattened himself against the tree, reaching down to feel blood flowing from the cut on this thigh.

And then Koren was too busy to worry about Lekerk. A bandit arrow aimed at Bjorn hit the horse's saddle instead, with the arrowhead poking through only a couple inches into his horse's skin. The animal reared in fright and pain, throwing Bjorn off its back, and as Bjorn fell to the ground his wildly flailing left arm smacked Koren in the face. Thunderbolt lurched to keep his master from falling off, and when the horse realized that wasn't going to work, Thunderbolt swerved to the side so that he wouldn't step on Koren as the young man fell.

Fast reflexes saved Koren from landing painfully on his backside, still he bashed his hip on the dirt road and rolled over, snapping his bow underneath himself in the process. Bjorn was not so fortunate, twisting an ankle and falling backward so his head smacked into the ground. He lay stunned, the breath knocked out of him, stars swimming in his eyes. Koren tossed the now useless bow aside and knelt beside Bjorn. "Bjorn? Can you speak?" The man's eyes were open and blinking. His mouth opened in a soundless gasp, but his chest neither rose nor fell. Koren was about to shake the man back to sensibility when Thunderbolt stuck his great head over Koren's shoulder and slobbered all over Bjorn's face.

"Ugh! Ah, yuck!" Bjorn gasped, sucking in lungfuls of air. "Oh, that hurt."

"Can you stand?" Koren asked, still concerned.

"I'm fine, you young fool," he waved a hand dismissively. "Go after Lekerk." Bjorn was in pain more from embarrassment that from physical injury.

"I'll need your bow, mine is broken," Koren explained.

"You're a better shot with a bow than I am anyway," Bjorn grunted, drawing his sword and using it to help himself stand up.

Koren couldn't see Lekerk by the time he got an arrow fitted to Bjorn's bow, but he had to duck to avoid an arrow flying at his head. The bandits who hadn't fallen already had taken cover behind fallen logs, rocks or whatever they could find, and were peppering the wagons with arrows. Two of the soldiers in the wagon had been hit, and one of the dwarves took a glancing blow from an arrow. The wagons provided poor cover and arrows were raining in from both sides. Concentrating on his breathing, Koren nocked one arrow after another, waiting until he knew, somehow *knew*, he would hit his target. A bandit who was shooting from behind a fallen log suddenly felt an arrow sticking out of his leg; the arrow having flown through the small gap between the log and the ground beneath it. Another bandit readied an arrow, looking through a crack in the rock he was hidden behind. As soon as he stuck his head up to aim at a wagon, an arrow took him straight between his eyes. An arrow that had left its bow even before the bandit decided to pop up above the rock.

As suddenly as it began, the battle was over. Of the twenty six bandits, sixteen were now dead or injured seriously enough to be out of the fight. Knowing there was nothing valuable in the wagons, the bandits had no incentive to continue the fight, especially now that the odds were no longer in their favor. They broke and ran, scattering in all directions.

"Barlen?" Koren shouted.

"We're fine here," the dwarf grimaced from an arrow that had bounced off his axe and cut into his right shoulder. "You go after Lekerk!"

"Go," Bjorn agreed, wincing as he tried to put weight on his twisted ankle.

Koren hesitated. Though it was difficult to see through the underbrush, he thought he could see the white and black clad figure of Lekerk limping away. Struggling to overcome his emotions, he shook his head. "No. Much as I want to, the odds of my capturing him alone are not good. I need you with me."

"Aye," Bjorn smiled in spite of the pain. "You're learning. I can ride." Calling his horse over, he used his good ankle in the stirrup to swing up into the saddle. "Let's go, you lead."

Koren did not need to spur Thunderbolt into action, the horse was nervously prancing with eagerness to charge after the bandit leader. As soon as Koren was seated on the saddle, the horse galloped along the road and easily jumped the fallen tree, turning right to dash into the woods. Koren had to duck down and lay flat on the horse's back as Thunderbolt crashed headlong through the underbrush. Soon, the horse had to slow as the footing became treacherous and the undergrowth became a tangled mass of interlocking branches. The bandits had chosen their ambush spot well; it was impossible to pursue them into the forest on horseback. "Whoa, whoa!" Koren patted Thunderbolt's neck. "Bjorn, I think this is as far as we can ride. Can you walk?"

Bjorn's face twisted into a grimace as he climbed down from the horse and tested his sore ankle. "Aye. It will be worse after I stop and it gets stiff, so we best get moving."

Koren told Thunderbolt to go back to the road, and the horse snorted unhappily before turning and leading Bjorn's horse back the way they'd come. It was slow going for Koren and Bjorn as they tried to follow the path Lekerk had taken. Although the bandit leader had pushed branches and vines out of the way as he passed, the undergrowth had sprung back, forcing the two hunters to bend down and in some places, almost crawl under the tangled brush. "Let me go first," Bjorn insisted, taking over his sword and hacking away at the annoying bushes.

"This is slowing us down," Koren protested.

"True enough. It's also making a clearer path for Barlen to follow us," Bjorn explained. "Unless you plan for just the two of us to take on nearly a dozen bandits?"

"No," Koren felt ashamed. Bjorn had so much more experience. "You're right."

The tangled underbrush grew worse, with bushes having grown up, over and around an area of downed trees. Even though they both could see fresh red droplets where the bandit leader had dripped blood on fallen logs, they could not go any faster. "Blast!" Bjorn cursed. "There must have been a hellacious windstorm here years before, to knock down all these trees."

Koren agreed. "The trees all fell in one direction."

"There's nothing for us to do but keep going," Bjorn's grumpiness wasn't helped by his sore ankle. "Oh, this isn't good." Ahead of them, the underbrush thinned out, but that was because ahead lay a swamp. The expanse of the swamp was littered with trees laying atop each other like toothpicks. "He went that way," Bjorn pointed to logs where the moss, algae and leaf litter had been stepped on, exposing the rotting wood beneath. Mucking through a swamp where he couldn't see what he was stepping on was not going to be good for his ankle.

"I'll cut marks in the trees, so Barlen can follow. Bjorn, do you really think Barlen and the others will be coming behind us?"

Bjorn chuckled. "With the price on Lekerk's head? You can be sure every one of them who can walk will be on our heels, fast as they can. They all want that reward money. We best get to Lekerk first, if you want answers. The others will prefer to put an arrow through his gullet and get it over quick and easy."

CHAPTER SEVENTEEN

Koren held up a hand, then put a finger to his lips. "Shh," he whispered. "I hear voices ahead." Bjorn froze, listening intently. He shook his head. "I don't hear anything."

"I hear it," Koren insisted.

"Aye, I believe you. Is your hearing as good as your skill with a bow?" Before Koren could answer, Bjorn pointed to the left. "If the bandits are ahead, we shouldn't stay on Lekerk's trail. We go around, until you find where they are."

"What then?"

"Then, we make a plan when we see the lay of the land."

Koren looked blankly at the former king's guard.

And Bjorn remembered he was not talking to a trained soldier. "I meant, we make a plan, when we see where they are."

"Oh." Koren lead the way, both of them moving as quietly as they could. The underbrush had thinned out enough that they had to seek concealment, rather than constantly fighting their way through. Ahead and to the left, the ground rose, and there was a jumble of large rocks, some of them large enough to stand under. That is where the voices were coming from, and Koren's sharp eyes detected movement in between the rocks. "There-"

"I see," Bjorn whispered. He pointed up to the left. "Thick brush up that way, we can get close."

They went to the left, losing sight of the bandits; once behind cover of the dense brush, they were able to crawl slowly and silently to within thirty yards of the rocks. Bjorn pointed to two bandits acting as lookouts, lookouts who were looking in the wrong direction. Their lack of discipline disgusted Bjorn, the two bandits were focused entirely on the direction from which they expected pursuit, and were ignoring any other possibility. "Can you hit those two?" Bjorn whispered. "You'll need to be quick."

Koren didn't reply. Slowly, carefully, he rose to one knee, taking two arrows from his quiver. Bjorn took one arrow, holding it ready, and slowly pulled aside the brush in front of Koren. Hitting two targets, so rapidly the second man would not have time to react and duck under cover? Koren thought that would be a challenge, even for him. He fit an arrow to the bowstring, unable to decide which bandit to target first. And he realized he didn't need to decide, as he swung his aim back and forth. It simply felt right to target the man farther away. "Ready?"

Bjorn nodded silently, poised to give the second arrow to his archer companion. It was good Bjorn did not blink, for the second arrow was snatched from his hand while the first was in the air. The second sentry barely had time to be startled by the other man's cry of pain when an arrow thudded into his chest also, and he tumbled off the rock he had been perched on. Bjorn took the opportunity to dash forward, running without caring about concealment, Koren on his heels. They were forced to drop to the ground behind a pair of rocks half as tall as they stood, as poorly-aimed arrows came flying at them. One of the arrows knocked a chip off a rock, Bjorn was pelted in the face by pebbles. Crouched behind the rocks, Bjorn tapped the quiver on Koren's back. "There are eight of them that I see, you have three arrows left. We need a plan."

"I have a plan," Koren said, though the shaky tone of his voice did not fill Bjorn with confidence. Koren popped his head around the side of the rock. Lekerk was not more than twenty feet from him, sheltered under an overhanging rock. The bandit leader was trapped; to get out of the rocks, he would need to come past Koren, or to climb. If he climbed, he would be exposed. "Lekerk! I wish to speak with you."

"Speak? You mean to kill me. Good luck to you on that, I count only two of you, while there are eight of us," Lekerk taunted.

"Your counting didn't work so well for you earlier," Bjorn shot back, thinking that Lekerk was either foolish or overconfident, to have confirmed the number of bandits they faced. "And you've been hit, we see the blood."

"This?" Lekerk laughed and pointed to the bloody bandage around his thigh. "There are mosquitos in the swamps that bite worse than this scratch."

"Aye," Bjorn retorted, "and you walked through the stinking water of that swamp with a leg sliced open. How many days until you are burning up with fever, and your leg begins to swell?"

That wasn't funny at all to Lekerk. "I can take care of myself," he snarled. "And my men will take care of me."

"Not when your leg begins to stink with gangrene, they won't," Bjorn laughed.

"That is my concern. The two of you must want that reward money badly, in order to follow me this far." Lekerk jested.

"I don't want any reward money!" Koren insisted.

That made the bandit leader pause. "Now you have my attention. I'm curious. Why else are you here? If you're looking to join my merry band of cutthroats, you've made a bad start of it."

"I'm going to stand up," Koren said slowly.

"Don't shoot at him," Lekerk ordered the other bandits, his curiosity overcoming his caution. "Not yet."

Koren stood, ready at any moment to duck behind the rock. He took the pendant from a pocket and held it up in the sunlight, dangling from its chain. "A serving girl at a tavern in Witheringdale told us you gave this to her. I'm going to throw it you." He bent down to pick up a stone, wrapped the chain around it, and tossed it underhand. It fell to the ground at Lekerk's feet, and the man stooped warily to pick it up, never taking his eyes of Koren.

"A cheap pendant?" He laughed. "Why would anyone care about this? I can buy a better one in any market."

Koren clamped down on his anger, clenching his teeth so hard that they slipped. and he bit the inside of his cheek. The pain helped him to focus. "That pendant was stolen, from a baroness who hired us to learn who stole it from her. We need to know where you got it," Koren repeated the tale he and Bjorn had cooked up while riding together.

"This little trinket?" Lekerk asked incredulously.

"There's a reward." Koren reached into a pocket and pulled out his coin purse, jingling it for emphasis.

Neither Lekerk nor his men could believe their ears. "You are going to pay a reward to *me*? For information?"

"That is the deal, yes," Bjorn confirmed. "It may be a cheap trinket," he made an apologetic glance at Koren, "but it's a family heirloom. The Baroness wants it back, and she wants to know which of her servants stole it. So, we tracked it to Witheringdale, and now we're here."

Lekerk shook his head in amazement. "And you set up an ambush for my band, just to speak with me?"

"No," Koren declared. "We joined the dwarf because he was hunting you, and we didn't know how else to find you."

"You found me," Lekerk admitted. "All right, I'll look at this, don't know as I can say for sure where I got it," he lied. He remembered giving that pendant to the girl in Witheringdale. And so he remembered where he'd gotten the cheap pendant. "As you can imagine, I handle a lot of jewels."

"We would appreciate you searching your memory," Bjorn said with dry humor. "My companion has a purse that is yours, if you tell us where you got it, and if we're satisfied with the answer. We do know roughly where and when it went missing."

"Could you give me a hint," Lekerk asked, holding the pendant up close and pretending to examine it. He wished to learn how much the two men seeking him already knew.

Bjorn chuckled gruffly. "My companion may be young, but neither of us was born yesterday. Lekerk, the truth costs you nothing. Tell us, give the pendant back, and you will have more coins in your pocket. And we'll be on our way. The longer you delay," Bjorn warned, "the more time you give for the dwarf to bring his people here."

Lekerk considered. This may be the one time in his miserable life that telling the truth would be of benefit. "Very well. I can't promise my men won't kill you later, as you've made them mad as a nest of hornets. But I will tell you what you want to know. I can tell you," he winced from the cut on his leg, "this is the strangest thing I've heard in many a year. I got this worthless trinket in Winterthur, it was near a village, it was, yes. It was near Tinsdale."

Koren's hands began to shake; he stuffed them in his pants pockets so the bandits would not see his distress. "Who?" He asked in a strangled voice. "Who had it?"

Lekerk smirked. "I can't tell you their names. A man and a woman, riding a wagon. They had a good amount of coins with them, if that helps you." He smirked. "Your baroness lost more than a trinket, I think. The woman in the wagon had this pendant around her neck."

Bjorn saw that Koren was unable to speak, and he guessed what question his companion wished to ask next. "You robbed them along the road?"

"Very good, master huntsman," Lekerk taunted. "As we are bandits, that is what we do. Yes, we robbed them, and if they were not so stupid and stubborn to resist us, they would be alive today. And so, alas, if they were the thieves your baroness seeks, they have both already paid the price for their crimes."

"Where," Koren breathed in a quavering voice, "was their wagon going?" He heard his voice, and it was as if another person was speaking. "There is a crossroads north of Tinsdale. Was the wagon headed north of the crossroads, or south and east?"

Lekerk truly did have to think about that for a moment. "North. Yes, I'm sure of it. We had a devil of a time getting that damned wagon off the road and hiding it," he added with an evil grin. "Is that enough for your baroness? I couldn't describe the man or women to you, it was so long ago, and there have been so many-" Lekerk stopped talking.

Koren's head spun, his knees gave way, and he staggered forward onto the rock, only a hand kept him from sprawling on it and falling over.

Lekerk saw his opportunity. Maybe the two mercenaries who had followed him with such dedication actually would pay a reward for the information he had provided. Maybe they would not. What Lekerk did know is that if he and his men killed both of the mercenaries right then, he would have their reward money, plus whatever money of their own they carried. And, in a twist of irony, he would keep the pendant. Keep it, to give to another girl. Most importantly, the quicker the two mercenaries were dispatched with, the sooner Lekerk and his men could get away. He knew that with the price on his head, the dwarf and those archers would be on his heels as fast as they could. Lekerk shook his left arm, letting a throwing dagger slip down from its sheath. He grasped it with his right hand and swung his arm back to throw.

Bjorn threw first, having watched not the bandit leader's hand but the expression on the man's face. Bjorn saw when Lekerk made the split-second decision to kill Koren; even before that, Bjorn had seen Koren go limp, and knew the bandits would seize their chance to kill. Lekerk's right arm moved forward in a well-practiced throwing motion and he released the knife just as Bjorn's own knife buried itself in Lekerk's chest. The bandit leader gasped with shock, reaching down to clutch the handle of the knife embedded in him. His eyes rolled back and he fell forward full length on the ground, the weight on him plunging the fatal knife in deeper.

Lekerk's aim had been thrown off just enough to miss Koren. The young man did not even hear or feel the deadly blade as it sliced through the air close enough to cut off a lock of his hair, and clattered against a rock behind him. "Duck, you fool!" Bjorn yelled as he tackled Koren to fall behind the rock. An arrow thudded against the heel of Bjorn's boot before he landed to sprawl on Koren. "Kedrun!" Bjorn slapped his companion's face. "Wake up and make that bow useful. You can ponder your troubles later!"

Koren shook his head, feeling the sting of Bjorn's hand against his face but not knowing the source of the pain. "Here," Bjorn thrust the bow into Koren's hands.

"Arrow," Koren said automatically, shifting the bow to his left hand. Without thinking, he took the proffered arrow and nocked it. He took a breath, two, three-

Koren popped up above the rock and let fly an arrow that caught a bandit dead center in the belly, then Koren was yanked down by Bjorn's hand on his shirt tail. "To the left, around that rock," Bjorn pointed to the danger. He had seen two bandits cross the gap to hide behind the rock. Both of the bandits had bows, and if they came at Koren and Bjorn from both sides, Bjorn did not like their chances.

Koren didn't speak, simply holding his hand out for the last arrow in the quiver. He set the arrow to the bowstring and waited, shifting his gaze from the right side of the rock to the left. There was a shadow moving to the right side of the rock and- Koren released the arrow aimed at the left side of the rock, where a bandit had leaned out to shoot at him. Koren's arrow took the bandit in the shoulder and the man dropped his bow.

"That's three of you dead just now," Bjorn shouted from behind the rock that provided their only shelter. "There's only five of you left. How many more do you-" Bjorn's question was cut off by a warning shout from one of the bandits. Barlen was crashing through the woods with another dwarf and more than a dozen men with him. That was too much for the remaining bandits, who could not run away fast enough. Bjorn gestured for Barlen's men to pursue the bandits, to make sure they didn't double back and cause trouble. "Lekerk is dead!" Bjorn called out.

Koren had dropped the bow and was on his knees, his stomach trying to decide whether to be sick. Bjorn knelt beside him and squeezed Koren's arm. "Ah, those people in that wagon Lekerk talked about," Bjorn asked softly. "They were your parents, weren't they?"

Koren nodded silently, then his body was wracked by sobs. Bjorn stayed with him, saying nothing, only patting his companion on the back for reassurance. Barlen, having satisfied himself that Lekerk was indeed dead, came over to speak with Bjorn.

What is going on, the dwarf mouthed silently.

Bjorn merely shook his head sadly, and Barlen took the hint to walk away. The Farlane Army men who had chased after the bandits came back, reporting that the bandits had horses corralled in a field close by, and the bandits had gotten away. With Lekerk dead, no one wanted to chase after bandits in the wilderness. The group was gathered around Lekerk's body, having gone through the bandit's pockets, when Bjorn walked into their midst. "Did anyone find a golden pendant on a thin chain? It may be on the ground."

The men shuffled their feet awkwardly, so Bjorn added "That pendant is worth no great sum to any of you, but it is precious to my friend over there. Anyone wishes to match swords with him, well, more the fool you are. And you'll taste my blade first," he said with a hand on his sword hilt.

"I found it," one of the Farlane men explained, and handed it over to Bjorn. "I figured it was part of the reward, like."

"You thought wrong," Barlen ran a thumb along the blade of his axe for emphasis. "Any loot you find around here goes into the pool, to be split as part of the reward." To Bjorn, he asked quietly "What's wrong with that other fellow?"

"He just learned that Lekerk killed his parents," Bjorn explained quietly .

"Ah," Barlen's sentiment was echoed by many others. "The pendant belonged to Kedrun's mother, then?"

"I think so," Bjorn guessed.

"It did," Koren said from behind Bjorn, wiping his red eyes.

"And you killed him?" Barlen asked.

"No, Bjorn did," Koren did not know whether to regret not killing the bandit himself, or to be grateful to Bjorn for doing it. "You saved my life," Koren said to Bjorn. "Thank you."

Bjorn shrugged. "It happens, in battle. You've saved my life more than once."

Barlen looked at Bjorn. "You two will be expecting a greater share of the reward, then?"

"No!" Koren said angrily. "I don't want any blood money. You can keep it."

"Are you sure, lad?" Bjorn didn't see any harm in filling their pockets with coins. They had hunted, trapped and killed a bandit who had plagued northern Tarador for years.

"I'm sure. You can take your cut, if you want. There's something else I want as a reward, Barlen."

The dwarf looked at him warily. Having one less person to share the substantial reward money with would be popular with everyone involved. If, that is, whatever Kedrun wanted instead did not cause worse problems for Barlen. "What is that you want, Kedrun?" He asked the young man who he barely knew. Although, he certainly knew Kedrun well enough.

"I want passage into your homeland. I have business in Westerholm."

Barlen looked at Bjorn, who shrugged again. "What kind of business?" Barlen asked.

"I need to speak with someone, that is all. I mean no harm. I will tell you who I seek, after I cross the border. You can provide me with passage?"

"And me. I go with Kedrun," Bjorn declared.

A message from Duke Falco caught up with Kyre as the battalion was preparing to load into barges, to float down the Tormel river. Going across the hills to reach the watershed of the Tormel had been arduous; wagons had broken down and horses strained against the steep grades on the rough roads. Captain Jaques had to order supplies taken out of wagons and distributed amongst the soldiers, who were already loaded down with heavy packs and their personal gear.

Kyre had again taken coins out of his own pocket to hire additional horses, mules and oxen to get the battalion over the hills. Even getting to the crest of one hill did not provide relief; the road went up a hill, down, and up another hill. In that area of Tarador, the hills that ran north to south formed part of the border between Anschulz and LeVanne provinces. There was no way west except to cross four ridges of hills, even though the royal road had been planned along the easiest route.

When they reached the banks of the Tormel, Kyre was heartily glad of it, because his backside was sore from being in the saddle for long days. He had gotten off his horse and walked several times each day, telling his officers that he wished to get to know the sergeants in the battalion, and as sergeants did not have horses, they had to walk. In truth, Kyre welcomed the walking to give his aching backside a rest. When his feet began to swell in his boots from the unfamiliar strain of marching long distances, he gingerly climbed back on his horse, and tried to keep the soreness from showing on his face.

Luckily, as the hired barges had not yet arrived, the battalion had only unloaded one wagon before the messenger from the Royal Army rode up the road, shouting for Kyre and Captain Jaques. "Lieutenant Reeves of the Royal Army, with a message for Your Grace," the woman announced, out of breath. She bowed, brushing her sweat-soaked hair out of her eyes as she handed a sealed envelope to Kyre, then saluted Jaques.

Kyre slit the envelope open with a knife, read it, and handed it to Jaques. The captain read it quickly and looked at Kyre in surprise. "We are hereby ordered to proceed south-south-west into Demarche, with all dispatch, there to join forces with Duchess Rochambeau's army along the River Fasse. Lieutenant," Jaques addressed the Royal Army messenger, "what is the situation in Anschulz?" The battalion's original orders were to support the Royal Army's defensive line on the east bank of the Tormel river in Anschulz, almost directly to the west. The battalion would have been able to float down the Tormel on barges most of the way to the new defensive line. Jaques considered that now, the battalion would have to go ashore where the Tormel made a sharp turn to the west, and march the remainder of the way into Demarche province.

"You haven't heard?" Reeves asked in surprise. "General Magrane attacked the enemy's flanks from north and south along the Fasse. The enemy column was cut off and defeated; we are now chasing down pockets of the enemy force between the Fasse and the Tormel. It was a tremendous victory. The queen," she then remembered that Ariana was not yet queen. "The new Regent allowed General Magrane to attack. We attacked!" She exulted. For an army that had been held on the defensive for far too long, it was a welcome victory over the enemy that had picked away at Tarador's defenses since their king had died in battle.

"Captain," Kyre observed, "regardless of our ultimate destination, we need to wait for the barges to arrive. Lieutenant Reeves, you must be thirsty, and your horse needs to be cared for. I will send for refreshments, and you will tell us of the battle?" Kyre and Jaques were burning to know details of Magrane's victory.

While sipping cold water flavored with apple cider, Reeves regaled an enraptured audience of the future duke, Captain Jaques and a half dozen Burwyck army lieutenants with tales of the glorious victory. Magrane's counterattack had come as a complete surprise to the enemy. Within half a day, the enemy force had been cut in two, with one half attempting to retreat across the River Fasse, and the other half encircled by troops from the Royal Army, Anschulz and LeVanne. Magrane had ordered the sinking and burning of as many of the enemy's boats and rafts as could be reached. Because of this, many of the retreating enemy were forced to swim across the Fasse, discarding their weapons before plunging into the wide and swiftly-flowing river. Those that did not drown were swept downstream, and found themselves set upon and killed by their own forces when they reached the west bank of the Fasse. The enemy did not know how to retreat, and the enemy commanders did not tolerate failure.

As Reeves fielded questions about the battle, a cheer arose from the riverbank. The first of the barges were coming around a bend in the river. Jaques sent his lieutenants away to oversee preparations for loading, then changed the subject. "Lieutenant Reeve, what of the situation in Demarche?"

Again, her face reddened. "I thought you knew, Captain, Your Grace. As Duchess Rochambeau did not support Ariana in the vote for the Regency, Her Highness has withdrawn the Royal Army east of the Turmalane mountains in Demarche. Duke Falco is sending you to support the army of Demarche along the Fasse, in anticipation of the enemy shifting their focus to Demarche."

Kyre could not believe that Ariana would be that petty and stupid. "Ariana is abandoning the western half of Demarche, because Duchess Rochambeau voted against her?"

"General Magrane has been ordered to pull back east of the Turmalanes, and to set up a new defensive line there," Reeves confirmed.

Kyre and Jaques looked at each other in astonished disbelief. "Where are the Demarche forces?"

Reeves almost squirmed where she was seated, so withering was the glare from Captain Jaques. "Along the River Fasse, Captain."

"Captain? Can they hold the Fasse, with our help?" Kyre asked, fearing that he knew the answer.

"It is doubtful," Jaques' face was grim. "I expect the duchess will order her army to fight a delaying action, up through the mountain passes."

"The Royal Army is evacuating civilians as they retreat back through the Turmalanes," Reeves offered as cold consolation.

"Your Grace, we will need to discuss strategy," Jaques warned. While Duke Falco had ordered the battalion to assist Duchess Rochambeau, the army captain could not believe his duke wished the Burwyck soldiers to sacrifice themselves in a hopeless battle. "With the enemy pushed back in Anschulz, surely their attention will turn south to Demarche."

Kyre looked to the river, where three barges were now in sight. "There will be time to talk strategy on the river. I need to send a message to my father, I think." He had the codes to send a secret message, the question was, what to put in a message? What did his father expect of the battalion, and of Kyre? There was not a telegraph nearby, he would need to send the message while on the march, after they left the river behind. Suddenly aware that Reeves served the Royal Army and was potentially a spy in their mist, Kyre stood, and forcing Reeves and Jaques to do the same. "Lieutenant Reeves, thank you for bringing the message to us so quickly."

"You are welcome. Oh, Your Grace, I have been remiss; I should offer you congratulations," Reeves said stiffly; her body language suggested that she was merely following formal courtesy, and did not think congratulations were in order at all.

"Ariana," Kyre said with a sour expression.

"What of our princess, Sire?" Jaques asked.

"I am now engaged to marry our future queen," Kyre explained bitterly. To Reeves, he added "I did not think the arrangement was common knowledge."

The Royal Army lieutenant's face reddened. "There was a rumor, Your Grace, then a formal message was sent only yesterday. It arrived just before I set out to bring you this message," she pointed to the paper held by Jaques.

"My congratulations to you, Your Grace," Jaques said in a neutral tone. His enthusiasm was tempered by not yet knowing exactly how this stunning news affected the Falco family and the duchy of Burwyck. And it was also tempered by the pained rather than proud expression on Kyre Falco's face. It was likely, Jaques thought to himself, that Kyre Falco resented being used to fulfill his father's dream of putting a Falco back on the throne of Tarador. By virtue of being Duke Falco's eldest child, Kyre was already in line to inherit the duchy of Burwyck. Now he would also become Prince Consort of the realm. According to the law, Kyre's first child would someday become king or queen of Tarador, and his second child would become duke or duchess of Burwyck after him. While others may envy Kyre, Captain Jaques knew marrying the crown princess would only cause more headaches for the Falco heir, and bring more pressure from his father.

Jaques did not envy Kyre. As he had risen through the ranks of the Burwyck ducal army, he had seen enough of politics to know he wanted no more of it.

Kyre Falco watched the Royal Army messenger ride away, wondering if he had been too hasty to offer protection to the new Regent and future queen. If Ariana's first act as Regent was to surrender the western third of Demarche province, in an act of childish spite because Duchess Rochambeau had voted against her, then Kyre's faith in Ariana was misplaced. Ariana Trehayme was not the steady leadership Tarador needed; she was a silly, spiteful girl. And Kyre was leading the battalion into a battle they must surely lose, at great cost.

What other mistakes had he made?

Kyre Falco considered that perhaps his father was right in striving to take the throne of Tarador away from the Trehaymes. Ariana's father the king had gotten himself killed in an act of foolish bravado. Her uncle Leese was lost in alcohol and whatever substances he could get his

CRAIG ALANSON

hands on. Her mother had been a weak, indecisive and ineffectual Regent. And now Ariana was allowing her personal feelings to overrule her common sense, and the advice of her generals.

Kyre hoped he could think of a way out of the awful mess, before he got the entire battalion killed for nothing.

It had been a long, tough march to Demarche, even though the land was mostly open and flat. For a full day, the battalion had marched on a road alongside a river, and with every step on the hot, dusty road, the soldiers winced at their sore, aching feet and wished they could be lazily floating along the river. But they couldn't, for the river flowed in the wrong direction. If it had flowed toward Demarche, they still could not have spent an afternoon being carried along the water. There were no boats, no barges and no rafts to be had in that part of Tarador. And no one to guide boats or barges or rafts, for the population had fled when Acedor's army crossed the River Fasse in Anschulz. Kyre rode at the head of the battalion, all the way to the border with Demarche, where they found the border station empty.

As they turned west and approached the valley of the River Fasse, the march slowed, because they ran into masses of refugees coming the other way. Kyre's horse was forced off the road, giving way to wagons grossly overloaded, as farmers brought with them everything that could move. Those who had fewer possessions either rode horses and even oxen, or walked. With the main roads clogged, the battalion split up and took a longer path toward the Fasse. Kyre noted that traffic on the roads thinned as they descended farther down into the river valley, until the river itself was a broad, silvery ribbon in plain view across the farm fields. The civilian population closest to the river had been the first to be evacuated, and all that remained now were stragglers. Royal Army cavalry ranged about the region in groups of two and three, herding the civilians along as best they can, and warning the reluctant that the Royal Army had already pulled back. Brief conversations Kyre had with the cavalry confirmed that the army of Demarche was all that remained between the foothills of the Turmalane mountains to the east, and the River Fasse to the west. On the west bank of the Fasse, a host of the enemy awaited.

Three days behind schedule, the battalion arrived at the rally point to find confusion, and far fewer Demarche soldiers than Kyre expected. And hoped for.

Under Barlen's direction, the group buried the dead bandits, then took Lekerk's body back to the Farlane army post to collect the reward. It took a full day of messages going back and forth on the telegraph, and a lot of arguing and threats by Barlen before the reward money was paid out from the thin coffers of Duke Bargann. But paid out it was, and Bjorn Jihnsson took his rightful share. While in the village, the entire group was treated to a feast at the finest, and only, tavern, with most people and two of the dwarves indulging in too much beer, wine and stronger drink. Right after the reward money was paid, Barlen insisted on riding north because he was wary of his companions having full purses and access to a tavern. The three other dwarves grumbled some-

204

what before getting on their sturdy ponies, and setting off on the road with Koren and Bjorn riding behind them. "Good idea that we move now," Bjorn commented quietly to Barlen.

"My fellows like to celebrate with a good drink. Or more," Barlen frowned.

"Aye," Bjorn agreed. "And, the longer we wait, the more time people up ahead of us will have to learn there are six people traveling with pockets full of reward money."

Barlen's eyebrows raised in surprise. "I hadn't thought of that, Bjorn."

"Lekerk's band may be scattered to the winds, but you can be sure there are other bandits eager to take over Lekerk's territory. I'll bet my whole purse there is someone in this village who reports to bandits on likely targets."

Barlen unconsciously checked that his battleaxe was securely attached to his belt. "It is good then," he grinned, "that we are well set for weapons." Out of his own pocket, Barlen had purchased a fine new bow for Koren, and a much better sword for the young man. Everyone had a full quiver of arrows on their backs. Every single arrow had been personally inspected by Koren, and Barlen was grateful for that. The young man had rejected three out of four arrows that were offered to them, explaining the rejected arrows were either not straight, not sound, or they simply didn't 'feel right'. "Bjorn, where did Kedrun get his skill? I've never seen anyone shoot an arrow like he does."

"You haven't seen him with a sword. He could cut lightning out of the air before it hit the ground," Bjorn boasted about his friend. "He told me he was apprenticed to a weapons master, and I didn't ask further."

Barlen was silent for a few minutes, considering what Bjorn had said. Barlen did not like unknowns, and Kedrun was an unknown. An unknown that Barlen had agreed to vouch for, so the young man could pass the border into Barlen's homeland. The dwarf reflected that, if Kedrun's intentions were not good, the young man would have tried to sneak across the border, rather than going through a border gate on a road. "Do you know why he wants entry to my homeland?"

Bjorn shook his head with a glance back at his companion. "No. I didn't know he is going there to speak with someone, until he told you."

"You have no business of your own with us?" Barlen asked, curious. "Why are you following him, then?"

"He saved my life. Although," Bjorn mused, "he didn't know it at the time. Then he saved my life again."

"Ah," Barlen nodded with understanding. "You have a debt to pay."

"Aye, there's that, to be sure. Also, I have a feeling this is where I'm supposed to be. I can't explain it."

"I know why I'm here," Barlen snorted. "The reward money. You won't see me or my crew risking our necks for nothing."

"Ha," Dekma laughed. "It was either this, or fighting orcs up in the mountains. They've been crawling all around our border like rats seeking cheese."

"Be quiet, Dekma," Barlen snapped. "Don't you go telling strangers about our affairs."

Bjorn took the hint. "I'm dropping back. I need to speak with Kedrun."

Bjorn did not actually speak with the young man he knew as 'Kedrun'. Koren was not paying attention to where they were going, which left Bjorn to watch the road for signs of danger. The ponies of the dwarves plodded along, and Thunderbolt walked behind them. While the great horse would usually have expressed his frustration at the slow pace, that day Thunderbolt sensed his master's mood, and merely walked along silently, avoiding potholes in the road so as not to jostle his rider.

Koren did not say much the rest of that day, nor when they stopped at an inn for the night. He did not even complain when he and Bjorn had to share a room with Dekma, who snored loudly. Halfway through the following morning, Bjorn cleared his throat. "You didn't know your parents had died?"

"I don't want to talk about it," Koren mumbled with anger.

"No you don't want to talk about it. You *need* to talk about it," Bjorn insisted. Koren did not respond. "Kedrun, listen to me. You can talk about it to your horse, or to the trees, but you do need to talk about it; the sooner the better. Listen to me. Are you listening? I suffered a terrible loss, and I blamed myself," Bjorn referred to when the king had been killed. "I should have spoken about it with my wife, or my fellow guards. I didn't, because I let my stubborn pride rule me. Instead of talking about it, with someone, I let a bottle do the talking for me."

Koren looked at Bjorn and nodded, but didn't say anything.

Bjorn understood the young man likely did not know where to start. "The wagon," Bjorn said as a way to start a conversation. "Why did you ask whether the wagon was," he tried to remember what question he had posed to Lekerk. "Was north of the crossroads or not? Why does it matter which direction the wagon was traveling?"

Bjorn's ploy worked; Koren had to respond in order to be polite. His mother would have wanted him to be polite. "Because," he took in a deep breath. "If the wagon had been headed south and east from the crossroads, my parents were leaving me behind. They were not doing that. They were going north, to get me. That's where I was. They were coming to get me, to bring me back."

"Because you ran away?"

Koren saw no need to tell Bjorn the full truth; that would come too close to the man possibly figuring out who he really was. He did not know how far the story had traveled throughout Tarador; the story of Koren Bladewell who had rescued the crown princess. Of Koren the jinx. Of Koren who had nearly killed Ariana Trehayme, and was now hunted by the Royal Army. Telling Bjorn that he had run away was close enough to the truth. "Yes. I thought my parents didn't come after me because they didn't want me. They *did* want me, even after what I did. They were coming to get me, to bring me back. And then," his hands tightened on the reins until his hands turned white, and tears flowed freely down his cheeks. Unashamed, he wiped them away. "He killed them.

I hate him. I *hate* him," Koren gritted his teeth and looked at Bjorn. "I don't know whether to thank you for killing him, or not."

"You should thank me. Kedrun, if he had surrendered, could you have killed him in cold blood?"

"I could- I don't know. I *want* to. I want to bring him back, and kill him, over and over again! Bjorn, I thought my parents abandoned me. Lekerk made me think my parents didn't want me. He made me think I was worthless. I hate him. Now he's dead, and I can't even get the satisfaction of imagining killing him. I feel, empty. Cheated."

"Kedrun, don't think about it. That kind of thing can eat you-"

"If I see more bandits, I'm going to kill them."

"You say that now," Bjorn cautioned.

"I mean it, Bjorn. They are all murderers. The bandits out there may not have killed my parents; I am sure they killed someone's parents."

Bjorn did not reply. His companion did not need a lecture, he needed time. And, perhaps, Bjorn thought, Kedrun did need another battle with bandits to give himself a measure of release. If that happened, Bjorn would stay by Kedrun's side. He hoped Kedrun's need for revenge didn't get them both killed.

CHAPTER EIGHTEEN

General Armistead unrolled a map of western Demarche and held down the corners with weights, against the breeze blowing through the tent. It was a warm late summer day; without the wind it would have been stiflingly hot under the campaign tent. She took off her helmet and set it on the table, pulling back her matted hair and tying it behind her neck. Using a dagger as a pointer, Armistead illustrated the situation on the map. "Forgive me, Your Grace," she said to Kyre, "I do not know how familiar you are with the terrain in this area of Tarador."

"In Burwyck, I know every hill and stream," Kyre said without resorting to a boast. "Here, I am lost," he admitted with no shame.

"The River Fasse here in Demarche cuts more deeply into the land on both sides than it does farther north. There are no bridges across the Fasse here, of course," she traced the line of the river on the map from Winterthur, down through Anschulz and Demarche to the seacoast. What bridges had existed had been destroyed when Tarador split from Acedor, and only remnants of their crumbled piers now testified to where the bridges had been in ancient times. "Because the bluffs on the east and west banks are tall and steep, it is only possible for the enemy to cross into Demarche in two places. Here, where the Urel flows into the Fasse," she pointed down close to the seacoast. "The enemy will not attack along the Urel, because the valley of the Urel is narrow and steep; they would be trapped after they crossed the Fasse. Here is the only place they can cross successfully." She pointed north, halfway from the seacoast to the border between Demarche and Anschulz. "The Little Fasse, or Fasselle, joins the Fasse from the east. The lower part of the Fasselle meanders back and forth before reaching the Fasse; it forms a broad, shallow valley in Demarche. There are marshes where the rivers join, that makes it impossible for us to fortify the area. Because the lower Fasselle splits into multiple channels, the enemy has many points to land boats, and the gentle current this time of year will allow enemy boats to travel up the Fasselle before landing."

Kyre and Jaques looked at each other. They both knew it was a very difficult place to defend, even if the Royal Army had been there in force. Jaques spoke first. "What is your plan, General?"

"With only the force I have here? To harass the enemy as they land along the Little Fasse, and then to conduct a fighting retreat, to delay them up through the mountain passes." She looked up from the map to Jaques, who nodded agreement. He could not see another possibility, without the involvement of the Royal Army. Armistead shifted her attention to Kyre. "What are your orders, Your Grace?"

"My father the Duke has ordered me to support you, and Duchess Rochambeau. Without the loss of the battalion," Kyre added, repeating his father's last instructions. His father had stressed the need to preserve the fighting power of the battalion, for it would surely be needed later.

"And not to place yourself at unreasonable risk, Sire," Captain Jaques reminded Kyre. That order had been given directly from Duke Falco to Jaques. If Kyre were in danger, Jaques had authority to overrule Kyre's orders and assure the Falco heir's safety.

"I understand," Armistead said simply. Regin Falco had sent the battalion into Demarche as a show of support for his political ally Duchess Rochambeau. "I do not intend to fight to the death here," she waved her hand over the relatively flat farmland in Demarche between the River Fasse and the foothills of the Turmalanes. "The real fighting will begin at the mountain passes. There are only two gaps in these mountains which can allow passage of a significant force."

"I can't believe Ariana is abandoning a third of Demarche, just to spite your Duchess," Kyre said with bitterness in his voice.

General Armistead was careful in her reply. She owed loyalty to her cousin the Duchess Rochambeau, but to speak openly against the Regent could be considered treason. Especially because this Regent would become queen. "With the Royal Army, we might be able to prevent the enemy from successfully landing along the Little Fasse. Or not. Regardless of our new Regent's intentions, the mountain passes are a better defensive line," she admitted. "Even if doing that surrenders the best farmland in Demarche to the enemy."

Two days later, and according to Barlen, two days' ride from reaching the border, they were riding through woods under a cloudy sky. Koren had been in a foul mood all that day; barely speaking during breakfast, and offering only short, grumpy responses when someone asked him a question while riding. It did not help his mood that the clouds were heavy, gray and low, threatening rain. The dark woods pressed in on the road from both sides, it felt oppressive to Koren. These woods, Koren told himself, had never been logged or cleared for farmland. The trees were broad and tall, their canopies spread out to form a dense cover, blocking out the sunlight. Between the thick tree trunks, the undergrowth was thin, not having enough sunlight to feed growth. Ahead of him and Bjorn, two of the dwarves were singing a song they apparently were making up the words to; it was endless. Koren could only stand it because he wasn't listening. Bjorn was not so fortunate. "If those two sing another verse of that damned song, I'm going to knock them on the heads with the flat of my sword. How could any-"

"Shhh." Koren held up a hand. "I hear something."

"Should I ask our dwarf friends to kindly stop singing?" Bjorn whispered.

"No, that would tell the bandits that we know about them," Koren whispered back. "I see them now. At least two on the right, at least three on the left."

Bjorn kept his eyes facing forward. "I don't see anything."

"I do. They're not doing anything; they're just standing there."

"Likely, they've trying to decide whether six well-armed travelers on horseback are worth the risk." Bjorn advised his younger companion. Whether the bandits attacked depended on how many of them there were, and how desperate they were. "They will leave us be, I think."

"I'm not leaving them be," Koren hissed.

"Kedrun, don't you go looking for trouble," Bjorn warned.

"And let these bandits attack the next group that comes along?"

"We are not the Duke's army here, let them chase these bandits," Bjorn pleaded.

"Stay here if you want," Koren said as he reached back for an arrow and urged Thunderbolt forward. Unlike Lekerk's band, these bandits had not chosen their ambush spot wisely. The thin underbrush made it easy for Thunderbolt to dash off the road into the forest. At Koren's direction, they went to the left where there were more bandits.

The bandits were caught completely by surprise, having decided to let the six riders go by unmolested. When a large black horse suddenly charged at them, they were totally unprepared, and the three Koren had seen panicked. Two of them raised their bows defensively, taking shaky aim. One of them shot an arrow that missed Bjorn, before Koren's arrow took that bandit in the chest and he fell. The other bandit archer decided to surrender before he could draw back his bowstring, throwing his bow on the ground and holding up his hands.

Koren had seen three bandits on the left side of the road; there were actually five, and one of them was now lying dead on the ground. The four left alive stood stock still, hands in the air, encircled by Koren, Bjorn and two dwarves. The bandits were herded into the road, where Barlen and Dekma had brought the two bandits who had been hiding on the right side of the road,

"Well, well, well, what have we here?" Barlen asked, with a seriously annoyed look toward Koren.

"Those are a fine set of boots you have there," Bjorn said admiringly to one bandit. "It's my guess they don't belong to you. Did you kill their previous owner?"

"I bought these myself," the bandit protested.

"And I call you a liar. You bought them with someone else's blood. Those boots look like they might fit me. Take them off." When the bandit hesitated, Bjorn snorted disgustedly. "Kedrun, these scum need a lesson. Put an arrow in this one's gullet."

"No! No! You want my boots, you can have them," the bandit said as he struggled to take the boots off. He tossed them to Bjorn, who inspected them and tried them on.

"Ah, these are fine boots," Bjorn said approvingly. "They fit perfectly. I'll keep them."

"Give me your old boots?" The bandit asked hopefully.

"No," Barlen spoke. "All of you, take off your boots. Take off everything, strip down to your britches."

When the bandits protested, Barlen growled and split one of Bjorn's old boots with his axe, slicing the leather cleanly in two pieces. "We'll leave you with your britches, and your lives.

I reckon that is a better bargain than you gave to any of the travelers you preyed on." Seeing the battleaxe got the bandits moving. "Dekma, while these idiots are cooling down from the heat of the day," Barlen smiled wickedly, "break their bows and arrows, and collect their other weapons. And their bowstrings, so they can't fashion new bows. In fact, collect everything."

As their ponies and horses trotted up the road, loaded down with the clothes and weapons of the bandits, Barlen turned in the saddle. "There is a pond up the road, a mile, maybe two. We'll toss this filth in there. We can use their swords to weigh down the clothes," Barlen added in disgust at the poor care the bandits had taken of their weapons. The swords were battered and tarnished and the blades had more notches than sharp edges. "Those blades aren't good for anything else. Wouldn't even be worth melting down for the metal."

"Good," Koren wrinkled his nose. "Whichever one of them wore these clothes, he hadn't bathed in a month. I'm afraid these clothes will give my horse fleas."

They all laughed at that. Bjorn took Koren's laugh as a good sign.

"What," Koren stopped, for he was laughing too hard to talk. "What do you think those bandits are going to do? Wait for wagons to come along, and stand half naked in the road, hoping for a ride?"

The dwarves got a good chuckle about that. "They'll need a ride, I can tell you that. Up here near the border, it's a long walk either way to a village."

"Aye," Barlen chuckled, and slapped Koren on the back. "And they'd better hope they don't run into another gang of bandits. They'd die of embarrassment."

"That was all good fun, but," Barlen wagged a finger at Koren, "don't you do that again. You pull another stunt like that, you'll find yourself facing a gang of bandits by yourself. There's no reward for that gang." The dwarf leader pulled out the leather pouch filled with coins and odd bits of jewelry he had collected from the pirates. "Here," he tossed it through the air to Koren, "there's your reward."

"We should split it," Koren protested.

Barlen shook his head. "It's little enough, compared to the reward money the rest of us got for Lekerk. Keep it, Kedrun. When you get to my homeland, you won't have any friends. Coins will go a long way toward getting you wherever you want to go."

"Barlen," Dekma spoke. "The reward. The other one. They deserve a cut."

"What other reward?" Bjorn inquired suspiciously.

Barlen was not pleased with Dekma. "The reward my big-mouthed friend here should have kept quiet about," Barlen growled. "Your Duke Bargann, and Duke Romero, offered a reward because Lekerk terrorized the roads in Farlane and Winterthur for years. My people lost wagons also, and there's a reward waiting for us when we get to the first keep across the border."

"Aye," Dekma added, "that's why we insisted on getting a signed statement from the Farlane army garrison commander, proving that Lekerk is dead. Barlen got them to send a telegraph message ahead of us, so we can collect the reward. And," Dekma hung his head sheepishly, "that's more than I should have said."

"It's the right thing to do," Bjorn said with a broad grin. He had not anticipated that following 'Kedrun' across the north woods would fill his pockets.

"Why does the right thing always take coins from my pockets?" Barlen grumbled.

"Two, three, four," Barlen counted out the coins as he dropped them into Koren's purse.

"Thank you," Koren jingled the purse, feeling its weight. He had never handled so much money in his life. The reward money from the dwarves, the coins he had from the group of bandits they had ironically robbed, and his pay from the *Lady Hildegard*. Plus the coins he had received from Kyre Falco; he had still not touched most of that money. He grinned, holding up the heavy purse. "I feel like a baron!"

"You may have more money than some barons I have known," Barlen observed. Being royalty did not mean all barons were rich; many were rich in land but poor in coins. If the land of their barony did not generate a substantial income, barons had to farm and hunt for their food like commoners, or engage in commerce. "Kedrun, I have kept my part of our bargain; I brought you across our border. Even filled your purse with coins," he glared at Dekma. "Now it is your turn. What business do you have with dwarves?"

Koren hesitated. He had turned stories over in his mind, but none of them were what he wanted to say.

"Kedrun?" Bjorn prompted. "I pledged to follow you. I would appreciate knowing where we are going, and why."

"All right," Koren's shoulders slumped in defeat. "I need to speak with a wizard. A dwarf wizard."

"A wizard?" Barlen was genuinely surprised. "Which one?"

"Oh, I don't know. I don't have a particular wizard in mind," Koren admitted. He should have put more thought into the whole idea of what he was seeking in Westerholm. "There is more than one wizard among your people?" He had only ever heard Paedris mention the name 'Dirmell' as a wizard among the dwarves.

"There is more than one wizard among us, yes," Barlen shared a laugh with Dekma. "What do you need a wizard for?"

"I need a wizard to, do, something," Koren stumbled over his words, "for me."

Barlen's eyes narrowed. "What?"

"That is my business," Koren insisted. "I don't mean any harm. It's, personal, is all."

"Suit yourself, then," Barlen said with a shrug. "It's a good thing you have money, then. You'll need it."

"Money?" Koren was confused. "Why?"

It was Dekma's turn to laugh first. "You expect wizards to do favors for you, for free?"

"Yes?" Koren answered weakly. Paedris had never asked for, or accepted money in exchange for his healing people.

Bjorn joined in the laughter. "What do you know of wizards, Kedrun?"

Koren, despite living with a powerful wizard, apparently knew little about them. "Not much." Now that he thought about it, Paedris received a generous stipend from Tarador, as the royal court wizard. He did not need to take money for his services. But, how did other wizards pay for their expenses? Not all wizards were given impressive towers to live in. "How much do wizards charge?" He hoped he had enough coins in his purse. Now he felt foolish for turning down Duke Bargann's reward.

"That depends on what you want from them," Barlen advised. "I'll make another deal with you, Kedrun. A wizard lives in our village," he pointed his thumb at Dekma. "For a silver coin, we'll guide you up there."

"A silver?" Bjorn feigned incredulousness. "Ha! You two are bandits, there should be a reward for capturing you. *Two* copper coins," he counteroffered.

Barlen looked at Dekma, who nodded. "Three coppers," Dekma said. "That's as low as we'll go, for the trouble of dragging you two long-legs up into the hill with us. If you don't like our offer, good luck to you finding someone else to guide you."

"Three coppers is fine," Koren said quickly. He had been hoping the two dwarves would tell him where to go, and now they were going to guide him. Three coppers was a cheap price.

Barlen took the coins from Koren, and they shook hands on the deal. "Kedrun, you'll need to leave your horse here," Barlen warned.

"No!" Koren exclaimed, horrified at the idea. Thunderbolt had traveled on his own through the wilderness to find his master. "I can't leave him!"

Barlen shook his head. "You can't come with us, then. In the mountains," he pointed toward the peaks that were tinged white with snow, "there are narrow paths along sheer cliffs, and bridges made of rope that span canyons deep enough you can barely see the bottom. Kedrun, no horse, no pony, not even a sure-footed mule could travel those paths."

"We will be leaving our ponies in the stables here," Dekma told Koren as a way of assurance. "They will be well cared for," he gestured toward one of several stables in the town around the keep.

"Those are *your* ponies?" Koren snapped in anger. "Or are they only nameless beasts you hired for your journey to hunt Lekerk?' The expression on Dekma's face told Koren what he wanted to know. "Thunderbolt is not only my horse; he is my friend. On his own, he sought me out. He traveled-" That was revealing too much information, Koren realized. "I will not leave him."

"Kedrun," Bjorn steered Koren away for a private conversation. "My horse has no name, but when I served the king, I owned several horses. They were good companions, trusted in battle.

They all had names. That was a lifetime ago for me, but I understand the bond you have with your horse. Let us talk to the stable masters here, the two of us. If you don't find someone you trust to care for Thunderbolt, I will remain here."

Koren considered Bjorn's offer. Bjorn owed him nothing; Koren should not ask the man to follow him into the mountains. It might be that staying in the peaceful dwarf town was the best thing for Bjorn. "We can try," Koren agreed reluctantly. "I don't know what else to do." He looked up to the forbidding mountains. "Anywhere I go up there will likely be no place for a horse. And I must go," he added, speaking to himself. "How long a journey is it up to your village?"

Barlen thought a moment. "For us, three days up, two down. You two, on your spindly legs, are not so sure footed on the mountain paths. Add two days for a round trip."

Koren looked at Bjorn sadly. Seven days. He would be leaving Thunderbolt for seven days. "Bjorn, let's go look at the stables."

In the afternoon three days later, Koren could not speak about Bjorn's condition, but his own nerves were shot by the time they reached the end of the narrow ledge and set their feet on a flat surface wider than Koren was tall. At no time had Koren felt he was in any danger; his sense of balance was good and always had been. As they were making their way along the ledge at what felt like going inch by inch, he had recalled when he escaped from the room where he had been kept in Duke Yarron's castle. Then, he had walked along a very narrow ledge, really a single course of bricks set sideways. He remembered his feet and toes cramping as he struggled to keep from slipping onto the hard stones of the courtyard below, and his fingers shaking from the strain on gripping cracks in the stones of the castle. When he had reached the roof there, he had been trapped. Only the wizard Lord Salva had saved him. In his mind's eye, Koren pictured the court wizard of Tarador casually strolling along the frighteningly narrow ledge of the castle wall, and the wizard had been carrying a tray of pastries in one hand!

"Oh," Koren gasped, bent over with hands on his knees. "I do *not* want to ever do that again."

"Ah," Barlen laughed as he slapped Koren's back. "That is nothing, compared to some trails up farther in the mountains. Here, we had a rope to hold onto."

"In places!" Bjorn complained. "There was rope in some places, and not in others! Where there was no rope, that is where we needed it!"

Barlen made an exaggerated shrug. "Things have been slipping 'round here, that's true. With the orcs raiding us constantly the past years, there's not been time and attention paid to proper upkeep of things like safety ropes. Besides," he gestured back toward the ledge, "we don't get many visitors up this way."

"I can see why you don't get many visitors," a shaken Bjorn retorted. "one might think you were trying to discourage visitors, making them walk a deathtrap path like that."

Dekma snorted with mirth. "Our children easily tread such pathways as soon as they are able to walk."

"Your children must be part mountain goat," Bjorn grumbled. Then, aware of how the dwarves might take such a remark, he waved his arms. "I meant that as a compliment. Is there no path that frightens your people?"

Dekma and Barlen looked at each other. "I've been to Linden, years ago," Barlen stated. "The streets there made me wish I were back home. Your carriage drivers pay no heed to anyone, I was nearly run down a half dozen times on my first day."

Koren shook his head and grinned ruefully at Barlen's distress. "The carriage drivers in Linden are renowned for their speed and daring. Especially carriages of the minor royalty. Every baron or squire will happily run you down just to make the point that they are of royal birth and you are not."

Bjorn looked sharply at Koren. "You were in Linden? When?"

"I, I," Koren realized with fright that he had forgotten not to speak of his past. "I passed through the city. And I was almost run over." Quickly hoping to change the subject, he asked "Barlen, how much farther to your home?"

The dwarf pointed to a cleft in the mountain peaks, where a thin column of black smoke rose. "Not far. A couple hours, and we'll be there. I warn you, it's a steep climb."

"Everywhere is a steep climb up here," Bjorn said sourly. "It will be dark soon, I hope your 'couple hours' does not turn into many more."

"That," Dekma declared as he hitched up the straps of his pack, "depends on how slowly the two of you walk. With long legs like that," he looked from Bjorn's feet to the cap on the man's head, "I would think you people could walk faster."

Dekma's unsubtle dig at the slow pace of Koren and Bjorn got results, whether the dwarf had intended it or not. Already, they had taken only three days to climb the mountain; as good as the dwarves had said they could do on their own. Now that the narrow ledge was behind them, the two dwarves set a punishing pace up the steep track that served for a road in the mountains. Huffing and puffing, Koren resorted to placing his hands on his knees to force his legs up the incline. "How," he gasped, "can they walk so fast?" The climb was not only strenuous, it was awkward. With the slope so steep that his heels did not touch the ground, he was walking on his toes, and the tendons across the bottom of his feet ached with the strain. When the pain of his feet became a sharp, hot needle, he switched to walking partly sideways.

"Never you mind them," Bjorn advised with ragged breath. "They were born up here. Their legs are shorter, but powerful. Take shorter steps, Kedrun, you're trying to stride too far. And up here, the air is thinner; we need to breathe harder."

"How," Koren gasped, "could the air be more thin?" Air was air, wasn't it, Koren asked himself. You couldn't see it, but wasn't it the same everywhere?

"I don't know. But the last time I was here, we had people fall sick. Even resting didn't help; people fell ill while they were asleep. Usually you become accustomed to it after a few days, but some people needed to be brought down off the mountain. The wizards, I think, understand why the air becomes thinner as you climb."

Koren nodded and did not reply. It must be the wind in the mountains that made the air thin, he told himself. Although, he had experienced strong winds at sea, and the air never seemed to be pulled from his lungs as it did while they climbed. One foot in front of the other, he told himself. He needed to put one foot in front of the other.

Kyre Falco was so exhausted that when a sergeant rode up to report and saluted to his future duke, Kyre was almost too tired to lift his arm and return the salute. What Kyre wanted to be doing was engaging the enemy directly. Instead, he had been racing back and forth across Demarche, keeping track of the enemy's advance, and rounding up scattered groups of lost and frightened civilians. It was important, and necessary, and the assignment kept Kyre out of serious danger, and it was also terribly frustrating. While the Demarche army and most of Kyre's battalion fought the enemy, he rode frantically around the countryside, dashing from one grove of trees to another. After each area had been declared cleared of inhabitants, or the enemy had advanced so far the area had to be abandoned, Kyre pulled his people back. As they retreated, they burned any stores of grain or fields of crops that might provide food and fodder to the enemy. When they retreated across bridges, they set fire to the bridges behind them, to make it more difficult for the enemy's wagons to supply their troops.

"Sergeant," Kyre stifled a yawn. He had not slept at all the previous night. None of the battalion had.

Nor had the enemy.

"Your Grace, Captain Jaques reports enemy cavalry has outflanked our position; they are now between us and the base of the Kaltzen."

That alarming news brought Kyre snapping to full alertness. "We must redeploy to-"

"Yes, Sire, Captain Jaques and General Armistead have already ordered redeployment," the sergeant boldly interrupted Kyre. "We are ordered to ride straight for the pass as fast as possible, to block the enemy's lead elements, if possible."

"Not all of us can ride," Kyre looked around at his men. The army of Demarche had provided horses for about a third of Kyre's battalion, and more horses had been taken from civilian refugees after they were safely in the mountains. With horses becoming weary from racing about the countryside, still only one out of three Burwyck soldiers had a horse capable of riding. Kyre had gotten out of the saddle and been maintaining a brisk march for the past two hours, to rest his own tired horse.

"Yes, Sire," the sergeant agreed patiently while glancing over his shoulder. "Captain Jaques suggests the foot soldiers retreat due east, up the mountain." He pointed to the rugged, thickly-forested slopes which began less than ten miles away. "Cavalry will not be able to follow up there, and we are still comfortably ahead of the enemy infantry."

Kyre cocked his head at the last remark. "We engaged enemy infantry not three miles from here a few hours ago. That is not a *comfortable* distance, Sergeant."

"Yes, Your Grace," the sergeant nervously scanned the farm fields and woods to the west, the direction from which the enemy would soon appear. "General Armistead believes we have done all we can here, and now we must focus our efforts on preventing the enemy from forcing past the Gates."

There were only two passes through the mountains in that part of Demarche which were broad enough to allow an army to march through. The Tiper Pass lay to the north, and to the south was the Kaltzen. The steep approach up the western side of the Tiper was a wide, V-shaped valley that would be almost impossible to defend, but once over the ridgeline, the road traveled through rough terrain of thick forests and jumbled rocks. Once through the pass, the road went steeply down and up three times, before descending into the gently rolling farmland of eastern Demarche province.

The Kaltzen Pass had an easier approach from the west, but it was more narrow, with the road passing through the Gates of the Mountains. The Gates were high, sheer rock cliffs to the north and south of the road, separated by only one hundred yards at the narrowest point. Beyond the Gates was a shallow, bowl-like valley which ended in a broad canyon that was the actual summit of the pass. Once over the summit, the road led down an easy slope into flat farmland that would provide no natural defensive line for the Royal Army.

If he were the enemy commander, Kyre would have chosen to send his force up through the Tiper Pass, and Generals Jaques and Armistead agreed. The Tiper was farther from the river crossing where the Fasselle met the Fasse, and the pass itself was longer, steeper, higher and less accommodating to a lengthy column of troops. But Kyre judged those difficulties were preferable to the effort required in forcing past the Gates of the Mountains in the Kaltzen pass. The narrow chokepoint of the Gates made the Kaltzen much easier for the Royal Army to defend; any attacking force would suffer substantial losses in fighting its way through the pass. That is why Armistead had originally concentrated her army, and Kyre's battalion, between the Fasselle river and the Tiper Pass.

To the surprise of General Armistead, her plan to conduct a fighting retreat up through the Tiper pass was defeated before it started, by the enemy's refusal to cooperate. By the end of the second day after the enemy crossed the River Fasse and came ashore, it was clear they were headed straight for the Kaltzen, not the Tiper. Royal Army scouts who came across Armistead's headquarters reported the Taradoran Royal Army had established a strong defensive line up the Tiper, while the defense of the Kaltzen was thin. As there were not enough soldiers to fully man both defensive lines, Grand General Magrane had been forced to choose where to concentrate his strength, and the enemy again chose not to cooperate. It was likely that enemy wizards gave their army a view of both passes, and their commander decided to attack the weaker of the two forces.

It was also true, Armistead thought sadly, that the enemy cared nothing about how many of their soldiers were lost in breaking Tarador's defensive line at the Gates of the Mountains. The enemy did not value lives, only power.

It took all night and half the next day for Armistead to get her army turned around and in position between the vanguard of the enemy and the entrance to the Kaltzen pass. Her army maintained contact with the enemy all the way up through the pass; harassing the enemy when they could, collapsing and burning bridges to slow the enemy's advance, cutting down trees to block roads. Such was the size and power of the enemy host she faced, that all her efforts barely frustrated the advance of the foul men and orcs. Her own scouts reported that the greatest difficulties faced by the enemy were not the army of Demarche and the lone battalion of troops from Burwyck. The enemy's problems were that the size of its own force overwhelmed the roads, and the soldiers of the enemy army liked to fight among themselves as much as they desired to fight Tarador. The necessity of keeping men and orcs apart slowed the enemy more than Armistead's comparatively small army could.

"Sire, we must hurry, if we are to reach the pass before the enemy," Kyre's guard Falzon urged.

Kyre nodded curtly, and swung up onto his horse. "Sergeant Garner," he called out, and instructed the trusted man to pass the orders for the Burwyck infantry to retreat directly up into the mountains. "We will meet you at the east base of the Kaltzen pass."

"Yes, Your Grace," Garner saluted, and hurried off to get his men turned around. It was going to be a long, hard march over rugged mountains, on short rations, for soldiers already exhausted.

Kyre took one last look to the west, where a thin trail of smoke wafted from a bridge unseen behind a treeline. Kyre himself had personally tossed a torch onto the oil-soaked timbers of that bridge less than an hour earlier, the bridge must have already burned down to the water line. "Falzon, Carter, lead the way, we must gather any mounted troops we can find. The Gates must be held."

CHAPTER NINETEEN

It was a hard ride to the foothills where the road up the Kaltzen pass truly began to climb; the point where the foothills closed in so that the road was hemmed in on both sides by increasingly steep slopes. Unfortunately for the defenders, the sides of the pass were treeless and horses could ride along the slopes almost up to the Gates of the Mountains. Kyre kept his horse to a trot after their initial gallop. Scouts ahead had reported the enemy cavalry was near, but Kyre's group was still ahead of them. Around him, Kyre had only a hundred and twenty soldiers; all that had horses capable of climbing up the pass before the enemy cavalry arrived. And all that were still alive after endless days of fighting. Most of the battalion's soldiers were either too far away, or were on foot; they could not help in the coming battle.

Kyre, his guards and a half dozen soldiers lagged in the rear; Kyre had ordered the swiftest riders to go ahead up the pass, to reinforce the defense at the Gates. Below, in the valley, horsemen of the enemy could be seen galloping across farmland that had not been stripped of valuables, and bridges that had not been burned. The speed of the enemy's advance had overwhelmed the defenders' ability to scorch the land of anything that might assist the host of Acedor.

"Sire!" Carter shouted an alarm, pointing down the hill to the southwest. From a treeline, a group of two dozen ragged-looking civilians emerged, running as quickly across a mountain meadow as their wobbly legs could carry them. Whatever possessions they might once have brought from their homes were now abandoned; mothers and fathers and older siblings carried young children and babies, stumbling across the stony and brush-covered field. "Stragglers!"

Kyre pulled out his spyglass, focusing on the trees behind the fleeing civilians. There was movement in the woods, and enemy horsemen were riding across another field to the west, headed for those woods. To the south, below Kyre and closer to the civilians were General Armistead and her headquarters troops. She had only a dozen soldiers with her, and before Kyre could speak, Armistead wheeled her horse and charged for the treeline, coming to the aid of the civilians of Demarche she was pledged to protect.

"To me!" Kyre shouted, spurring his horse to race down the hill.

"Sire! No!" Carter pleaded, obligated to follow the young man he was sworn to protect.

General Armistead's group reached the fleeing civilians first. With their horses already tired, and keeping in mind that defending the pass was more important than another laggard group of civilians, Armistead ordered her soldiers to take the young children on their horses. She urged the adults to run; there were not enough horses for everyone. If the civilians could reach the trees at the top of the slope, they would be safe, for the enemy cavalry would not bother to follow. The enemy, even cruel as they were, would not waste time in killing civilians when the greater prize of capturing the mountain pass lay in sight.

Killing civilians would not divert the enemy cavalry, but the possibility of killing the Demarche army's commander would. As Kyre raced to help, enemy cavalry burst from the treeline into the meadow. They did not attack the running, stumbling civilians, they did not split right and left to encircle the civilians and their defenders. No, the enemy focused on capturing or killing General Armistead.

The enemy could scarcely have mistaken their target, for Armistead and her personal guard stuck out like a red wine stain on a white tablecloth. At the direction of Duchess Rochambeau, the commander of Demarche's army wore the colors of the duchy's crest; gold and blue, with a polished gold-plated helmet. One of her guards carried a large Demarche flag, also blue and gold. The uniform and flag were impressive in a parade or any peacetime military review. In combat, they were a hindrance. To the enemy, they were a beacon.

Kyre's father required his high-ranking officers to be similarly outfitted, which Kyre thought foolish. One of his first orders to Captain Jaques had been for the man to put away his shiny helmet in favor of the more practical helmet of an ordinary officer. And the Burwyck flag was to be flown only when the battalion was in camp; otherwise it was to be carefully furled and stowed away. Not having to carry a flag gave the battalion one more mounted, and useful, soldier.

As he charged across the meadow, holding the reins with one hand while reaching back for an arrow, Kyre's heart was in his throat. Armistead was quickly besieged, having seen the danger to herself too late. Thinking the enemy would ride straight for the civilians, Armistead had positioned herself to strike the flanks of the enemy cavalry as they raced by. Instead, a hundred yards before the first enemy riders reached the civilians, they wheeled to the right and charged directly at Armistead.

When her soldiers realized their commander was the target of the enemy, those protecting the civilians broke off to assist Armistead. But they were already too late, for more of the enemy blocked their attempts to reinforce the guards protecting Armistead.

The only chance to save the general was Kyre's group, coming from the opposite side. Kyre had time only to fire off two arrows; the first missed entirely while the second struck an enemy in the shoulder, causing the man to drop his sword. Then Kyre had to toss the bow aside and draw his sword, for he was in the midst of the swirling, chaotic battle. What he remembered later was concentrating not on killing the enemy, but of forcing them aside, to get to Armistead before she was overcome. The Demarche general was surrounded by more than a dozen enemy, with only a half dozen of her guards still in the fight. Armistead was personally tangling with two enemy soldiers, hindered by a bloody cut to one arm.

Kyre hacked at the enemy until he was in the middle of the fight, matching swords with an enemy soldier who had a large X-shaped scar on both his cheeks. He was a large man and strong; blocking the man's sword blows made Kyre's sword arm ring with pain. Spinning his horse around to gain space, Kyre saw that Armistead was beset. She parried the sword thrust of one enemy, but another was poised to stab her undefended back. The general wore light chainmail as did Kyre; such lightweight protection would not stop the point of a sharp sword. Desperately, Kyre pulled a dagger from his belt and threw it, the poorly-aimed throw struck the enemy across the bridge of his nose with the side of the blade, rather than with the point as Kyre intended. The razor-sharp blade still cut deeply so that blood spurted from the man's sliced-open nose; blood blocked his vision and his sword thrust fell on empty air as Armistead dodged aside. The momentum of his sword swinging through the air threw the enemy off balance and he fell from his saddle, to be trampled under Armistead's horse. Her horse stumbled, saving the general's life because as she fell backwards, a sword cut clanged off the top of her helmet rather than chopping her head off. Her head was jerked backwards and she fell heavily to the ground, her horse bucking and running off in panic.

Kyre spurred his horse and charged forward, as the enemy who had knocked Armistead off her horse saw the opportunity to stab her in the back while she staggered back onto her feet, using her own sword to support herself. She was too dazed to see the danger of the sword plunging down between her shoulder blades. Kyre swung his own sword underhanded to force the enemy's blow aside; he was successful but the shocking impact sent Kyre's sword spinning through the air and he was momentarily defenseless.

The enemy, enraged that Kyre had blocked him from the glory of killing the Demarche army commander, turned his attention to the unarmed heir to the duchy of Burwyck. The enemy did not know who he faced as an opponent, but it was clear Kyre was some sort of Taradoran royalty from the fine clothes he wore.

Kyre's right arm was cramped and numb from the ringing blow of losing his sword. He had no time to reach for a dagger with his left hand; his only remaining dagger was on the left side of his belt and awkward to reach with his left hand. In a panic, he realized the enemy's long sword meant the enemy could cut him from farther away that Kyre could reach, so he wheeled his trusted horse closer to the enemy. As the enemy drew back his long sword for a killing blow, Kyre in a panic ripped off his own helmet and used it as a club to batter the enemy's face. The man rocked back in the saddle from the unexpected attack. Again Kyre punched the man with the helmet, then the man pulled his horse back and Kyre's horse stumbled on a rock. The enemy's sword came arcing through the air at Kyre's unprotected right side; the Falco heir knew he could not swing his helmet around in time to block the sword cut.

Then the enemy jerked upright as the tip of a sword stuck out of his chest. Kyre's guard Carter withdrew his sword from behind the man, using a leg to kick the dying enemy aside. "Sire! We must go!"

"Falzon!" Kyre shouted to his other personal guard as he jammed the helmet back on his head. "Get General Armistead!" Kyre knew he had not the strength, with his right arm still numb, to assist the Demarche commander onto a horse. As Carter and Falzon awkwardly got Armistead on the back of Falzon's horse, Kyre reached out for the reins of Armistead's horse, and galloped off up the hill.

During the short battle, more soldiers of Demarche and Burwyck had come to the rescue; they now outnumbered the enemy, who pulled back to the treeline. Dead and injured on both sides littered the field, there was no time to help them, as more and more of the enemy arrived by the second. As soon as they had ridden a safe mere hundred yards away, they halted briefly for Armistead to transfer to her own horse, then the entire party turned up toward the Kaltzen pass, as quickly as the weary legs of their horses could carry them.

Kyre looked back to the meadow, to where the enemy cavalry now ranged freely, killing the wounded soldiers who Kyre had been forced to leave behind. Above the meadow, the civilian stragglers who had been the reason for the brief battle scrambled up the steep hill toward the treeline, using hands and knees when needed. The civilians, Kyre thought, would escape safely, at least they would not be pursued by the enemy horsemen.

Was it worth the cost? A handful of civilian lives saved, against the cost of a dozen soldiers lost from the armies of Demarche and Burwyck. And almost the loss of the commander of the Demarche army and the heir to the duchy of Burwyck. Worse, the action had delayed their reinforcing the defense of the Gates of the Mountains.

Kyre thought, as his tired horse slowed to a trot, that in the future, he needed to weigh the cost before he rode into action. Harsh as it may seem, Tarador would have been better served if Kyre and Armistead had kept to their mission, rather than following all-too-human instincts to protect the defenseless. To his right, Armistead was wrapping a bandage around the injury to her arm. Falzon rode up to Kyre's left, holding out a sword. "It is not your fine blade, Sire, but it will have to do. You cannot fight all your battles with a helmet."

Despite everything that had happened, everyone around Kyre laughed, Armistead especially so. "Your Grace," she said through a grimace of pain, "you will need to teach your helmet-fighting technique to my army. It was, unique?"

"That will be easy," Kyre grinned through his own pain, feeling hot fire from the wrist to shoulder of his sword arm. "All it takes is the right mixture of clumsiness and desperation. Carter, Falzon," he addressed his two personal guards, "thank you for saving my life."

"Thank you for saving my life, Your Grace." General Armistead said, as she used her teeth to pull tight the bandage on her arm.

"You are welcome, General," Kyre replied. "I think my Captain Jaques would not be pleased that I-"

"General!" A Demarche soldier called out as he rode swiftly toward them. "I have your helmet!" The man proudly held up the now-battered gold-plated helmet.

"Ah, yes, my helmet," Armistead observed with disgust. The heavy, gaudy, conspicuous helmet that she had never liked to wear in the field. "It is too bad," she said, "that it was lost during the battle."

"But," said the soldier, confused.

"Yes," Kyre agreed, "it *is* too bad that your helmet was lost in the battle, and that we had no opportunity to recover it."

"Oh, yes," the soldier caught onto their meaning. "Perhaps the enemy will fight over it," he said as he threw it down the road. It bounced and rolled, coming to a stop in a ditch.

Armistead tested the range of motion she had in her bandaged arm. With the damage to her forearm, she could not grip a sword, but she could hold a shield. She contemplated the dent in her former helmet, a dent that could have been in her skull. "If it delays the enemy even a moment, my helmet will have served us well."

The Gates of the Mountains loomed above them in plain view, when the ride up the pass became a desperate race. With all of their horses exhausted from racing about the countryside, they could manage no more than a brisk walk up the mountain. In stretches of the road that were particularly steep, Kyre hopped down and ran alongside. General Armistead was about to follow his example, but Kyre and the general's guards urged her to stay on her horse. The blow to her head, although blocked by the gaudy helmet, was causing her an intense headache. At times, she had difficulty looking straight at a person she was speaking with; her eyes tended to wander to the side and lose focus. Kyre exchanged worried looks with the general's guards, they feared she had a concussion but there was nothing to be done but to push on up the road to the Gates. Hopefully there, Armistead could rest and receive medical attention. Even with what little Kyre knew of the commander of Demarche's army, he doubted the woman would allow herself rest at all, until the Gates of the Mountains were securely held against the oncoming enemy.

The road flattened a bit, and Kyre climbed back into the saddle, urging his horse to a trot. Ahead and above, the Gates towered to each side; sheer cliffs of whitish-gray granite. From Kyre's location, the road up through the Gates was unseen, only the cliffs created a gap in the mountain ridge. Kyre had only been through the Gates once, when he was so little that he had ridden with his father on the front of his saddle. Back then, he remembered thinking that the Gates soared up into the heavens, especially at the point where the road squeezed through the narrow gap. Kyre had not measured the Gates back then, he had only held onto the saddle and gawked in awe at the cliffs. According to the map provided by General Armistead's headquarters team, the width of the Gates at the road was roughly one hundred yards. Actually, it was more narrow, because rocks crumbling off the cliffs had created a debris field on both sides; the road had to constantly be kept cleared of boulders that flaked away from the granite cliffs and tumbled down. Most of the boulders crashed to the ground and rolled down the road to the west, bouncing and rolling, dangerous to anyone on the road going up to the Gates. But enough rock stayed at the bottom of the cliffs that the road would have become completely blocked, without the tireless efforts of Demarche to keep the precious road open for traffic.

It was the narrow size of the Gates that made them the perfect spot to defend the Kaltzen pass. The gates were not the actual highest point of the pass; that lay more than a mile farther up the road. Beyond the Gates was a broad, bowl-shaped shallow valley; a mountain meadow the residents of Demarche called a 'park'. On the east side of the park, the ridge of the mountain crest was an escarpment ranging far north and south, with the escarpment looming above the valley. The road went through a gap in the escarpment, a gap much wider and more gently sloped than the Gates.

Kyre stood in the saddle, as much to give his sore backside a rest as to get a better look at the Gates. He still could not see the base of the Gates, where the road cut through the narrow gap, because there was a hump in the road before the Gates. That was something Kyre remembered from going up the road as a little boy; how frustrating it was that you could not actually see the road through the Gates until you were almost upon them. As he stood, a soldier behind him shouted a warning, and Kyre looked back down the road. No enemy riders were in sight directly behind them, for the road curved and dropped off. Where the road went around a spur of the mountain perhaps a mile away, Kyre was surprised to see the road fairly clogged with enemy cavalry. He pulled out his spyglass.

The enemy was approaching rapidly, on horses much fresher than the tired mounts ridden by Kyre and the soldiers accompanying him. Armistead had pulled her horse to a halt, to steady her own spyglass. She lowered the glass and looked at Kyre. "They have wizards with them."

Kyre again studied the enemy cavalry, he had not seen any wizards among- Yes, now he saw them. "Two wizards, at least!" Kyre cried out. As he watched through the shaking image of the spyglass, one of the wizards looked up. Directly at him, it seemed, and for a moment, Kyre felt sheer terror. From a mile away, Kyre thought it not possible the wizard could have singled him out, but the wizard was clearly shaking his fist at the group from Demarche and Burwyck.

"We ride!" Armistead ordered. "Your Grace, we must go!"

Kyre tucked his spyglass away spurred his horse, but the animal could not manage more than a trot on trembling legs. The enemy's galloping pace was gaining on them; Kyre looked to the Gates to judge whether they would pass through before the enemy caught up with them. "How far to the Gates?" He asked breathlessly.

A Demarche soldier answered with a worried glance behind. His horse was also soaked with sweat and laboring, glassy-eyed. "Three miles, slightly less, Your Grace."

When the road through the Gates was still just beyond sight, perhaps half a mile away, wizard fire shattered a rock on the side of the road, and the company turned as one in the saddle to see the imminent danger. Two wizards were in the lead, with black-clad cavalry close behind, shouting war cries and brandishing spears and swords. Their onrushing horses kicked up clouds of choking dust from the road, and a few arrows flew from their midst, falling far short of any target. Even for wizard fire, the distance was still too great for accuracy. No matter, the enemy wizards did not care to hit any particular person, merely to sow terror among the defenders. Another ball of magical fire was flung and this one splashed in the road, panicking several horses. All the horses, even those trained for war, flared their nostrils at the acrid stench of wizard fire, and their fear gave them fresh legs.

Wizards! The thought sent fear coursing along Kyre's spine. He had been trained to fight with a bow, a sword, a dagger, a spear, and axe and all manner of other odd weapons he may use or be faced with. He knew the strengths and weaknesses of each weapon, how to use them, how to defend against them. He knew how to use a stronger opponent's strength against them, and how to use his own strength and speed. What he did not know was any practical way to fight a wizard. Advice from weapons masters was to run when faced with magical power. A shield may provide temporary protection against the crudest form of power; wizard fire. Against more arcane arts, an ordinary soldier had no protection, and wizard fire could eat through the strongest shield if hit more than once.

The only tactic taught in the Burwyck army, if forced to fight a wizard, was to use the advantage of numbers. Even the most powerful wizard could fight only a certain number of opponents. Massed soldiers, brave to the point of suicidal, could overwhelm a wizard, if any of them survived to get close enough. A wizard could block an arrow, or two or three, but a full volley of arrows could get through a magical defense. When faced with a wizard, Kyre's weapons instructor had told him, the only thing to do was accept that you would die, and do your best to strike a blow, futile gesture though that may be.

All that ran through Kyre's mind as he raced toward the Gates. Surely the Gates were well defended, and surely that defense included wizards, many wizards.

So Kyre was utterly shocked when he came over the crest of the road, to find less than a hundred soldiers defending the Gates, and most of them were people Kyre and Armistead had sent ahead of them. Where was the Demarche army?

Where was the Royal Army?!

Their horses stumbled the final hundred yards to the ragged line of soldiers milling about between the towering Gates. A brisk wind blew right in their faces from the east, snatching the breath from Kyre's mouth, forcing him to shout and even then, soldiers cupped hands to their ears in order to hear him. "We must hold the Gates!" Kyre demanded. "Where are your fellows?"

"Begging your pardon, Your Grace," said one Demarche sergeant with a pained expression, "we have orders to pull back. There's not enough of us here to hold the Gates, and the Royal Army is still climbing the other side of the pass."

"What! No!" The gap at the true summit of the pass was ten times, more than ten times as wide as the Gates. If the Gates could not be held with the soldiers on hand, how could the summit of the pass be secured?

The sergeant took off his helmet. "Your Grace, with all respect, I am a soldier of Demarche," he looked at General Armistead, who was slumped in the saddle of her horse, supported by guards on either side. The valiant woman was barely awake, mumbling something to herself.

"Get the general to safety," one of her captains ordered. "Who gave you these orders?" The captain demanded to the sergeant.

"General Magrane himself," the sergeant said defensively, drawing himself up on his toes and squaring his soldiers. "He told me there is not time to set up proper defenses here before the enemy arrives," the soldier pointed down the road, where the enemy was no more than half a mile away, their panting horses struggling to maintain a gallop up the road.

"The defenses should have already been here!" Kyre exploded.

"Yes, Your Grace," the sergeant was now less deferential, having absorbed scathing criticism from too many officers over the past hour. "Seeing as they were not when I arrived, I am following orders. We might hold for a time against that cavalry," he held up his spear, "but not against wizards."

"Your Grace," the Demarche captain said in a defeated tone, "he is right. The Gates are lost. We must pull back on General Magrane's orders, and-"

"No!" Kyre's youthful emotions shown through. "We will not lose our nation, just because our new Regent is a spoiled, petulant little girl! She may surrender Demarche to spite your duchess, but the army of Burwyck will stand firm! Burwyck! To me!" He wheeled his exhausted horse, feeling the beast slow to respond. So too were his guard and soldiers, he noticed. The prospect of fighting a desperate battle against endless numbers of enemy cavalry was not what caused his soldiers to hesitate.

It was the prospect of fighting wizards.

Kyre snatched a spear from the Demarche sergeant's hand and took the lead, riding back west to the absolute most narrow point of the Gates. When his soldiers, no more than thirty, formed up with him, Kyre tried to think of inspiring words. This is where his father would truly command his army; but to Kyre, no words came. He wheeled his horse back and forth, trying not to admit to his own terror at the onrushing enemy.

Indulging himself, he looked up at the Gates, the powerful mountain wind buffeting him in the saddle. The sky, which in the valley below had been pleasantly sunny, was now clouded over, promising a storm. The wind was chilly, making him shiver in his sweat-soaked shirt under the chainmail.

This, he thought, is where I will die? Far from home. Not to save his nation or to ensure victory, but in a futile gesture.

Kyre considered that he should regret that if Tarador survived, the princess Ariana would have to marry his younger brother Talen.

And he found himself thinking that spoiled brat Ariana deserved his bully of a brother.

How could he, Kyre asked himself, have ever been so *stupid* and gullible as to pledge featly to an untested princess he barely knew?

The enemy neared, letting out a blood-curdling battle cry, and Kyre opened his mouth to shout a defiant reply.

His shout was cut short by a fireball smashing into the rock face of the Gate beside him, throwing him off his horse, and then all was darkness.

CHAPTER TWENTY

The enemy poured through the Gates, marching across the broad, shallow mountain valley meadow before the Kaltzen Gap, as the actual summit of the pass was known in Demarche. The ranks of the enemy swelled, concentrating in the center but so many of them were there, they were forced to spread out across the valley. In the Gap, more and more Royal Army soldiers were arriving, to reinforce the meager ranks of Demarche soldiers. The defenders formed a line across the wide Gap, only four rows deep. Pikes were set into the ground to menace the enemy cavalry, swords made ready in the first two ranks, with archers behind them. There was no point to archers climbing the escarpment, for the top of those cliffs were so high above the valley below that no arrow could aimed accurately at the valley floor, and the swirling mountains winds would blow even the most carefully aimed arrow wildly off course.

The enemy cavalry tried an initial charge of the Gap to test the defenses there, and found those defenses too stout for comfort. The army commanders of Acedor had no qualms about ordering their entire cavalry to their deaths, merely to wear down the numbers of defenders, but with thousands of infantry marching through the Gates, there was no need for wasteful slaughter. Better to wait until Acedor had overwhelming numbers, then let infantry march on the Gap and crush the defenders by sheer numbers. Cavalry would be held in reserve to exploit the opening forced by their infantry and race down the other side of the pass, into the heart of Tarador below. Already, the enemy commanders judged they had a four to one advantage in soldiers at the Kaltzen pass. In wizards, their advantage was even greater, for only three were seen in the ranks of Tarador, while Acedor could boast of seven wielders of magical fire.

Among the wizards of Acedor, there was no boasting. There was fear. Fear and doubt. True, the seven of them faced only three, and behind them was the power of a demon. What nagged them with fear and doubt was recognizing one of the wizards on the side of Tarador.

It was the woman from the faraway land of Ching-Do, the wizard known as Madame Chu. The enemy knew of her, feared her, had tried to kill her over the years. Tried and failed.

"I can't *throw* a fireball," Olivia protested to Chu Wing. She had not yet mastered that skill, and Lord Salva had warned her against trying. The technique Olivia had developed allowed her to create a larger fireball in her hand, but she yet lacked control of it. Whenever she tried to throw it, as soon as it left her hand, it shrunk to a pinpoint of light and then snuffed out. Madame Chu thought the problem might be that because Olivia was using artificial means of growing the fire-ball, the magic was not properly contained. Although, when Chu tried 'pulling' a fireball using Olivia's technique, she created a fireball larger and more intense than she usually did, and the power remained when she threw it. Chu had told Olivia that she simply needed to work on her concentration with a small amount of magical fire, before she tried throwing anything powerful.

"You don't have to throw anything," Chu assured the young wizard. "Stand here, in view of the enemy, particularly whenever their wizards are watching, and just hold fire in your hand. We only need to make them keep their distance from us." Madame Chu had already forced the enemy back by creating an especially large fireball, and hurling it into the ranks of the enemy. After that, they had pulled back the front rank. The crisped bodies of the dead provided a marker for the unwary.

"What if they charge us while you're busy?" Olivia asked fearfully. She was not concerned for her own life; she was afraid of failing in her assigned task. Even though it was a task that should not have fallen to an apprentice wizard.

"You will be fine, Olivia," Chu held a hand above her head, let flare a truly impressive fireball, then let it snap out of existence. Her strength was needed elsewhere.

"But what if-"

Chu stepped down behind the barrier, and crouched so the enemy would not see where she was going. "If the enemy charges now, all is lost anyway. Take care of yourself, and stay out of the army's way." Without a backward glance, she hurried a short way down the road to where a tent had been set up for her, shielding her from prying eyes. Sitting cross-legged on cushions, she closed her eyes, slowed her breathing and reached out for Paedris through the spirit world. "It is time."

Paedris, accompanied by Cecil, was on top of a ridge slightly above and to the south of the Gates of the Mountains. When he felt Chu Wing reach out for him in the spirit world, he smiled to himself, and sent a wave of warmth back to her. Then, he spoke. "Lord Mwazo, it is time."

Cecil shuddered, breathing deeply from the strain of the magic he had been wielding. "You may have my strength, what is left of it. Paedris, what of your own strength?" The other wizard had been feeding power to Cecil all day, and parts of the previous days.

"It will be enough," Paedris' face reflected the great strain he was under. "Whenever have we wielded great power, unless it is in great need?" A good part of a wizard's training was to pull power from the spirit world while the wizard was very tired, even utterly exhausted. That was when mistakes were made, and power could become dangerous, even deadly, to the wizard him or herself. "Let us begin."

Paedris closed his eyes, feeling the power from Madame Chu and Lord Mwazo; at first two streams of a warm, liquid-like caress, quickly growing to a blast of furnace-like fire. In the mountain valley below, the enemy wizards could not have missed such raw power being used, and they saw their danger.

Too late.

Paedris used the power of his fellow wizards, and added his own. With his mind, he reached down into the rock that lay under and supported the great weight of the Gates. Many years ago, when passing through the Gates, Paedris had sent out his senses deep underground, and found faults. Places where the rock foundation was weak, cracked, crumbling. Over the course of his many travels in Tarador, he had several occasions to ride through the Kaltzen pass, and each time, he had explored and tweaked the underground faults. Paedris had told General Magrane about the weakness of the Gates, and the general had thought it might someday be useful to collapse the Gates, to prevent an enemy from using the pass and gain entry to the heart of Tarador that way.

The new Regent of Tarador knew of the weakness underlying the Gates also, but she had a very different idea about how to use that knowledge.

Let the enemy pass through the Gates first.

The host of Acedor, having passed through the Gates and now standing in the valley, awaiting orders to charge and force their way through the pass, all jerked as one as they felt the ground rumble under their feet. In terror, they saw the solid rock cliffs of the Gates *ripple*. And then, as they began throwing aside their weapons and running in terror, the faces of the twin cliffs began to slump, toppling down and over to the north. The air filled with screams and billowing dust and flying shards of rock as the enormous columns of rock gave way, collapsing to fill in where the Gates had been, and creating a landslide wall of rock rushing across the floor of the valley. Paedris had chosen well, the underground faults he split open began in the valley and ran west under the Gates. As the faults grew wider and wider, the west half of the valley floor gave way in one sudden catastrophic collapse, land falling away twenty feet or more. Great cracks opened in the valley, swallowing men, orcs and horses, before the land shifted again and the cracks closed on those un-fortunates.

"Paedris!" Mwazo shouted in alarm, as the ground beneath them also shifted.

Lord Salva's eyes snapped open, but for a moment his awareness was still in the spirit world. Shaking himself back to the real, he grasped Mwazo's arm to steady the both of them. "Have no fear, my friend. We are up here because the rock under this place is solid." The ground beneath them lurched.

"Perhaps not as solid as you supposed?"

"It is solid as I expected, Cecil," Paedris pushed himself to his knees. "The problem is, I may have used somewhat too much power. The spirits were more than eager to help us."

"Somewhat?" Cecil's eyes grew wide as he contemplated the chaos in the valley below. Most of the valley was now wreathed in dust, as were the Gates. Or, where the magnificent Gates used to be, for the once-impressive cliffs had collapsed entirely to fill in any gap. In the valley, with the ground still shaking, those enemy still alive were stumbling, crawling, rolling on the ground and trying to get to the east, but in that direction lay archers of the Royal Army of Tarador. The choice was either deadly arrows to the east, or being crushed to death by falling rock to the west.

Most of the enemy soldiers, without guidance from their wizards or orders from their leaders, chose to risk the arrows, holding their hands up in fearful surrender.

"What have I done?" Ariana gasped in horror from her viewpoint above the valley.

General Magrane had no such regrets. "You have given us a victory, Your Highness. And now, if you will excuse me, I must go down to the road, to see to the enemy's surrender. Or to finish them." Magrane had a preference, which he did not express aloud in the presence of the crown princess. She had seen enough ugliness for one day. Let the enemy surrender, if they would. If they *could*, given the demon they served.

If not, then enemy would soon discover the Royal Army of Tarador was not so weak in the Kaltzen pass as their leaders had thought, for Magrane had thousands of soldiers hidden just down the road. Soldiers who even then were polishing the edges of their already razor-sharp swords. Soldiers seeking revenge.

Soldiers eager to kill the servants of the demon who sought to slaughter or enslave them and their families.

Grand General Magrane very much preferred the enemy not to surrender.

Ariana walked slowly through the line of large tents of the hurriedly set up Royal Army field hospital, which held cots full of wounded soldiers. She briefly greeted the doctors first, mindful they were extremely busy, then walked through each tent. With soldiers who were awake, she knelt beside them, inquired about their injuries and simply listened. It took her many hours to go through every tent, then she had to visit one particular wounded soldier; a person she had been putting off visiting.

Kyre Falco.

When she came into the section of the tent which held Kyre, she saw that a haggard-looking Lord Salva had just finished checking on the heir to Burwyck. The wizard acknowledged the princess with a nod, and walked to her slowly, wiping his hands on a clean towel.

Whereas before, when among the wounded soldiers, she had been outwardly cheery and trying to project confidence, now she appeared to have shrunk. Her shoulders were stooped, arms hugged tightly across her chest, her face downcast. "How," she let out a long breath. "How is he?"

Her inner conflict had not escaped the attention of the court wizard. "He will recover fully," Paedris assured the Regent. "More quickly if I had the strength," he added with great weariness, "I did what I could for him. He needs rest, which, since he is a generally healthy young man, he will not allow himself." Paedris looked at the crown princess, trying to judge her emotions. Her face was a mask, unreadable. "Your Highness, his injury was grave, he could have died. I do not know whether it pleases you that I saved his life?"

"No. I meant to say, no, it does not displease me. Or, I don't know," she sighed. "I am to marry the heir to Burwyck, and Kyre's younger brother is worse." She looked up at Paedris, and had they been alone, she would have appreciated a reassuring hug. "Talen Falco is a bully, and every inch his father. Kyre," she shook her head. "I thought I knew him. Now, I'm not sure. With the Falcos, you can never tell what is real, and what is a careful show for my benefit."

Paedris was about to remark that was true of most royalty, but he held his tongue. "His Grace wishes to speak with you, Your Highness."

Ariana blushed. "Please, call me Ariana. You are the only person who will."

Paedris straightened. "Perhaps when you are serving me tea and sweet biscuits. Here," he gestured around the tent, "you command Tarador, Your Highness. I would prefer that Kyre rest, but I know that if I don't let him speak with you, he won't be able to rest. Please be brief. And then, Your Highness, you and I must speak privately."

Ariana made a short, stiff bow. "Yes, Lord Salva," she said without a trace of a smile; her focus was on the figure grimacing as he pushed himself upright in bed.

As the crown princess approached, Kyre struggled to swing his legs off the bed onto the floor. "No, stop!" Ariana hurried forward, waving her hands in genuine concern. "Lord Salva told me you were gravely injured. You need to rest."

"I am not so injured that I can't stand in the presence of my future queen," Kyre said in a voice much weaker than he would have wished, and tried to push himself up.

"Stop! That is a command from your Regent," Ariana ordered automatically, not knowing what else to say. To her surprise, it worked. Kyre sunk back to sit on the bed.

"Your Highness, it is you who were gravely injured, by my thoughts and things I said about you, to myself," Kyre couldn't look at her as he spoke. "I should have trusted you."

"Oh. Kyre," then she remembered that this conversation should be kept formal. "Your Grace, I am sorry. The deception was necessary."

"I understand that now." He looked away, thinking of the soldiers who had died or been injured, not to stop the enemy, but to maintain a deception. A deception that he now knew was indeed absolutely necessary. General Magrane and his Royal Army had counterattacked the enemy along the River Fasse in Anschulz, and the royal force simply lacked the strength to have stopped a second invasion. A much larger second invasion. The only reason the enemy had not pushed their way across the Turmalane mountains into the heart of Tarador, was because the enemy had been lured into a trap. Those soldiers of Tarador who died to maintain the deception had sold their lives dearly, for their sacrifice had drawn the enemy to their defeat.

That might be of cold comfort to the dead.

Ariana kept talking, feeling she needed to justify her actions. "Duchess Rochambeau knew the truth, but her army commander did not."

Kyre did not react openly. "Did my father know?"

"Yes," the crown princess looked away. "He was sworn to secrecy; he could not have told you, though I expect he wished to?"

Kyre laughed bitterly. "I am not in good favor with my father at the moment." Would the Duke of Burwyck have preferred his eldest son to have died in glorious battle, so that Talen could become the heir? Kyre was certain the thought had crossed his father's mind. "Your Highness, I said some very harsh things about you, when I thought you had abandoned Demarche out of spite. I judged you unfairly."

"You were supposed to, silly," Ariana's smile was genuine. "If I couldn't deceive you, how could our enemy have been deceived?" She lowered her voice. "The, *wizards*," she whispered, "helped to maintain the deception. You were not alone, Your Grace. The wizards assured me they used their utmost power to convince the enemy that we had abandoned Demarche, and that the Kaltzen pass was only lightly defended," she repeated the words General Magrane had used when explaining his final plan to her. Chancellor Kallron was constantly reminding her that she needed to speak like an adult if she wanted people to take her seriously as Regent. "I am sorry about the people we lost, I do regret that."

"Don't, Princess," Kyre said groggily, his eyelids fluttering. The effort of staying awake was becoming too much for him. His head nodded onto his chest, then he jerked awake, embarrassed. "I saw what happened when the enemy crossed the river. If we had tried to stop them west of the mountains, it would have taken your entire army, and we would have had nothing left now."

"That is what General Magrane told me."

"It was his idea to trap the enemy behind the Gates?"

"Yes, he and Lord Salva have been talking about the possibility of doing something like that for years. It was my idea to make the enemy think I was punishing Duchess Rochambeau because she snubbed me in the Council vote," Ariana added with pride. "To lure the enemy in past the Gates."

"I'll bet Aunt Sally wasn't happy about that," Kyre giggled, half asleep. The Duchess of Demarche was distantly related to him, as most of Tarador's royalty were related in some way or another. Salvanna Rochambeau was not Kyre's favorite aunt, but she was the most powerful. "She hates you."

"I know."

"No. She really, *really* hates you," Kyre giggled again. Whatever Paedris had done to him in the healing process, it had made Kyre free with his words. Very much unlike the careful training he had received since he was a baby; to use every word as a weapon to get what he wanted. "She must super hate you right now. My father doesn't hate you," Kyre's head nodded again, "I think he kind of admires you. He probably wishes you were his child instead of me right now. He just," he lost his train of thought, "what was I saying? He sees that you are in his way. He will kill you someday, you know that?"

"Yes, Your Grace," Ariana replied quietly, knowing Kyre was slipping away into sleep. She hoped when he awakened, he would not remember the conversation.

Kyre reached up to hold her hand, but missed twice, his hand kept flopping onto the bed. Ariana took pity on him, holding his hand lightly, while glancing around to check if anyone was watching. People in the hospital tent were either asleep, or too busy to notice or care what the princess was doing.

"Don't you worry," Kyre said so quietly that Ariana had to bend down to hear. "I'll pro- protect you." His hand went limp, his head lolled to the side, and he fell into a deep sleep.

Ariana patted his hand, and placed it gently on the bed. The young man who she would be forced to marry, the young man who was the heir to a family that had been bitter enemies of the Trehaymes for centuries, was drooling on the pillow. Ariana stifled a laugh. Laying there like that, a matted lock of blond hair curled like an 'S' on his forehead, his hands twitching in sleep, he looked almost- Cute, she had to admit.

Then she frowned, and stood upright. A sleeping bear might look cute also, until it awakened and decided to kill you. Kyre was a Falco, and he would always be a Falco. Despite his words, she reminded herself that Kyre would, in the end, fulfill his familial obligations. His words meant nothing; a person like Kyre never said anything unless his words gained an advantage for him. And for the Falcos.

Ariana wiped her hands on a towel, wiped them clean of the sweat Kyre's hand had left on hers. The Falcos and the Trehaymes were enemies and always would be. Someday, Kyre himself might kill her. If she hadn't killed him first.

A tiny part of her, the part that was still a girl rather than the cold-hearted leader of her nation, took one last look at Kyre's sleeping form, and wished things could be different.

"Lord Salva?" Ariana asked later, much later, when she had finished walking through every tent in the field hospital.

"Your Highness," Paedris wearily began to push himself up from the folding chair.

"No, please, sit," Ariana waved a hand. "I'm sure you are weary."

The court wizard nodded gratefully. "Never before so in my life," he admitted. "Or so it seems. Please, sit," he pointed to a folding chair next to him. They were in a tent that had been set aside for the use of the wizards, only five of them were in the tent at the time. Paedris and Madame Chu were awake, slumped in chair and sipping tea, while Lord Mwazo and two others were collapsed on cots, snoring softly.

"Thank you," Ariana said, but she stepped over to check on the three sleeping wizards before sitting down. "Will they recover?"

"After a while," Wing was barely able to keep her eyes open. "We are concerned about Cecil," she shared a glance with Paedris. "The burden of deceiving the enemy fell entirely on him; only he has that ability. He was able to fill the minds of the enemy commanders with confidence that they could easily push their way through the Kaltzen, and he made them think the Tiper pass was too strongly defended."

"He succeeded," Paedris agreed, "at great cost to himself. And then he and Wing lent me the last of their strength to topple the Gates of the Mountains."

"We did," Wing closed her eyes and rested her head on the back of the chair.

"You gave too much of yourself, my dear," Paedris reached out to caress Wing's hand, but the wizard from Ching-Do had fallen asleep. He took the teacup from her lap and put it on the floor. "She has the power of healing, which many wizards do not. Wing should have rested after we brought down the Gates, but she could not rest while people needed our help."

"You should have rested also, Lord Salva."

Paedris could not argue with that sentiment. "I am blessed with the gift of healing; I cannot ignore people who need me, simply because I am weary. Your Highness," he smiled, "you said we should drop our formality when we were speaking privately."

Ariana looked puzzled; she herself was tired enough that her thinking was slowed. "Yes, *Paedris*."

"Thank you, *Ariana*," he chuckled.

"We won a great victory today, thanks to you, and your fellow wizards."

"Mostly due to Cecil's efforts, I feel I must say," Paedris drained his teacup. "Because he does not show his power in the form of fireballs, people think him a lesser wizard. They are wrong. I do not have the skill, or the strength, to wrestle with the minds of our enemy. Ariana," he rubbed his eyes and could not stop from yawning, "we won a battle today, no more. I fear that, in fighting this battle, we may have lost the war."

"*What*? Why?" The Regent asked, shocked to her core.

"You, and General Magrane, have now crushed two invasions of Tarador. One in Anschulz, and now here. The battle in Anschulz was merely a test for the enemy; to establish a crossing of the Fasse so that a much larger force could come across the border unopposed. The battle here was not the enemy's intention; they were lured into fighting in Demarche because their commanders saw an opportunity that was too tempting to miss. Or, because Cecil persuaded them this opportunity would not happen again, and the enemy needed to strike before they were ready." Paedris leaned forward and poured himself more tea, too weary to think of offering tea to the princess. "Our enemy is filled with cowardice and fear, Ariana. The demon's heart is filled with destruction, and it fears its own destruction. It is ancient, it remembers a time before this world, a time before time. Because it is ancient, time means nothing to it, even though it burns inside to make this world its own. The demon has been content to wait until it is so strong, and we have become so weak, that it takes no risk in conquering us. It had been my hope to forestall the final battle until Koren," he paused to make sure no one was listening outside the tent, "could use his full powers in our defense. Now, I fear, the enemy has measured our strength, and found us lacking. We are weaker now than the demon supposed."

"What does that mean?" Ariana asked fearfully.

"The final blow will fall on us, sooner than I had hoped. The enemy will not wait for winter; Cecil has seen this in the enemy's heart. Orcs are coming down from the mountains in the north; already the dwarves are fighting desperate battles through their lands. Across the Fasse from Anschulz, the enemy readies a host that makes the army we crushed here today seem a mere battalion. The enemy now knows they can cross the River Fasse in Anschulz; they know where and how to do it. This time, they will not leave themselves open to counterattack, and this time, we will not be able to stop them. They are too many, they have prepared too carefully, and they have the power of a demon behind them."

"We have you, Lord Salva," she reached out and squeezed his hand, more to reassure herself. "Your strength will grant us victory. Can you do anything at the river to-"

"I will not be at the Fasse," Paedris explained. "The time for pitting strength against strength is over; we would lose badly if we continue along that path. Wing," he reached out to stroke that wizard's cheek affectionately, "will remain with you. Cecil and I must embark on a perilous journey into the heart of Acedor, I fear."

"No! You must not-"

"I must. *We* must," Paedris insisted. "Our only hope is to sow fear and confusion in the mind of the demon, so it hesitates to strike the final blow into the heart of Tarador. As I have said, I have no ability to do that, among us only Mwazo does. He must be close to the demon to get inside its mind, and I must go with him, to conceal our presence in Acedor and to lend my power." What Paedris did not say was that he and Mwazo likely would not be returning to Tarador; the hazards of the journey were too great for them to survive. Paedris and Cecil had not discussed it, even between themselves, but Mwazo expected they would be discovered in Acedor, despite the best efforts Paedris would make to conceal the two of them. In fact, Paedris suspected being discovered was part of Mwazo's plan. When the demon detected two wizards from Tarador had slipped into its territory and gotten close, Mwazo hoped that would add to the demon's sense of fear and paranoia. Finding two powerful enemy wizards on its very doorstep might hopefully cause the demon to pull back its army to protect itself. Paedris and Cecil would die, but they would buy time for Tarador, and for Koren Bladewell to become the incredibly powerful wizard they knew he would someday be. If he were sure Koren was safe and being guided into his power, Paedris could die happily. As it was, Paedris would die in the hope that Shomas would find Koren.

"There is no hope, then?" Ariana was not ashamed of the tears which stung her eyes.

The wizard squeezed her hand. "There is always hope. Koren is out there, somewhere, and Shomas is searching for him. While Koren lives, and he is not in the clutches of the enemy, there will always be hope."

"How long?" Ariana asked, forcing herself to put her emotions aside and focus on the practical need of keeping Tarador from being overrun by its ancient enemy.

Paedris was confused, his tired mind not following her meaning. "How long for what?"

"For Koren to become powerful enough to help us. To help you. How long will he need?"

Too long now, Paedris wanted to say. He could hear there was more than hope for Tarador in her voice; she still longed for Koren to return. Return to her. "Only a few short months ago, I would have told you Koren needed five years, at the very least. He is still too young to control his power; it would be dangerous for him to attempt using it. His power could kill him now, even with an experienced wizard guiding him."

"We do not have five years." It was not a question.

"No. We do not. Even if Cecil and I are successful," and likely die in the attempt, "the enemy would delay no more than a year or two."

"Two years? But Koren needs five years. You said we have hope?"

"The hope is that, somehow, Koren is able to transcend the usual path followed by apprentice wizards. That he comes into his power, and can control it, with a speed far beyond that of any wizard before him."

"That is not much hope," Ariana was disappointed.

"More than you may think, Regent," Paedris said with a wink. "Only a few short months ago, I would have thought you could not come to power until your sixteenth birthday. Yet, you found a way to transcend the legal restrictions upon you, and now you have led us to victory here. You were able to rise above the usual path of a crown princess. Do not be so quick to dismiss Koren's abilities. *You* came to power with a speed far beyond any monarch in Tarador's history," he reminded her. "A thing is impossible only if it cannot be done. Koren has not even tried. Koren Bladewell is a mystery. His power is immense, and somehow, his power went unnoticed for years longer than it should have. Your Highness, I suspect that the normal rules do not apply to Koren. *That* is my hope."

CHAPTER TWENTY ONE

As the sun approached the ridge of hills to the west, the two dwarves and the strangers they were guiding came over a rise, and saw the source of the black smoke they had been walking toward all afternoon. It was a town, a substantial dwarf town, situated in a narrow valley. At the far end of the valley was the town; a jumble of stone, brick and wood buildings, all jammed closely together. Along both sides of the valley, caves led into the hillsides, the caves being entrances to mines deep underground. At the near side of the valley was another mine; this one a pit. Over many years, the pit had been dug out to expose whatever the dwarves were mining. There were wooden towers along the rim of the pit, with cables leading from the bottom of the pit up to the rim, buckets on the cables brought up rock. And what else, Koren asked himself? "Barlen, what are they mining?"

"Iron ore," Barlen replied with pride. "The finest iron ore in the world, we have up here. They bring up rock with the raw ore, crack the rock in those buildings over there," he pointed to large, dark wood structure. "The rock we can't use gets dumped down the hillside over there."

Koren peered over the edge, to where a pile of rocks was being dumped. "You dig a hole here, and fill in that valley below with the rock you can't use?" The scale of the mining operation impressed Koren; he had no idea an industry of that size could exist so high in the mountains.

"That's the idea," Dekma winked. "Mind your step and follow us, we're going around the rim of the pit to the town. Don't stand under a cable when there is a bucket passing overhead; sometimes loose rock falls from buckets."

"Oh, no." Koren groaned when they reached the town. On the hillside above the town was a keep, with a tall tower made of a type of stone that glowed faintly yellow in the light of the setting sun. It was a grand building, compared to the rude structures that made up most of the town. It was also high above the town, at the top of a path so steep that parts of the path had steps carved into the rock. "We have to go all the way up there?" He was half considering the idea of finding a place to eat, a place to sleep, and walking up to the wizard's tower in the morning.

"Eh?" Dekma asked, puzzled. "Up where?"

Koren pointed. "The keep. The wizard's tower up there."

"Wizard?" Barlen pointed to the smoke-blackened rough timbers of the shop they were standing in front of. "*This* is the wizard's place."

Koren's eyes grew wide. "This wizard lives *here*?"

"He lives there, next door," Barlen jerked a thumb toward a modest two story house. "This here is the wizard's workshop."

"Oh," Koren's face grew red. "I thought a wizard would live in a tower, like Lord Sal-" Too late, he realized he had said too much. "This looks like a blacksmith's shop."

"It *is* a blacksmith's shop," Bjorn said, peering in the doorway. While the forge was cold and silent, there was no mistaking the tools and implements inside the shop. Although, the shop held many strange things he did not recognize.

"Yes, so?" Barlen said scornfully. "The Lady Zara is a metalsmith wizard," he explained. "Not all wizards cast fireballs and make silly potions."

Bjorn nodded. "Dwarven magic is why your metalwork is the finest in the world."

"Dwarven metalworking is a secret," Dekma said without humor. "You'll not learn our secrets here."

"I doubt *you* know anything about the wizardry of working metal," Bjorn retorted. "I have worked as a smith, have you? We know what you call secrets, we know how you work metal. The reason we can't create fine metalwork like you dwarves is not a lack of knowledge. What we lack is the best materials, the special equipment, and the techniques."

"Aye," Dekma folded his arms across his chest. "And you'll not get any of it on your visit here. If you came up here to-"

Koren interrupted, wishing to avoid an argument. He held up a shiny, jagged black stone that he had picked up from a bin in front of the wizard's shop. "What is this?"

"That?" Dekma said as he snatched it from Koren's hand and tossed it back into the bin. "It's coal. And it is not any of your business."

Koren held up his hands to show he had meant no harm. "What is coal?"

"It's a rock that burns," Dekma explained, glaring at Bjorn.

"A rock that burns? Now I know you are joking with me," Koren said sourly. Where they also joking about the blacksmith shop being home to a wizard?

"It's no joke," Bjorn declared. "I've seen it before. The dwarves mine it out of the mountains up here. You see how few trees there are in these mountains? There isn't enough timber to use for fires, they need what they have for building," Bjorn nudged the wood timbers of the blacksmith shop with a boot. "Coal burns much hotter than wood, it's one of the secrets to their ability to work metal. They also do something with coal that removes impurities from iron, to make stronger steel. That is something I don't know about."

"Why don't we use coal?" Koren bent down to pick up a chip of coal on the ground beside the bin. He handed it to Bjorn. A rock that burned? Amazing.

"We don't have enough of it," Bjorn examined the chip of coal and tossed it into the bin. "The only supply of coal in Tarador is in Winterthur. I hear the smiths there use it. But the cost of transporting a wagon load of coal is too expensive. And there is plenty of firewood in Tarador, unlike up here."

Dekma still felt he needed to defend the honor of dwarven metalworking. "Coal isn't our only advantage. We use magic also, magic your wizards don't know how to use. Our wizards can make blades that never go dull. Blades that will not cut their owner, no matter how sharp their edges may be."

"I had a sword like that!" Koren exclaimed.

"You?" Barlen cocked his head. "Where did you get such a special weapon? A blade like that would cost more than-"

"It wasn't *mine*," Koren backtracked. He needed to remember to keep his mouth shut! "I, I only touched it," he lied as Bjorn and the two dwarves stared at him. "I saw how it sliced through stiff leather, but when the sword's owner ran his hand along the edge, it didn't leave a mark. That was dwarf magic?" He asked the question to divert attention away from himself. "The Lady Zara makes swords like that?"

"Yes, she does," Dekma confirmed with pride, although in truth he had little knowledge of exactly what sort of magic Zara performed in her shop.

Bjorn glanced at the sun, which was setting over distant peaks to the west. "Barlen, are you going to introduce Kedrun to this Lady Zara?"

"I'll see if she is in," he said with doubt in his voice. When the wizard was at home, the forge was almost always glowing with fire. He knocked on the door frame. "Hello?"

From a back room of the shop came a dwarf woman, with long, beautiful silver-white hair tied in a braid. "Yes? What do you-" She recognized the two dwarves. "Oh, it's you. Hello, Barlen, Dekma. Who are your two companions?"

Barlen bowed slightly. "Bjorn, Kedrun, this is Frieda. She had been Lady Zara's trusted servant for, nigh on forty years now?" He guessed.

"You're making me sound old," Frieda said with a laugh.

"Frieda, this is Bjorn, and Kedrun. They helped us kill a bandit who had been vexing our merchants for years. Kedrun has some business with the Lady."

"Eh?" Frieda looked at Koren with suspicion. "What sort of business? The Lady is not here, she has gone northwest, to assist with our defenses there. If you are not here to waste my time, I may be able to help you, young man."

"How can you help me?" Koren asked, disappointment clear in his voice. He had traveled so very far, and the wizard was not at home. "You said you are not a wizard."

"If I judge your need worthy, I can send a message to Zara. What do you want with the Lady?" Frieda asked suspiciously.

"I," Koren looked at his companions. "Could we talk inside?"

"You can pay?"

"Pay?" Koren was still uncomfortable with the idea of wizards charging for their services. "Yes," he pulled out his purse and shook it. "I can pay."

"Hmm. Whether you can pay enough, for whatever you want, is the question."

"He can pay enough," Bjorn growled. "I have a purse also, if needed."

That convinced Frieda. "Very well, young man, come inside."

"We'll be going then," Barlen told Bjorn. "There's an inn down the street, you can seek lodgings there. Good luck to you."

As Koren followed Frieda into the shop, Bjorn settled on the lid of a coal bin to take his boots off and rub his aching feet. The wizard not being at home was annoying. He had pledged to follow 'Kedrun', but he would like the young man's business to be concluded successfully, whatever it was that Kedrun wanted.

Then? Bjorn had no idea what to do next. He would figure that out later. Hopefully, the near future held a hearty meal and a comfortable bed. Beyond that, the future would take care of itself, eventually.

In the shop, Frieda closed the door behind them, and gestured for Koren to sit at a rough but spotlessly clean table. The air in the blacksmith shop held a faint whiff of an acrid smell Koren remembered, from when Paedris was practicing magic in his awkward old tower.

Frieda sat on a chair, but did not relax at all. Strangers showing up unexpected on her doorstep were usually trouble. Especially when the strangers were not dwarves. With dwarves, if she did not know them, she usually knew their families, or their clan. With 'Kedrun' she knew nothing. "What do you need from Lady Zara?"

"A spell was cast on me. I want it, fixed. Removed. Taken away, however wizards do that."

"If you think someone cast a love spell on you," Frieda remarked with disgust, "then you have come a long way up here for nothing. There is no such thing as a love potion. Zara gets requests for that once a week, at least."

"No, it's, it is not a love potion," Koren replied, embarrassed.

"Anyway, why don't you ask the wizard you paid for this spell? Whoever cast the spell on you would be the best person to undo it."

"I can't ask Lor-, I can't ask that wizard. I didn't pay for the spell, I didn't ask for it. I didn't even know a spell had been cast on me, until I was told about it."

That got Frieda's attention. "A wizard cast a spell on you, without your permission? Kedrun, this is a serious matter. This must be reported. The Wizards' Council forbids the use of magic on anyone who-"

"No, please don't report anything. It's my fault. Partly my fault. I just want the spell undone. Or I want to understand it, if it is dangerous to me."

"Hmm," Frieda sat back in her chair. Koren had her intrigued. "What is the nature of the spell?"

"I have," he glanced toward the door. "I have been given magical fighting skill."

"Ha!" Frieda laughed.

"It's true! I have," Koren protested with sudden anger.

"No, you haven't, you young fool," Frieda said gently, seeing on Koren's face that he truly believed what he said. "You're either a complete fool, or someone has played a trick on you. There is no spell to make anyone fight with the speed and skill of a wizard."

"I can! Ask Bjorn! Or Barlen. Bjorn called me a berserker, and I was not even showing him all of my speed or skill. I may not have the fighting skill of a wizard," he did not know what level of skill that could be, "but I have bested a weapons master when I had no training."

"Kedrun, there is no such magic," Frieda scoffed. "If that is your business with the Lady Zara, you have wasted your journey. And my time."

"There must be," Koren insisted. Had his long journey all been for nothing?

Frieda shook her head slowly. "There is not. There is not a month that goes by without someone asking Zara to make him or her faster, for greater skill with an axe or a sword or a bow. Zara turns them all away, because there is no such magic."

"Is that because Zara works only with metal? Should I ask another wizard?" Koren asked innocently.

"You question my Lady's power?" Frieda's eyes flashed anger in the candle light.

"No, I, I do not mean any offense. I know little of wizards. Please, you have to believe me. I had never touched a sword before, and I was able to fight like a champion my very first time. Ask Bjorn. Or Barlen or Dekma, they've seen me fight." Then he corrected himself. "They've seen my skill with a bow. I never miss. Never."

"Never?" Frieda asked with an arched eyebrow.

"*Never.*"

For the first time, Frieda paused to consider the young man. Whatever the truth, Kedrun very much believed a wizard had cast a spell on him. A spell Frieda knew did not exist. Then she had a startling thought. "Your skill with a bow, when did this start?"

"I've always been good with a bow, ever since I was a little boy. I've never missed, not since I was very little."

"*Never?*" Frieda repeated, skeptical.

"Not that I can ever remember," Koren answered truthfully.

Frieda knew it could not be true, but she also saw that Koren fervently believed in what he was saying. Whatever the truth was, the young man was frightened, and he needed help, and Frieda could not turn him callously away. She could not help him, but she could humor him, and perhaps provide some comfort. And a dose of reality. Or, possibly, a shocking truth? No, that was not possible. "Stay here, I need to get something." She went into a back room and returned with a copper-plated box. Before opening it, she lit a lantern and set it on the table. "Here," she opened the box and began taking out various items. "Set these on the table behind you."

The first item Koren was given was a heavy ceramic bowl, stained dark with years of use. He set it carefully on the table, and reached for the next item; a simple stone with a rounded top and a flat base. It was not large, and to his surprise, she tossed it through the air to him. As soon as it fell into his cupped hands, the stone flared into dazzling light. Koren yelped in surprise and he dropped the stone onto the wood floor. It bounced and rolled under his chair. "What was that?"

Frieda seemed to be just as surprised as Koren. "It won't hurt you. Pick it up and put it on the table." Seeing he was reluctant to touch it again, she reached under his chair and picked it up. Frieda moved to put the stone on the table, but flicked her wrist and dropped it in Koren's lap.

The stone flared light again, not as bright this time, but Koren could feel the heat of it tingling the skin on top of his thighs. In a panic, he scooped it up with both hands to toss it across the workshop. As before, as soon as his bare hands touched the smooth stone, it flared with light, but this time the light grew blinding, searing Koren's eyes though his eyelids were tightly shut. He had not time to heave the stone upward before the light grew unbearably intense, and the stone shattered into three pieces.

Koren's fell over backwards, his chair toppling to the floor, sending him awkwardly flailing his arms until he crashed heavily onto the rough wood planks of the floor. "What was that?!" He shouted in fear, feeling around blindly to set the chair upright. His vision was coming quickly back to normal.

"What did you do?" Frieda asked from the floor where she had also fallen, dazed.

"I'm sorry," Koren almost sobbed. "It's my fault. I didn't mean to break it. I'm a jinx. I have always been a jinx."

"You *broke* it?" Frieda screeched, shaking her head to clear the spots swimming in her eyes.

Koren's vision had returned quickly. Not wishing to touch the stone again, he used a metal rod to push the pieces across the floor to Frieda. "It shattered. I didn't mean to do it, I swear. I'm a jinx. I will pay for the damage," he offered.

"Pay for-" Frieda asked in horror as she pushed the three pieces of the stone together on the floor by feel, her vision still dazzled by spots. "Do you have *any* idea how much a focus stone is worth? It's priceless!"

The door burst open and Bjorn rushed in. "What happened? Are you all right?"

"No we're not all right!" Frieda wailed. "Your idiot wizard friend here broke Lady Zara's focus stone."

"*Wizard?*" Bjorn's mouth was agape in astonishment. "Kedrun is no wizard."

"I'm not a wizard." Koren was just as surprised.

"You have lied to me from the moment you darkened my door," Frieda scolded, waving a finger at Koren.

"I am *not* a wizard," Koren insisted. He turned to Bjorn. "She played a trick on me, and the stone broke. I'm no wizard."

"No?" Frieda scooped up the pieces of the focus stone and offered them to Bjorn. "You take it. You'll see."

Bjorn gingerly let her put the three pieces of stone into his cupped hands. Nothing happened. "See what?"

"Exactly!" Frieda pointed to Koren. "Now make him touch a fingertip to one piece."

Koren recoiled, holding his hands behind his back. "I'm not touching it again," he pleaded with Bjorn. "I already broke it."

"Kedrun," Bjorn looked askance at his young companion. "I think you need to do as she says." When Koren hesitated, Bjorn added softly "It is already broken, what could be the harm?"

Barely holding one eye open, Koren reached out a shaking finger and brushed it against one of the shards of the focus stone. It flared to light in Bjorn's hand, but faintly, no longer having the power to blind anyone. "Do that again," Bjorn requested, intrigued.

Koren tapped a fingertip to the shard, then held his finger lightly on it. The shard glowed with a warm light, flickering. "Why does it do that?"

"It's a focus stone, of course. It *was* a focus stone," Frieda snapped. "You know damned well what it is, master wizard."

"*I* don't," Bjorn declared. "Tell me."

"Wizards use focus stones to concentrate their power. The stone pulls power from the spirit world, through the wizard who touches the stone. I don't know how it works, I'm not a wizard. Lady Zara uses this one to infuse magic into metal, somehow. She *did* use it," she glared at Koren. "It's broken now!"

"I said I was sorry," Koren was now angry at her. "You shouldn't have given it to me, if you knew it was going to break!"

"How did it break?" Bjorn asked.

"I don't know," Frieda admitted. She looked at the shattered pieces in Bjorn's hand, and took them back from him. "It shouldn't have happened. All I have ever seen it do is glow. When Zara used it, the stone only ever had a dull red glow to it. It's never been blindingly bright like that. What did *you* do to it?"

"I didn't do anything!" Koren repeated his protest. "How could I do anything? I'm not a wizard?"

"Then why does the stone shine when you touch it?" Bjorn asked. On impulse, he picked up a piece and squeezed it tightly. Nothing happened. But when he lightly pressed it to Koren's forearm, light pulsed from the shard of stone. "Kedrun is not a wizard," Bjorn told Frieda confidently. "What could this mean?"

Before Frieda could repeat that Koren certainly must be a wizard, Koren made a guess. "Could the stone be pulling power from the spell within me?"

Frieda stomped a foot on the floor. "There is no-"

Bjorn interrupted. "What spell?"

Koren shuffled his feet and stared at the floor. "You called me a berserker? My speed and skill come from a spell a wizard cast on me. That's why I need to see a wizard, to have the spell removed, before it burns me from the inside."

"There is no such spell!" Frieda shouted, raising her hands in frustration.

Bjorn took a half step backward, away from Koren. "She is right, there is no such spell."

"But-"

"Kedrun, I was a king's guard. If there were a magical way to give a soldier the fighting ability I have seen in you, we would have been given it to protect the king," Bjorn declared with certainty. "What does this mean?" He addressed the last to Frieda.

She held up her hands. "He is a wizard, I told you. Kedrun, you said a wizard gave you magical fighting power with the sword, but you also told me that you never miss with a bow? That you have never missed, as far back as you can remember? That started before you say a wizard cast a spell on you?"

Koren did not like the answer he had to give. "Yes."

Bjorn was not convinced. "I've known archers who *say* they never miss. Kedrun, you have remarkable skill with a bow, but-"

Frieda had enough. "I'll prove it to you. Come outside."

Outside the blacksmith shop, it was now fully dark; the last tinges of sunset had faded from the western horizon. Overhead, stars twinkled brightly in the inky black sky; the stars rippling as a strong breeze blew down the mountain. In the streets, lights shone through windows, and lanterns on posts beside the street swung back and forth. "Do you see that yellow sign there," Frieda pointed away from the town, toward the pit mine that was now dark and empty of workers. "It is round, and hangs just below the lantern?"

"That one?" Bjorn looked toward a post closer to the shop.

"No, the one at the edge of the mine pit. The yellow sign is there as a warning to avoid the edge," Frieda explained.

Bjorn squinted. The sign was too far away for him to see anything other than a faintly yellow dot that swung wildly in the breeze. "I see it. What about it?"

"Kedrun," Frieda instructed, "put an arrow in that sign."

"Impossible," Bjorn snorted.

"Can you do it?" Frieda demanded. "If you can, I will send a message to Zara."

Koren unlimbered his bow and peered at the sign. When the breeze blew strongly, the sign was edge on. Only when the breezed slackened momentarily was he able to see it as a full circle. "Yes," he said slowly. "I can hit it."

"No," Bjorn scoffed. "It would be a miracle. In this wind? How could you time such a shot?"

Koren nocked an arrow and drew the bowstring back. "I don't time it. I just," how could he explain what he did not understand? "I wait until it feels right, then I-" His fingers released the bowstring without him commanding them to do anything. In the darkness, there was a distant "thunk" sound, and the little yellow disc of a sign now had an arrow embedded in it.

Bjorn's words echoed the words Koren had heard aboard the *Lady Hildegard*. "That was not an amazing shot. That was an impossible shot, Kedrun."

"It's not impossible! I did it," Koren thought that fairly obvious. "I can do it again, if you like. It's not so difficult."

"How could you possibly know to aim, at so distant a target?" Bjorn unconsciously took a step back from Koren. "A moving target?"

Frieda touched Bjorn's arm. "He doesn't know, not consciously. Zara explained it to me one day. A wizard who holds a bow can draw on the power of the spirit world, and bend them to her will. Or his will, in Kedrun's case. The spirits know which target he wishes to hit, and they guide him. When the spirits sense the time is right, the bowstring is released, even if the wizard does not know it."

"But the wind!" Bjorn shook his head. "This wind would send any arrow off course."

"The vagaries of wind are no mystery to the spirits. They know when to release the bowstring, because they know the exact moment when the winds will blow an arrow to its target. And powerful wizards can bend the world to their will, so that even the winds do their bidding. You," she looked at Koren with a mixture of awe and fear, "are a *powerful* wizard. Why have you come here, to my Lady Zara's home?"

"I can't be a wizard. I would know!" Koren protested again, but less surely. "Wouldn't I know?" How could a wizard *not* know of his own power?

"Come back inside," Frieda invited them, pulling her shawl around her. "Nights can be chilly here in the mountains, even before the summer has passed."

Inside, the two men sat silently at a table while Frieda went to get a teapot and cups. Koren busied himself with tapping one or another piece of the focus stone, watching the shards glow briefly. "Bjorn, I'm scared. This can't be."

Bjorn touched the focus stone, and nothing happened. "You think a wizard put a spell on you? I think you need to tell me who you really are."

For the first time, Koren regretted accepting Bjorn's offer to come with him. "Koren. My name is Koren Bladewell."

That seemed to satisfy Bjorn, for the man nodded and held out a hand to shake. "Pleased to meet you, Koren Bladewell. I'm still Bjorn Jihnsson."

"Sorry," Koren said sheepishly. "My name, um, doesn't mean anything to you?"

Bjorn thought for a moment, and shook his head. "No. Should it?"

Koren had to remind himself that, while he had briefly been famous within the small circle of the castle in Linden, few people in the wider world of Tarador knew or cared who the court wizard had as a servant. "Do you know of Lord Salva?"

"Yes, of course." Bjorn sat up straight and squared his shoulders. "I was a king's guard. I lived in the castle barracks for many a year. Lord Salva knew me by name, we shared meals together in the field many times. Why do you ask about the court wizard?"

It surprised Koren how big the world was, and at the same time, how small. "I was Lord Salva's servant. Until-"

Frieda came back into the room, carrying a tray laden with a tea setting. Koren rose to take the heavy tray from her. "Lord Salva?" Frieda asked. "What about him?"

Bjorn shared a look with Koren. "Kedrun asked if, since I was a king's guard in Linden, I had ever met the court wizard. Frieda, you are certain that Kedrun must be a wizard?"

Koren dropped the shard of focus stone he had been playing with. "I can't be a wizard. Wizards, don't they *know* what they are?"

Frieda poured tea into three cups, and removed the cover from a bowl of sweet biscuits. "Kedrun, has anything strange ever happened around you? Something you couldn't explain?"

"Not real-"

"After the focus stone shattered, you said you were a jinx, that you've always been a jinx. What did you mean by that?"

It took more prompting, but Koren told them of how he knew he was a jinx. He did not mention the crown princess, or the incident with the pirates. He told them of the bad things that had happened to a boy in a small village; bad things that could not be explained as anything other than a supernatural jinx. Himself.

Frieda turned away, wiping at her eyes. "Kedrun," she said quietly as she sipped tea, "you are not a jinx. There is no such thing as a jinx. You are a *wizard*. All those incidents you mentioned are your magical power manifesting itself, without you being able to control it. Or even knowing of it. That is why wizards are supposed to be discovered when they are very young; so an adult wizard can guide their power, and protect them from being hurt by their own power. No wizard ever came to your village?"

"Oh," Koren stared at his teacup with guilt. "We lived in a very small village, our farm was a long way from the village center. We didn't get into the village much," he explained. "I remember hearing a wizard was coming to our village one time, and I was excited about it. But the wizard was to come through our village during harvest time, and we were busy, and one of our cows was sick. So I stayed at home." And his father had declared that having a wizard look at Koren, to find out whether the boy was a wizard, was a foolish waste of time. Bodric knew his boy was not a wizard; anyone could see that. The law stated every child in Tarador was supposed to be tested for magical power. The law said a lot of things, Bodric had said scornfully, and not one of those laws helped a poor honest farmer to make a living.

CRAIG ALANSON

Koren recalled being completely miserable back then, not only at missing out on seeing a real wizard, but miserable at hearing everyone else in Crebbs Ford later talking about how amazing the wizard was. "And it was only that one time, I think," he added. He was very sure a wizard passing through the tiny poverty-stricken village of Crebbs Ford had only happened once; he would certainly have heard about something exciting like that.

Frieda was not pleased. "Wizards are supposed to visit every village at least once every three years, in Tarador. Here, our wizards come to every village two years apart, at the most," she declared with pride. "And we dwarves have fewer wizards."

"My village was very tiny, ma'am," Koren was embarrassed to say.

"That is no excuse," she said with disgust. "Your power should have been discovered when you were very young. It is not your fault."

"It doesn't matter," Koren shook his head. "I'm not a wizard. I can't be. I have never cast a spell, or, or made a ball of fire with my hands."

"Not all wizards can throw fireballs," Frieda admonished. "Some have power for healing. Or they can work with animals, speak with them, almost. I remember one wizard who-"

Koren seized Frieda's arm. "Speak with animals?" He asked slowly.

"Yes, why? Can you do that?"

"They don't *talk* to me," he whispered.

"No, animals can't actually speak," Frieda explained. "Zara told me wizards are able to make animals understand when they speak, understand their thoughts. And wizards can calm an animal when they are frightened, and use their power to heal a sick animal. Have you ever done anything like that?"

"No?" Koren said, as he thought back to when he had sat up all night with a sick cow. Or more than all night. People in Crebb's Ford had remarked on how good Koren was with animals. His touch had calmed many animals. Even Thunderbolt, now that he thought about it. And Thunderbolt had an uncanny ability to understand Koren. "Maybe?"

Could he be a wizard? It could not be. But-

"Kedrun," Bjorn prompted with a nudge of his boot. "Frieda asked you a question."

"Oh, sorry, ma'am. What?"

"I asked, how do you know you can't make a fireball? Have you tried?"

"How would I do that?" Koren stared at his palm, without realizing he was actually contemplating the possibility that he might, just might, be a wizard.

"I don't know," Frieda placed her hands upright on the table. "*I'm* not a wizard."

"I'm not a wizard either!"

"Kedrun," Bjorn held up a hand to forestall an argument. "I followed you all the way up here, without knowing your purpose. Now I'm asking you to try. Just try it."

"When I can't do it," Koren demanded, "will you stop telling me I'm a wizard?" He looked to Frieda. "Can you give me a hint?"

248

"All I know is, I once heard Zara say she wills the spirits to pull power through her."

"Through her," Koren mumbled to himself. "That is not much help." Shomas Feany had once made a fireball appear in his hand, and that wizard said it was difficult for him. What had Shomas done? Koren squinted and stared at his right palm, willing fire to appear there.

And also *not* willing a ball of magical fire to appear, for if it did, Koren's life would turn upside down.

"Is there something I'm supposed to say, to make the fire appear?" He asked, imagining fire hovering above his palm.

"Concentrate," Frieda suggested. "I truly don't know how it works."

Koren willed fire into existence, and-

Nothing happened.

"I told you-"

Koren fell backwards on his chair again, his feet kicking in surprise as an orange spark flickered just above his hand.

"Whoa, whoa," Bjorn held onto Koren's shirt and hauled him back upright, then the three sat in stunned silence. Koren pushed his right hand away from him, holding it away with his left hand around his right wrist, as if he didn't trust the magical fire not to appear again. A gust of wind came in through the half-closed window shutters, making the lanterns flicker. For a moment the workshop was plunged into darkness before the lanterns flared back to life.

Koren broke the silence, staring open-mouthed at his right hand. "Did that happen?"

"It did," Bjorn said in a hoarse voice. "We all saw it." Kedrun, or Koren, the lost young man who snuck into a warehouse where Bjorn had been trying to drink himself to sleep, was a wizard. A wizard who did not know he was a wizard!

Frieda reached across the table and squeezed Koren's hand. "Now do you believe me?"

"I'm a *wizard*. How could that- If a wizard had discovered that I have power," Koren still did not fully believe it. "When I was young, in my village. What would have happened to me?"

"You would have been taken as an apprentice by an experienced wizard, to teach you and guide you into understanding your power and how to use it."

"Taken me away from my parents?" Koren did not like the sound of that. "But, they needed me to work the farm."

Bjorn chuckled at that. "Kor- Kedrun," he kept up the ruse in front of Frieda. "There is a reward for the parents of wizard. Your parents would not have needed to work a farm ever again, not unless they wanted to act as lord and lady of the manor."

"They would have been rich?"

"Rich?" Bjorn laughed along with Frieda. "Yes! They would-" Bjorn halted his thought. "I'm sorry, Kedrun."

"Why?" Frieda looked at Bjorn. Koren's head was down, a tear rolling down his cheek.

Bjorn spoke for him. "Kedrun ran away from home. Later, his parents were killed by bandits."

"I'm sorry," Frieda squeezed Koren's hand. "It must be-"

Koren squeezed her hand, hard, then snatched his hand away. "Any wizard who knew me, would have known that I am a wizard?"

"Yes, assuredly,' Frieda answered, puzzled. "That is what I do not understand. You thought a wizard cast a spell on you, so you must have known a wizard at some-"

"I did," Koren stood up abruptly. "I did know a wizard, and he lied to me. They all lied."

"Would you like me to send a message to Lady Zara?" Frieda asked quietly.

"No," Koren touched a fingertip to a shard of the focus stone again, as if to assure himself that he had not imagined a flicker of fire appearing in his hand. "Bjorn, we need to go."

"Go?" Frieda frowned in concern. Whether Koren wanted her to or not, Frieda knew she needed to tell Zara about the young wizard who did not know he was a wizard. "Go where? You can't walk the mountain paths in the dark. You could stay here tonight," she offered.

"Frieda, thank you," Koren made a short bow to the kindly dwarf woman. "I need to speak with Bjorn."

Frieda protested several more times, but Koren would not be swayed. Outside, he and Bjorn looked down the street at the lights in windows of the tightly-packed buildings. "Koren," Bjorn whispered, "I think we do not say anything about this to Barlen, or anyone else. And Frieda is right, we can't go anywhere tonight," Bjorn realized he had no idea what Koren's plans were now. "Where are we going now?"

"Linden," Koren said with spite. "In Linden, there is a wizard who needs to answer for his lies."

CHAPTER TWENTY TWO

The next afternoon, after they had again left the narrow ledge behind, they saw plumes of smoke coming from beyond the foothills in front of them. The valley could not be seen over the crest of the foothills, yet it was clear that was where the smoke was coming from. Without any discussion, Koren and Bjorn picked up their pace, hurrying down the steeply sloping trail as quickly as their aching legs could carry them. Neither Koren nor Bjorn had been able to sleep much the previous night, and not only because the beds at the tavern were too short.

Bjorn's sleep had been interrupted by waking with one eye open, to peek across the room in the darkness to where Koren was sitting up in his too-short bed. The young man had been either staring out the window at the night sky, or staring at his palm, willing a fireball to appear. Only once in the night had Bjorn seen a tiny, weak glow of magical fire appear. "Koren," Bjorn asked to satisfy his own curiosity, "you keep looking at your hand. Are you able to make a fireball?"

Koren didn't answer at first. He clenched his fists, not being aware he had been looking at his hands. His attention was focused on the plumes of smoke rising into the sky to the south. If it was possible to run down the rugged mountain path, he would have. The loose rock and steep slopes forced him and Bjorn to walk carefully; a turned ankle or twisted knee in the mountains would be disastrous. Ahead of them were two flimsy, frightening rope bridges over deep chasms. On their way up the mountain, Koren had balked at crossing the first bridge, insisting there had to be another way up the mountain. The two dwarves had strode confidently across, showing it was, they said, perfectly safe even as bridge swayed alarmingly in the gusty winds. It had taken Bjorn walking easily across the bridge to shame Koren into trying it. He was not looking forward to crossing the pair of bridges in a downhill direction. "I tried a hundred times to make another fireball; it only worked again twice. And it wasn't anything I would call a fireball," Koren said sheepishly. He had tried off and on all night to make another flicker of flame appear above his hand, only managing to create a twinkle of dull red so faint, his sleep-deprived mind thought it might have been a reflection from lamps in the street outside.

When he had wakened, just as an orange glow in the east announced the sun would soon rise, he had wondered if the previous day was a dream, Surely he could not be a wizard. And then, on his very first try that morning, he made an orange ball of thin fog the size of a walnut appear. No matter how many times he tried after that, he could not do it again. "I don't know what is different when it works, and when it doesn't," Koren gritted his teeth in frustration. "I don't know *how* to create a fireball! I'm guessing."

"Don't wear yourself out," Bjorn was worried about Koren. "Magic is dangerous, and you are right, you don't have any idea what you are doing. Leave it alone, until you can find a wizard who will train you properly."

"They were supposed to have trained me properly already! They were-" Koren's voice cracked, and he fumed silently.

"Koren," Bjorn said after letting the young man by himself for a while. "I'll go with you to Linden, and I won't ask questions until we get close to the capital. What I ask is, whatever you intend to do there, think it through first."

Koren didn't reply. He had plenty of time to decide exactly what he was going to do when he returned to Linden. All he knew right then was that he felt used and angry and betrayed. Paedris must have known about Koren's power. If the court wizard knew, surely the Regent also knew. And likely crown princess Ariana knew also. All of them had lied to him. All of them had denied him a proper reward for saving the princess. And for finding the Cornerstone. The betrayal of Carlana and Ariana Trehayme did not surprise him; they were royalty and they cared nothing for other people. But Paedris? Paedris was a fellow wizard. The Wizard's Council should have discovered Koren's power when he was a little boy. His parents should have been living like royalty. Instead, they were dead. They were dead, and Koren had thought his parents rejected him, abandoned him.

Koren did not yet know what he was going to do when he got back to Linden, and there was still the problem that the Royal Army had orders to kill him.

The only thing Koren was sure of was that someone was going to pay for betraying him. Pay for the death of his parents. Pay for making him think he was cursed to be a jinx.

"Koren!" Bjorn's call jolted Koren from his enraged reverie. "Look!" The former king's guard pointed down the trail, to where two dozen dwarves were struggling up the mountain.

As they grew closer, the dwarves began gesturing, waving as if they wanted Koren and Bjorn to turn around and go back up the mountain. The dwarves were shouting something that could not be understood due to the distance and the wind. One of the dwarves got the others to halt, and he hustled up the trail by himself. When he was close enough, he halted, cupped hands around his mouth, and shouted. "Go back!"

Koren followed Bjorn's lead, holding hands up in a peaceful gesture, but continuing down the trail. "I'm Bjorn, this is Kedrun," Bjorn shouted.

"I'm Abelard. Turn and go back, we're all coming up the mountain!" Before Koren could ask why, the dwarf gestured to the pillars of smoke. "Orcs invaded the valley from the east, yesterday. We're cut off. Some of us went north, others south."

"My horse!" Koren exclaimed. "My horse was in a stable there!"

"Don't worry about your horse," Abelard advised. "We had enough warning to clear ourselves and our animals ahead of the orcs; most of them fled south."

"We need to get back to Tarador," Koren said breathlessly.

Abelard shook his head slowly. "You'll not get there going down this trail. After the last of us crossed the lower bridge, it is going to be dropped into the gorge to stop the orcs from following us." He looked up at the sun. "That was this morning. Without that bridge, the next closest way across the gorge is twenty miles east. There's likely orcs crawling all over land to the east; they came at us with a full army, this wasn't any raid."

"How else do we get across the gorge?" Bjorn asked, holding Koren's shoulder to steady the young man.

"If you're headed for Tarador?" Abelard scratched his beard. "You'll need to go back up this trail, go toward Westerholm, then south from there. That's," he considered, while watching the other dwarves continue up the trail, laden with everything they'd been able to carry from the foothills. "Three, four days?"

"Another four days?" Koren exploded. "We can't-"

"I wouldn't go, if I were you," Abelard grimaced. "Those orcs are heading west; they'll likely be there in force by the time you could get there."

"But-" Koren's protest was cut off by Bjorn steering him away, and speaking quietly in his ear.

"These dwarves have just lost their homes to orcs; and likely family and friends also. Our concerns mean nothing to them. We will get to Tarador, it will not happen today. Understood, my young wizard friend?"

"Understood," Koren hung his head in shame and disbelief.

"Abelard," Bjorn adjusted his pack, "how can we help?"

CHAPTER TWENTY THREE

Regin Falco ate supper by himself in his study. As he picked at his food, his gaze alternated from the messages on the table, to the royal castle on the hill beyond the window of his Linden estate. There were two messages. One spoke of triumph; the destruction of the enemy force in the Kaltzen Pass of the Turmalane mountains. The first message was an official communication from the Royal Army to the leaders of Tarador, and had arrived early that afternoon. All of Linden, indeed all of Tarador rejoiced wherever that message had reached. Regin's genuine joy at the victory was tempered by his knowledge, provided by officers of the Royal Army, that the enemy had another entire army still west of the River Fasse, an army perhaps even larger than the force lost in the Kaltzen. While Tarador's victory was impressive, it was not the final battle in the war, nor likely even the final battle before winter that year. For this reason, Regin had not announced a celebration that evening. There would no doubt be an official royal feast day when the Regent Ariana returned to Linden; until then Regin would wait to see what followed the victory at the Kaltzen.

The other reason Regin wanted to be alone was the second message on the table. The second message had arrived hours later, a private message from Captain Jaques to Duke Falco. The message stated that Kyre had bravely risked his life, in an ultimately futile attempt to prevent the enemy from forcing their way through the Gates of the Mountain. That Kyre had been injured by an enemy wizard, but had later been healed and was now recovering.

Regin's heart nearly had stopped when he read that his eldest son had been struck by a wizard. He intended to compose a message back to reprimand Captain Jaques; any such a message from Jaques should have opened with 'Kyre is well', before stating that the heir to the duchy of Burwyck had led a charge and been seriously injured.

Knowing his son would regain his full health had mollified Regin only the span of a moment, for the message went on to state that after the battle, Kyre had confronted the Regent. That meeting, tense at first, had ended with Kyre renewing his pledge of loyalty to Ariana Trehayme! Regin Falco's heir had sworn an oath to protect the enemy of the Falcos.

After dinner, a meal he largely pushed away, the duke took a glass of wine and walked the parapet of the estate. His guards knew not to engage him in conversation or make eye contact when their duke wished to be alone with his thoughts. The sun set, stars appeared in the sky, and Regin retired to his bed chamber.

But he did not sleep. Rather than taking to bed, he sat in a chair by the window, slowly sipping a glass of wine. And attempting to decide what he should do. What he needed to do. His carefully laid plans were close, so close, to bearing fruit; to putting a Falco back on the throne of Tarador. Now his son, the instrument of the impending Falco victory over the Trehaymes, had betrayed him. Openly embraced Regin Falco's enemy. That Kyre had demonstrated exceptional courage mattered nothing to his father.

The Falco estate became quiet as its residents took to bed, and still the duke sat silently, staring out the window. The only sound was the occasional footsteps of guards echoing in the walled courtyard below, the only movement visible was the flickering of torchlight.

The duke of Burwyck went rigid, wine glass poised halfway to his lips. The glass fell from his stiff fingers, falling into his lap, then rolling off onto the thick carpet, barely making a sound. Red wine pooled in Regin's robe, soaking into his pants and the chair beneath. Unable to breathe properly, his mouth tried to open and close, but the only sound was a faint rattling gasp.

With eyes open wide and staring fixedly in front of him, he saw the heavy curtain next to one window slowly push away from the wall. A figure emerged, clothed in black silk. It was a man, or it had been a man at one point. Now the figure was hideous. Its long fingers were crinkly gray skin over bones. Under the black hood that shrouded its face, its skin that was also gray, with dark circles around its eyes.

A wizard.

A wizard of Acedor had slipped into Duke Falco's bed chamber, unseen. Regin, still unable to move, mentally prepared for death. He was unable even to close his eyes, not that he would have done so. Confronted by an agent of the enemy, Regin would have glared defiance at the wizard of ancient evil, showing that Falcos would not surrender to fear.

"Duuuuke Faaaalco," the wizard hissed, and waved a skeletal hand toward Regin, releasing the paralyzing spell slightly.

Regin gasped for air, only able to take rapid, shallow breaths. "I," he struggled to speak as he exhaled, "do not fear you."

"Yes, you do," the wizard's voiced hissed through gnarled teeth that were even more stained and yellow in the light of the candles. "You do not show it, to your credit. You should fear my master, for his power is unstoppable."

"He," Regin took as deep a breath as he could manage, "has been stopped."

The wizard laughed; a rasping choking sound that made the hairs on the back of Regin's neck stand up. "A truly minor setback. Tarador has showed the full extent of its strength, and you were barely able to defeat a tiny part of my master's forces. It was foolishness, not lack of power, that lead to the loss of our army in the Turmalanes. Our commanders were lured into a battle that was not necessary, because of their incompetence and overconfidence. They and their families have paid with their lives. There will not be any such mistakes in the future."

"Empty words," Regin tried to put disdain into his voice, fighting with the only weapon he had left. "Say what you wish after your army was crushed in battle, your words change nothing."

That angered the enemy wizard, for his hand rose again, and Regin writhed in silent agony as a spike of fire-like pain stabbed through his heart. He tried to scream, but no sound came out. Then the pain stopped as suddenly as it began, and Regin panted to catch his breath. "You should be wary of insulting my master," the wizard hissed. "You see only what is before your eyes, and not the greater truth. Behold!" The wizard put a hand over his eyes, and-

For Regin, the room in his Linden mansion disappeared, his vision rushing forward through the night, as if he were flying across the landscape of Tarador. He soared over hills and rivers he vaguely recognized, and unseen behind him, the sun rose. In the light, he saw what he knew was the River Fasse in Anschulz, seeing the distinctive bend in that river where it looped back on it- self. He saw destruction and the terrible remnants of a great battle on the east side of the river; Royal Army troops mopping up defeated and scattered groups of the enemy. His vision zoomed over the river, continuing west, where an enemy encampment on the west side of the river had few fires burning. The encampment, which stretched for miles along the river, had been occupied by the army which had crossed the river and been decisively defeated. As Regin's disembodied sight floated silently overhead, he could see the enemy camp was split between men and orcs, with a swamp between them. Even in his disorientation and fright, Regin smiled inwardly to see how divided were the armies controlled by Tarador's ancient enemy; the men of Acedor and the orcs of the north would fight each other at every opportunity.

Then the camp disappeared and Regin was flying over a forest of sickly, gnarled, stunted trees. Even from on high, he could imagine the unhealthy stench of the decaying woods. The forest con- tinued west up over a chain of hills, and Regin gasped.

Just beyond the hills west of the River Fasse was another camp of the enemy. Only this camp made the one along the river look like a cluster of tents housing a mere hunting party. Tents and fires lay everywhere from the hills to the horizon. Everywhere Regin looked, he saw more tents, more corrals of horses, more men and orcs training for battle. The movement of his vision slowed, until he hovered over the center of the enormous camp. From the west, along every road, men and orcs were marching to swell the ranks of the camp. Strings of horses and oxen pulled huge wagons laden with supplies and equipment for war. Regin had never imagined an army of that size.

With a snap of the wizard's bony fingers, Regin's awareness returned to his familiar bed cham- ber outside the capital city of Linden "You see?" The wizard hissed. "You have seen the host my master had prepared to invade across the river into Anschulz. Your Royal Army cannot stand against such a mighty army. And what you saw does not include the army poised to invade Lev- anne, or the legions of orcs who will sweep through the dwarves, and split Tarador down the mid- dle from the north. Duke Falco, the Royal Army of Tarador, and the armies of your seven prov- inces, and all your wizards, are as nothing compared to the hosts my master will throw against you. Soon, you will be duke of nothing; duke of a scorched wasteland. If you are still alive, you will bow before my master, and you will beg for him to be merciful to your family. He will show you no mercy, if you have resisted his rightful desire to protect himself against those parasites, the Trehaymes."

"The Trehaymes?" Regin asked, surprised.

The enemy wizard's mouth moved silently, as if chewing on something unpleasant. "Much as it would please me to destroy scum like you, my master sent me here not to kill you, but to entreat with you. Do not think my master does not know your plan to retake the throne by your son marrying the princess, and then killing Ariana when she becomes queen."

"Your master disapproves?" Regin did not bother to deny his plan.

"My master would greatly reward anyone who kills the princess, but your plan will never come to fruition. Your son will not be controlled by you; the Falcos will never regain the throne through him. You have now seen the mighty hosts my master will soon throw across the border into the heart of Tarador. None can stand against him, and no one in Tarador will survive his final triumph. Ariana will never become queen; there will be no throne of Tarador for you to take back for your family."

"What," Regin asked with a voice starved of air, "do you wish of me?" The wizard said his master wanted to offer something to Regin, in exchange for, what? What could the demon of Acedor want that the duke of Burwyck could possibly give?

"My master is wise and merciful, except to those who take up arms against him. What my master offers you is the throne of Tarador. The throne now, for yourself. While there is a throne to be offered. You may take the throne in your own right, and you will save Tarador from destruction."

Regin Falco should have refused the enemy's treasonous plans. Instead, he considered the temptation of fulfilling, after generations, his family's quest to regain the throne of Tarador. "How?"

"My master wishes peace, not conquest," the lies dripped easily from the wizard's tongue. "You will assist my master in killing the crown princess, the usurper of the throne Ariana Trehayme. Once she is dead, my master will support you taking the throne, and we can pull back from the brink of this unnecessary war. Terrible bloodshed can be avoided, Tarador will be saved, and the Falcos will once again take their rightful place at the leadership of your nation. Think on it, Duke Falco. My master chose to entreat with you, because of all the dukes and duchesses of your seven provinces, he judges you are strong. And because he recognizes your claim to the throne, the throne that was stolen from you by the treacherous Trehaymes. The treacherous and foolhardy Trehaymes, who have brought Tarador to the precipice of utter destruction. Think on it, Duke Falco. My master offers not only the throne to you; he offers life for the innocent citizens of your nation. Why should they pay with their lives for the aggressive actions of the Trehaymes, the Trehaymes with their endless desire for conquest?"

Regin shook his head. Was the enemy casting a spell to break his will as the wizard spoke? Or did the enemy merely understand what lay deep inside Regin's heart, his greatest desire, the desire that consumed him and blocked out all other concerns?

The duke of Burwyck should have rejected the enemy's offer to support treason. Instead, he persuaded himself that he, and he alone, could save Tarador from complete and final destruction. He had indeed seen the unstoppable armies that the enemy could soon throw across the border. It was an army the wizard assured was only part of the enemy's force. And Regin believed. He believed, because he had his own intelligence sources, both from his own army and within the Royal Army. And because he wanted to believe that defeat and destruction for Tarador were inevitable, for only that could justify his treason. "Your master offers me the throne? Throne of what?" He struggled against his own instincts and desires. "A land of slaves?"

"I said my master is merciful, and desires only peace. The peace of not being threatened by Tarador. My master will sign a treaty of peace with you, once you are king of Tarador. You must surrender all lands west of the summit of the Turmalanes, as a buffer between our nations, to protect the peaceful people of Acedor. Tribute must be paid to my master every year, to compensate for the threats and insults Tarador has given him over centuries. And Tarador will be banned from maintaining a standing army, for the only purpose of such an army would be to threaten my peace-loving master. You may use a force of sheriffs to maintain peace and good order within your border, of course."

"Of course," Regin repeated. "My son. My son Kyre. He has taken up arms against your master. Kyre acted on *my* orders," his voice faded.

The wizard's mouth moved again, gnashing his teeth against having to say something that greatly displeased him. "I told you that my master is merciful; part of his mercy is not to blame the son for the sins of his father. If you repent of your hateful aggressions against my master, your son will be spared."

"And the others of my family?"

"You ask much, Duke Falco!" The wizard roared, and Regin's heart was again spiked with fire. The wizard jerked like a puppet on strings, and the searing pain left Regin. For a moment, the wizard wavered on his feet, and when he spoke again, his voice was a pained whisper. "Your family will be safe, if you keep to your promise to my master. If any of your family continues to act against my master, they will answer for their crimes."

"Understood," Regin said quickly, ready for another sharp pain.

"Do we have an agreement?"

The duke of Burwyck did not answer. In part, he was playing for time to decide what to do. If he agreed, he would have the possibility of gaining the throne of a country enslaved. But he might be able to save the life of his son. Making a deal with the enemy might be the only way to save Kyre's life, for if Kyre continued on his current course, Regin may reluctantly have to order his own son killed. Kyre's youthful emotional foolishness could not be allowed to destroy what the dukes and duchess of Burwyck had striven for over hundreds of years.

And, most importantly, Regin despaired of Tarador's survival, having seen the almost endless army the enemy could use against the already strained and meager forces of Tarador. Ariana may be a far better leader than her mother, but she was also far too late to save her nation.

Regin's heart was filled with despair. This was the end of everything he had hoped for, the end of everything he held dear. "Does your master need an answer tonight? This is a very serious decision for me to make."

The wizard smiled, a horrible sight that made Regin's skin crawl. "There is no need for an answer, Duke Falco. My master knows what is in your heart. You have already decided."

Regin found that he could move again, and he took deep breaths, his head in his hands. When his head was no longer spinning, he looked up at the emissary of Tarador's ancient enemy. The emissary of the demon of the underworld. "What do you wish me to do?"

THE END

Contact the author at craigalanson@gmail.com
https://www.facebook.com/Craig.Alanson.Author/
Visit CraigAlanson.com for blogs and items such as T-shirts, coffee cups etc.

Made in the USA
Middletown, DE
27 September 2021